AMERICAN ODYSSEY, BOOK ONE

*For Dorothy and Dick
A Tale from the Mists
where the Rivers run*

AMERICAN ODYSSEY,
BOOK ONE

*E. P. Roesch
Ethel Roesch
Paul Roesch*

E.P. Roesch

Xlibris

Copyright © 2000 by E.P. Roesch.

Library of Congress Number: 00-192613
ISBN #: Softcover 0-7388-4057-2

All rights reserved. No part of this book may be reproduced or transmitted in any form or by any means, electronic or mechanical, including photocopying, recording, or by any information storage and retrieval system, without permission in writing from the copyright owner.

This is a work of fiction. Names, characters, places and incidents either are the product of the author's imagination or if a real event or person is represented it shall be in a way that could not be deemed libelous.

This book was printed in the United States of America.

To order additional copies of this book, contact:
Xlibris Corporation
1-888-7-XLIBRIS
www.Xlibris.com
Orders@Xlibris.com

DEDICATIONS

*In Memory of
Dr. Lorenzo J. Greene,
professor, Lincoln University, Jefferson City,
the man of Missouri who years ago admonished the authors
with his impassioned,
"Never give up."*

*For our family
who supports and indulges our writing,
who listens and hopes with us,
Paul, Nancy, Scott, Kari
Brian, Sara
Lynn, Arthur, Andrew, Amanda
Carol, Rod, Cynthia, Christopher
Dwight*

Praise for E. P. Roesch's novel Ashana

"This is a strong rendering of the exploitation of native Alaskan culture by foreigners . . . the broad, sweeping tale enlightens and astonishes."

Publishers Weekly

". . . a lyrical novel woven of Alaskan shadow-spirit and Russian reaiity . . . This haunting novel will interest Y[oung] A[dults] who are not put off by complex tales . . . its richness will hold those interested in folklore."

School Library Journal

"Cultures clash in this lyrical first novel based on historical fact . . . Alaskan legends and traditions, interwoven within the text, add resonance and depth to this haunting tale."

Kirkus Review

"*Ashana* . . . is a blanket of documentable, historical fact and fiction woven to perfection, using legends to uphold the tale. It is a haunting, lyrical saga . . . a tragic love story."

The Ojibwe News

"The rape of innocence was never more hauntingly portrayed than in this story of Aleksandr Baranov, the embodiment of Russian Imperial adventuring, and Ashana, his unwilling concubine . . . a major contriution to the literature of that northern land."

James Michener

EPIGRAPHS

We hold these truths to be self-evident,
that all men are created equal,
that they are endowed by their creator
with certain inalienable rights,
that among these are Life, Liberty, and the pursuit of
Happiness.

Selection from the Declaration of Independence,
July 4, 1776

Now o'er the restless waves there came a sound
As of a mighty crashing—fraught with fear,
Which shook both shores in the vast profound,
Like to the raging of a mighty wind.

Alighieri Dante, Italian poet (1265-1321)

Selection from *In the Footprints of Dante*,
compiled 1907 by Paget Toynbee, M.A.,
D. Litt., Oxford University.

ACKNOWLEDGMENTS FOR *AMERICAN ODYSSEY*

Our grateful appreciation goes to descendants of George Bush who shared with the authors papers, artifacts, history, and intimate details about the Bush family.

We extend sincere appreciation and thanks to the curators and staffs of the archives, libraries, research facilities, and museums during the many years when the story of George Bush, black pioneer, has been in process. Our particular thanks go to the following:

>Amistad Research Center, Dillard University, New Orleans, Louisiana;
>Bancroft Library and Archives, University of California, Berkeley, California;
>Cabildo Museum and Historical Society, New Orleans, Louisiana;
>Clay County courthouse records, Liberty, Missouri;
>Clay County Historical Society, Liberty, Missouri;
>East Tennessee Library, Knoxville, Tennessee;
>Fur Trappers Museum, Chadron, Nebraska;
>GSA, National Archives and Records Service, Seattle, Washington;
>GSA, National Archives and Records Service, Washington, D. C.;
>Historic New Orleans Collections, New Orleans, Louisiana;
>Historical Archives and Records, Kansas City, Missouri;

Huntington Library, San Marino, California;
Jesse James Museum, Liberty, Missouri;
Lewis & Clark Museum, Astoria, Oregon;
Lincoln University Library, Jefferson City, Missouri;
Louisiana State University, Baton Rouge, Louisiana;
Museum of the Fur Trade, St. Louis, Missouri;
Oregon State Historical Society, Portland, Oregon;
Schomburg Archives and Library, New York;
State Historical Society of Missouri, Columbia, Missouri;
State Capitol Museum, Olympia, Washington;
Tennessee State Historical Society, Nashville, Tennessee;
Tennessee State Library and Archives, Nashville, Tennessee;
Timberland Regional Library system, Olympia and Lacey, Washington;
Tulane University Library, New Orleans, Louisiana;
U. S. Census Bureau, regional offices;
University of Missouri, Columbia, Missouri;
University of Washington, Seattle, Washington;
Walnut Street Historical Archives, Philadelphia, Pennsylvania;
Washington State Museum, Tacoma, Washington;
Washington State Library, Olympia, Washington;
William Jewel College, Liberty, Missouri.

E. P. Roesch

American Odyssey

HISTORICAL CHARACTERS

(in order of their appearance)

George Bush
Matthew Bush
Captain Stevenson
Free black men and women, unnamed in history
Reverend Allen of the Philadelphia Free African Society
Free man from York, Pennsylvania
Mrs. Preacher James
Isabella (Ibby) James
General Andrew Jackson
Kentucky lawyer, a runaway slave
German gunsmith
Slaves sold at auctions
Slave men and women, unnamed in history
Captain John Lewis
Colonel Edwin E. Booth
Colonel William Tunnell
East Tennessee Muster Roll copyist, Crosby
Levi Lee
General William Carroll
Tennessee militiamen
Rachel Jackson, Mrs. Andrew Jackson
Flatboat pilot
Zadok Cramer, author of *The Navigator*
William Duane, author of *A Handbook for Infantry*
Robert Jackson
Skipper of the *Pittsburg*

Major Gabriel Villeré
Colonel de La Ronde
Jean Lafitte
Dominique You, Jean's brother
Major Latour, engineer
Sir Edward Packenham
Sergeant, Free Colored Battalion of New Orleans
Sanité Dédé
Preacher James

1

"Stop where you are, George Bush," a voice snarled from my cabin door.

Reining in my horse near the pasture fence, I dismounted and headed through my yard to see who had shouted at me.

"I said, stop. You fool! Stop!" A big man in a dirty, loose-fitting jerkin kicked my cabin door wide open and stomped into my yard. Spitting a stream of tobacco juice in my direction, leveling his musket barrel at me, the stranger bellowed, "I'm Hank Lucas. I've bought this here place. And I'm tellin' you easy like to git off my land. Now, George Bush!"

"You have it wrong. I rent this farm from Zeb Turley up in Knoxville. And he agreed . . ."

"The hell you say. Myrtle, git up to that window with your gun. Git ready to shoot this black bastard." His snarl spit between teeth decayed to stained brown stubs. Tobacco juice dribbled down his chin.

From behind the haystack to my left, I glimpsed a third gun aimed at me. But I kept my eye on the stranger who called himself "Hank Lucas." Dirty pants hung ragged over scuffed boots. A soggy yellow straw hat sagged onto matted hair. His huge grog-blossom nose stuck out from a scraggly whiskered face.

"Cain't you hear? Clear out, Boy. You're nothin' but a squatter. You ain't got no title. We bought this here place from Zeb Turley and figure to git it in shape for next year." Lucas moved closer, his gun aimed squarely at my chest.

"Zeb Turley rents to me, and . . ." My voice choked. I wanted to shoot the stranger with my Jaeger, but I had left it hidden in my pack. Me, a free Negro, raising a gun at a white man? A violation of Tennessee law. That would give a court reason to brand me guilty of assault and order me sold into slavery.

The East Tennessee sky, bright blue with fleecy white clouds scudding across it, had for me lost all light.

The minute seemed an hour.

Scraping his tongue across his lips, then pulling it back, Lucas moved his tobacco cud from one side of his mouth down to the hollow in front of his stubbed teeth. He sucked in his cheeks and spit a thick stream of tobacco juice that slopped onto the ground close by.

My legs, stomach, back, and sides tightened. My mind struggled with figuring how to best him. I reined in my rage, and kept my voice civil. "This land is my land. I rented it fair and square from Zeb Turley. A few weeks back, I handed him another six month's rent across the counter of his store in Knoxville. Cash."

The abandoned cabin, broken-down fences, rotting barn roof—everything had needed a lot of fixing when Turley let the farm to me. I had worked, labored, sweated on the place going on two years, brought it to the point of making a decent home. I needed its meadows for my cattle business already in the first stage of promising good returns.

Lying in a lush valley among the rising hills and ridges of East Tennessee, Turley's vacant land had looked like one of the finest places around to start a farm. When I had first ridden across it, the land had looked productive, its grass green and tall. My recently purchased cattle added the touch of permanence. A few months after arriving from Philadelphia, I spent time checking land prices, then had offered Zeb Turley a fair price to buy his acres.

"Well, take your time, George Bush. Finish fixing up my place. See how you and I get along. Next year, we can likely talk about you buying me out," storekeeper Turley had said.

I was suspicious at the time. But I thought there would not be much pressure for buying this raw frontier land. Zeb Turley had appeared to be an honest merchant. I was too blinded by my passion for land to see through the old crook. That day when I left Turley's store thinking I had a spread of good land, I had felt a calm glowing as if my turmoil was fading to an end.

"Roy?" The man in my yard yelled.

"Yeh, Pa. I'm over here by the haystack."

"Git your gun cocked. Shoot this crazy fool full of buckshot when I tell you."

The woman at the window had a gun. Lucas and his son had guns. Every gun cocked to shoot. Three to one. Poor odds even if I had my gun and wanted to risk the law. And how many more did I have against me? I asked myself and answered: Could be a whole patrol of white men hiding around here, in a fume to do a lynching.

Threatening to shoot, Lucas backed me to my horse. I grabbed the horn of the saddle—for support, for escape, I was not sure. My whole being boiled with rage as I struggled to hold myself from exploding against the thief. I stood a head taller than the man, my muscles tight and strong from months of work with the cattle and the buildings. I knew I could squeeze the thief into submission, but he had the gun.

"Hurry, Myrtle, this here stupid cur don't look to have no respec'," Lucas hollered to his wife. "No respec' at all for a man."

My mind tumbled. Anger smoldered deep inside. I fought for a way around the intruder, a plan to force him to back off. But I knew there was no reasoning with him. Hank Lucas had been lying in wait, ready for any move by me. "I'll take my things in the cabin and . . ."

"We picked up all your personals. Every stinkin' rag. Don' want no darky stuff around our house. Tossed 'em in bundles by the fence. Now, pack up and git out, Boy."

Strike out. Smash his face. My fists clenched, I glared at the man, choked back words. Wild thoughts raced through my head: Defend your land, George Bush. Hit him. Strike him down. I looked him dead in the eye, knew a braggart coward hid behind the gun barrel. His stench stained the air.

"Go ahead, jis' try somethin.'" Lucas dared me to take a swing at him.

* * *

Rage beating through me, I forced myself to pick up my bundles dumped beside the fence. Taking my time, I strapped them onto my horse. Just like that. Give up my place. Jimmers, I hated to let my land go. Against what I faced, an urge deep down still drove at me commanding, Knock him down if he leaves you an opening. I crunched my teeth and bit down hard on my inner cheek. I tasted blood.

Too easy for Hank Lucas, white man. Ride in. Steal my place. Settle down. No recourse for George Bush, free black man. Ride out. Give up my home. The guns and the laws are white. I may have been born free, a free Negro from the free state of Pennsylvania. But in America in 1813 free for what?

* * *

At the corner of my cow pasture fence, I decided to salvage what I could and head away before Lucas pulled his trigger and cut me down. Starting to walk toward the gate, I turned to the son-of-a-bitch and said with as much faked politeness, faked humility, as I could conjure up, "I'll just take my cows and be gone, *Mister Lucas.*" "The hell you will," Lucas snorted. I had taken but a couple of steps when he yelled, "Roy, jump over to that corner post. Keep your gun on the nigger scum."

I stopped in my tracks. To the side of me, Lucas's son slouched from behind the haystack, his musket aimed straight at my head.

"Jis' try stealin' our cows, and I'll put a bullet through your thick skull," Roy hollered.

"Them cows ain't yourn." Lucas shuffled toward me, his finger on the musket's trigger. He had the gun cocked, and I knew it was loaded. At point-blank range, he rasped, "Like I said, I bought the land and the whole kit and caboodle from Zeb Turley. Cattle and all. Done it legal. Git off my property!"

"I bought those cattle. Every one. I own them. They were never in my land deal with Turley," I snarled back at Lucas.

"You callin' me a liar, Boy?" Without turning his head, Lucas shouted, "Myrtle. Git down in the yard where we need you. This here is one stubborn fool."

* * *

So, Zeb Turley had never intended to sell the farm to me, just schemed to to have me clean it up for him. No wonder he would never listen to my requests for a long-term lease and evaded talk of selling the land to me. I knew it would be useless for me to challenge storekeeper Turley in court. No judge would listen to my word. The law barred a free Negro from testifying against a white. I had no right to the land.

Although I had come to Tennessee knowing I could stand fast in any fair fight, I rode away from those three guns and away from my farm. Hate for what the man had done etched a fissure into my mind.

2

My mind spinning, to keep from going beserk and killing Hank Lucas, I forced myself to ride away from my stolen home and head toward my friend Sam's cabin. To control the spinning, I turned my mind back to my first Tennessee turkey hunt that Sam and I had taken some weeks before.

One day, Sam had laughed at me, "You be too serious, George Bush. Alus thinkin'. Alus worryin'. Time you and me goes huntin'. Take yo' mind off yo' trubbles, Young Man." Sam had handed me his old squirrel gun. "Use dis. Dat rifle yo' hab be way too pow'ful fo' shootin' turkeys."

Scamp and Turner, Sam's hounds—I had learned not to call Tennessee hounds plain "dogs"—struck our trail through brush and tall trees. Racing ahead, Turner had taken the lead.

"Dat ol' cold-nose pot likker sho' will find de scent of any turks." Sam chuckled deep down, pride in his hounds showing. "Den, dat Scamp. Him has English hound blood in him. Him takes da trail close afta Turna'. Bred fo' huntin', bof dem hounds is. Only way dat plantation Brown gib dem to me, dey's so dam ol' him figure deys about to drop. Ol' same as me."

Sam had sat for a spell, quiet, a faraway look in his eyes. Shrugging his shoulders, he went on, "In de ol' days on de big hunts on Brown's plantation where we be slaves, I runs a whole pack o' dem hounds. Had tre, many as five hush-mouths wid dem two up dere.

"Yes, those hush mouths, dey be de best of hounds. Dey gots de bes' blood, pointer bird and bull terrier. Some shepherd blood, too. De best of hounds. 'N kin dey run? Streak light'nin, dey wuz. Fasta' den de English houn's. Dey'd take up de scent and follow de animal fo' miles. Stays right wid 'im. Stays right wid a slave on da run, too. A hush-mouth treed me dat las' time I runn'd."

Rain of several days had left the ground soft. Trickles spilled downslope and over rocks below where Sam and I had stopped and posted ourselves under thick foliage bordering the edge of a good-sized meadow.

From our protective cover, while I was loading the gun, we had watched Turner and Scamp race ahead, noses in the air, then to the ground. Before long Turner stopped, sniffed, turned around, circled toward the opposite edge of the clearing, Scamp close behind. Sam and I crawled several feet along a ditch, waited again where a small grove screened us.

As I had started to stand up, Sam pulled me down, whispered, "Sssshhh. Let de houn's do it. Dey'll stir up turks, but dey'll keep dem from runnin' into dat undda'brush down da ravine."

Some minutes passed while I scanned the bushes for birds. Then motion from behind a decaying log caught my sight—two turkey heads bobbing close together. Their rich reds, blacks, and browns glistened whenever a fleeting ray of sunshine slithered down and brushed their feathers. "Git 'em," Sam whispered.

My Jaeger ready, scanning the distance, figuring it about a hundred yards, maybe a little more, I waited until both turkey heads bobbed as one. Then I fired.

"Two birds wid one shot. Some shootin', Son. Da Lawd be praised." Sam's excitement had matched mine as he picked up the turkeys.

* * *

As I rode away forever from my East Tennessee farm that Hank Lucas now claimed to own, the thought of how peaceful and happy this land should have been left me sick. This East Tennessee that I had adopted for home. "Tennessee"—the name sounds music from *Tenase*—a Cherokee village on the banks of the Little Tennessee

River. Freedom should have ridden the air in the mountains of East Tennessee.

But instead, this Tennessee is a crazymaker on free Negroes, the same as it had been in Philadelphia where I was born. The first time I had begun to learn what the word race meant and how free Negroes were treated, came one sultry day on the Philadelphia docks when I was age nine.

Sitting on those docks, I was watching a free Negro unload a wagon filled with barrels. One slipped over the end of the wagon bed. It cracked, spilling sugar onto the ground. The merchant who owned the barrels yelled, "Boy, you stupid fool."

The lash fell several times before the free man grabbed a board and struck back at his boss. The merchant skidded on the sugar, stumbled, and fell. As the free man ran, some whites rushed to pick up the storekeeper. Two whites showed up with guns and yelled, "Kill the nigger! Kill him!"

Only by his quickness did the man escape, hiding the better part of a week among our free people on the fringes of the city of Philadelphia. To save himself, he slipped away, never to return.

He had escaped, and the blacks in the area talked about how they hated the whites. Some said they always kept guns hidden and would use them if a white made it necessary.

* * *

I went home and asked, "Father, what is a nigger?"

Father did not hesitate in getting to the explanation. "George, people seem to need someone they think is lower than them. So white people look down on our people and call us something that makes them feel higher than we are. That's how come that white was whipping that black driver. And he'd be sold into slavery or at least put in prison a long time for hitting that white merchant." Father paused, hurt and misery filling his words. "Aye, you asked about *nigger*. Whites use that word as a way to push us down and lift themselves up."

"Father, how does treating our people so bad help the whites?"

"Well, George, the whites brought most of us to America chained on slave ships. They needed to think we are less human than they are so they don't have to feel bad about keeping us slave. But, George, don't never forgot one thing, as long as you live."

"What's that, Father?"

"That man on the docks was one brave man. He hit that white man back for whipping him." The way father explained happenings, I began to realize that he was a man of more courage than I had thought. Father stood as erect and sturdy as the mast of a sailing ship. I was young, but I knew I should listen and learn from him about life in Philadelphia.

* * *

From then on as I played with friends, I watched the streets of Philadelphia with a wiser eye, a cautious eye, and wary.

I began to grasp the fact that a big part of the world was not like my quiet, well-provided boyhood home. I began to understand more about my best boyhood friend, Isaiah Curry, nearly eight months younger than me.

The Curry family, brothers and sisters, parents, grandmother, lived in a red frame house on Philadelphia's Water Street. Isaiah's house seemed half buried in the ground; and summer rains and spring thaws filled its yard with pools of putrid stinking water. Isaiah's home may have been simple, but it was much better than most free Negro family homes.

Great numbers of our black people in Philadelphia lived in cramped wooden shacks—pens, smaller than my stolen East Tennessee barn. Leaky roofs. No windows. Only a square-foot hole beside the door for the smoke to escape. Much of Philadelphia stands on low land, and water soaks through the rotten floor boards. Children run around, their feet always wet.

I was growing up in the stately house of Captain Stevenson, a white sea captain. His sailing ships circled the globe. His house on

Walnut Street was a mansion. It was built of red brick and stood high amid gardens and fruit trees with a cow pasture in back. Captain Stevenson, a white man, and my father, Matthew Bush, a free black man, sailed the seas together.

"Matthew Bush, my right hand man," Captain Stevenson often said. But I remember my father as a servant for the way he said "Yessir" to the Captain.

Weathered by sea spray and wind, the Captain looked to be tougher than his sailors. His white hair roamed his head like a seacap on the ocean. His eyes flashed the blue plucked from the sky. Stevenson made his command law over his crews; and his long-fingered hands held the power that managed the ship's wheel with my father always at his side.

Father loved the sea, never happier than when he and the Captain hoisted their sails and slipped out from Philadelphia, down the Delaware River, into the Atlantic Ocean, to face the winds sweeping the ship. Trips north to Boston and Portsmouth. Voyages to the West Indies. Jamaica. Trips across the sea to Europe. England. Spain. Exotic far eastern ports. His pleasure in telling me of the long trips bordered on sheer excitement. About Trinidad, father said, "I saw great ships in port from all over the world. They brought spices and goods." I remember his voice shook, "And people in chains."

I watched their tall sails come back into port on the Delaware River. The odor of their spice-filled crates and pungent curry mixtures from India filled my nose enough to last for days. These years later, I still hear Father, "Cinnamon and other spices are not used only for flavoring on the ships. They cover the taste of spoiling meat when we're at sea for a long time."

Among the strange and wonderful things they put in our house, I remember most the rugs they said came from Persia. I can still see that long, red patterned Yomud rug, a runner stretching the full length of the shiny front hall in the Stevenson home.

The tales my Father and the Captain brought home! I listened to every detail of the tales about pirates. The two sailors filled me with stories about the devils swinging cutlasses and roaming the seas. Bloodthirsty, vicious, unattached to any country's flag, those turbaned, sometimes masked, rascals, killed people and seized their treasures. But the Captain's ships were well armed with cannon and tough sailors and always defended themselves. Isaiah Curry and I listened to the stories with awe. Rattling in our heads, those tales kept us awake nights as we lay talking about some day seeing those lands and people.

* * *

Isaiah and I spent hours on the Philadelphia docks, for it was from those docks that Father and Captain Stevenson sailed. We waded, swam, and fished in the Delaware. It was on the docks that we played our boyhood games. One of our favorites was to choose sides with our neighborhood friends and fight a battle of the Revolutionary War. We found old uniforms stored in Stevenson's attic; a few were worn and ragged, but perfect for the fray of our battles. I had grown tall. The legs of my uniform were a full three inches above my ankles, the sleeves too short. But my uniform was the envy of the fighters for it had an officer's badge sewn high on the right sleeve and bore a bullet hole through the left shoulder.

One afternoon, black boys our age from another neighborhood wanted to join us in a battle so we had a larger group of fighters than usual. That time, Isaiah called off the names for each side. "You three be on our side. You four can be with the side over there."

"I ain't bein' on no side of no part-white," the tallest and blackest of the strange boys yelled, sticking out his tongue at me. "You be a clabber boy." He glared at me like I had done something wrong.

"What you talking about?" I yelled louder than he had.

"You ain't even no black boy and I don't even think you got no mama." He dove into me and knocked me to the ground, but not before I could drag him down with me. I got in two good hits to his stomach as we landed, more by instinct than by even realizing

I was in a fight. Then we both lit into each other as hard as we could. By the time we began getting too tired to pound each other much more, I was realizing that somebody actually hated me for my skin color being about two shades lighter than his.

Back home that night, Jonah and Mahala, Captain Stevenson's two house servants, cleaned my cuts. Mahala explained how it was that many people looked down on people who were part white and part black. "But usually, it's only them that ain't as good as you anyways. They has to try and call you somethin' to make you wus than them. And there's no one can make you wus than them if you know you ain't."

"But Mahala, why does it have to be like that?" I asked. "My Father is strong and black. Better than any of them. And you know my father says my mother was a strong and good person. So what if she was German and white?"

"Well, you'se goin' to have lots of worry about that all your life cause that's jist the way people is. An' it ain't right. Ain't none of this crazy black-white stuff right." Mahala's voice, powerful as always, shook with emotions beyond what I could understand.

We finished our evening meal. Then, Mahala said, "George, I got to tell you again how all this crazy foolishness started. It changes every time a storyteller speaks it. You know how that is."

As grownup as I believed I was getting, I still listened whenever Mahala started a tale with, "My Old Uncle said it began in a very long ago time. Long before Philadelphia was born. *Man-Who-Started-It-All lived in a large forest in Africa. The land was beautiful. Flowers bloomed everywhere. Their colors were red and pink and yellow and white. There fragrances pleased him. Birds sang. Their songs drifted far across the land. One day, Man-Who-Started-It-All fell asleep. He slept a very long time. When he woke up, he was sitting beside a large mound. It was not there when he went to sleep. He saw bird feet tracks on the mound. He muttered to himself, "This clay must be soft. It must be pliable." He pulled a blob of clay off the mound. He had never really seen himself . But he remembered how he looked when he stared down into a pool of water. He remembered that his hair was long and* black and curly. He rolled the blob of clay between his hands. He made it long and narrow. He called it a body. Then he made two legs and two arms and a head, and fixed them onto the body. He spent a long time putting on the hat. He made it long and curly. He took the thing home and put it behind his fire pit. Every day for a long time, he made more things and put them behind his fire pit. He worked for ages, perhaps for many ages.

One day a terrible wind blew across the land. It blew so hard that it made a deep hole in the ground behind the fire pit. Then the rains came. They fell so long and hard they filled the hole the wind had made. It made a big lake. After a long time, the rains stopped. Man-Who-Started-It-All climbed down from the tree where he had stayed during the wind and the rains. Behind his fire pit, he found the things he had made all buried in the mud. He dug them up. He set the things on the shore of the big lake. He washed them off. He saw the ones that had been nearest the fire in his pit had baked dark black. Many farther back from the fire had baked yellow and brown. Others had stayed white because they had been left far from the fire and out in the cold.

It was always at this point in her story that Mahala paused and shivered for the things left out in the cold. Jonah would say, "Mahala, My Darling"—he always called her that—"don't waste time pitying the white things."

* * *

It saddened my Father as he watched my growing realization of what race meant. He wanted me to have a free life, but he told me of things that I had never guessed.

"George, life is getting much worse for us here in Philadelphia," he said one evening in the kitchen. "I think whites are getting worried about all our people running north from slavery and coming into the city the last few years. The law in Pennyslvania still requires children of free women servants to be bound as servants till they are twenty-eight years old.

"Every day you see the whites making more accusations against us free black people. Now there are a lot of accusations that we hide our people behind forged freedom papers. By law, us Negroes got to carry legal freedom papers. If we don't, we can be seized and locked up. Then the whites will sell us south into slavery."

I was actually growing prouder, though more afraid, to be Negro as my Father kept talking and explaining. How could whites be the way they were when we did no offense to them?

"One of the worst problems, Son, is that since 1800 there's been more and more kidnapping of us free Negroes," my father continued. "White men will kidnap a free black right off the street when no one is around. Then they sell the man or the woman down south into slavery before anyone can find out and prevent it. Sure, the legislature made a law against it. But the way the slave patrollers do it quick like, they rarely get stopped."

"George, you need to know that some people will do anything for money. That's how slavery started. Because selling black people made a lot of money for the traders." Father worried about what might happen to me while he was gone on a sea voyage. He always ended our talks with, "Remember one other thing. The Free African Society right here in Philadelphia has got a lot of people who can help you if you need them. Go there for help."

Always controlled, Father did not frown or swear as he talked. "You know, Son, I have spent my life serving Captain Stevenson. Pennsylvania is a free state. It was long ago in 1725 that the legislature passed the law making Negroes free people. But Captain Stevenson gave me papers anyway to make freedom sure for my family forever. A freedom paper for you, too, George. Maybe he did not trust those men who made the state laws. And because we respected each other, we have always stayed together." Father seemed lost a spell in memory. "The sea has been more a free life for me than the city. At least, I get a lot of respect from many people on the ships. But even on the Captain's ships there are sailors who have been on slaver ships. And for whatever reason they hate us."

In time, my father made a decision. "George, I want you to learn the sea as a trade. That will give you some independence from white control."

* * *

At the age of thirteen, I took my first sea voyage.

Captain Stevenson thought I would be the sailor my father was. But I hated every minute of it. I can still see the deck of the ship where my father and Stevenson stood talking during a fast run to Kingston in Jamaica. I can even hear their words.

"George is maybe too young for the sea," the Captain said.

Father agreed. "Yessir. He stays in my bunk a lot. Gets seasick too often."

"George does not seem to be the sailor I had hoped he would be." I remember the Captain frowned as he spoke.

The ship pitched hard under me. But greater misery struck from being the son of Captain Stevenson's favored "boy." It made me the brunt of many sneaky pranks by the regular sailors. Too much spice dumped in my food or drink made my stomach turn at a slight roll of the ship. Simple riggings snarled in my hands. I heard sneers when I could not handle the heavy ropes. And there were the same sneers of scorn I had heard from the boys on shore.

"You stupid brown boy."

"You part black bastard."

"You clabber boy, you ain't got no mother."

So it was not only the crazy pitching roll that made me hate sea voyages. I used to cry in my bunk at night, slashed by the insults.

I decided to fight my own battles without telling the Captain. Resentment was brewing in me, and I began to feel uneasy around the Captain. I did not think Stevenson had done right treating my father as belonging to him, not exactly slave but not free either. So the Captain never knew the real reasons I did not like his brand of freedom on the high seas. I preferred to leave the sea with the

Captain thinking, "Just a mere stripling, Matthew. Young George has a lot to learn of the sea and my ships."

My father and I talked about the sailors' attitudes. I asked him, "Why do the sailors say the mean things they do?"

A patient man, Matthew explained again, "Like I told you, Son, there are many low people in this world. They have to try and find a person on the bottom. It pushes them up if they can put someone down. And it is the same when it comes to race. In fact, these sailors that used to be on the slaver ships are hating us more."

I had taken my last voyage. The Captain and father understood, each from his different view, because neither one of them argued with me. Rather, they talked about my future.

"What are we going to do with you, George?" Father had asked.

"You must learn to read better. To improve your writing. They are skills a lot of people never have." Captain Stevenson had always been concerned with my education. "Preparation for life," the old Quaker liked to say. "You have to study hard to gain those skills. Learn from the books on my library shelves."

"You must not waste your time while the Captain and I are away at sea." My Father supported Stevenson's insistence that I read and improve myself.

* * *

There was little chance I would waste any time, for Captain Stevenson's library opened itself to my own fiery brand of desire. The Captain and my father had already sent me to a Quaker school for free black children in order that I become literate. So I knew how to make use of the Captain's library. His books reflected his broad interests. A Bible. A geography of the world. William Penn's *No Cross, No Crown*. A history of navigation. Law books. Shelves full of books on an array of subjects.

William Penn left England in 1682 for America to found the Commonwealth of Pennsylvania. He had received a vast area of land on the west bank of the Delaware River from Charles II of

England in return for cancellation of the King of England's debts to the Penn family. How would it feel to have a king owe me such a large sum of money? I used to think about that as I read Penn's book. *No Cross, No Crown*, I admit, was difficult going for me, even after the drill of several terms in the Quaker school. But as I read the book and figured out its words, I could understand most of it. I remember one of its statements, "True Godliness don't turn Men out of the World but enables them to live better in it, and excites their Endeavors to mend it."

Mahala often spoke the same thought.

There I was back in Philadelphia, the Cradle of Liberty where my people are called "niggers." I could stay and mend the world. But how could a person do any mending when, like the sugar barrel driver, you are chased by guns? That shattering day years later in East Tennessee, facing the Lucas guns, I saw the same thing. Mend the world? Not a simple task.

As a boy in Philadelphia, I had kept asking myself, "With so many free Negroes in Philadelphia, why isn't there more mending going on?"

I never forgot the sugar barrel driver forced from Philadelphia on pain of death, prison, or being sold into slavery. I had a sickening nightmare whenever I thought of him. *My dreams would take me to a place where I was sitting on a dock with a sack of food. I sat there for days without eating. I got hungrier and hungrier. Finally, I would reach into the sack. Just at that moment a white man in a merchant's outfit would point a gun at my head and yell, "Not for you, Boy. Not a bite." My hand could never quite grab the food for fear of being shot. But time and again I would think I could grab the food quick enough so that maybe the man with the gun would not see. My hand would sneak just inside the sack, but the man with the gun would always see and begin pulling the trigger. I had to stop on the brink of death. My hand drew back.*

I would wake up soaked in sweat, crying out from wondering which way I would die. Memory of the nightmare clawed at me through the day. I felt that I was hanging on the edge of a terrible abyss.

*   *   *

My father was old. His hair shone as white as the new sails the Captain's crews unfurled in home port. I watched those sails take their first bite into the sky above the Delaware River, sails that drove the ships beneath them across distant seas, ships borne by the whip of the winds. Through all his last years, voice strong, mind sharp, iron-willed in fending the quips and the insults, Matthew Bush held to fairness among all people as the guiding rule of his life. Father passed to me—stated in one way or another that he believed I would understand—the great fund of learning he acquired from the many seas he had traveled.

Almost blind in his last years, Captain Stevenson walked with a gold eagle-headed cane. But his voice still had the power to roar orders, to command wharf hands across the docks on land or sailors high in the masts at sea.

As I grew older, I wondered why the doughty old Philadelphia salt had ever worried a whit about educating me. Why would any white man teach a Negro, free or slave, to read? Reading unlocks secrets, spreads thoughts, reveals ideas whites never meant my people to learn or to understand.

It bothered me that Captain Stevenson often said, "George Bush, you have a quick mind. You need to keep improving it. Get school training while you are young." Training me to read and write merely for my own good? No. I figured that he wanted me to know enough to serve him in his business, do his bookkeeping, his records, his daily office chores. I saw the Captain educating me as his cynical, scheming method of binding me to him in the same way he had taken my father's entire life for serving him.

My passion to learn always burned far stronger than doubts of the Captain's motives for exposing me to the school training. As the years stretched behind me, I gained more and more respect for the Philadelphia Quaker blab school that had earlier taught me the basics of reading, how to sound out words, learn their meanings, create logic in my talk. The schoolmasters guided us students in reading aloud, a way of making certain each pupil kept to his studies. The blabbing continued throughout the day. A noisy method. At night, I would hear voices in my sleep. Blab and drill. Drill and blab. Blab and drill, and we learned to read. Training in the Quaker blab school served me well, but in different ways than the sea captain had thought.

* * *

Captain Stevenson's wife had died when young, leaving the house to be ruled by the Negro couple, Jonah and Mahala. Through the years, Mahala proved a strong friend, like a mother to me. She often said, "George, learn from the Captain's books. They might lead you out from misery." While my father and the Captain were at sea, she urged me to spend time reading in the library.

Mahala would always make us wash our hands before touching the books. The Curry boys would make fun of her as being too much of a fat old nag. The Captain's library was our favorite room. We spent many afternoons flat on our stomachs with me as "teacher" helping Isaiah sound out words while the younger ones listened and mouthed the words along with us.

Isaiah's favorite story came from a small book. It told of a man named Sisyphus trying to push a big rock to the top of the hill. Near the top, it always slipped down. He tried again and again, shoving it high up the hill. Sisyphus spent his life shoving, pushing, lifting the rock. And Isaiah roared with laughter as he pantomined the man's struggle.

My "teaching" in the library done, we would pull a kitchen raid before the Curry children left for home. We stationed a little brother at each door watching for Jonah and Mahala—"Jonah and Whale-a," Isaiah had nicknamed her. We older boys sneaked into the kitchen and pulled out a loaf of her delicious bread. "Scram, here comes the Whale-a" would send us out the back door and into the safety of the cow pasture, laughing, screaming, gobbling up the bread as we jigged a preposterous "Jonah and the Whale-a" in the mud.

When I returned home after such an escapade, Mahala greeted me with a stern, "You been in the kitchen. I knows cause some fresh bread has been et. Now you spending too much time inside reading and playing around. You got to git outside." She would order me to do chores—weeding the garden, cutting dead heads off the flowers, or feeding our cattle.

I cannot say that going outside to work was altogether bad for me. But it did make me realize how little I had time to learn from the books when I had to do menial labor. This is part of what they were saying at Free African Society meetings. The white man keeps the Negro at hard labor. He prevents us learning to read, so he keeps ideas away from the Negro.

With the ideas I kept finding in the Captain's library, I could not wait to race back in for more reading. Pretty soon Mahala would relent, laugh at me, and say, "Hah, you scamp, you can go back in and read. Only you got to tell me what you be reading."

The Declaration of Independence.

The Constitution.

Milton. Donne. A few lines here and there.

Shakespeare, one of my favorites.

The classics. Dante was hard going, but filled with wisdom.

The law books. Blackstone. Treatises on maritime law. Books on State law. United States law. Although not a lawyer, the Captain had his own volumes and always checked up on his Philadelphia lawyers. "Know the law thyself," he told me. "Never rely on others."

These two men whom I knew as parents had long been planning for my future. One day, I listened to them talking me over.

"Thee will be well provided for when I am gone, Matthew," the aged Captain used to say to my father who was as old, or older, than he was.

"Aye, and I thank thee, Sir," my father would answer. "But my time be as short as thine."

'Tis, then, for the lad George we provide. We've sailed these oceans, the two of us. Many happy years 'tis been. And we may as well sail out together to our last port."

So it was that through the years while they sailed from one port to another they left me with the books to build a good reading ability they hoped would help me understand this crazy world.

3

While my two "parents" sailed the seas, I often visited the Free African Society for Father believed it a suitable place for me to spend time. Through the Society I made good friends and learned from the older people who were members. Isaiah learned along with me. A close friend, cheerful, Isaiah saw the best side to everything. His vibrant laugh when we walked about the city would ring out, cause ladies to rush to their windows and brush back their curtains to see who was going by.

Isaiah and I fished from the banks of the Delaware River, many times anchoring our poles in an overhanging branch while we went swimming, the water swishing cool and clean against our naked bodies. Later, we would lie on the bank of the river drying in the sun, sometimes questioning the difference in our color—Isaiah's body the darkest black, a glistening slender boy in the sun, my body long and black, too, but a few shades lighter.

Isaiah joked once about it, "Deep in your soul you must have got some clabber from white milk in there."

I took a friendly laughing shove at him. "Well, I am a true mixture of America. That means I can catch more fish here than you can 'cause I am more natural hereabouts. I'm a true native son, made of white and black."

Just then Isaiah's fish line jerked taut. He laughed at me, "You big mouthed talker. See, this proves it. I am better." He jumped for the pole, but the fish got away.

"The only chance of you catching one is because the fish will probably die laughing at both of us scrambling around like darn fools." I laughed at him.

Isaiah's deep black eyes sparkled. His rich laugh spilled out and rolled down the Delaware River.

* * *

One late night in a meeting of the Free African Society, Isaiah and I listened as a fiery pure black man recounted his experiences a few weeks earlier. He had just fled from York, a city a little less than one hundred miles west of Philadelphia across the Susquehanna River. "Some time back, we burned eleven buildings to the ground! Those cussed whites had been starving us. And they made charges that some of us have forged freeman papers. They don't hold to their contracts with us, and we can't testify in court about it. Our kids have no doctors. We live in slums. Our only jobs, the very lowest, dirty, with little pay. Some of my friends and me went out to destroy the white men.

"So we burned those eleven buildings down! Six different places in the city we started big fires. I was one of the men who escaped, but twenty of my friends were caught to stand trial.

"The whites are not any one of them a Christian even though they say they are. There is no way a just God would have them be over us the way it is. Race haters are mixing with devils. We Negroes had better not mix our blood with them. Them whites are a devil race."

His words seared my heart. From the sad day I had first begun to learn what race meant, I had fought enough dark-skinned Negro boys who had taunted me with the words "part-white clabber" that I now felt sick in my stomach hearing the same feeling come from this fiery man whom I admired.

That night at home in bed, I woke up in a terrible sweat. I sat up, another of my nightmares tearing through me. In this one, *I am walking, and the earth seems almost to end. I am at the edge of it with nothing around. I am standing on a high ridgelike rock that falls away to nothing on all sides. A winged milk-white horse with a skeleton rider flies by again and again, kicking at the rocks, knocking more rocks away. A rock crashes onto my foot cutting it half off.* I awoke with the pain of it.

A native son of Philadelphia, I grew up afraid for us free Negroes. Mulatto or all black, most of the free Negro people were in trouble, trouble because a smoldering fire seemed always to scorch the relations between white and black. When my father's ship lay in port at its dock, his free Negro friends came by our house. Or he would visit with them at meeting places for the Free African Society and its many members. They talked about conditions like those spoken of by that obsessed man who had helped burn York.

I was about fifteen when I heard that the Free African Society had asked the Pennsylvania state legislature to remove some of the restrictions on free Negroes. In Philadelphia like in York, we free Negroes were still restricted from the good jobs. Low wages caused the poor living conditions for my people. The whites were not paying them enough for work. Many of our men went for weeks without any work at all. How could our parents keep feeding their children?

Every day we suffered stinging insults from the whites. Even at death, those of our people who still attended white churches could not be buried in the same church yard. The whites ran their own churches and were so disrespectful that our Negro families pulled out and set up their own. Even in our separate churches, worship services were interrupted time and again. Well-dressed white men stormed in, threw stinking wads into the stove, laughed when the noxious smell started people coughing and drove them from their church.

Another stinging insult wounded us deep—the free black fire brigade band could not play its music along with the white band.

My father figured that the whites were trying to drive all the free Negroes away from Philadelphia.

I knew why York burned!

*　*　*

Isaiah's parents were delightful folks. They knew how to live above the meanness and the "keep your place" insults. Many people lived in the Curry house, but all one family. It seemed as if every time I visited the Curry's someone new had been taken in, and I wished—often said it out loud to them—I had a family like that. For some reason, my father was an "only one" as I was. Unusual that our family in the good-sized brick house was just father and me, for the black families I knew always had many members.

Isaiah's father was a bright good man, able to do anything, fix chairs, buggy wheels, cabinet making his strong forte. The only work for pay open to him was menial—cleaning rotting fishheads, dead cats and dogs, human debris off the docks. His work paid little, kept him working daylight till dark. Yet the Curry house rang with laughter when the whole family, me included, gathered around the table for dinner at noon.

For a lone child like George Bush who lived in a house of grown-ups strict in manner and spare of talk, the open Curry home meant *family*. With Isaiah's clan, I grew toward young manhood. I loved the home, its noise and happy chatter, everyone in it. Even if no tablecloth covered the scarred pine table and the chairs were old benches worn smooth by many children's bottoms sliding back and forth, I fitted with the Currys. Learning the difference between my well-to-do household and the frugal one of my best friend seemed to draw me closer to him.

As we grew older, Isaiah and I would spend hours on Front Street where curiosity about the sailing ships drew us to the docks. It gave me pleasure bragging to Isaiah about the foreign ports I had seen, the strange people. The languages had been beyond my understanding, but I remembered that the smiles of people in the many different ports we visited spoke a common tongue. Isaiah followed me as I pointed out the river docks where ships sailed by my father and Captain Stevenson had ridden at anchor. Sitting on hawsers tying the ocean vessels to the docks, we talked about sea life, watched the cargoes being unloaded: fabrics and furniture from Europe, porcelain from China, iron goods, spices, other barrels filled with articles strange to us. Isaiah was the only friend I cared to tell about my misadventures at sea. His wonderful rich laugh roared out over my adventures to faraway places and strange people. Even my poor sailing sounded quite ridiculous as it grew distant in time and place from the happenings.

* * *

One day, a couple of sailors stopped and began telling jokes to us. One leaned against an anchor post, drew an old pipe from his dungaree pocket, and started puffing smoke into the air. They offered to take us on board to look at the docks from the pilot's nest. I declined. I could not force myself onto a strange ship with men I did not know.

The hours passed. Dusk slowly settled over the Philadelphia docks. Knowing we should be home, Isaiah and I paused at the corner of a warehouse, looked back over the waterfront. The last rays of sun touched the top fifth of the furled sails, drawing an eerie whiteness into the sky from them.

From my spot a step or two in front of my friend, I heard Isaiah's gasping cry. I wheeled around as a tall man with a rope threw it around me and clamped his hand over my mouth. I jerked my elbow into the man's stomach, grasped his arm and, using it as a pry, twisted myself out of the yet loose rope and away from him.

"Run, Isaiah!" I screamed as I saw two men dragging my best friend out of sight.

I rushed toward them to help Isaiah. Another man swept from behind a storage shed, knocked me to the dock. Kicking, slugging with my fists, I thrashed at my two assailants. As if I were an animal, they pushed me to the planking, tied my arms and legs.

Familiar with Front Street, I realized in the dimness of early evening that activity on the waterfront had shut down. No hands would be around until sometime before sunup. I struggled, fought back, as the strangers threw Isaiah and me into a wagon behind the most remote warehouse on the docks.

Bound and gagged, fear stabbing from his eyes, Isaiah tried to say something to me, but the gags muffled his words.

Three men climbed into the wagon, whips in hands, pistol butts jutting from holsters. I arched my back, aiming to turn toward Isaiah, but a kick struck me flat onto the wagon bottom. Our captors sat on a bench at one side of the wagon. I stared. I determined to fix their features in my mind, but the dim light flattened all three faces into the same gray-bearded monsters. Finally, the man closest to me shouted an order to the short squat figure on the driver's bench, and the wagon turned from the city street onto a trail. The tight bindings wore into my skin, and my arms and legs grew numb.

Fear beat through my head. Sweat itched my armpits. Words streaked through my mind: *kidnapping . . . man-stealers . . . sold in the Southlands . . . slavery.* I knew we were heading away from the main part of Philadelphia. Crazy that Isaiah and I were not home at the Curry house. Crazy that we were not part of the chatter around the Curry table. Crazy that we were not diving into his mother's steaming pepper pot stew. I tried to figure how it could be possible to turn time back, pulled my legs toward my chest, tried to sit up. A fist dropped me flat.

As the wagon jolted onward, the dim light we had left at the docks deepened into total darkness. I estimated time, knew that we had been at least an hour on the trail when the wagon slowed, turned, and pulled to a stop.

Two of the men yanked me to my feet, roughed me up. I swung my body around, butted as hard as I could against one of them, hit against his solid shoulder. Yanked by my hair, I screamed unheard into my gag. Without water from afternoon into the night, the dryness in my throat made it impossible to swallow.

Kicked and pushed into a small hut, Isaiah and I fell against each other in a heap. The air reeked with human stench and dirty straw. The door closed leaving us with our terror. We had been thrown into a rats' nest. I felt their claws skittering over my legs, a tail sliding across my neck. I smelled their foul, unclean stink.

Time drifted. An hour passed? Two hours?

The door opened. Holding lanterns at arm's length, keeping their distance from us, a couple of men stepped into the hut, looked us over. The younger man, big shouldered and short, stood beside an older man without a cap, his hair close-cropped.

"They're jist the right age. Good strong bucks, both of them," the older one said. The light of the lantern reflected from his leather boots and the large diamond ring on his finger.

"You got food coming. But don't try anything or we'll shoot you both." The younger man handed the lantern to his companion, removed my gag and ropes, then Isaiah's.

Despite the threat, I pulled my feet under me, firmed my muscles, shot myself against the man holding both lanterns. His lanterns jerked loose, fell at the side of the room. The dry straw burst into flames. The man kicked at me. I side-stepped his boot, grabbed his foot, and threw him onto his back. Isaiah had slammed the younger man against the door, shoving it wide open.

As we dashed for the cover of trees nearby, pistol shots streaked over us. A searing hot stab into my left shoulder turned me half around. Gasping fresh air into my lungs, I stumbled against a tree trunk. Isaiah screamed as the big-shouldered man punched him and dragged him back toward the rats' nest. Silhouetted against the flames of the burning shack, I saw three men rushing at me. Stretching at half length on the ground, I let my body sag. I knew my only hope was to lie limp, look dead.

A boot kicked me over. A hand twisted me around by the leg and swiped through the fresh blood gushing from the wound down over my chest. A violent slap bruised my nose, but I held myself breathless.

"Damn us, John. 'Pears we've finished this one."

"No worry. The river's close by. No more shootin' tonight. We best avoid drawing attention over a dumb darky. We ain't got no time to see about patchin' him up. You and Fred kick him over the bank. Shove him into deep water. Quick now. Get a move on."

Still sagging as they dragged me by my feet, I could scarcely hold back screaming out when one of the men struck me hard on the head with a pole before forcing me into black water.

Treading water at first, keeping my head mostly below the surface so they would think I had sunk to the bottom, I knew the night and the black water were my best protection. The bleeding left me weak, nauseated. The pain, almost unbearable, held me back from swimming with any power in my strokes. Then, paddling slowly, without noise, avoiding ripples on the surface, I moved along the riverbank. I blacked out time and again. The motions brought squirts of blood from the wound, and sharp pains shot through every fiber of my chest and shoulder and head. I managed to pull my aching body into the reeds and marshes along the Delaware's bank, near where Isaiah and I had often fished.

As soon as I could move, biting my cheeks against the pain, keeping alert for sounds, I swam back to where I had been thrown into the river. I hoped to see the wagon. It was gone. The half-burned shack stood empty. My wound throbbed. My head felt as if it had cracked open.

My agony was more than physical. Isaiah.

Back in the city, screening myself with protecting shadows, I slipped from one street to another, felt the wound tear open again. Bursting through the Curry door, I screamed, "They stole Isaiah." I sagged onto a bench, my blood puddling on the floor.

Father Curry rushed to find men he could trust, men close to him in the Free African Society. They searched for Isaiah— along the riverbank, through abandoned boats and buildings knowing he was not there. Kidnappers waste no time departing with their prey.

* * *

Isaiah had vanished.

The bright light that had shone over Philadelphia had been pinched out. The warm family laughter that had sounded in the Curry house died. The gutter stench that always hung over the streets pressed in, overpowering, strangling. Thinking back, the stench was more than gutter debris. The stench was people.

Aye, I know, the state of Pennsylvania had outlawed slavery. Honest folks struggled with laws and rules trying to make manumission work. But under it all lived a horrible truth: Slave patrollers roamed our free state. Most operated at night, but many took the guise of respectable businessmen. As my father and the free Negro from York had told me, traders made money by kidnapping free Negroes and selling them to the deep south slave markets.

Kidnapping was illegal and despised by many whites. Nevertheless, the practice thrived. Some white Philadelphians would slip information to those traders about where to snatch free persons. A strong young man like Isaiah—"good Negro stock"—could sell for as high as five thousand dollars at one Natchez slave mart; forty-five hundred at another one. Strong, young bodies—a valuable commodity.

"It's my fault. I should have saved him," I cried out day after day. "I should have gotten out of the river right away. I should have followed him." Even though both of Isaiah's parents told me it was not my fault, guilt overwhelmed me. The awful realization that Isaiah had fallen into a slaver's clutch struck the Curry family as if spikes had been nailed into their hearts.

Nightmares lashed me. *I heard Isaiah's laugh. I ran for him. Dirty hands jerked him away. I could never reach him.*

* * *

Several months after Isaiah had disappeared, the Captain and my father sailed back up the Delaware River into port with stories of a new type of piracy on the high seas. They spoke of English piracy called impressment. The Britishers (not loved at any time that I could tell after the Revolutionary War) had begun stopping Yankee skippers at sea, forcing Americans off their vessels at sword's point, forcing them into the British navy. "Impressment," it was called.

Captain Stevenson said that English deserters were being hidden on American ships, so the English claimed the right to stop our ships. My ability to read had already allowed me to follow this situation in newspapers when my father and the Captain were at sea. Mahala and Jonah would sit in the kitchen and listen as I read to them. The newspapers screamed that the British, as the Captain had said, were impressing American sailors because their own deserters hid on American ships.

How different from what I had learned at the same time through the Free African Society! The truth, as we had come to understand it, was that international law had forbidden the African slave-ship trade in 1808. The British navy now claimed it had the duty to patrol the high seas to uphold international law. It claimed a duty to board American ships and seize men as deserters.

But while the Captain railed against the English—"Piracy," he called it—the impressment at sea was not what panicked father and me. It was the piracy rampant in Philadelphia. *Isaiah stolen. No law protected him.* And Father cried, "What law will protect you, George Bush?"

As the days passed, I lost patience with British impressment talk. "Isaiah has been stolen," I screamed at my father time on time.

Father spent hours talking with me, listening to my ravings about that awful night. Father was sympathetic, but that sympathy did nothing to ease my pain and guilt about Isaiah. And I felt adrift on a roiling sea.

I did not always understand Father's advice in our late night talks, but I remember his words. "George, life is an ocean of eternal change. Do not let the whitecaps roll you over. Take courage. Swim through the whitecaps."

* * *

Captain Stevenson, in port from his last intended ocean venture, wanted to enjoy his remaining life ashore with time to read his books and look back on his many trips sailing the seas. He had survived less than a year. A few months later, Father followed, as if one old Philadelphia sea dog could not live without the other.

The Captain's Last Will left his estate to Matthew Bush who passed it down to me. The Captain's hand-penned, angular, solid letters, "Forever Free," guaranteed the freedom of our Bush family. Even in death, the Captain held a skeptical and wary hand on the Pennsylvania lawmakers. He feared they might undo the Gradual Emancipation Law of 1780 and slip me into slavery for he knew considerable numbers of Pennsylvania citizens frowned on the freedom given us by that old law. Faithful to Quaker beliefs, Captain Stevenson lived his rejection of slavery by those words, "Forever free."

Old shipowners of those days left debts. Tremendous debts. Captain Stevenson's estate fared no better. Many men filed claims for cargoes lost at sea years past. Settlement of Stevenson's affairs required sale of ships and cargoes, payment of crews and banks. Every obligation had to be reconciled. But even after the Captain's accounts had been applied to satisfy those huge sums, I received a goodly amount giving me a decent start in life.

I had the funds. Now, I could search for Isaiah.

Suddenly, it appeared as if I had more friends, white as well as black, than I had ever known. Those last Philadelphia days I forced myself to keep an alert head on my shoulders as I turned down offers to use my inheritance for an apothecary shop, a tailor shop, a market stall on the river, and many more. The most expansive and requiring by far the greatest outlay of dollars was a sea trading venture, the schemers clever enough to work on my Stevenson ship experience. The offers always came from an "expert" who could take my dollars and run the outfit for me, but my plans did not include dumping money into the pockets held open for me by those high-scheming, easy-figuring business folks.

"A rich nigger," I heard some men say. Because I pushed aside all offers, I also became known as "one stingy, aloof nigger. An arrogant clabber bastard."

Philadelphia! Cradle of Liberty! Bondage city! Thief of Isaiah! My birth city a bondage city. Bondage for my father. For all our people. Wherever I walked, I heard from past years the echo of the slave chains on the backs of my African family. For my lost friend Isaiah, the stench of slavery curdling the air of the city made me sick. No longer the *Cradle of Liberty*. Or perhaps, it never had cradled liberty.

I determined to move away from the city where we Negroes could not get enough pay for work to stay out of poverty. The city that stole Isaiah.

* * *

Through the Free African Society, I had heard that East Tennessee was a region of small farmers having only a few men and women wealthy enough to own slaves. Mostly wilderness, that state was the opening west, the frontier, a place where a man could search for a new start in life.

Word was that in Tennessee Negroes could own land. And the Tennessee Convention of 1796 gave free black men the right to vote, the same as in North Carolina. That meant something! Perhaps, those Tennessee laws meant there could be decent folks on the frontier.

Naturally, the Free African Society members and I talked about the fact that there was some slavery even in the hills of East Tennessee where I thought of going. A minister, Reverend Allen, a leader in the Free African Society, gave me the most hope. He said, "We ministers have our own message system. I have already sent word to my brothers in the Southland. If Isaiah can be found, we will find him. It takes a long time for such cases. I believe we can locate Isaiah. Then we will send word to you. Young Man, you can not do this alone. You must be careful. Keep wary. Do not let rage destroy you, George Bush."

Those Free African Society leaders knew that the cotton gin had opened up the west part of Tennessee. Cotton fields brought large scale slavery. I read some about that myself. But if any Negro could find a way to live peaceably on the frontier, I could. The hills of East Tennessee looked to be the place where I could carve out a farm.

In those hills, I planned to build a base to start looking for Isaiah, a place where he could bide his time and heal when he became free. Oh, the anguish of those late nights when I talked with Mother and Father Curry. We tried to figure the best way to find Isaiah and bring him home. While we waited for word from the Free African Society, we dreamed and planned for the day we would hear again Isaiah's deep toned laughter in the Curry home.

Thinking that way, I started getting a better feeling that maybe my horrible nightmares of being always on the brink of the abyss would not have to be. I believed the wild Tennessee frontier to be a place for me if my efforts counted for anything at all in this world. We heard that East Tennessee had come into existence as "The Revolutionary State of Franklin" founded on the liberty ideas of America's break from Great Britain. East Tennesseans had refused to bow to an unjust king. That place had to have good people.

* * *

I settled the money I had inherited from Captain Stevenson in accounts secure in the Philadelphia bank. It was then I began packing my clothes, blankets, the red Yomud runner, and favorites from the Captain's books. During the weeks following Stevenson's death, I explained to Mahala and Jonah about the Captain's involved affairs, read them his will passing all he owned to my father, then to me. I explained how the law worked in such matters.

The past couple of years, with more slaves escaping from the South into Pennsylvania and the tightening of openings for us

Negroes for work and social relations, the two had drawn some closer to me, natural in the milieu of the times. Understanding that I did plan to head south, our evenings became long talks about their future, my future, what, if anything, compatible with whites we could expect.

They shared my grief over Isaiah. They promised me they would lend a hand to Currys whenever they needed help. Both Jonah and Mahala had mourned with me from the day Isaiah had disappeared. How long since Isaiah and I had laughed in the library, teasing "Jonah and the Whale-a!"

* * *

An evening during my last week in Philadelphia, carrying a live plant I dug from the Stevenson yard to give the Currys, I walked toward their home on Water Street. Duty to tell them I was leaving had pulled at me for several days. Now I had to face saying good-bye to them. In spite of the closeness between me and the Currys, it haunted me to face them. Isaiah seemed to be all around the place, splashing beside me as we ran across their yard, sitting at their table, teasing his small brothers and sisters.

Mother Curry opened the door to my knock. "Gracious sacks! Come in, George. We just be sitting down to eat."

The family warmth I had known with the Curry family flowed around me. Our talk held subdued, and I felt that each of us searched for words to cover feelings. The fresh home made bread and clam chowder had never tasted better. The lighted candles at the center of the table carried a message of hope. In the undertow of their voices, I heard Isaiah's laugh from days we had spent on the wharf.

As the meal drew to a close, I said, "Friends, I have made up my mind. I am leaving Philadelphia in a few days. I have decided to settle in . . ."

"George Bush, if you . . ." Mr. Curry's voice broke. He kept tear filled eyes on me, his unspoken words pleading.

"I am going to search for Isaiah and bring him home. I will not come back till I find him."

Silence bound us for several moments. I swallowed the emotion I could not put into words, then turned my talk to facts.

"I have made inquiries about places in the Southland where I believe I can get along with people. My friends at the Free African Society have given me good advice about people in East Tennessee. The country there is an open, frontier region. Few slaveholders. I believe it offers a place for the base I need to begin the search."

As she recognized my will to do as I said, Mother Curry wiped tears from her face. "Our hearts and prayers go with you, George Bush."

Hugs from each of the children brought tears to my face. Final handclasps made with father and mother Curry, I stepped through the door and eased into the shadowed streets of the City of Brotherly Love.

* * *

The next day, I found Mahala sitting beside the kitchen table crying. I stood a few moments waiting. As she glanced up, tears streaming down her face, she sobbed, "Isaiah's still gone. Such a rascal. Oh, George, I used to hear the two of you laughing, calling us Jonah and the Whale-a. I knew it was his words. Sometimes it made me so mad. Isaiah so naughty, even when he was a small boy. But such a happy scamp. That loud laugh of his. Who could help loving him? I did. I loved Isaiah. We both did, Jonah and me. Go find him, George."

Then, Mahala reminded me of our people's ancient story of creation. In her telling, she always hung her tale on Man-Who-Started-It-All and the people he created from clay. That day, she said to me, "Man-Who-Started-It-All lived in the most ancient time. You remember him, George. He was the wisest of all. He found the clay mound." She thought a moment, then the gracious

Mahala smile lighted up her face. "They's got to be good people out there in East Tennessee. We all be made out of the same clay."

Mahala and Jonah had been lifetime servants to the Captain, trusted by him. I think the three of us regretted not having been more understanding of each other those years we had lived together in the Stevenson house. Out of respect for Stevenson and Matthew Bush, knowing the housekeeper and her husband would need refuge away from the growing sentiment against our free people, my last act in Philaldelphia was to sign over to them the Captain's home and furnishings. I sensed their sorrow when I was ready to leave, saw Mahala wipe away tears, felt the touch of her heart in her rare hug as I said a few words and stepped out the door.

Overriding everything I had done those days, the fact was that somewhere in the Southland Isaiah slaved. I had been carrying a heavy load of guilt staying in a city in the North while Isaiah lived South in slavery. In East Tennessee, I would be closer to him and could keep my ear open for news about him. Maybe, just maybe, a way to find him would open. A long shot, I knew. I began daring to hope that the Reverend Allen's minister message network would locate Isaiah.

But one thing for sure, I would never find Isaiah Curry if I stayed north in Philadelphia.

With some of Captain Stevenson's estate money, I could buy a few acres of East Tennessee land. I would begin building a way to overcome the uncontrolled feeling, the powerlessness, the loss that surrounded all free Negroes in the City of Brotherly Love. Maybe there would even be a town where I could become friends with a few of the folks living there. Looking for ways to build friendships could always open doors.

Negro by color and by pride, I left Philadelphia, that rat's alley where deadmen lost their bones.

4

Etched with narrow valleys, East Tennessee presents the face of a remote, homegrown region. Heavily-forested foothills range the land, a country ridged by mountains—the Great Smokies in the east, Appalachians to the south and west, Cumberlands to the north. Hills and mountains covered with snow during winter months offer a spectacular show of flowering shrubs and trees through spring and summer. During autumn the red and yellow leaves of hardwoods flood the land.

The great valley of East Tennessee stretches from Virginia far south into Alabama. Bordering sparkling rivers spread the fertile lands of the Cumberland Plateau. Southwest from King's Mountain, John Sevier had routed the British during the Revolution. And in those Cumberland Mountains rich with coal deposits, people took the fertile land for homes and farms. Families of Revolutionary War soldiers provided most of the settlers, people who hated the oppressive "East" of North Carolina about as much as they hated the British.

The East Tennessee frontier called to all levels and ranks. Hunters. Traders. Adventurers. Outlaws. Free Negroes. Outcasts. Preachers. Missionaries. A region of fervent evangelism and frontier brawling. A tough folk-stream. A self-reliant society. A land of people who built their log cabins in remote enclaves among the ridges so they could live free.

* * *

When I set foot in the frontier village of Knoxville, it offered me no public accommodations. For a few days I had looked the town over, careful not to seem a loiterer or to give anyone an excuse to accuse me of vagrancy. As I rode through Knoxville streets, I found myself comparing the small frontier village on the Holston River in the foothills of the Great Smokies with the Pennsylvania city on the Delaware up to this point the most important place in my life.

Houses were small. Cattle and pigs roamed the streets. Dust from countless feet and wagons coated everything. Knoxville people had a pioneer home-spun and buckskin look about them. A far cry separated that settlement from Philadelphia, city of history and wealth and importance, but a city of sorrow.

Aye, always the memories rode with me. Philadelphia with its grand public buildings: City Hall, St. George's Church, American Philosophical Society. Banks and mills, fine homes on tree-lined streets, the carriages of rich people. The Delaware River docks from which Captain Stevenson and my father had sailed to foreign lands and returned with exotic cargoes. Men well clothed and sporting manners. Women in dresses and finery imported from France and other European lands. And foremost, Independence Hall where the Constitution of the United States had been created.

Philadelphia, where Isaiah had been stolen.

I listened to the talk in the Knoxville stores. Different from what I knew and spoke, the speech flowed so thick with accents of Elizabethan English that I found it hard to understand. Sometimes passing a house, I heard ballads carried long ago from the Old Country, songs, no doubt, passed down from one generation of singers to the next.

After a time in Knoxville, I gained speaking acquaintance with Joseph Young, owner of the Wild Turkey Tavern. When I felt easy talking with the man, I began asking questions about places to live.

Young suggested, "Go talk to Sam Brown about boarding with him." Then his tone turned patronizing as he finished our last talk with, "Sam's honest. One of the most respected freedmen hereabouts. He'll likely take you in till you move on."

Move on? Hell, I had come to East Tennessee to stay.

* * *

At the sound of my horse's hoofbeats, a lean, elderly man limped out the door of an old barn. "Welcome, heah, Stranga," his high-pitched voice greeted me. His iron handclasp reinforced the warmth of his words. His two hounds—"Scamp and Turner," tails wagging—barked their friendly greeting.

Dismounting, I walked with Sam to his house, a rundown hutch of ill-fitting boards and logs. I received a more subdued welcome from a small thin woman, hair tied in a faded red headcloth. I was not sure if I could stop with them, but true to the tavern keeper's words, Sam insisted I stay with him and his wife, "Sally," he called her. I tried to press a few dollars on them for my room and board, but they refused.

That night, Sam and Sally told me they had been freed from slavery three years. They had neither time nor money to fix up the small place. The daily chores for survival pushed them to their limits. I read the two as good and gentle people, so I figured it better that I move on. I did not want to impose on them.

After a spell, Sam agreed I could help him fix up their house and pay for the supplies and materials needed. We cut and skinned trees, shored up the cabin, chinked the gaps between logs with a mixture of Tennessee clay and straw, added on two lean-tos. One lean-to provided more space for Sally's cooking. The second gave me a place where I could store my gun and the belongings from my pack, a bedroom base while I looked around the country for my own land.

Quiet, more cautious than pleasant at first, Sally appeared neither ready to understand nor to trust me, a wanderer from the North. Only when she saw her new kitchen and fireplace taking shape did she warm toward me. Her hands, always working, never ceased their restless busy motions. Tiny, those hands had a strength uncommmon for her size, strength built from lifting the heavy iron kettles, digging carrots from her garden. A small quick woman, sometimes her voice sounded vinegar, sometimes honey. Her eyes seemed hooded, wary, unreadable. A Tennessee wild rose, that Sally.

For a man who spent little time away from his home, Sam Brown knew much of the Knoxville talk and happenings. Sam told me what farmers had cows for sale, what men were honest, which ones to avoid. Farm holdings in the region, except for a few, were small, the owners sometimes difficult. Aye, my old friend, I carry his image in my head wherever I roam. Lean face, leaner than most men his age. Gray wool on his cheeks, fuzzier than sideburns. The hair on his head standing straight up. His walk a bad limp.

Sam Brown proved to be all that the Wild Turkey Tavern owner told me he was. A man full of wisdom, his talk drew from memory a truism I had learned in my Philadelphia Quaker school reading exercises: Outward appearances seldom show what dwells within.

* * *

"Free men he'bouts gots to be mighty kerful how dey speaks." Sam cautioned me as we worked in the pasture through the weeks and months. He worried about my traveling across the countryside. He squinted at me one day, "George, dat freedom papah ye showed me. I gots none. Dat plantation Brown what owned me, him jist say I be free. N'n lemme go. I took his name Brown fo' me'n Sally. I did not know me own. So, hey I be."

Unsure why he seemed puzzled over my papers I let him talk, listened carefully to his words.

Finally, he said, "Son, I knows dat Penns'vany be a free land up north. Me tried runnin' dere." The lines in his worn cheeks drew tight. "Dis Ten'see be in slave country. So, I gots to ask, Why did you leave dat free land to set yo'sef down hey?"

The moment he asked my mind flowed with the memories of Philadelphia. The anguish torturing the fiery young man from York, my agony for Isaiah sold into slavery, rose in my mind.

"Sam, how a land is—free or slave—depends more on the people than the laws they make. You know, people's attitudes fix how laws are used. In the process the laws often get twisted. The same kind of people you have here as slaveholders are everywhere. They try to bring down us free Negroes."

His ax knifing into a stump, Sam added, "Us folks doin' all de white man's hardes' wuk. Anywhere we go dey tries to overpower us."

"It all hinges on the white people being afraid of us. You are right, Sam, Pennsylvania is a free state. The laws in 1780 ordered gradual emancipation. But the whites see any free Negroes as a threat to them. They say there's far too many of us free people living in the city of Philadelphia." I pontificated. I have a tendency to pontificate. Perhaps Stevenson's law books taught me something.

Sam frowned. "It sounds like a matta of feah and control. Jist like in slavery."

"That's right. They made new laws and kept control of the good jobs," I said. "That way they keep us down. And because many Negroes in the city have no jobs, they say we are lazy even though most of us are skilled workmen."

"Crazy, George. But me knows. Me bin tru' it here in Ten'see," Sam appeared drawing from his past.

"And so they could control us, they hated those of us who could read . . ."

"*Read?*" Almost a screech. "George Bush, kin you read?"

"Jimmers, yes."

"Who larnt you?"

"Like I said, I went to a Quaker school. Several different times. I also helped teach Negro children how to read. Sure is true that Negro children can learn as well as whites. Most Philadelphians hated all of this. They let it come out, clear and strong, that they did not want Negro children learning equal to whites." Excited at our talk, I began pounding my club on the fence post, unmindful that Sally had come with her apron full of ginseng roots and stood listening.

"You be soundin' like a preacha'." She laughed, her tone more friendly. "Mighty good talk. You be right, George."

"Unfortunately, in the set of the times, white folks distrust free Negroes." I was so steamed up, had so much to say, I wanted to spill out my thoughts. I held back certain words, fearing to raise distress in my new friends.

"Yes, we got's to know dat readin' and writin' if'n we spec's eber to gain eny uv our rights. I neber had da chancet, George. You soun' real good." Sam gave me one of his searching looks. I had the feeling he was studying me, trying to figure out if I believed everything I was saying.

Those first weeks in East Tennessee with Sam limping beside me, many times I compared Sam with my father for I saw in Sam the same bizarre pattern. Masters hold their slaves until they are too old to work, then free them. Like with my father, Matthew Bush. Aye, Matthew Bush was a free man. But he spent his entire life as an aide, a servant, to the Philadelphia seafaring Captain Stevenson. Release came for Matthew at the end of his life when he had burned out all his energy and was of no more use for the hard sea voyages, too old to understand or enjoy his freedom. Sam, too, had been used to the limit, then shucked aside, "freed" so his owner did not have to provide support for a slave no longer productive.

* * *

Sam sounded like my father when he told me time and again his view that a free Negro should not be too blunt. That could cost him his life and make lots of trouble for the other free Negroes in the region. "We all gots to be kerful. Mighty kerful. Make 'em tink we keeps our place. Den we can do tings dey nebber knows about. They tink I keeps my place real good."

"How'd you get your freedom?"

"Git me freedom? Oh, Suh. I's bin free onliest nigh on tre years comin' up Jan'ry one."

The idea of "git me freedom" struck Sam in strange and bitter fashion, and his laugh rocked the cabin walls.

"How'd you get it? Your freedom, yours and Sally's?"

"Wuk'd fo' it. An' buy'd it. Yes, Suh. Wuk'd fo' it an' buy'd it. Me used to do special jobs." Sam's wrinkled forehead tensed, a rasp overlaying his usually soft words. "Brown, him what owned me, he kep back a little cash fo' me ebry time I earn it an' save it fo' me 'gainst my freedom. When I had 'nuf, I buy'd us. Me an' Sal."

"Bought yourselves?"

"Yes, Suh."

"How long did it take?"

"To git us freedom? Les see. I calc'late nigh to fo'ty year. Gib or takes a few. Me bein' slave all dat time. But, Son, is I free now! Got dis yer piece of ground from old man Brown for s'long's we live. An' me two houns. Scamp and Turner. All dat an' freedom I gots now. I knows da land hain't mine, but hey we is and hopes to stay."

Give? Sam had no title to his land, no paper to protect him. Give? Forty years? "Be careful, Sam. Brown—anyone else—can yank it away." My friend Sam was quite a man. He never gave up. He had found those small keys to freedom that warmed him and Sally with some joy the last years of their lives. A strong man, the kind to tread the winepress alone.

But his crippled leg? Finally, I asked him outright what had happened, why he had only a stub instead of a foot.

"He don' like speakin' 'bout it none," Sally cut into our conversation, one of the few times she interrupted our talks. "It happen long 'fore dat Brown buy'd him. Dat's why he gots him so cheap. One cheap niggah, he." She laughed up at Sam, poked him in the ribs. "Sam, him runned many time when he be young. Dey says he runned ever chancet he git. An' he massa see dat whippin's don' stop Sam from runnin'. So, de owner gits so mad, he jist up an' chop off Sam's foot. Hacked it half right off. Den Sam kin run no mo'. Dat's how I cotcht him!" Her black eyes flashed. "George, iffen you gits you' foot chopt off in Ten'see, maybe you can get yo'sef cotcht by a wife."

* * *

Sam had helped me locate the Zeb Turley place. Sifting the black earth from hand to hand, he pronounced, "Da soil be good, George." But he had seemed much more leery than I of Zeb Turley ever selling to me. He reminded me that it was the custom generally to rent land to free Negro men only for short periods of time. My hopes centered on owning land. I had let Sam's cautions drift past me. I wanted to believe that when Zeb Turley saw my cash, how much I improved the place, he would sell to me.

As I had worked the Turley acres, I had questioned how much to do, for I did began to wonder if Turley would sell to me; but my questions did not stop my work. About nine months after I had started improving the farm, I went back to Turley to explain what I was doing and that someday it would be good to own it. I said, "I'm putting in a lot of sweat on your place. I'm starting to like it."

"Just fix it up good. Maybe you'll have a place to buy."

"I want to buy it from you now."

Turley's eyes blinked as he said, "Keep up the place. We'll talk later about you buying."

While I had talked to Turley, a tinge of distrust slid through my mind that I should have heeded. Why did I ignore the care I had learned to use in dealing with a white man? Why did I fail to read Turley's eyes or the tone of his voice? The thought plowed sharply that I should hold back on the matter of buying. But I had reached desperation about getting on with freeing Isaiah. I had convinced myself to use the farm as the base in my hunt for Isaiah and the place where I could hide him.

Later, on the trail to my farm, like a slap in the face it had struck me—a craziness, the same crazymaker of the Philadelphia attitude—". . . Idle, sloathful . . ." Zeb Turley's double-talk had tinged with the same insults.

Riding back to my rented acres that day before the Hank Lucas affair, I remembered worrying, How can I protect myself for all my labor and expense? How can I make a safe place to hide Isaiah?

* * *

During those long seasons of work shaping Old Turley's place into the farm I had imagined owning—good land in wide open country, pasture for cattle, a place to gain independence—my dreams became almost real. I saw my home growing before my eyes. I savored the feeling of *free*.

Working the place, many days I would stop to hear a meadowlark sing, then crane my neck skyward to watch a bald eagle dip and soar in flight, its huge wings tracing a timeless pattern against the azure sky. Majestic, regal, the eagle—deadly in its dive for prey.

Rotting fence posts had needed replacement. My cabin's ramshackle condition made it cousin to Sam's hut. Torn up, dirty inside, every inch had to be cleaned, ashes scraped from the fireplace, loose and broken bricks replaced, rotten smelly clothes thrown out and burned. After the house, I tackled the barn. Sam made me a shovel and a kind of drag sled to haul away the damned manure; that helped, but the stench made this city transplant one sick man. There were times I had doubts about my being a farmer if mucking out the barn were what it took.

"What's the matter, George Bush?" I used to ask myself. "Can't you take it?"

"Of course, I can," I had answered my own question, held my breath and bent to the shoveling.

I knew exactly what life I wanted. Filthy muck in an old barn would not deter me from becoming a top-level farmer who knew the law. When the time came right, I would buy Turley's land and look for more.

I became obsessed by land: acres and acres of land. Everything I did, thought, planned, centered on visions of owning fertile acres. I knew that in years to come I would possess my own place. American men worked, bought, squatted on, aye, even stole, land that they might claim independence.

Own land, George Bush. You will have your independence. Freedom for you and Isaiah.

Cattle were not plentiful in East Tennessee, so I figured how to develop a cattle-trading business to keep myself in cash, thereby avoid digging into my Philadelphia money. I had to be certain every one of my deals came out clean, clean in every letter of every word—no hole into which a white cattle owner could stuff me by claiming I cheated or failed to keep my part of the bargain—each an offense against him. If any white man accused me of a less than honest deal, I could be punished by a long term of servitude, a bondage the same as slavery—term after term after term as long as the flimsy whim of a white man could accuse me.

But I asked myself, How, George Bush, can you make a clean deal unless the other man deals clean with you? Then I would remember my father's words, "Swim through the whitecaps."

* * *

Shortly after first renting the Turley land, I had decided to move fast on Sam's advice. "Preacher James, he gots de skinniest cattle in East Tennessee. But you kin deal wid him, George Bush. Hear he gots a couple fo' sale jist now."

I decided to take time and look at the James cows even though my pasture needed more fencing. If the critters proved worth buying, I would make a deal with the Preacher, pay the cattle's board for a week or two, then bring them home when I had the pasture cross-fenced. I could have put them in the meadow with my other animals, but Sam told me it was not too good an idea to pasture strange cattle together. "Makes mo' sense to keep dem apaht at fust."

The trail to the preacher's farm had led through weeds and bushes that almost obscured it. Small rocks rolled under my horse's feet, and he stumbled several times. I had picked my way with care, annoyed by the yipping curs that rushed out to meet us. Those hard-time, back hill, scrabble farms always had the worst starved out, mean looking runts. Give me a fat Philadelphia lap dog anytime! There I went again, comparing Tennessee to Pennsylvania. I knew I must guard against that attitude.

I had left Philadelphia in anguish over Isaiah and the barriers set up against us. But I knew I still bore deep within me the feeling of superiority for being a native Philadelphian. I believed that my big city beginnings assured me I was a cut above unlearned East Tennessee backwoodsmen. Sam said that attitude, snobbishness, I guess he meant, would guarantee making me unpopular. Aye, the feeling was a streak deeply ingrained in me. Only a few days back, I had caught myself ready to tell one farmer about the superior milk cows Captain Stevenson owned.

No one showed to my knock at the Preacher James house, but a tall thin woman swung open the barn door and walked toward me. Mrs. James wasted no time when she heard the purpose of my call. "Pa's gone a'preachin' down the valley." She wiped her hands on her apron, pinned a wisp of faded red-brown hair into the bun at the back of her neck, squinted at me through red rimmed, pale, almost colorless eyes. "He says we should sell a head or two if'n we has the chance. I'll have my boys fetch the two below the barn."

Parched tan weeds, gray with dust, choked against the broken fence and ramshackle barn leaning several degrees to the west. An air of poverty hung over those hill acres. Fatigue and despair clung to its unkept field and buildings, an all over dismal color of gray-tan, dried grass, bleached soil. I wondered about the man who could leave his wife and children to eke out their living on that scrabble hill farm while he rode off saving souls.

Chased by a couple of freckled-faced boys as thin as they were, two skinny cows rounded the corner of the barn. I studied the animals. I figured they would fatten quickly on the lush green meadow grass on my rented acres. Although wary, the boys answered my few questions. I decided to deal for the cows. Desperate though the Preacher James woman must have been for cash, she drove a hard bargain. We finally settled the price, including board for the cows for a time.

"I'll need you to sign these critters over to me." My Philadelphia law reading took hold, and I meant to tie the deal legal and proper. "Here. I'll write out the paper, and you can sign it," I said, reaching into my saddlebag for a blank sheet and cash.

What gave me the hunch to have Mrs. James sign a bill of sale for the cows I bought from her? I had failed to get anything in writing from Zeb Turley for renting my land or from the other farmers who sold me cattle. Perhaps I felt easier asking for a paper from a woman than from a man. I don't know. Something must have been nagging at me.

"Huh?" More of a screech than a question.

"A paper giving me title to the cows. A bill of sale, Ma'am. I need you to sign it."

She backed away, her eyes on the wad of money and the piece of paper in my hand. "No. I hain't fer signin' nothin'."

"I have to make the deal legal for me. You must sign the cattle over. Please, Ma'am, just write your name on the line." I steadied the paper on my saddlebag, waited.

"No. Like I jist tole ye. I ain't signin' nothin'."

"Too bad. The deal is off." I made myself sound like a lawyer at his best. Why should I explain to her that the reason I needed a signed bill of sale was that if I were found with the cattle and no proof of ownership, any white crook so inclined could take them away from me? I could do nothing. No. I could not say anything to Mrs. James. Either she knew it or she was too ignorant to understand. I folded up the paper and shoved it and the money back into my bag.

"Wait. Wait." She turned and screamed, "Ibby! Ibby! Come here. Fast." Facing me again, her eyes glued to the saddlebag containing the money, she spoke in a voice so low I could barely hear her. "My daughter, Isabella, she kin write. She'll write my name like you said. I need the money, need it real bad. But ye' see, I hain't larnt to write."

George Bush, I scolded myself, sometimes you are too full of yourself to understand anything else. As if somebody had punched me, I realized, This woman is ashamed to admit she cannot write her own name. Play Philadelphia lawyer. Be a big man with a fistful of money. Think how she feels with her half-starved kids stuck here on this godforsaken hill!

* * *

Isabella James. I received the second punch for the day when the daughter joined us, a squirrel gun in her hand. She put her arm around the older woman's shoulders as if to protect her. Ibby's flashing blue eyes blazed into mine. I read her message clear and loud. Don't you make fun of my mother. Don't go pitying us. We don't take charity from no one.

Ibby James swung long, thick red hair to the side as a hint of laughter raced across her face, its freckles seeming to bounce out at me. Her only words, "Yes, Ma. What do you want me to do? Shoot him?"

Drawing back from the punch of her words on me, I paid for the cows, took my bill of sale, headed home with the promise that I would come back for the animals as soon as my cross-fence had been finished.

Half way down, I stopped and looked back. In the distance on that East Tennessee hilltop, Isabella James stood silhouetted against the afternoon sky. I had never seen anyone like her. A sight burned into my memory. Young. Feisty child of a tough land. Isabella stood slim and tall, as far away from me as the setting sun splashed against the sky, wild strawberry red hair blowing in the wind.

* * *

From the James house, it was a long trail home to my cabin on the Turley acres. I remember thinking that day, Your farm needs its own new name. Quit calling it the "Old Turley place." I had camped out, started riding early that next morning. Pushing my horse hard, I had covered the miles, stopped to rest him on top of the hill in sight of my cabin. I had slid off his sweaty back to let him graze while I leaned against a tree and surveyed my domain in the valley below. I did not know it that morning; but what a fool I was to think, If things go right for me this fall, I believe Zeb Turley will let me buy this spread outright rather than renting it. I reminded myself that Sam had sounded skeptical when we had discussed the idea of my buying, but I kept telling myself money would talk with Old Turley when he got used to the notion that I did have ready cash.

Another picture painted in my mind forever. I remember standing on that high crest looking down the oak-covered slope, imagining my home as it would look when I finished fixing it—the barn, the outbuildings, the fences. My fields. A garden. My herd in the pasture, new heads of cattle penned at the side of the barn for a few days: What a way to make money! Buy skinny critters. Graze them for a short time on my fertile bottom land. Sell fat cattle in Knoxville for a good price. Doing most of the chores outdoors avoids the stench that hangs in the barn even though I regularly scrape out the cow dung. Hard labor involved, but not that bad. I was independent. I was free.

The dreams I had. The old cabin was temporary. Some day I fancied that on the high knoll overlooking my valley I would build a two-story, shuttered, red brick Philadelphia house. Sometimes, in my imaginings that house changed into a stately white-pillared mansion like Governor Blount's house in Knoxville.

Damn peaceful, these East Tennessee hills, high ridged with their few farmers nestled deep within the valleys, I had thought.

My head swam.

I remember I was tempted that morning to ride back to the preacher's farm, although I had to admit to myself, it was not the cattle I was thinking about. That redhead. What did her mother call her? "Ibby?" Strange names Southland people have.

I had dreamed about the redhead during the night, but I took myself in hand. Wait a minute, George Bush, you crazy fool. You have trouble enough as it is getting started in this new country.

Don't go begging it. Maybe that old woman cannot write her name, but she will sure as hell shoot you on sight if you so much as look at her daughter. Leave that feisty redhead up there on the hilltop. Find yourself a woman of your own kind.

I looked at my hands. Big, burnt umber. Ran my fingers through my hair. Black, tight curls. Over my face. High forehead, solid lean cheeks, stubbled chin. Nose and lips thinned down a little by my German genes. Of my tall, broad-shouldered frame, my father had often said, "A handsome physique." Sally had teased me, "You too good-lookin'. A fine black gal be sho' to find you. Nab you." A free man newly arrived in a slave state, rather than dream about someone forbidden, George Bush, you should listen to Sally, find a woman you can love legal. Aye, yes, but . . .

In the early hours of that morning before I had tangled with Hank Lucas, I remember standing on that hill a few strides above the river, my mind meandering about Ibby James, dreaming for a little while, but I stopped it. Aye, I knew: Stay away from the redhead on the scrabble hilltop. She is trouble for you. Find an African girl. So far, I had seen no freed woman. No *free* girl. The only Negro beauties I had noticed were slaves, and slave masters wrapped hate around a free northern man messing with their property. "Free men spell trouble. Cause unrest. Make slaves want their freedom," all of them said. "Talking to slaves about breaking out, rebelling, running. Free men spread ideas slaves should never hear."

* * *

Forever etched in my mind: my cabin, the fresh green meadow, cattle grazing, the cresting ridges all around, the wild pink roses. I smelled the fresh green grass of Tennessee. The wild mint. I felt the peace of the land. I heard the meadowlark's song. So far, I thought, it is just "a place." A woman would make it "a home."

East Tennessee settlers built their remote cabins with a small window high on the wall. It made for a dim, smoky room. I had wanted to cut a new window, lower and larger to take in the view from the river; but Zeb Turley had vetoed the idea.

"Large windows are open invitation to Indians when they go on the rampage," he had said. "They shoot their arrows right into the house, and you don't have a chance. Besides, the high, small openings can serve as sentinel posts in case of attack."

"I haven't seen any Indians since I've been out here," I had countered.

"You need to have them call on you only once," Turley had snarled.

I could not argue with the owner. I bided my time. Having learned the shortcomings of the place, I had made up my mind to put in a number of changes as soon as I had my hands on the deed.

The Indian argument had struck me as specious, I recall, and it should have warned that Turley was not dealing squarely with me because I had heard that there were no Indians in the region. Everywhere I went people talked about how Andrew Jackson, as the Tennessee Militia Major-General, had destroyed the Creeks and secured the frontier against Indian attacks. Tennesseans swelled with their bragging about Jackson—the great Indian fighter who had led his troops in the killing of hundreds of Creeks, then after the battle took into his home as his ward one three-year old orphan Creek found crying in the ruins of his village, his entire family slain by the militia. A man of contradictions, Andrew Jackson.

I hoped what people were saying about the Creeks held no truth. In this big, open country, no one need be pushed out or destroyed. Indians were no worry to me. If one of them visited me, I aimed to make friends, share the bounty of my farm with them, live at peace side by side. I could do all that on my acres, my good farm in East Tennessee. Be friends. Be fair. Welcome the Creeks, if there were any, on my place. Let them share the good soil, green meadows, trees. Fish in my river. Cattle in my pasture. My home. For me, the best place in the U. S. Plenty for everyone. That day, I reveled in the knowledge that George Bush had found the place to sink his roots. Young, darn happy with his life. Living free. Living free. Living free.

My horse rested, I had jumped on, given him rein, and galloped down the slope. I can still feel my horse under me that morning. We were one, together, riding home. It was when I rounded the turn of the trail toward the cabin that I had seen the two strange horses and the loaded wagon in my yard. Eerie, I remember thinking, no one in sight. Must be some passer-by. Guess I won't have to eat alone tonight.

Then it had happened.

I will never forget, "Stop where you are, George Bush."

My land and cattle stolen from me at gunpoint.

Hank Lucas, a name forever burned into my soul.

* * *

Later that day, beyond gunshot of the Lucas clan, I had stopped my horse, dropped onto a log beside a mountain stream. Rage had ridden in the saddle with me all morning and all afternoon, and I still could not absorb my loss. I picked a cranefly orchid, held it in my hand, then let it go. Water murmured close by. A goldfinch sang overhead. Pristine beauty, fresh mountain air, pressed upon me. I staggered up the ridge topped with oak, looked over sloping hills to rivers and valleys below, then into the distance to lovely mountains as far as I could see. The sun was sliding behind the highest ridge. Twilight of a perfect summer day swelled around me. The peacefulness, the warmth, mocked me. Despising myself for being a sucker about the land, I glared down the hillside toward the stream. A timber rattlesnake slithered over my boot and slipped under a rock.

* * *

When new from Philadelphia, I had ridden that first time into Sam Brown's yard hopeful, confident, maybe even a bit cocky in my quest for land. But the day Hank Lucas shot down my dreams, I crawled to Sam and Sally on my belly. I spent the evening grieving with Sam. We two, a couple of men, one *free*, one recently *freed*.

Sally left us alone for awhile. Then, figuring I had spent enough time pitying myself in my loss, she flung the door open, stood framed against the outside light, head thrown back, hooded eyes flashing. Her face lined with the hurt and misery of a lifetime of slavehood for herself and Sam, she stared a long moment at his mutilated foot.

Facing me, she shook her wooden spatula, cried out, "Wha's da matta', City Boy? You gots bof you' feets half chopt off?"

5

In the weeks that followed the Hank Lucas fiasco, the reality of my loss too painful to absorb, I let memories wash over me, carry me back to an earlier time and place.

Father Matthew Bush. Where his people came from, I do not know. Try as I might, I have had no success in learning about them so I cannot give a precise answer when asked about my African ancestral beginnings. I wish I could, but Father never told me. I believe he did not know. The facts were scarce. Father's life seemed a remote affair he preferred not to discuss.

My mother's life story was a closed book to me. She had died at my birth and was never mentioned in my boyhood home. I have heard that the words "indentured servant" were used to describe those early German single people who came to America. White women and men laborers in England and Europe were willing to bind themselves into years of service in return for passage to this country. My mother may have been one of them.

Our Bush family has been in America since the beginnings of white settlement on this continent. One of the first slaver ships must have brought across the Atlantic to these shores an ancestor of mine, bound and shackled, wild at being torn from family in Africa, an ancestor too far back in time for me to know firsthand. I do believe that much.

We later men carrying the blood of that Bush ancestor were born in America. Our people helped lay out this country. We turned the soil by hand for crops. We cut the trees, skinned the logs for houses and barns. We sailed her ships. We fought in her war for independence. We built cities brick by brick, stone by stone. Philadelphia: America calls it the "City of Brotherhood. City of Liberty." My birthplace.

Another reason I know father was not born across the sea: the slave ships. I have seen them. Human beings chained in stink holes, like so many logs, dumped together in vomit and filth. If my father had been stolen from Africa, the slave ship would have made him hate the sea for life. He did not. He loved the sea.

* * *

The 1725 Pennsylvania law rode with me in Tennessee, its beating constant in my head: ". . . 'tis found by Experience, That free Negroes are an Idle, sloathful People." Those words were penned by the fathers of the men who on March 1, 1780, wrote the law providing that no child born in Pennsylvania after that date would be slave. Gradually emancipate them, the law ordered. The change took about ten years. By the time I came along, I was born free.

Crazy? Crazy that I lost my farm? I had worked hard on Zeb Turley's East Tennessee acres. I was neither "idle" nor "sloathful." I had skinned my knuckles and bent my back on that farm, up before daylight, to bed only when I could no longer see.

No free Negro was really free. Tough to gain any learning. Tough to fit life to fact.

Being a man with lawyer know-how gives power to a man, but it certainly failed one Kentucky man. A for-sale ad in the *Louisville Courier* told his story:

> "A valuable yellow man, . . . stout and active and weighing 175 pounds. A very good rough lawyer; very healthy, and title good—said negro is not fitted to practice in the Court of Appeals or in the Court of Chancery, but take him in a common law case, or a six-penny trial before a County Magistrate and 'he can't be beat.' Said yellow man can also take depositions, make out legal writings, and is thoroughly adept at brow-beating witnesses and other tricks of the trade."

* * *

I remember how often I had walked the streets of Philadelphia from my home on Walnut Street, along Eighth to Spruce, turning on Third to cross Dock Street, holding my breath against the sewer smells, then right onto Chestnut to wander Front Street and watch the ships on the Delaware River. I stopped at Captain Stevenson's old docks and questioned if I had been foolish not to continue in his business. With every step, the laughter of Isaiah had haunted me, and remorse overlaid with anguish that I had not rescued him tore at my guts.

"Land For Sale."

Philadelphia newspapers had printed columns about many opportunities in Tennessee. From what I had read, it appeared to be the place where land speculators were making it big. I doubted most of the claims by unknown people promising great wealth. Andrew Jackson's advertisements kept drawing me, and I tended to believe what he put into print. For me, Jackson's status as a former U. S. Congressman from Tennessee lent credibility to his words, and I had figured his ads must be honest.

I remembered that Captain Stevenson had admired Andrew Jackson because he took the floor in Congress and criticized President George Washington over the mild treaty negotiated in 1794 by his special representative to the British, U. S. Supreme Court Justice John Jay. Then, too, Captain Stevenson had never ceased burning over the arrogance of the British impressment policy. "Piracy," the Captain called their policy of boarding our ships and pulling off sailors they claimed to be "British." So to my way of thinking, Andrew Jackson wanting to be tough on old England and the rights her navy claimed set him right with me. From what I read in the newspapers Andrew Jackson spoke for Tennessee.

Losing my land and cattle in East Tennessee smacks of a different brand of piracy. Un-British, certainly unkingly, but for me, personally, more high-handed and malicious, more calculated and destructive, than what is happening on the high seas.

* * *

With every step I took, my friend Isaiah walked beside me. The Quaker Society, the Free African Society, and the Methodist Church had sent out pleas for help in finding him, but no word had come back to Philadelphia by the time I left. No word came to me in East Tennessee. In my nightmares, I saw Isaiah slaving somewhere in the South. My grief for failure to save him mixed with grief over the loss of my farm.

The last time I had talked with Reverend Allen before leaving Philadelphia, he had warned me: "Keep your freedom papers sewed inside your shirt. Next to your heart. Beware the stranger. George, I worry about you heading into the Southland."

The preacher's hand had trembled when I handed him a paper empowering him to withdraw funds from my account to pay the costs of the search for Isaiah and, if necessary, to buy him.

He said, "When we locate Isaiah, we'll force his freedom. We'll go to the governor. To the president. We'll get statements from white folks saying he is a free man. That he is a good man. That he was kidnapped from us. Your money, George, will be used to find him, wherever he is. To free him."

The men I talked with at the Free African Society had sounded clear warnings. They and I knew that Tennessee might not be much different from Pennsylvania, but we kept reminding ourselves that in 1796 the Tennessee Constitutional Convention had given free Negroes voting rights. We had heard, also, of the Tennessee revivalist Methodist camp meetings of the early 1800s. The Methodism of John Wesley professed equality and control of one's own destiny. That brand of religion might make it a more fair-minded place—certainly a contrast with the Pennsylvania Methodist Church congregation which the Negroes had been forced to leave around 1786 because of ill treatment. I had left Pennsylvania knowing the dangers of being Negro in America.

I was young. I had hope.

* * *

My friends at the Free African Society believed that a gun would help me survive on the frontier, a safeguard for me in making my first move. Sure, most states had laws that said Negroes could not carry guns; but carry them we did. Made by a German gunsmith in Pennsylvania, my gun had bored riflings so the shot would spin out faster and follow a flatter trajectory to its mark than did the older guns without riflings. The gunsmith called the rifles "Jaegers"—proud of their highly polished stocks and silver inlay—in honor of the sharpshooters who fired them in battles in Europe. He had a reputation for "a sharpshooting eye." Needing to develop skill with a gun, I enlisted the German's help in learning to shoot. He taught me to raise the barrel and sight, relax and let out a breath, then squeeze the trigger. With this fine Jaeger, over the span of only three months I had become a dead center bull's-eye shot.

As fortune would have it, the Pennsylvania gunsmith's shop had served as a sort of headquarters for groups of German immigrants coming off boats from Europe. One day several Germans came in who had been met by land speculators when their boat had landed. Hearing the talk about land for everyone in Tennessee, the new arrivals agreed that was where they meant to settle. The gunsmith had helped them with provisions and advice. He warned them that for safety they should have a single man or two riding with them in case of Indian attack. He recommended me, "George Bush is a good shot. You can depend on him."

Those immigrants I had led over the trail from Pennsylvania through the Cumberland Gap were poorly equipped for the trip. Still exhausted from their long ocean voyage, they were apprehensive at fitting into the new society. Unable to speak but a few words of scarcely understandable English, their tongues tripped over the word "Tennessee." Their blue eyes and light hair failed to bridge a single gap between them and the settlers along the way who could not understand their strange language and did not trust the foreigners. I, too, had one difficulty after another bargaining for supplies to meet the bare needs of the party.

One day, during the crossing of Kentucky, near crude pens holding human beings, I saw a poster advertising:

"SLAVE SALE.
"MOST LOCALLY BRED AND REARED STOCK. SOME MARYLAND OR VIRGINIA STOCK. ALL STRONG AND HEALTHY. WELL TRAINED.
5 BUCKS, AGES 18 TO 28
1 BUCK, AGE 47, HUNTS WELL WITH DOGS
2 WENCHES, BOTH GOOD COOKS
1 WENCH, WITH 7 MONTHS OLD PICKANINNY
1 WENCH, WITH 2 AND 3 YEAR OLDS
14 BUCKS, ASSORTED AGES, 10 TO 17
OWNER LEAVING FOR MASSACHUSETTS, A FREE STATE.
TERMS: CASH.
OWNER: REUBEN THOMAS."

The United States flag lazing in the breeze, the day sunny, freedom should have been in the air. Instead, brought in from all over Kentucky, some from Maryland and Virginia, the slaves were closely guarded, chained together. I had stood back of the Germans, pretended no interest in the proceedings while I searched for sight of Isaiah, but he was not among the slaves. My good sense told me he most likely would never be put up for sale in Kentucky, too close to home, but I had to search.

The poster had advertised mostly local slaves. As far as I was concerned, the word "local" meant nothing. Anyone who would sell a human being could lie about the origin. I read anguish on the faces of the shackled young boys and girls, wondered from how many parents they had been stolen. Seeing the people on the block, listening to the bidding, the Stars and Stripes waving its message of freedom and justice overhead, I suffered for my country. Shame seared me in facing the Germans. I wondered if the Germans intended to buy a slave. If they did, I would leave them. They seemed only disgusted by the proceedings.

They had stared at me when we started the wagons again, questioning, no doubt, why I, one black man, could move freely about the country while others of my brothers and sisters agonized in chains. Mercifully, they did not ask. I was not called to explain America's sins. For the rest of our journey, I kept myself well buried among the immigrants. I knew that in 1807 Kentucky had prohibited entry of free Negroes into the state, and I took no chances of being picked up. Fortunately, no law officers stopped us on the trail.

During that long ride with the Germans from Pennsylvania's civilization to the East Tennessee wilderness, I sometimes laughed aloud wondering what my travel companions would have said if I had given them some facts. "Hello, Brothers. Well, here we are. I am part German, German like you." But the immigrants were a sober group, lacked humor. After seeing the slave sale, I did not feel much like joking either. Although the leaders kept strict discipline and divided food fairly, bickering and fights broke out. I was relieved when we passed through the Cumberland Gap, the Germans going their way and I taking the trail alone toward Knoxville.

* * *

Those weeks and months after Hank Lucas and his family stole my farm, I had wrestled with myself. I had struggled trying to figure the best approach to Zeb Turley. He had the law on his side. He held the deed. I had no rights to the land. I could have sued him in the courts of Tennessee, but the fact that I could not testify in court against him made that a futile gesture. Several different days, I started for his store; but each time my feet felt as if bound, and I turned back. Finally, the grating inside had scraped me raw, and I did force myself to Knoxville to confront Turley.

His clerk fended me off. I knew he had instructions, "Git rid of that George Bush." Hell, I could plant my feet squarely in front of that clerk, look down at him, some six inches shorter than I, but the law did not stand on my side of the counter.

Defeated, I went that same day to the courthouse. Sheriff Dunbar would not listen to my complaint about Zeb Turley and Hank Lucas. He pushed aside what I said, challenged me. "You tell me you have freedom papers. From Philadelphia. Let's see them. Ain't many what claim sich kin prove their words." After spending a long time checking my papers and talking to a couple of men in the back of the room, he faced me. "You better carry these with you, George Bush. Always." He threatened, "Don't get caught crossing county lines in this state without them or without registering. You'll get an ear sliced off for your carelessness."

Or worse, I knew what the Sheriff did not put into words—sold into slavery like Isaiah or Caleb. The story about Caleb had often been told at the Free African Society. He had been stolen from Maryland and ended up in a Nashville jail in 1810. When a friendly deputy sheriff had let him write his friends, they started to gather his free papers and build a fund of money to get him out. But before help could reach Nashville, Caleb was sold "down the river" into deep South slavery, chances nil of his ever being heard from or found.

Stirrings began prodding from deep in my mind. There are no boundaries to hell.

* * *

Sally and Sam had saved me from committing mayhem or worse when I lost my farm. Living with them framed in stark reality for me what victims slavery makes of people. I heard Sally cry out at night for her children, "Sold down the river." She had no idea where her lost ones were. She had no means to make a search for them. There were no boundaries to Sally's hell.

In the not-so-deep South, my life became involved as it never before had been with the suffering decreed by the American system of slavery. The thought cut across my mind as sharply as streak lightning blazes the dark sky that I could never know freedom until all the Sams and Sallys were free.

In living close to my cabin companions, I learned to understand Sally, her moodiness, her loneliness, her unreadable eyes. I realized that she missed the contacts with other women, contacts that could only happen during the religious meetings held around the countryside.

"She wants to go, but she cain't walk that fur. 'En I cain't ride a hoss, nohow iff'n I had one."

Not ride a horse? One of the few times I heard Sam complain or admit a lack.

"Where is the meeting?"

"Down by de Truegood place. Next to ol' Brown's plantation. Next Sunday. Den de folks won't be wukin'."

"Who's doing the preaching?"

"Fo' de white folks, dat Preacher Truegood, I rekun, him what owns da place. Him preaches for his white folks. I hears him buyed a preacha, Toby Moore, from down Virginny way for de slaves. Our people say Preacha Toby wuks ha'd in da week and preaches pow'ful strong cum Sunday."

* * *

I had seen a used buggy for sale in Knoxville, and a plan formed in my mind. I bought the buggy. Sam and I fixed and polished it into good condition, then I hitched my horse to it and escorted Sally to the meeting in style.

We arrived early. The white congregation seated on benches outside an old house listened to Truegood preaching at peak fervor. In back of them stood my people. Truegood appeared to me as quite a slick man. Slicked down hair, smooth slick face, his black coat slick. He did hold his eyes steady as they swept over the worshippers.

The Reverend Truegood's exhortations stretched long and loud. His high nasal twang rode them. I could not hear much of what he said, but enough filtered through for me to know he told the story of Samson whose courage he said was true, whose strength was great.

We sat in the buggy, waiting, Sally and I. Sam had declined at the last minute to come with us. I wondered at the heartsick look on Sally's face as we waited for Truegood to end his sermon for the white family, supposed it was because Sam had refused to come, so said nothing to her.

Truegood's slaves had built him an imposing mansion farther up a hill, and the preacher allowed his aging unkempt house to be used as a church. "So many peoples be comin' to de meetin's in de summah, so dey allus be held outside," Sally explained as we sat in the buggy, her indigo blue hand-woven shawl drawn close around her, her bonnet pushed back so she could see.

His sermon finished for the white folks, most of the people filed out after Truegood, but several stood talking and joking in loud voices for a long while.

The overseer and a few white men lounged in the background. Eyes ranging over the crowd, they listened as my people drew close around the slave, Preacher Toby Moore. I allowed myself the hint of a smile. A round man, Moore looked to be all arms and legs and head. Our people hummed softly while he prayed. One of the white men joined the humming for he knew the tune as well as anyone else. Perhaps he had heard the slave songs all his life.

The humming and the prayer melded into a Tennessee song I had never heard: "O de Lamb done been down here an' died, De Lamb done been down here an' died. Sinner won' die no mo'. De robes all ready now."

I tried to pick out the lead voices, for there were both men and women singing the phrases, "Sinner won' die no mo'," and the entire gathering answering, "De Lamb done been down here an' died. Sinner won' die no mo'." Verse after verse ignited my people. Then the Preacher's voice took over in another prayer, and the singing again faded to a soft humming as if a background chorus of angels supported Preacher Toby Moore, his round face reflecting the warmth of his soul.

It seemed that his sermon rose from the words of the song as Preacher Toby began telling the story of Jesus. Suffering. Obedience. Forbearance. Be good in this life, and you will go to a better place in the next. The listeners knew the story so well, they kept chorusing "Amen," "Ain't it so?," "Yes, Lawd."

"Be good chilluns. *Good* means you obey de masta'," Preacher Toby exhorted, and the overseer nodded and smiled. "Work hard fo' like de song say de robes all ready now. Be good, for de masta has the *right* to whup you if you are not."

Like the clapper of a bell, responses at this point struck with a solid moaning, "Yes, Lawd," "Amen." "Ain't it so?"

"De Lamb done been down here an' died," the humming rose and fell, its rhythm punctuating the preacher's words, his feet stomping the beat now and then, his hands sometimes swinging toward Heaven as if he were receiving "de robe" for being good and working hard.

Preacher Toby Moore held to the bible message of "Be good chilluns" as long as the white men lounged close and listened. As they became bored and drifted away, the preacher lowered his voice, shifted the thrust of his message, and spoke words pleading that the people be strong. Be ready for the better day. His last words spread through the tepid air and urged the golden voices to help all of us, ". . . see dem ships come a-sailin', sailin', sailin'. / O see dem ships come a-sailin', / De robes all ready now."

The trees swayed in the late afternoon heat. As the sun traced its path westward, the Philadelphia skeptic I was saw "dem ships come a-sailin'" as clearly as any Tennessee singer.

* * *

The day after the preaching, Sam said to me, "Yeh, dat Brown, him brags him giv'd me my freedom. Dat be hogwash. I wuk'd nigh to fo'ty years to buy messef. Den I buyed me Sally."

My lost farm. Sam's chopped off foot.

"What was Brown like when you were his slave?" I asked.

Sam limped to a hickory tree, steadied himself against it with one hand, stood looking down the lane a long while, came back, sat down, picked up a chip, chewed and spit it out. I thought he had forgotten the question or would never answer it, then he spoke on slavehood in a way I have remembered to this day.

"Old Brown? He owned me. I be his animal. Take a dog. A dog kin love his massa. I cain't love a massa. A dog ain't no human being. I is. I don' respec' a massa. Dey's de whip. De gun. De dogs. Or wust. I dun have sev'rl chilluns. Massa use me for many women. Massa done brek my famblies up. Sold dem down de ribba'. I cain't respec' him." Sam shook his long, crooked forefinger in my face. "Respec' for a massa? Dey be only digrees of dispisement."

Isaiah's image swam before me, echoes of his laugh made me shudder. Slavery, Isaiah's life?

"Some slaves always hates da massa. Others gits so dey don' care, don' care much 'bout nuthin'. Most takes one day at de time. We all be different. We gots no wher' to go.

"White folks say we be lazy. But I tells you, George, on de plantation it nebba pay for us to pull 'head of othas. Dat on'y make our wuk harda. We wuks jist enuf so we stays alive. We be satisfy wid dat.

"Some slaves jist behaves, wuks ha'd de bes' dey kin. Us mens, we say 'bout dem, A pig what keep him head down de deepes' grubs de best roots.

"Someunes stand it better'n od'ers. Slaves like my Sal wuz, dey gots religion. Her escape be in 'Yes, Jesus!' Her hope dat 'de robes all ready now.' Religion be de sweet suga' tit slave massas has used to keep us down. Hold us in line. Make us behave an' wuk ha'd. Dey reads from de Bible dat slaves gots to obey massas, or dey be whupp'd. Dey say if we be good an' wuks ha'd hey in dis life an' not gits sassy, an' not runs, den we'll go to de Promised Land an' dance all ova' God's Hebben. Dat be what de white preacha' say. Dat what Toby Moore say when de white folks be listenin'.

"Old Brown, him nebba' say it to us. But some folks claim dat bein' niggah be punishment in dis life for bein' bad in 'nudder. Dat we be condemned to be servants, lowes' of de low. An' if we be good niggahs now, an' wuks ha'd on dis earth, we done will have a betta life in de nex place. Hogwash! I know my Sal nebba' did no wrong on dis earth or in any otha! So, I don' believe none of it.

"All I eva wanted was a betta place heh an' now. Dat's why I runned so much when I be young. Dat's why otha' slaves runs. Runways, dey be de ones what cain't take bein' slaves an' don' believe dey be any use to be a good slave cause dey be no truf in de Hebben teachin'.

"So, da bes way to ansa you be to say dey be as many ways of standin' up to slavin' as dey be slaves.

"I say if dey be a God smart 'nuff to take me to Hebben, he sho' be smart 'nuff to let us all live free. He'd let me go free. But de Lord neva' freed me. I had to wuk fo' my own freedom. Like I tol' you, I slaved fo'ty year fo' it. I earns it. Now, I jist makin' de best of ebba day dat I kin." He stopped, scratched his head, stretched both hands out toward me, palms up, fingers spread. "Nope. De man what say he love his massa, he be a liah an' a fool. Like I tole you, George, de be only digrees of dispisement."

* * *

There was little I could add to Sam's analysis of slavery, but pestering in my mind was Sally's stony silence the night Preacher Truegood had sermonized to his people at the meeting. If religion were her comfort and help in time of trouble, the words and charisma of the Reverend should have uplifted her. It did not. Troubled, she had sat still and quiet, waiting for him to finish. Not until Truegood had left, and Preacher Toby began, did she smile.

"What about that meeting, Sam? It was plain to me Sally did not like hearing the Reverend Truegood preach. I don't think while he was holding forth that she enjoyed herself a single minute."

"Did you see dat Truegood? Heah dat white man preach, George?" Sam's look was like the one on Sally's face when she and I sat in the buggy. Something bothered her at the meeting, bothered Sam when we talked.

"Yes, I heard a few words. But we were too far away, and there was too much noise to make sense out of what he said. Kind of an old windbag, isn't he?"

"Windbag? Dat be too good a name fo' him. He is wus. Much wus. Preachas like him be why I don' have no truk wit religion. Like dis, Son. Me and Sally knows 'bout him. He be a sinna' wus den you or me evah wuz."

"Sinner, why? Couldn't find bigger sinners than us, my Friend." I laughed at him, tried to lighten his heavy mood.

"Don' tink you knows what goes on in dese Christi'n plantations, George. Don' know iff'n I should tell you. If you wud unnerstan'. Yo' bein' young, and from up No'th, 'en all."

"Go ahead." I had to be careful not to press Sam too hard. Sometimes, he wanted only to bide his time, thinking, keeping to himself. Today, he seemed filled with need to talk.

"Like dis." He looked around, made sure Sally was in the house out of hearing. "Dat Preacher Truegood, him whut you heerd, be a pow'ful sinnin' man." He hesitated a moment, then his words tumbled out, fast, as if they blazed his tongue when he said them. "He goes afta all de young slave girls. Waits 'til a young'un gits to be around twelve or so. Den he takes her, misuses 'n abuses her. Fust one, den anuder."

"Rape?"

"Dat be right. Onliest we cain't say dat word to him. De whites pertends not to know. No ones of us kin do enny ting to him. He be 'n awful man. Dere be many chilluns on his place what wears his face. When he gits tired of a girl, he marry her off to anotha' slave, no nem'mind if she wants or not. Sometimes, his abuse has bin so bad da girl dies. One time a girl run, 'n da dogs found her. 'N she tried to run from dem 'n dey bit big chunks out'n he' legs. Da sores festered, 'n she died. T'war'nt no medicine cud hep her den. She bin too fah gone. Po' chile.

"Dat man Reverend Truegood preachin'? All dose white folks listenin' to him? Tinkin' him be a godly man?"

No wonder my friend Sam refused that brand of religion.

"Don' make no dif'runce to de white folks. If'n dey knows, dey tink it be his'n right. Afta all, de slaves be his'n prop'ety. Him kin do whut he wants wid dem. No one kin complain 'bout him. Slaves hain't 'lowed to hev der say in court. Yo' knows dat. Ain't no law gonna stop men like dat old basta'd Truegood. Him has de full control."

No wonder Sally had sat in our buggy listening to Reverend Truegood, her face as gray as a piece of marble dug out of the quarry in the great mountains of Tennessee. And as cold.

6

A nightmare badgered me during the low hours of night. It had long torn through my restless sleep following Sally's torment over the Truegood preachings. For whatever reason, each of us held that torment a private, deep inside feeling.

The nightmare bedeviled me, and I could not cast it aside. In the hazy midhours of the nightmare tearing my sleep, a spirit took hold of me. *A skinny, ashen-faced scarecrow, the spirit rode with me for miles following an out-of-the-way trail I seldom cared to use. It ran along the often rocky trail that ended in the marshy, reed-grown edge of a swamp many miles east of Sam's cabin. Out among the cattails, grasses, and sedges we pushed our horses until they stood belly deep in the matted wild grasses.*

The spirit pointed to the right at a gnarled ancient hemlock that grew at the rim of the swamp. The hemlock seemed to spread an intense eerie glow behind a patch of its soft flat needles. The needles shiny dark green on top, their whitish bands on the lower surface turned up whenever the breeze blew stiff. Given time, my eyes adjusted to the absence of light. From the scaly reddish plates of the hemlock's bark, Isaiah's face stared at me. Sometimes misshapen. Other times smooth and round. On occasion leering but more often stern. His face stood out boldly, then faded away. The images repeated as if speaking to me at different times and places. His laugh, long and mocking, turned high-pitched. Resonating, repeating endlessly, it always sank into a dull and barely audible intonation.

On awakening, I knew that Sally's talk of the loss of her children stirred my loss of Isaiah. No word came from the Free African Society. That meant no one had located Isaiah. I feared East Tennessee had for me become another land of rats' alleys where people lived and dead men lost their bones.

* * *

Midnight? No. I had fallen asleep early one night several weeks after my last meeting with the spirit, and it must have been just an hour or so past dark. Sam shook me, "Wake up. Wake up, Son." When I sat on the side of my bed, my head in my hands, he laughed, "You cain't fight de demons all by yo'sef, Young Man. Here, hab a cup of coffee." Sam's brew of chickory and dried wild peas left a taste something like tar and mud in my mouth, but the hot liquid woke me up.

When he said, "Cum wid me fo' a walk in de woods," I was glad to get out of the house. Sam would disappear often at night. "For a walk," he always said the next morning. I never questioned the purpose of his midnight excursions, only presumed he was something of an insomniac out for his midnight stroll.

Sam took no leisurely stroll that night. We hurried past the sycamore tree in his yard, across his garden, crawled through his rail fence, paused to pet a sleepy cow, then struck down a lane through the grove of ash and beech, past a chestnut tree or two. We stopped long enough to carve a chew from the gnarled bark of the red gum tree, then picked our way through the thick woods beyond where we had shot wild turkeys. I could see no path to follow, but Sam seemed to know exactly where he was going.

Deep in the woods Sam halted, put his hand out to keep me from charging past him, spoke in a half whisper, "Now, Son, you's gwine to meet some friends uv mine. Mens who meets yere when peoples sleep. We sits yere and speaks whuts on de mind. Onliest men we kin trust comes. You be one I trusts now, so I brung you. To speak wid us. Dey wants to heah of de freedom land up North. How fah away it be. De bes' place to go. Enny ting 'bout freedom yo' kin tink uv to tell us. Enny ting."

He rushed ahead. Evidently, I was not to be given the opportunity to debate whether or not I wanted to speak to anybody about freedom, or anything else, in the dark of night. Sam had reasons for whatever he did, reasons I had learned not to question. I followed him.

* * *

On the riverbank, sheltered by a canopy of branches of a towering maple tree, in a place so dark it took several minutes for my eyes to adjust and pick out the shape of first one man then another seated on the ground, I entered my first clandestine slave-freedman meeting. Meetings that struck terror in the minds and hearts of slave masters. Meetings forbidden by slaveowner edicts and by law. Clandestine meetings carrying horrible penalties—tarings, buck beatings, chopped off feet.

A few questions about my reliability from voices in the shadows drew Sam's ringing assurance. "My friend, him I trust like iff'n he be me own son. He be from de free land up North. From up in Penns'vany. Him kin tell us all 'bout bein' free. Enny ting any mens wants to ask him. Enny ting. He kno de truf 'bout it, my friend George Bush duz."

No fire blazed for the meeting. No cleared space in the forest marked the place. Men who lived nightmare lives waited in dark silence.

Below us the river sang its timeless melody. Somewhere under the bushes cricket chirrups counterpointed the long bass notes of the Tennessee toad. No response to Sam's invitation to ask me "Enny ting" came from the men. I began to feel as out of place as a politician haranguing in a Quaker silent meeting. I was about to bolt away, when the first question came, an abrupt, tough one. "If ye be from freedom land, why does yo' come her' to dis slave country?"

The same question Sam had asked me early on, a question that has baffled people throughout my life. I remembered what I had said to Sam. To those men, I tried to clarify my reasons, be more forthright, speak less like a textbook than I had back in Sam's cabin. Somehow, I had to convey to those men that life in Philadelphia had not been perfect, that our free people seemed always to swing on the short end of the pendulum. But I had to be sure they understood I regarded freedom as precious. However risky and poor in Pennsylvania, freedom was richer than slavery in Tennessee. I better not pontificate to the strangers in the dark, but I had to say all that and not down talk to my unknown audience who listened, hanging onto every word I said.

"Freedom is richer than gold. But as long as one of us is in slavery, no man's freedom is worth anything. That is as true for Pennsylvania as it is for Tennessee," I said, then told them about Isaiah Curry. I hoped they understood and believed that I was sincere.

"A peculiar institution," someone had written about slavery. Peculiar? Bosh. Deadening is more like it. Aye, life threatening.

Slavery may be deadening, but those slaves who spoke their minds to me that night were far from dead.

"If dat Philadelphia be free, why do it hab all dem laws agin' free folks?"

"Whites are afraid of us, afraid we will step on their rights. Aye, they do not want us to share their rights. Rights owned by whites, they believe, because they come onto this earth in a white covering." I echoed words my father had years ago told me.

"I knows we cain't change what color our skins be. Not dat I eber wants to. But we be men and women. And we shud hev da sam' rights de whites has. Dat Independence Dec'ration sez so." I could not be certain by voice sound who the speaker was but I figured it was Jim, Sheriff Dunbar's slave. I had seen him cleaning the jail the day I had pleaded for my land and had heard that same voice calling to a customer.

I wanted to stand up and shout, but I kept my voice low. "I believe that, too. You asked me about leaving a free place. I have to tell you. Pennsylvanians are no different than white folks most everywhere in our country. They forget that the United States fought the Revolutionary War against England for freedom. America spent its blood to build a nation dedicated to human rights for every human being. That is what the Constitution says. And that Constitution was written in Philadelphia. Yet this nation has cut men like you and me off from those rights. I say, No person has any right to own another person. Everyone of you should walk free in America. Slavery is sin." My Father's words about people flowed into my head, and I spoke his thoughts that night of questions.

In the dark, I heard a mutter, "Slavery is hell."

I waited for the man to go on. He said no more, so I finished with, "Because they are slavers, once they free us, whites do not understand that human freedom can never be set with boundaries. When they set limits on us free people different than what they set for themselves, it is unfair. Bottom level treatment. We resent it. We boil."

"Bottom lebel treatment." That time Sam echoed my words. "Dat be what me and Sally, all us, had."

"White folks in the North curse us free men as troublesome creatures, too ready to spread ideas, and they . . ." I was beginning to feel comfortable talking almost under my breath.

"White folks in the South bless us as being cheerful. Faithful children too dumb to learn." A muted voice broke into my sentence, a voice ridden with sarcasm and speaking with the contradictory statements that have come to grace the language of my race because so often we dare not speak what we mean.

Evidently, the men had begun feeling easy with me. Their responses rang true. The crickets and frogs had stopped, perhaps listening to the strange words drifting in the trees of their forest land.

"White peoples be mighty 'shamed of holding people slaves. Dat's why dey make so many bad rules on us. Dey be jist plain 'shamed, so dey covers demsefs by sayin we is no good. Dat we be dumb brutes. Dat we has to be protected." Jim had more to say.

"Den why don' dey jis let us go free if'n dey feel so 'shamed?" a voice interrupted him. "Why, friend, why?"

Again struggling to put my words clearly, becoming more involved, I said, "Some people have twisted their thinking around, so they claim it is their responsibility to care for us. Like the man said, whites figure they have unlimited rights to control us by whatever laws they want to make. White is superior to black, so they claim. The white men's laws mean rights for themselves, not rights for all people."

"What you say sounds true, Friend. But I reckon it's more simple. The whole mess boils down to this. They want us to do all their work for them." A strange voice spilled out words in a stream, and a litany took hold of the meeting.

"Yeh, build da white folks houses."

"Plow da fields."

"Nurse da babies."

"Groom da horses."

"Drive dem carriages."

"Sho', we do all de wuk. Dat gives dem time to sit 'round writin' fancy words for demsefs."

"We folks be da reason dey kin read 'n write so many purty promises. All for demsefs."

"We slaves fer dem. We gots no time to larn de readin' and writin'. Dey gots de time. Purty promises . . ."

"Sho' not for us slaves."

"Not for us free men, either. I want to hear more, Friend. How did you live in Philadelphia?"

Us free men? I had not known another free person was in the neighborhood. I heard the strong voice of a man I should meet.

Philadelphia. My boyhood home. The garden and shade trees. My clean yard. The smelly, stagnant water in the Curry yard. The shanties they called homes. The knowing-you-better-step-off the walk to let white people pass. Mr. Curry's day-to-day rat race to put food in his children's mouths. His son, my stolen friend, Isaiah Curry. Those thoughts and many more tumbled off the end of my tongue at his question. I told the men the truth of a free man's life. Again, I told them not to quash their dreams of freedom. I repeated, "Being a free man is not perfect. But it is far better than being a slave. You do breath air that you can call your own. That is what I always try to remember."

"Even if they ride in and steal your farm?"

"Even if they ride in and steal my farm." Then I set out another idea. "You know, wherever there's repression, given time, rebellions will break out."

I waited awhile, wondered if anyone had such thoughts or knew about slave rebellions in other places. Or did they live so isolated in the back country of East Tennessee that no word of struggles in other sections reached them?

But I did not have to wait long.

"You know, Friend, down South Carolina way, where I comes from, we had three uprisings or more in the 1700s. My grandpappy told me about them."

Another voice picked up the idea. "Remember, just a few years back that slave Gabriel organized eleven hundred slaves. Dey figured to finish off Richmond down in Virginy. He be a real hero." A cough strangled his words. "Dey took his life."

"We knows dey be repressin' us all ober de southlan'. We boils. And some boils ober." Hard words struck through the darkness. "I knows. Old massa tuk me down de Mississippi fer tradin'. New Orleans be in a big stir. Jist a short time before, I tink it been 1811, slaves a few miles up de ribber boils up. Killed de massas. Many peoples on both sides die. Dose slaves burned ebberting. My massa done his biznis, and we gots out of dere fast as we culd."

Listening in the dark forest to the fellows under the maple tree, I realized that deep in their souls eternal fires blazed for freedom. "Those festerings weren't just in the south. Before slaves were free in the north, that part of the country had its problems," I said. "Right in my own state the town of York burned, and people died. Long, long ago, in New York City, the slaves rose up in great numbers. People died. Lots of buildings were burned. Thirty years later, another rebellion was put down, and more than sixty of our people were executed. All such a long, long time ago, but people still remember."

"And you know right now in the swamps 'roun Georgia an North Car'lina there's camps of runaway slaves in control. White folk don't be fool enough to go into those parts."

An ominous silence hung in the woods. My voice little more than a whisper, I warned, "There's terrible risks for our people. Whites have the guns. That's where the power is."

We had said enough to put the damper on more talk. We sat for a long time knowing we risked our lives in the clandestine meeting under that tree. If any white person had overheard us, we faced death. All we said and did was against the law. That night, I, myself, had espoused ideas to slaves that from the beginning of slavery the masters had forbidden. *Free men are dangerous. They spout ideas that slaves should not hear.* The white men who voiced those fears of free men or freedmen voiced fact. Us frees were, indeed, dangerous.

In the distance, a dog barked.

"It's Blue. Truegood's hound. I've got a hunk of meat in case . . ." A man from the Reverend's place hurried away to head off the dog.

Quiet wildcats of the forest, one by one, the men, most of them barefoot, slipped from the sheltering canopy of the ageless maple tree into the woods, leaving Sam and me alone.

* * *

Summer of 1814 drew to a close. One day I gathered the last of the black walnuts that had dropped to the ground, stopping now and then to crack a particularly plump one and eat the tongue-tingling nut. Sam had finished extracting his maple syrup. Sally had promised us a fat black walnut-maple sugar cobbler as reward for our labor. A good, lazy day. Black walnuts must simply be the best eating nut, I thought, as a shadow crossed my hand when I reached down to pick up my full basket and head for the house.

He had slipped quietly from the woods. I had not heard him come. I faced a thin, small, barefoot man carrying a squirrel gun in his hand. The biggest coonskin cap I had ever seen covered his head. When he spoke, from the sound of his voice, I knew it was the man who, the night of the meeting in the woods, had said "Us free men" and then, later, had asked, "Even if they ride in and steal your farm?"

I offered him a handful of nuts. He broke one between his teeth, spit out the pieces of shell, swallowed the meat, finished all the nuts so fast before saying a word that I knew he was near starving. While I waited for him to introduce himself and state his business, I looked across Sam's garden. The cornstalks were bleached almost white. Scraggly, most of them had fallen down with our harvesting of the cobs. The pumpkins still sprawled on the ground. In the middle of the patch, Sam's infamous scarecrow ruled: a fright made of crossed sticks, Sally's worn-out broom for a head, clothes the spare rags from the house, rags that flapped wildly in the breeze to scare off vagrant birds bent on stealing kernels of corn. With the exception of his coonskin cap, my visitor looked cousin to the scarecrow.

* * *

Sam recognized our visitor. It developed that after he had been fed one of Sally's meals, all he wanted were directions from me to find his way North. Traveling alone, feet bare, without money, intent on leaving "slaveland" by the fastest route possible, he wanted to stay only long enough for me to draw him a map of the safest route out of slave country. He had come to East Tennessee following the *North Star*, he claimed. I am loathe to admit it, but listening to him, I began to doubt his "free man" status. But folded into his shirt pocket, he carried a worn and sweat-soaked paper. A freedman, freedom was his by writ of his Alabama master.

"How'd it be dat him freed you?" Sam asked.

"How'd it be? I save de massa's life. Stoppt de run'way hoss what was draggin' him down de road. Dat hoss be a-gallopin' 'n I got his reins and held on. Save de massa's life, I did. 'N him freed me."

But with the man's freedom had come no means to sustain him until he could find work to pay his way. No doubt more than a smattering of trouble followed his freedom because, if Sam and I understood him, he had been ordered by the Sheriff to leave the state of Alabama forever.

Our visitor might be free, free by a few lines scratched on a piece of paper. But it was impossible to have true freedom in slave country, least of all, for a poor, illiterate, jobless free black person. Our guest had learned that whites look down on us free blacks. Even those whites staring from the deepest layers of poverty put us on a level lower than theirs. The young slave had saved a white master's life, and had been freed; now he must run to keep that freedom. Those Lucas bastards took my home. Fields I had sweated over. Cattle I had bought with my good money. From the looks of the Lucas outfit, poor white trash, I know I could buy them several times over. But they were white, threatening me from their low level. Drove me off with their law protection. And their guns.

I wondered then, How long will it take black and white America to straighten up our mess?

In the flames of the burning shack beside the Delaware River, I saw again the low, filthy polecats binding the cords and dragging Isaiah away.

That's insanity. Crazymaking.

Smiling over a sack of provisions given him by Sam and Sally, pleased to have a map and some cash from me, the man took up his run north. For several nights after he had left, I awoke sweating, fuming over the theft of my land and cattle at gunpoint. I knew the issue cuts deeper than guns. The law of the land backs the gun. Force and rule by the white man. Faced with the killing power of the gun, a people can be forced to do anything the gun owner desires. Write the law to frame and undergird those desires. Set up the rule of law exactly the way you want society to work for you. *Free or freed*? Did it matter? You have a rule of law—white man rule based on force and violence. America.

* * *

Poor Sam! I used him as a sounding board for all my questions and ideas and lectures. He would listen to me, then end our long talks with a shake of his head and practical advice. "Rememba you be a free man. Keep yo' freedom, George. Guard it wid yo' life." Full of wisdom, Sam knew much that I did not. He cautioned me, "You gots to be kerful, George. Freedom kin be dangerous fo' you. Don't be so open wid yo' talk. Be quiet. Obey de rules on de outside. But rememba' inside yo'sef', 'til all us be free, you ain't a free man."

"Sam, I am free. I carry a freedom paper."

"I know you be free. But de trick is, George, make dem tink you keeps yo' place. Show dem a happy grinnin' face. Tink, plan, how we all kin be free. Keep yo' mouf shut. Quit buckin' de odds." And always, the old admonition, "Keep yo' place."

I had learned, *Freedom is not liberty.*

7

A long letter from the Free African Society waited for me when I rode into Knoxville for supplies in November. I ripped it open. A line of compact handwritten words in the middle of the letter stunned me: "Isaiah Curry is reported to slave on a plantation in the Southland somewhere near New Orleans."

"I just been biding my time," I said to Sam that evening after reading the letter to Sam and Sally. "Now I got to free Isaiah."

Sam gave me one of his long questioning looks. "George Bush, stop and tink. Ain't safe, you goin' to New Orleans. You got to have a plan. Don't jist spin off like a loose buggy wheel."

Sam and I had mended the last cracks in their cabin walls, cut up the last log for winter firewood, dug the last turnip, butchered a couple of pigs and were smoking them. The old couple could enjoy a warm winter, secure in knowing that they had food to last out the cold months. My final purchase was a spinning wheel. In her kitchen as she spun her thread for Sam's new linsey-woolsey shirt, I could hear Sally humming "De robes all ready now."

* * *

"Dat Jackson Proc'mation. What 'bout it?" Sam struck directly with what had been stirring at the front of his mind. "If Andy Jackson takes you in de Ten'see militia, dat be de mos' respek'ble ting you kin ebba do. Put you in real good wid de locals. 'N dat gibs you a plan. Bein' in de militia. It could hep you trabble wid dem safe to New Orleans to find your friend."

Sam had listened to my readings of Andrew Jackson's invitation from his army headquarters at Mobile, Alabama, in September 1814:

> "To every noble hearted generous brave freeman of colour volunteering to serve during the present contest with Great Britain, . . . $124.00 in Cash and 160 Acres of Land. . . ."

In my saddlebag, I carried a copy of General Andrew Jackson's proclamation I had found lying on a table in Knoxville's Wild Turkey Tavern. I clamped onto the idea that I might take up Old Hickory—that is the way people referred to Jackson, "hard as old hickory"—on his invitation and join his militia, although fighting the British was not my idea of the best way to come by my farm or Isaiah's freedom.

In between my rides looking for a place, buying a few cattle, Sam and I debated every pro and con of my enlisting. We understood the General's invitation spoke specifically to the "freeman of colour" of Louisiana. I felt a bit of rebellion arguing, "Andy Jackson will welcome any freeman of colour from his home state. Any man from Tennessee who has a gun and provisions." I figured the "160 Acres of Land" should provide a title no man could steal. But more, like Sam said, "George, yo' be crossin' county lines and state boundaries in de deep south. So, de militia gibs you cover you needs to git to New Orleans 'n begin lookin' for Isaiah."

* * *

War news traveled across the country. America was suffering in the east. British troops had driven the government out of Washington City and burned the buildings. White American soldiers were resentful of the long drawn out war with few victories. Desertions ran high. Reenlistments dragged. New Englanders threatened secession from the Union. Our Second War for Independence fared badly.

In Knoxville, we had begun hearing that thousands of British soldiers trained on the battlefields of Europe had rendezvoused in the English colony of Jamaica—to me a land not just a spot on a map of the Caribbean in Stevenson's library for I had sailed there years ago. In Jamaica, British veterans from battles in the north of our country had been ordered to join forces with troops transferring from Europe. Our generals believed the British aimed to storm the beaches of the Gulf of Mexico, take Mobile and New Orleans, seize control of the Mississippi River valley for Great Britain.

Tennessee men swore that a foreign power must not control the Mississippi. The great river provided the main artery for Tennessee and interior America to reach the outside world and its commerce. Anger swelled against the British. Patriotic fever swept across the countryside.

Since being appointed regular army commander for the U. S. Seventh Military District in May 1814, so no longer the Tennessee state militia commander, General Andrew Jackson faced the problem of too few white men to fill out his army. His call for the state militias had been answered; but he found his white troops deficient in numbers, lacking in training, low on arms and ammunition.

The General saw us free Negroes as an untapped pool of available men. We had bolstered America's whites fighting her northern battles. Negro sailors made up a quarter of the crews that had helped Admiral Oliver Perry win his victory on Lake Erie. In civilian life, Andrew Jackson had bought, owned, and sold black people. He knew well the work capacity of slaves. He had no doubts but that Negroes could provide large numbers of men to fight in the defense of his country. The use of white officers would provide adequate supervision and discipline, assurance of keeping us blacks in our place while we fought to safeguard the boundaries of America's "free" society. So, as the solution to his problem, Old Hickory issued his proclamation to the free Negroes of the Southlands.

The citizens of Louisiana feared that with guns available to them the blacks might spawn slave revolts. They had objected to

Jackson's use of "men of colour." The General refused to listen. "I know blacks can be trusted," he said. "Better they join us than the British."

To a regular army paymaster questioning the General's right to pay Negroes, he stuck to the point, closing the matter without room for opinions. Old Hickory wrote, "Be pleased to keep to yourself your opinions upon the policy of making payments to particular corps. It is enough for you to receive my order for the payment of the troops with the necessary muster rolls without inquiring whether the troops are white, black, or tea."

* * *

Early, a few mornings after Sam had brought up the matter of militia service, he pushed aside the blanket covering my entryway. "Git up. Git up. Dey be recruitin' at de old musta grounds down by Knoxville. You goin', George Bush?"

Our discussing the validity of free black's fighting a white man's war to acquire the ". . . 160 . . ." was over. Hopes for rewards and fears of risk were pushed aside.

I enlisted.

It proved easy. Sam stood at my side, assured the militia officers, everyone a white man, that I shot straight, owned my own gun and horse, and could supply ammunition, food, and clothing for myself. He knew the Tennesseans, most of whom had been callers on plantation owner Brown during the years Sam had slaved there. Watching Sam talking with them, I gained a small inkling of the trust the recruiting officers placed in my friend. Sam said I was a good man. They took his word. "'N him be a sharpshooter. I seed him tuk two turks wid one shot. Nigh unto two hun'ert yard, it wuz."

I never ceased to be amazed at Southland society, a complicated structure of races, a collection of states where laws were written against us Negro people that were too awful to be believed.

Yet, the white officers took one skinny old black man's word. They knew Sam and trusted him.

Still, before permitting me to sign on, the captain in charge ordered me to prove my sharpshooting ability. I stood at the back of a row of raw recruits waiting my turn.

I lifted my beaver hat a couple of inches, ran my fingers through tangled hair, then set the hat firmly on the back of my head so that the broad felt brim would not shade my sight. My tongue, pushing around from my bristled right cheek, played briefly against my lower lip, could not work up enough moisture to relieve the dryness inside.

Maybe the fact that I had been challenged, or that I was the last of the raw recruits to take his shot at the target, or that the militia officers kept a close watch on me, set my nerves on edge as I took my place. My fingers felt stiff, my muscles tense. I might be the end of the line, but I determined to show them that I was the best shot. I took hold of myself.

After mentally calculating the range to the target, to load my Jaeger I dropped the butt to the ground and rested it, barrel up, against my buckskins. From the powderhorn, I dribbled gunpowder into the palm of my hand a hair's-breadth above the life-line wrinkle, measuring the exact amount needed for firing. Next, I trickled the powder into the barrel. With my thumb I pushed in on top a lead ball wrapped in greased leather, then reached for my ramrod. My hand shook.

Scolding myself as I ramrodded ball and greased leather into place, I slowed the thoughts racing through me. Ramrod that ball too hard, George Bush, and she'll flatten and spin lopsided out of the barrel. You'll miss the bull's-eye. Likely cancel your chances of joining. Captain Lewis has the reputation of being so tough he will never sign on a recruit who misses the target, no matter who vouches for him.

Although the late November chill crawled up my spine, sweat broke out over my face. I licked a couple of beads off my upper lip and forced my hand steady, waited.

"Fire!" Captain Lewis ordered.

For an instant, I held myself immobile. Then, with motion almost too quick for the eye to see, I raised my Jaeger, aimed, fired. The tiny shred of bull's-eye red left by other East Tennessee recruits who had fired before me disappeared from the center of the target.

* * *

As I stepped back from the firing line, the veterans of the 5th Regiment, East Tennessee Militia, watching the test shoot, made no sound. A slight and careless shuffling closed their ranks. A few nods indicated "This one will do," as much approval as I could expect from the seasoned militiamen.

"Huzza! Huzza!" Several young white recruits cheered as I took my place among them. A broad smile spread over the face of the one on my right. But I caught a blank stare from the one on my left. I looked right through him, pretended not to see the man. Mindful of our lack of experience, we new untrained enlistees stood somewhat to the rear of the veterans of the East Tennessee Militia. Relief showed on our faces. Each one of us had hit the target.

* * *

The next morning I stood in the muster line ready to sign up, but nearly bolted out of the place at talk I heard behind me. A group of men sat watching, chairs tipped against the wall of the old building, their voices so loud, words so clear, they seemed to ricochet from the wall to where we recruits waited.

Joseph Young, the Wild Turkey Tavern owner who had told me about Sam, sat with them. I heard him say, "Jackson is an army general. He does not make the law."

"No court in the land will uphold his proclamation to use free Nigras," another man drawled.

Their words piling together, I lost track of who said what.

"Too dangerous. Those free niggers in the militia."

"Yep. You're right. Dangerous even letting them live in Tennessee. They shouldn't be allowed in this here state at all."

"Too many free niggers around. They spread their freedom tripe. They're all a bad influence."

"Worse. Arm the free nigra. Train them to shoot. And we'll have an armed revolt on our hands."

Loud as they were talking, I pretended not to hear, but nearly turned on them at Joseph Young's words. "That promise of one-sixty acres—do you think it will hold up?"

"Shucks, never."

"Nope. Never. Andy Jackson must be desperate for men. He'd never write such a promise if the British weren't giving America a hell of a licking."

"You mean he doesn't intend to make good on his word?" Young questioned again.

"Hell, you know, he just needs bodies to go up against the enemy. Figures to use the free nigra. But land for them? Never."

Although the men talked as if I were a tree stump, or, at best, stone deaf, I knew the conversation was for my benefit. Reaching into my sack, I took out Jackson's Proclamation, wheeled around, stared straight at the men.

They just laughed.

Joseph Young looked away, would not meet my eye.

I bit down hard on my cheeks, hoping my face looked as blank as the slate in the old Quaker blab school. I stood without moving a muscle. Rage boiled through me. My innards felt like a kettle of badly scorched grits. My hands clutched my gun until the knuckles stood out grisly purple.

An authoritative-looking man thumbed through papers in his hand, then read, "Gentlemen, the law of the United State clearly states, and I read from the statutes of the Second United States Congress, '... each and every free able-bodied *white* male citizen of the respective states, resident therein, ... of the age of eighteen years and under the age of forty-five years ... shall ... be enrolled in the militia by the captain or the commanding officer of the company . . . '"

The man left the group, strode over to me, snarled, "See here, Boy. Didn't you hear the law of these United States says *white male citizen*? With all due respect to Andy Jackson, that Proclamation's not worth the paper it's written on. No mention is made about enrolling a nigger, slave or free. Not in our Tennessee Militia." His eyes narrowed, paused on my hands, then slowly scanned my face, "Even if he's a half-white clabber type."

Clabber. This was Tennessee. This was a militia muster—closed to me by law. But as the white tormentor turned back to his circle of friends, there thrust into my mind the meeting of the Free African Society in Philadelphia. I heard again the same insult spoken by the obsessed free man from York.

Are both White and Black telling me I am a man without a place? A marginal man between White and Black? Not wholly one? Denied by both? An endless wanderer haunting the landscape? Am I the scarecrow of my own nightmares?

* * *

Captain Lewis had been standing by the company table closely following the talk. His impatience mounting, he silenced further argument. "Gentlemen, we're wasting time. Tennessee is Jackson country. We follow what the General says. He has ordered three thousand militiamen to join him immediately in the Southlands. Andrew Jackson told the U. S. Army paymaster white, black, or tea. We need every man we can sign on." The Captain turned to me, "Got money enough for your gear, George Bush? Your clothes? Provisions?"

"Yes, Sir," I stammered, trying to pull together my fractured thoughts. I knew the Tennessee Militia was so broke it could not provision its members. Not more than one out of ten men could furnish his own gun and gear.

"Sign him on," Captain Lewis ordered Mr. Crosby, the company copyist.

Colonel William Tunnell stepped beside Lewis, leaned toward Crosby, directed, "Sign George Bush on as my waiter."

Waiter! Waiter? The word beat through my mind. Why a waiter? No waiter bondage for me. I started to object. Pulled back. After all the bickering, if I refused the militia assignment, it could be used as an excuse to send me out of the state. Jackson needed sharpshooters. I had proved my gun. But I would not bend my back to be any man's waiter. I better say so now.

If I let the officers sign me on as a waiter, easy for them to steal my freedom papers, it could open the door for slipping me into slavery, the word "waiter" proving my servile state.

Isaiah stood beside me, his voice deep in my ear, *Hang tough, George.*

Holding in rein the rage that boiled, I looked straight at Colonel William Tunnell, my voice hard but polite. "Sir, I am volunteering to fight the British. Not to be a waiter. I will not join if I must go as a waiter, and I . . ."

"Hold on, George Bush. Let me clarify. I take no waiters or servants to the battlefield. We need every gun at New Orleans. I saw you hit that target yesterday. Dead center. You go with us as a sharpshooter. That is the *only* reason the Tennessee Militia will enlist you," Colonel Tunnell spoke, his words firm, unhurried. "I am signing you on as my waiter so you will have my direct protection when we head across the state to Nashville. No goldarn sheriff can lock you up for crossing county lines without complying with the county registries for free Negroes. You know that's the law here. So you'll carry proof you're with us. And I'll vouch for you if any sheriff raises question." The officer's eyes met mine, not staring past me as most white men did. I sensed that he saw me as a man. "I give you my word. I have no use for a waiter where we are going. When the firing starts, we need every sharpshooter we can muster. Now, George Bush, let's swear you into the Tennessee Militia."

I give you my word.

A white man's word? I had told him how I felt. In my mind, I questioned if Colonel Tunnell leveled with me. I had no assurance he would keep his word. Would he break it like Old Turley had done with my farm? I had to admit that Tunnell seemed like a man I could trust. Aye, Zeb Turley had once seemed that kind, too.

"Raise your right hand," Crosby cut through my thoughts.

The taking of the oath was over in seconds. I watched as copyist Crosby, on the official militia form, enrolled: "George Bush Pvt, Captain John Lewis' Company, Col. Edwin E. Booth's Regiment, Tennessee Drafted Militia. (War of 1812.)" My enlistment extended from "Nov. 13—1814 to June 5, l815." Mr. Crosby noted "Present" and under "Remarks" listed me as "Waiter to Colo Tunnell."

Mr. Crosby's handwritten entries stood clear, decisive, angular, against the precise square shaped printed lines of the Company Muster Roll.

* * *

My belongings stashed in Sam's house, only one piece of business remained unfinished before I rode away with the Tennessee Militia: my cows at the James place. Sam had room for them in his meadow. The cows would provide Sally and him with milk and cream for the winter. If I did not come back, they would belong to my friends because I wrote out a paper giving them the animals, legal.

* * *

Red sunset splashed against a cloud-dusted blue Tennessee sky. Red hair blowing free. Blue eyes. White homespun dress windfanned against the tiny breasts of a long-limbed girl standing high on a Tennessee hillside. A dream? A vision? Mind wanderings?

No.

I saw Isabella James again for a brief moment the third morning after my enlistment.

We rode to the preacher's house together, Sam and I. As we galloped in, Mrs. James and Ibby met us. The boys chased my cows into the barn, and Sam fastened lead ropes around their necks. No words passed between Isabella and me, but the longing I had buried deep since the time Hank Lucas drove me off my farm surfaced again. How could a man feel that way about someone forbidden, a skinny red-headed spitfire whose opening words had been, "Shoot him, Ma?"

All-seeing, all-knowing Sam sensed the tension in the air. "My God, Son," he threw at me, his first words as soon as we had ridden out of earshot of Ibby and her mother. "It be a good ting you gwine head out o' Ten'see in de mawnin'. She bad trubble for you. Don' you know dat? Bad trubble. You no nem'mine dat white gal."

Trouble? Isabella James trouble? Deep inside me I knew all I wanted was to touch her, run my hands through her wild red hair.

Half-black. Half-white. The pull to touch her was so strong it was almost as if my white half had covered my black half. But I snapped the pull. Broke the thought of Ibby James. Rode away into an ocean seething with whitecaps.

8

Fog drifted across the old horse-racing grounds north of Nashville, elongated ghostly shapes that wheeled and turned, hung motionless, then drifted again closing around us militiamen. The eerie shapes mingled, drifted, merged, shading the late afternoon sun a dull silver.

We Tennessee Militia recruits had little time to worry about either sun or fog. Every morning, sunup barely having reached us over the horizon, William Carroll of Nashville, commanding general of the Tennessee Militia, set the officers drilling our squads. He knew what he was about. Rumor had it that General Carroll spent hours figuring how to perfect his understanding of maneuvers and drills. In spite of the General, at first confusion seemed to be the order of our days. The officers, most of them fresh from farms and out of stores, had no idea how to drill a squad of men. They neither knew nor understood military commands. They called out the wrong orders, even forgot them, marched us in the wrong directions, backwards, sideways, turned us right when they meant left, their embarrassment obvious to us men who did not help matters with our sometimes intentional crossups. I began to wonder if joining the militia were a wise move. Would these men provide the cover I needed, the means to get to the deep South to search for Isaiah?

* * *

William Carroll proved a gentleman. When he appeared on the parade ground, he did not correct or interrupt the officers. We all had the feeling he saw every wrong turn, caught every misstep, recorded in his mind every mistake. We respected him for correcting his captains later in the privacy of his tent. For General Carroll, there would be no marching "half seas over" as Fortescue Cuming, an author-traveler, pictured the militia units he had seen on the roads and trails to Nashville in November of 1814:

> "On the road I met in straggling parties . . . horsemen with rifles . . . [from] . . . a militia muster, for the purpose of volunteering, or of being drafted to serve against Britain . . . Most of them were above half seas over, and they traveled with much noise—some singing, some swearing, some quarreling, some laughing, according to their different natural dispositions . . ."

I have always needed to know the man who walks close to me, takes part in my life. But militiamen have no choice as to the officers who command them. We were fortunate. William Carroll must have used the same care in running the militia that he had in managing his business, a large nail manufactory and ironmongery in Nashville.

Some men said Carroll would rather serve as an army officer than work as a businessman. He had the bearing of a military man: tall, athletic, dignified, with a touch of dandyism. Proven courageous under fire awhile back, William Carroll and his men had stood in the middle of Enotachopco Creek and held off the Indians in tough hand-to-hand fighting during Andrew Jackson's campaign against the Creeks. In 1813, he had served General Jackson as a brigade-inspector on a river expedition that had terminated at Natchez. His accurate, meticulous records and accounts for the expedition won high praise from the General. Only natural, then, that when the regular U. S. Army appointed Andrew Jackson as its Major-General charged to protect the Southlands against the British, the Tennessee State Militia officers would elect William Carroll their new commander. Few men in Tennessee were as popular as Andrew Jackson, and Carroll carried the respect and pride of the men necessary to take over Jackson's militia command.

* * *

At the order dismissing us, men grasped their rifles or muskets and headed back to the encampment where the odor of many barbecues soon spread thick in the air. All across the campgrounds, men stirred their stew and grits, chowed down their barbecued meat. Not only squirrels turned on the spits that night. Sniffing around, it smelled to me as if the farmers hereabouts had lost a few chickens and pigs. That was life in the militia. A man took what he could from home and foraged the countryside for the rest. No Tennessee chicken ran safe with the militia in the neighborhood.

Too tired or too lazy to hustle more than a quick dish of grits for my evening fare, I dumped a helping of cornmeal into my kettle, stirred in a little water, hung it over the fire. Weariness set in as soon as I relaxed. I felt uneasy, out of place. Their meals over, most of the regiment members relaxed with their friends drinking grog. A few rolled themselves in their blankets, tried to get some sleep.

Leaning against a hickory tree a few feet away, Will Briggs, one of the men who had talked against my joining back in Knoxville, sat drinking with a friend. I heard him say, "Niggers gotta be the laziest people on earth. Back on my farm, I gotta watch my slaves all the time to get any work out of them."

His companion, a white farm hand whose name I did not know, the swing in his voice speaking of origins in Louisiana, drawled, "Yeah, and I don't see why any of them northern niggers should be allowed in this here country at all. Sure not when they ain't enough jobs for us white men. Niggers ain't no part of our community. Free ones, anyways. But they walk in and grab jobs from us. A free nigger had better stay out of my way. In this man's militia, same as any place else."

I kept quiet, listened as the farm hand droned on. "Niggers with guns better not look cross-eyed in no battle. If I get a little oneasy, I'll cure that by plugging 'em full of lead."

"Shore is spooky havin' to shoot the British and look over our shoulder at the same time to make sure no nigger ain't shootin' at us," Briggs backed up his friend.

I knew Will Briggs for the man he was. "A sharp un," Sam had said, and warned me against buying cattle from him. The Briggs farm provided a skimpy living for his family. Anyone, "white, black, or tea," who posed a threat to his established, hard life would meet trouble.

Sam said, "Dat Briggs, him hates us freedmen. Figgers us be a big danger to how he live. Him tinkin' him be better'n any of us." Sam knew his man. "Dat Will Briggs be a mean one. Folks tell'd me dat him be in de patrol what kilt a freedman or two down by a ribber west of Knoxville."

The farm hand with Briggs looked to be a drifter, a man who would blame his poor state of affairs on anyone but himself. A ne'er-do-well who would work awhile, get fired for shiftiness, he would move on, cursing others for his bad luck. Two of a kind, I figured, Briggs and him. As Sam had cautioned me, I remember telling myself to stay clear of them. A few more *kind* remarks, and Briggs and his friend slouched away, their message battering my ears.

The night sat unclamoring on the countryside, a far different creature than the darkness that had covered our noisy tramp from Knoxville. Three thousand militiamen encamped on the old horse-racing grounds near Nashville, men who had walked or ridden from all over Tennessee—"half seas over" most of us. Those nights before we moved out for New Orleans and the fighting, I believed many felt the way I did, uncertain, uneasy, not wanting to think that perhaps there would be no returning.

But more than the ghost of war sat on my shoulders. The realization almost crushed me down that I had placed myself squarely in the middle of men who saw me as a threat, who despised me for my color, who would finish me off at a whim or fix an accusation on me that could tangle me with their law. To them, I was nothing but a marginal man, a scarecrow haunting their countryside.

To survive among them while keeping my self-respect, aye, that was my problem. All my book reading had not provided me with any words of wisdom, any platitude, to shore up my sagging feelings. Always, I questioned the wisdom of my joining the militia. Was it logical to think it would really help me find Isaiah?

The shadows hid men. The air hung heavy. The mist that had dampened the campgrounds most of the afternoon loosened upon us a steady drizzle. A few voices sounded muted. Men sat bound by private thoughts and fears.

From nearby, someone began a ballad that had grown out of America's Second War with England. I looked around, could not fix on the singer. I could pick out only outlines of tents silhouetted against the campfires, and beyond, the forest, awesome and hidden.

One gift, among many, that I lack is any ability to carry a tune. But that night, as the song pumped out its martial air, I decided I sounded no worse than the rest. I joined the militiamen who challenged Great Britian:

"Ye parliament of England
Ye lords and commons, too,
Consider well what you're about
And what you're going to do;

"You're now to fight with Yankees,
I'm sure you'll rue the day
You roused the sons of liberty
In North America.

. . . .

"Go tell your king and parliament,
By all the world 'tis known,
That British force, by sea and land,
By Yankees is o'erthrown."

I could feel the mood change throughout the encampment as the song ended. "Huzzas" rang out. Groups of men strode closer to their fires, talked of the adventure ahead, shared hot grog and coffee. Mugs raised, cheers of "Tennessee" and "Andy Jackson" streaked through the "Huzzas." Jokes ribbed the British. Insults derided them.

Trying to forget the long hours of marching imposed by our officers, the monotony of discipline, the confusion of drills, the strange life of the military, we drowned them in the hot grog. A combination of heat and drink seeped deep into tired bodies, and the effects shone in reddened noses—"grog-blossoms"—the mark of every seasoned militiaman.

We sang together about the "... sons of liberty in North America." Here stood one "son" who loved her, who would fight for her, but who would also be fighting for the promised one hundred-sixty acres of her land. But "liberty?" "... sons of liberty ... ?"

Liberty for Isaiah?

Waiter. The word on my muster paper bedeviled me, throbbed through my head by day, woke me at night. Maybe Colonel Tunnell knew Tennessee better than I did. He might figure it would not be used against me, but I worried.

* * *

Rumors spread throughout the camp that General William Carroll had great uncertainty about how best to move us three thousand militiamen to New Orleans. His superiors had ordered him to march as fast as possible to the defense of lower Louisiana, instructions not received from the government until October 19th. His dilemma: If he marched our militia to New Orleans on foot, overland, he would have no time to teach us military tactics; if he floated us south on the rivers, he would violate marching orders from top ranks.

March us militiamen? That would mean tramping the Natchez Trace. Men died on the Trace. In winter, the Trace plagued travelers with dysentery, fever, hunger, swampy mud, impassable stretches, bitter cold. Marching would allow no stops for drills, even though drill was absolutely essential to shape us raw recruits into disciplined units.

I did not envy the General his problems.

Outside his tent one morning, General William Carroll squinted into the raw cold wind sweeping across his face. "Colonel Tunnell, assemble the officers," he directed. "I have made my decision."

Scattered in lines behind the officers, we militiamen listened as Colonel Tunnell read his orders directing the officers to hold all men in camp ready for the long river journey to New Orleans on flatboats. The men next to me shifted from one foot to another, talked in low tones, caring not a whit about our officer's words. The Colonel paused, coughed, but did not look up as the undertones faded away.

"Sure sounds good to me, George," said the militiaman leaning against a post after dismissal from the talk. Levi Lee by name, a string bean of a fellow, I had met him on the Nashville muster grounds.

"A relief to me, too," I said. "I was not looking forward to walking all the way to New Orleans."

But, jimmers, the thought of a pitching sailing vessel still made my guts boil. I swore when I quit Captain Stevenson's ships never to get on another boat. Never again. I had drunk too much Atlantic salt water. Enough to make my stomach heave right here on dry land!

Levi, neither as tall nor as muscular as I, appeared a few years my senior. From his looks, he needed to put on several pounds to stand the trip and the fighting ahead. He wore his long, dark brown, almost black hair straight and tied in the back with a thin rawhide strap. I remember the sometimes quizzical looks in his eyes, blacker than his hair. His corncob pipe never far from his mouth, he often blew smoke rings into different shapes as he talked.

"You been on the river before?" I asked.

"Short trips. Forty, fifty miles, maybe some more," Levi replied. "Easy travel."

"This will be one long ride, all the way to New Orleans on the river."

"That's true. But it can't be as bad as sloshing through the mud on the Natchez Trace." He paused, intent on the work of the boat carpenters. "You know, I think I'll keep me a diary. I want my father to know I was part of all this."

"A good idea." At Levi's mention of father, I had a sudden flash of Matthew Bush, a flash so real I could have touched him, but the image faded as suddenly as it had appeared.

"Like I said, I was in the militia before. And when they discharged me, I got on to teach school for three months. Started the 4th of July and ended the 14th of October. After that I wasn't working."

Levi paused, then spoke again of the young lady for whom he still felt a romantic interest. Coming across to me as a sensitive man by nature, Levi had told me he pained deeply over her refusal to have him as her suitor. He had taken reenlistment as his way of easing the break with her. She must have remained much in his thoughts because a remark about her dropped often into our talk, Levi conjecturing how different his life might have been with her.

Although no woman had nudged me toward enlisting in the militia, I allowed to Levi, "There's a girl near Knoxville I'd sure like to see again." Then recalling Sam's prodding about the redhead on the hill, "She be trubble. Big trubble. Bes' you be gone," I decided not to say more about her, certainly not mention her color. "Levi, I really came because of that one-sixty acres that can be mine for militia duty."

"Yeh, I read about the land bonus. I'm going to make me a claim. Be kind of nice to own a piece of ground. Even if I go back to teaching school. There's no money in that. But there's nothing better than helping children learn. Reading. Grammar. History. Figures. A bit of drawing, although I couldn't draw a face if my life depended on it."

"I did my learning in a Quaker school back in Philadelphia. A blab school. We read all our lessons out loud."

"I hope your school was better than mine. So much for pupils to learn, so little time. My school terms were always too short. Three months a year at the most. I couldn't teach everything so fast." Then Levi changed the talk from his own work. "You, George, you told me you had been a farmer?"

Deep inside caution rose to guard further talk. An uneasy feeling always forced me to ask myself how much I wanted to say to a white man. I had met Levi during the singing. He seemed plain enough, friendly whenever we talked, I thought. But I figured always to watch what I said.

"I raised cattle for trading and some corn and oats. I aim to own land. So I'm interested in Andrew Jackson's promise." Wondering whether or not Levi Lee listened, I paused.

He watched me closely. Perhaps, after all, he did see me as a human being. I recalled, though, that he had told me the only Negroes he knew were slaves. I talked straight out to him. He looked me squarely in the eyes. I thought, If he treats me like he would any other man, I'll do the same with him.

"This militia service gives all of us a chance for a chunk of ground. One we don't get very often." I stopped, that was enough to say to him about plans. I relaxed as the thought skipped through my head that Levi apparently had his passion in school teaching, the same as I had mine for land.

"You know, my stomach feels like meal time again," I headed off further talk.

"Mine too."

Turning up the bank away from the Cumberland River, we saw three or four chickens pecking seeds at the edge of a clump of bushes a few paces to our left. We sneaked close, cornered one, grabbed it. Laughing, we tramped toward the campgrounds to broil our newly snatched grub on a spit over a fire of hickory wood.

* * *

Creating a fleet of flatboats—gathering materials, building, repairing—had made great demands on General Carroll's time and temper. Frustrations and uncertainties had badgered him at every turn. Delays because of timber not delivered when needed. Having to bully people to get work done. Shortages of carpenters.

We militiamen shouldered part of the load of muscle and sweat to bring the fleet into reality. Long straight cottonwood and poplar were shaved into the planking necessary to replace decayed and badly knotted timbers of the weakened bottoms of old flatboats. Split and broken spikes were augured out, new spikes driven in. Rotted planking of decks and stalls were torn out, good boards pegged down. Heavy batches of caulking were applied to cracked seams to withstand the battering currents of the Mississippi River.

Captain Lewis complained of the time taken to repair the old boats. "No reason to fix them. Poor flatboats to begin with. Get rid of them. We best put our time into building new ones."

Easy to suggest. But with the shortage, William Carroll needed every flatboat he could lay hands on. He ordered men not only to keep fixing the old ones but also to build new craft. The construction moved all too slowly as time for transporting the militia to New Orleans reached the critical point.

While putting in hours working on the boats, I learned about a far different breed of man: the pilot of the rivers of the West, a rootless, lawless, swearing, hard-fisted, eye-gouging river-rat always looking for a scrap. "Half alligator, not human"—the common slur applied to a pilot, and the man relished the insult. He might be the lowest of the low, but he was white, and he could license himself to be a river pilot. I could not.

On board, a pilot's sole duty required that flatboats be kept afloat. Working his way down the Mississippi to New Orleans, the river pilot earned his pay from flatboat owners for his special knowledge of the channels of the river, for his nerveless challenges to its threats and dangers lurking in the huge waterway. Once in New Orleans, the river pilots sprouted legends by their carousing. They fought anyone foolish enough to answer their challenges. They took on any women available. Bored, they drank themselves into howling demons, then into stupor. They wagered bets with abandon and lost them. Money spent, they made their way north by boat or trail to hire on for another downriver ride.

Each river boat boasted its champion pilot who displayed a red turkey feather in his cap, a challenge to every other bully up and down the river. It was said that when boats moored for the night, the rival pilots stalked the camp, itching for a fight. Our officers ordered us militiamen not to tangle with them. Gouged eyes ruined a sharpshooter.

Time was running out. We knew Andrew Jackson needed us in New Orleans. Finally, on November 14, 1814, General Carroll could count forty-seven flatboats riverworthy, ready to transport three thousand Tennessee militiamen and supplies to lower Louisiana.

* * *

"Hurry! Git yer gear stowed!" River boat pilots shouted orders, taking every opening they could to scream at us militiamen climbing onto the flatboats.

"Git your butts movin'!" The pilot on a nearby boat bellowed. "Git yer gear stowed quickern 'n alligator kin chew a pup!"

"Blast your hides! Move!" Boomed the devil standing on our deck. "To ketch my boat you gotta move fastern a nigger in a thunderstorm!"

My fingers tightened on my Jaeger. Every muscle in my body hardened. Backed by that inner charge that pushes a man beyond reason, makes him dangerous, I set myself for attack. Aware of nothing but the words "nigger in a thunderstorm," I snarled back at that pocked face, my glower fixing on a livid scar just under his right eye. I needed to strike out, beat him down, smash him with my rifle butt.

Then as he had at the militia muster, Isaiah stood beside me, warning: *The river boat pilot may be the lowest of the low, but he is white. Never forget that, my Friend. Hit him? Exactly what he wants. He begs for a fight. But you? You will be in trouble with the law. Locked up or dead. The end of your militia service and your land claim.* I felt the presence of Isaiah so real that I believed somewhere he must still be alive.

Jerking my eyes away from the pilot, I turned, glimpsed a side view of a burly man in loose fitting hunting jacket hoisting himself onto the deck of the flatboat tied up nearby, yanking his pack up beside him. He stared at me. Hank Lucas! Him on a militia boat! Thank God, not on mine. My mind rolled over. He better stay on that other boat. The river pilot is just a come-one, come all river-brawler. But Hank Lucas? Hank Lucas had the smell of skunk about him. It was more than his stink that made me almost throw up. The man was too low to be likened to a skunk.

Will Briggs shoved the butt of a nearby sweep into my ribs. "Heh! Don't stand there gawking, Boy. Pick a spot and set your pack down. Our boat's movin' out."

Boy. Boy? You got it wrong, my Tennessee Militia comrade. I heard you now, as I had heard your warning the other night.

Isaiah's presence was gone, but he had shored up my reasoning. I kept repeating: Don't make trouble for yourself on this trip, George Bush. Stay put. You may claim being a free man, but you know you can't hit him back. Stick it out for now. These sons-a-bitches are not worth making trouble for yourself. Finding Isaiah is your goal, even if it means fighting the British. Keep your record clean. Hang on to your right to claim that one hundred sixty. Prove yourself. Make it easier for the next free man.

I swallowed the urge to drop Will Briggs flat on the deck, but the bitter thought struck that countless are the times necessary to "prove yourself." Sam knew. He had warned, "Keep yo' place."

And that meant learning to keep a face so smooth, so unreadable, so controlled that no one could guess that flames burned within.

Stuffing my anger deep inside, I bent to stowing my gear, then moved away and stood behind a group of men leaning on packs in the middle of the flatboat. Other men along the edge of the craft called farewells to loved ones on the riverbank. I searched the deck of the next boat but could see nothing of Hank Lucas. I pulled my beaver hat low over my forehead. I dared not allow any man to see the rage boiling inside. Damn good that Lucas was on another boat or I would have . . . But I am a sucker, I clearly remember telling myself, if I think no *Hank Lucas* rides with my outfit.

I have already heard from a few of the bastards. Boy?

* * *

Departure of flatboats from Nashville usually offered pause for festivities. Departure became a social event of parties and drinking. Relatives and friends picnicked on the river front waiting for the boats to be loaded so they could line the bank and bid safe journey to the travelers.

Embarkation of forty-seven flatboats with militiamen from all over the state set our departure apart as a historic event—not the usual carefree affair, for we departed for combat. The banks of the Cumberland River crowded with officials and relatives. "Goodbye," "God bless you," "Come home soon" mingled with shouts of men waving from the flatboats.

A carriage drawn by a pair of matched racers approached our embarkation point and stopped near William Carroll. A short, chunky, middle-aged woman stepped from the vehicle and greeted the General.

"That's Mrs. Rachel Jackson," a man in front of me said.

"You mean that plain looking one? She, General Andrew Jackson's missus?" another asked.

"That's her all right."

"She don't look like no general's wife."

"You might not think so, but that's her talking to General Carroll."

Rachel Jackson spoke alone for several minutes with the General. We heard later that she had given him a message for her "Mr. Jackson." Then she shook hands and greeted the folks who stood close by.

"From what's said, Mrs. Jackson does a whole heap of good for a lot of people."

"She sure does. Most for them that's sick and orphan."

"And them that just needs some kind of help."

"But she's been in some real scandal, too."

"Yeh. What's all this you hear about Andy Jackson marryin' up with her when there weren't no divorce from her first husband?"

"My pa used to talk about it. He said Robards what first married her plain lied about the state assembly giving him a divorce from Rachel when it hadn't."

"Maybe Robards was tryin' to trap Jackson."

"So? Jackson bein' a lawyer, seems he'd have sense enough to check."

"Folks is going to jaw over that Jackson and Robards tale for a long spell."

As did other Tennessee Militia wives whose men ran off to duty, Rachel Jackson took her husband's place on their plantation during Old Hickory's absences. She kept the Hermitage in full operation, supervising the slaves she and the General owned. She walked the fields—managed the plowing, the planting, the harvesting. Rachel grew brown in the sun, her eyes smarted, her legs tired. The burden of war on the home front sat heavy on Rachel's shoulders, but it opened for Andrew Jackson his path to glory.

Slaves packed stores of provisions onto the flatboats. Bellowing cattle resisted being dragged on board. Whinnying horses, mounts reserved for our officers, flailed front feet high before being forced into stalls.

As the last militiamen climbed onto the decks, the crowd sobered. Proud as the Tennesseans were of their militia, they knew that when the troops returned countless men could be missing.

For a long time, I sat on my pack on the open deck, watching. Although I had no purpose in writing a diary like Levi, I still wanted to keep track of time, so I cut a small notch into a plank to begin a calendar of my days on the rivers.

"Come home soon!" The words repeated, echoed in my ears. To what? America was my birthplace, but never really could be home for me until I found Isaiah Curry and returned him to his family in Philadelphia a free man.

* * *

"Shove off!" The flatboat pilot's command sounded above the goodbyes of the crowd and the sluicing of the Cumberland River. With several other militiamen on orders for deck duty, I grasped the handle of the closest broadhorn sweep as the pilot yelled again, "Shove her off!"

Feet braced on the deck, muscles straining, I pushed the handle and felt the bite of the broadhorn against the riverbank; but the eighty-foot boat stuck fast. Militiamen lined opposite sides of the flatboat to prevent capsizing until it would float free into the river current.

The pilot stomped back and forth, screamed insults at all of us, damned our ancestors, then stopped beside me. "Git a move on, Boy! Use them mutton fists! Man the broadhorn!" We glowered at each other, hate etching his face. No "nigger in a thunderstorm" this time, but again the urge steamed in me to strike at him. Caution turned me back to the work at hand.

On the broadhorns, we militiamen strained, pushed, gasped for breath. We shoved, shoved again. Pushed hard several times. Inch by tortured inch the flatboat, heavy with men and supplies, moved away from the bank. Built alike at both ends, the craft had neither bow nor stern; the end that happened to swing downstream first would be the bow. As the boat began edging several feet from shore, the river took hold. Caught in the pull of the current, the flatboat drifted around almost a quarter of a circle, drew back toward the riverbank, finally turning to float free into the center of the Cumberland River.

In my copy of Zadok Cramer's *The Navigator* that I had bought for a dollar at William Carroll's store in Nashville, I read about the Cumberland the day before shoving into its current. Through Sumner County, Tennessee, the river roams southwesterly to Nashville, thence northwesterly to Clarksville, pursuing northerly and westerly courses and widening to a breadth of about two hundred and fifty yards where it enters the Ohio. Boats passing down the Cumberland River, most of them bound for the New Orleans market, carry a variety of cargo: flour, gunpowder, apples, pork, poultry, butter, lard, bacon, salt-peter, coarse linen, cotton, corn, cattle, horses, hogs, hides and—certainly not the least—whiskey and slaves.

Levi Lee wrote in his diary:

> "November the 13,th 1814, I started this present Campain and on the 21st day we landed At Nashville, and joined the Army Command by William Carroll Major General At Nashville we marched into our boats And took in our provision for 60 days, and moved on down to Clarksville. And the 24th of No,br we left Clarksville, on the 26th we went out of the mouth of Cumberland on the 27th we arived at the mouth of the ohio."

* * *

Bone-chilling, moisture-laden wind swept the flatboats as they floated among islands and around bends in the Ohio River. The Cumberland several miles behind us, we floated past a broken willow bar near the left shore of the Ohio, our pilots keeping the fleet well to the right of the river channel opposite that bar. Further along, we saw a scattering of cypress, the first trees of its kind on the Ohio.

Beyond the point of the Tennessee River's confluence with the Ohio, two islands split the Ohio's current into at least three channels. Our pilot warned that a big sandbar posed danger, safe passage a tricky maneuver. He let loose his usual round of curses and damnations at us men working the broadhorns.

On a high dry bank viewing the river for miles and surrounded by a few cabins and several small fields, Fort Massac crouched above the Ohio. A minor, out-of-the-way, western military post, Massac rated only a captain's command. Stagnating water from the yearly Ohio floods that collected in pools and swamps made the region too unhealthy to attract settlers, Cramer reported. As we floated by, Fort Massac's soldiers did us a courtesy. Lining the bank in formation, they fired a salute, the first official recognition on the river for our Tennessee Militia. We did not stop. Holding to the middle of the channel, we avoided the shallow rocky shore to the left.

Stretching on deck one morning after pole duty, I wished I had eaten more, although an hour had not elapsed since the early morning meal of fatback and coffee. Memories of Hank Lucas forced themselves on me. Jimmers, I had never expected to see him again. But as a "white male citizen" who owned a gun, it was his privilege and duty to enlist for militia service. If he or any of the others came after me . . . Confined as we were, to avoid insults or worse without being seen as a sniveling coward posed a problem.

* * *

Ever since we had assembled at Nashville, we had known that William Carroll studied *A Hand Book For Infantry*. Published in 1812 by Adjutant General William Duane, the book instructed on the principles of military discipline and on the drills taken from the French system that Napoleon Bonaparte perfected.

While we had waited at Nashville, General Carroll ordered his officers to read sections of Duane to us men. He needed to impress recruits that the orders inflicted on us had a source other than their personal imaginations.

One of those principles of war had been taken directly from the manuals of Napoleon:

"It is military discipline, . . . which constitutes the glory of the soldier, and the power of armies."

The days of the real business of our downriver trip began somewhere on the Ohio. Every morning part of a company worked deck duty while the rest of the unit drilled.

"Attention!" At Captain Lewis's bark, we jumped to our feet, stood in a line, listened to him read from the William Duane *Hand Book*:

> ". . . By means of the cadence, you will always be able to regulate your pace at pleasure. If all march equally to the cadence, all will march over an equal distance, by an equal number of paces in equal times. . . .
>
> ". . . [training] by acquiring the cadence, or marking of time, by the stroke of each foot alternately, and together in time, to the sound of . . . one, two . . . one, two . . . one, two . . . by the officer who has charge of the drill. So soon as they strike time tolerably, they should be faced to the right, and to the left, and to the right about, and to the left about; and so constantly, until the ear becomes habituated to wait for the word, and not to anticipate, nor delay after it is given . . ."

Glory? Power?

"Drill duty today will be to learn cadence, the ability to mark time. Each one of you will do so by practicing to step each foot alternately, in place. Then, all of you together, in place. Always in time, to the order of . . . one, two . . . one, two . . . one, two." Captain Lewis paused, looked us over. "Any questions?"

"You mean, Captain, we just stand still, stomping our feet up and down?" A militiaman drawled, skepticism in his voice.

"That's what we do to begin with. Stand in one place, but move your feet up and down to the count. Learn to step all together. Move your feet in unison. That's what cadence means. Now, let's do it."

One, Two. One, Two. One, Two. Hit the deck with the left foot when the Captain commands *One.* Hit the deck with the right foot on *Two. Up and down. Up and down. Mark Time! One, Two.*

I had known some strange situations, but this cadence drill beat them all. Grown men standing in one place, stomping up and down. *One, Two.* No sense, but we had nowhere to march. *One, Two. One, Two.* Where could we go on that flatboat? *Mark Time. In Place. One, Two. One, Two.*

Jimmers! Watch your feet, hit the damn cadence, I scolded myself. You're getting behind. Should be stomping your right foot down on *Two.*

The man beside me seemed worse off than I was. The man ahead had quit stomping altogether. *One, Two.* The count went on. *One, Two. One, Two.*

The boat lurched sideways. I lurched with it, missing the count with both feet. Shuffle, shuffle again, I ordered myself, hurrying my feet to catch the next counts in order. *One, Two. One, Two.* Whoops, miss. Miss again. *One.* Shuffle. *One, Two.* Catch the step.

Down the Ohio River. Oarsmen poled to correct sideways drifts, swung the boat to avoid snags—shifts causing me to lose count again and again, putting confusion on all of us, driving every man to reshuffle steps.

Cadence? I was not sure exactly what the Captain meant. *One, Two. One, Two. One, Two.* The officers barked, we stomped, hour after hour, day after day, sweating in the cold dampness that hung over the river valley. Then, somewhere out there on the Ohio, I began to feel a rhythm I did not have at first.

"Huzza! Huzza!" The Ohio flowed into the Mississippi. Our boat swung wide around Willow Point covered with a dense thicket of green supple willows. For hundreds of yards, the almost clear waters of the Ohio flowed into and merged with the whitish, muddy, turbid waters of the Mississippi. One vast sea of swells and whirlpools roiled southward.

"Huge, the Mississippi. Never saw anything like it." My voice was lost in the noise of the waters swishing their beats against the flatboats. I began to realize the value of the river pilots, why the boat owners put up with their insults and violence, why General Carroll had insisted that the militia hire only the best and had warned us to disregard their beastliness. Carroll depended on their experience with the steering oars to guide our fleet through the swells and boils of the river without the mishaps I had heard plagued smaller boats with less competent pilots.

Passing several islands we floated southward to New Madrid. "Levi, Cramer writes that the whole country was wrecked by that 1811 earthquake."

"Sure was. Looks like a giant hand reached down."

"Squashed the barns. Tossed the cabins around."

"Pulled up trees."

"Frightening." I joined Levi at the deck's edge. "That riverbank has been wiped out. Water spills every which way."

"The river has made a new channel, new islands."

"When you think about it, some mighty strong forces were at work in that earthquake. Mighty strong."

"Many people fled. Left behind buildings and fields."

"Yes, but I remember hearing some people refused to leave. They looked like ants crawling around rebuilding. Another kind of strong force."

* * *

Studying details in *The Navigator*, I gained respect for its author. Jimmers, that Zadok Cramer must have spent his life traveling the rivers. On the written pages and maps, he had marked every navigation detail a man needed to know: Where the snags and hidden trees hung in the river. What parts of the channel were navigable. What parts dangerous. Where best to put to shore. Every twist and turn flatboating southward to New Orleans.

Between drills and my turn at the sweeps, I tried to memorize parts of *The Navigator*. Surprising, the number of islands in the Mississippi, their names descriptive of shapes and events, sometimes humorous. "Dickey's Elbow." "Devil's Race Ground." "Council Island." "Nine Mile Reach." "Paddy's Hen and Chickens." "General Hull's Left Leg." I wondered, What happened to the General on that island?

One, Two. One, Two. One, Two. Miss. Shuffle. Try again. *One, Two. One, Two.* Long ago in the Philadelphia Quaker blab school, the teachers had drilled us, drilled every day. They made us repeat words and lines of words, until sounds and words echoed in our heads, filled our thoughts, and identified themselves with the forms and shapes on the printed pages. That drill had taught reading. But the drill on the boat, stomping my feet in one place, I did not see what it could accomplish. Perhaps General Carroll thought learning cadence with our feet would improve our sharpshooting eyes and trigger fingers. After learning cadence, then what?

Criticism of officers became the favorite gripe for us militiamen in the long hours before sleep took over. Quite a few men griped at each other about having to miss Pacolet's race back in Nashville. Drill. Drill. Drill. *One, Two. One, Two. One, Two.*

Pacolet, General Jackson's race horse scheduled to run in Nashville, drew high bets among militiamen. Levi bet against him, warning me, "Pacolet has stiff competition. Tam O'Shanter. Maria. Doublehead. Fast horses with good riders."

Bet money on this race? Most of the riders were slaves. Many jockeys commanded as high a price at the slave auctions as the horses did at theirs, a source of pride to the owners.

* * *

Levi Lee cut into my thoughts. "George, does your book say how far it is to New Orleans?"

"You mean from the Ohio?"

"No, clear from Nashville?"

"Lemme see. I'll add up the miles marked down by Cramer. It'll take a few minutes." Turning pages, adding in my head, I had the answer. "About one thousand two hundred fifty miles from Nashville."

Levi whistled. "Maybe I need to know how far from the Ohio, too."

More figures added in my head. "A thousand miles, give or take a few, from where we left the Ohio."

"Great. I just won me a bet." Levi hurried off to collect his money from another militiaman unaware of any book on board as authoritative as *The Navigator*.

* * *

Meanwhile, on the command flatboat, General Carroll continued his concentration on the principles of military discipline. Duane's *Hand Book* instructed:

> "To learn how to do anything well, we must always keep in mind the end for which the thing is to be done. The intention of discipline is war, or to produce in a body of armed men, such knowledge of a common and uniform mode of movement, in combined numbers, as will give the whole of a large force the same impulse and direction in any manner that may be required by the general."
>
> "This principle applies to every species of troops with their respective arms . . ."

We militiamen listened as the General directed his officers to divide the men on the boats into squads to explain Duane's principles and to show us how to execute them. No doubt in a more formal situation at a fort such instructions would have been given to officers apart from the common soldiers. No such privacy was possible on the flatboats. It was back to drill, drill, drill, drill.

Drill until the ear heard fully, the mind responded completely, the body automatically. Duane wrote, and our General believed him to the dot:

> "All good discipline begins with learning to *march in time*, and to a *given pace*, . .
> "The intention of all discipline is to supply a kind of artificial instinct, and to make this uniform throughout the whole mass of an army, . ."

Uniform throughout the whole mass of an army. I hoped other American troops would listen to Duane and learn that *artificial instinct.*

Uniform throughout. The British already knew uniformity as trained bodies of men, a skill they applied to personal experience, our officers claimed. Enemy troops gathering to assault the American Southlands were conquering veterans of campaigns in Europe, military operations in which masses of foot soldiers and horsemen did the fighting. Their officers had risen to commands because of superior ability for instilling into their troops "a kind of artificial instinct." Our own officers expressed concern that we green militiamen would not hold our lines against the massive British firepower we would confront at New Orleans.

How could our officers supply uniformity throughout three thousand frontier men lacking formal military training? Teach them "artificial instinct" while they tried to march across the decks of flatboats floating down the Mississippi?

"As individuals you are expert marksmen." Colonel Tunnell took Captain Lewis's place for a session. "General Carroll's instructions are that we must learn to volley in unison. Fire all together when we face the enemy. Learning to act together as if hundreds of us were one man will put us in shape to do what we have to do on the battlefield. We have a slight problem. We cannot practice to volley here. We have no powder or shot. But we will learn." He paused, let his words sink in. "When our day on the firing line comes, one thousand of you Tennessee marksmen will volley at the same time. Step back. The next thousand, step forward and fire. A deadly volley. Step back. The next thousand. Step forward, fire. Think of it. Remember, *One, Two* . . . *One, Two* . . . *One, Two*. General Carroll demands that our units learn by practice to volley in unison as a single man. So, if you have been thinking the drills are just foolishness, kick the idea out of your heads."

"Take over, Captain." Tunnell turned to Lewis, then walked to the side of our boat to watch.

Volley with what? Why worry about ammunition? I knew most of the militia had no guns.

"*One, Two. One, Two.*" The Captain drilled until dark, dismissed us with, "Tomorrow, we start an hour earlier. Time is getting short. The wind and rain have robbed us of several days. From now on, you will have continuous drills. Forget the weather." Nothing more was said about volleying.

The everlasting *One, Two* badgered us. Our officer's orders echoed into the night until fatigue took over and sleep came. The flatboats had none of the rising, falling, sideways jerking and rolling motion of a sailing ship so I slept. I believe that difference kept me from developing on the river the same sickness that had plagued me on Captain Stevenson's ships.

* * *

Although our forty-seven flatboat fleet was so large it seemed to command most of the river channel, other travelers plied their way alongside, moving up or down the Mississippi. Traders headed south with piles of produce from Tennessee farms. Families lived on boats with slaves poling them, slaves cooking meals, slaves washing clothes, slaves tending children playing on decks. Families hanging out washing on their boat decks during days found energy for dancing at night to fiddle music. They were never-give-ups like the people at New Madrid.

It appeared that quite a number of folks lived on the river, the mighty waterway the only home they knew from one year to another. Always, a man lounged at the edge of the flatboat deck, gun across his knees, watching for an outside marauder or guarding so that his faithful, much-beloved Tom or Mary would not slip into the river to freedom.

The most intriguing boats drawing my thoughts away from all else were the pirogues of the mountain men and fur traders gliding north against the current. At times, they stroked the long slender pirogues close enough for us to hear their greetings shouted in a mixture of French, Indian, and English—a trade jargon, I figured. Trappers and mountain men who had delivered their furs south, they were rowing back to St. Louis. After outfitting themselves, they would strike out again into beaver-rich streams of northern Mexico's mountains or fan out along Missouri River tributaries for another season of trapping. Weathered by their outdoor life, most of the men looked French like the merchants I had seen in Philadelphia.

I envied those western outdoor men their freedom. I needed to talk to the *voyageurs*, find out about trapping and trading, where they went, what they did. I watched them stroking their long slender pirogues to the cadence of melodies brought to North America by the early French fur traders. I watched them until their pirogues no longer could be seen in the haze and shadows that hung over the Mississippi. They sang as they rowed, strange, haunting, unforgettable melodies rooted deep in ancient French:

> "Who is it cries in the dawn,
> Cries when the stars go down?
> Who is it that comes through the mist,
> The mist where the rivers run?

> Who is it
> in the dawn
> and the mist?"

* * *

Treacherous currents deviled us for many days. Then, late one afternoon, with indications of worse waters ahead, we tied up along the shore. The next morning, not a streak of first light showed, but our officers were already at their plans. Before they ordered us out for the day, ready for drill, I rolled over, listened to a discussion between Captain Lewis and our river pilot, along with two men from other boats.

"Three weeks ago when I passed through, the old schute above Flour Island was jammed full of snags and sawyers," one of the pilots pointed out.

"What you sayin' we should do, Mike?" A second river guide asked.

"Run the new schute. On the other side. Can't be no worse than the old one."

"Let's git back to our boats, and shove into it."

"Hold on a minute," Captain Lewis commanded. "Have any of you been through the new schute?"

"Hell, no, we ain't, Mister," a pilot answered. "Mister" was as far as any pilot would acknowledge the status of Captain Lewis as an officer. "Sir" from the pilots was not a possibility. The officers ignored that no river pilot would address them with respect for rank. "Like I was sayin' the old schute's plumb dangerous."

"You say the new schute has just opened up. How do you know it's even as clear as the old one?" our Captain asked.

The three river rats glowered at the officers. How far they dared push the Captain required canny judgment, something given short shrift by a river pilot. Riding the river was their business, not managing men. But none of them wanted to raise the anger of

Captain Lewis who had the direct ear of the no-nonsense General Carroll, a man they knew to be a favorite of Andrew Jackson. Get in trouble with that trio and likely a man would lose all his piloting hire for the government.

"Well?" Captain Lewis persisted.

"We're tryin' to figure what's best, Mister," one of the men said. "We think we better run the new schute."

"You know time is vital to us. We trust you to pick the best course."

"That's what we aim to do, Mister." Our pilot headed to his post. "Let's git the boats goin' and run 'em through."

Directions boomed out. Our men on duty strained their backs, pushed the boat into the current, poled along the right side of Flour Island into the Mississippi's main channel. For awhile it looked as if chaos had taken over. Several boats were forced to run the left schute, crowding together toward the east bank. Curses mingled with the pilot's yelled instructions. Men on the broadhorns strained to keep their flatboats off newly formed sandbars.

Better pay attention, George Bush. Brace your feet against the deck. I acted none too soon. The boat tilted to a drunken angle, then with an abrupt drop jolted against the river current. Shouts and commands merged into the roar of the torrents. The pilot grasped one of the broadhorns, added his weight to the efforts to guide the boat. By a hair, we missed collision with two flatboats.

Drill suspended, we battled the river, freed nine flatboats snagged on sawyers, huge trees swaying loose in the current. The stubs of the sawyer limbs, broken off and sharpened by the swift flowing water, struck into the wooden flatboat planking like sharp saws. One boat swamped. The men on it grabbed what gear they could, jumped onto other boats. Several men pulled themselves aboard with us. My God, Hank Lucas! Ignore him. No time to deal with him while we run the chute.

Limbs of sawyers scraped our sides again as we hurtled past the south side of Flour Island into less turbulent current. Luck held with us. Years earlier, boats heavily laden with flour for the

Southlands had wrecked against the sawyers. Their white cargos washed ashore giving the chunk of land in the river the name "Flour Island."

* * *

Then it happened. A sweep smashed across my back with a powerful shove toward the side of the boat. I caught a glimpse of Briggs's sneering face. "You damn smart northern nigger. Think you can march better'n us." Hank Lucas spit at me as I lost footing and crashed overboard.

Belly-flopping into the swirling water, my fingers touched bottom. I swung upright. Using my feet as a spring, I plunged toward the surface, treaded water, flailed my arms, spit out a mouthful of grit. I reached for the side of the boat, missed, floundered. A loose log grazed my head sending me under water again. I was stuck in the sawlike arms of a huge sawyer that bounded up and down swamping me each time I went under. The Mississippi has currents no man can see from the deck of a boat. Those currents took me into their grip, spun me around, twisted me over.

Time wove an endless web, it seemed. I fought the river, tried to gain footing, lost it, the water too deep. The cold numbed my feet and arms and began to sap my strength. Whatever the reason, the gulped cold water, the shove of the sweep, the blow from the sawyer, my limbs seemed out of control. I could not work up the strength to swim after my boat as it drifted southward. My head became groggy, my eyes water-strained. The faces of the two who had pushed me in leered at me. Struggling to keep my head above water, I pumped my legs, felt myself weaken, sink down, then up again, each time weaker, slower.

Don't let them . . . get away . . . with it. Don't . . . Don't . . . , I heard Isaiah gasp. *Tread water. Stay afloat. Start swimming. Swim. Swim.* Each time I lost control, the swirling current sucked me down.

After what seemed an eternity, a man using strong, fast strokes swam toward me, yelling, "Hey, keep pumpin'." A hand grabbed mine. "Hang on, Brother. I'll pull you in." He dragged me to his flatboat. Helping me shinny up a rope hanging over the side, he half carried me on board, a sodden waste too bruised, too tired to help.

"I'm Jim. Remember me?" my rescuer asked. I opened my eyes to stare at Jim, the Sheriff Dunbar slave whom I had met in those night talks with Sam and friends deep in the East Tennessee woods. I had seen him on the overland trip to the muster grounds, but he had ridden with a different squad. In Nashville, the Sheriff kept him in strict attendance so we had found no chance for even brief talk. "We was near enough so's we seen them guys try to do you in. You sure put up a fight in that water 'fore I could get to you. Bad business. Reckon those bastards aim to do us all in 'fore we're through."

Jim. Aye, Jim had a force and an understanding few men possess. A short, stalky man, he had the powerful shoulders and arms of a smithy. Always held to business by Sheriff Dunbar, Jim knew he could not stray from his owner's side. His "duties" the same as those given to other slaves carried south by our militia left no opening for him to jump off the flatboat and swim to freedom in the wilderness lining the west side of the Mississippi. I wished I could stay and talk with him. As soon as I could stand, I was rowed back to my militia boat.

I needed to know Jim. But even on the flatboat, the closeness of one militiaman for another, a place where new friendships formed, I could not stand any closer to Jim—him slave, me free. The bars held as strong on the great river of the west as they did back in Tennessee. Masters never ceased complaining that free Negroes associating with their slaves made the slaves valueless. "Free nigras spread too many ideas," the man had said at the Knoxville muster ground. But in spite of restrictions, friendships did form. I aimed to follow up with Jim. Perhaps in New Orleans. In camp. Somewhere.

* * *

One day about one hundred seventy miles south of the mouth of the Ohio River, we passed Chickasaw Bluffs, the site of ancient ceremonial grounds of the Chickasaw Indian tribes. The Bluffs ranged along the left bank of the Mississippi for several miles. They rose one hundred fifty to two hundred feet high. Glistening in the sun, the broad and jagged masses of rock painted a spectacular parade of pink and orange and yellow.

"No doubt we will see Chickasaws in New Orleans," I muttered to Levi Lee.

"Sure enough, George. Jackson has promised each Chickasaw warrior a blanket or two for joining him to fight the British."

"Got a question for you, Levi. Why is our service worth one-sixty acres plus some cash, but an Indian gets only a blanket?"

"And that probably an old army issue."

A bluff sloughed off; splitting into chunks, it fell into the current. With loud rumbling, another mammoth section larger than several flatboats settled into the river. The incessant force of water beating and swirling against its base had loosened it. Gigantic spouts and geysers rose from the surface of the river. I jumped back from the edge of the deck, but a wave of spray soaked me. Tons of rock and soil kept dropping into the current, baring the fresh face of the bluff. Its colored veins shredding in contrary directions glowed bright yellow and pink.

* * *

"Devil's Race Ground!" Our pilot roared. "Grab yourself a rope! Tie down the horses! We're shovin' through."

The hiss of roiling waters in the narrowing channel rose to chilling pitch. Tying the rope around my waist, I took my post on the broadhorn.

"Watch that island!" The pilot shouted. "Hang right!"

Ahead, sawyers and snags jammed the river. Planters, giant trees rooted in the bottom of the river, often not visible from our low decks, scraped against our boat.

Strain on the broadhorn. Fight the river.

Driven by boils, swirls, and powerful undercurrents, the flatboat careened through a narrow channel between the bank and an island. The boat shoved against a tangled mass of snags and was forced directly toward land. No time that day to check *The Navigator* for the island's name and size.

"Devil's Elbow," the pilot yelled. All of us, anchored by ropes, sweated, strained, pushed hard on the sweeps.

We were grounding.

I jabbed with my broadhorn as the flatboat struck a high sand and willow bar. Our forward speed floundered.

On our right, a large whirlpool rose to the surface as its force sucked the flatboat back into the swirling current. "What's happening?" I yelled. No one could hear to answer. "We're worse off than if we'd grounded on that sandbar."

Disappearing downward, whirling around, the murky waters hissed to the surface again. Grimy and thick with mud sucked up from the river bottom, water tossed high into the air as if thrown by a giant hand.

The channel narrowed.

Caught in the whirlpool, the side of the boat raked by huge sawyer limbs, our sweeps hung useless. The river in control, we drifted a mad and twisting course.

Again the strange sucking hiss, the surge, the pull of the whirlpool, the swirl of the current. One of the men lost his footing; and thrown against the corner of the hatch, lay in a heap, unconscious or dead. Levi started to crawl toward him to see what could be done. The entire river swooshed sideways, and our flatboat lurched as river currents slashed against its side. We hung suspended for a moment, my hands frozen to the broadhorn. Then we crashed down hard against a mass of snags almost wrenching the sweep from my hands.

"Use that pole, Nigger Boy," a nasty voice rasped in my ear. Hank Lucas, feet braced on the deck, lurched toward me.

"I said use that broadhorn, you lazy nigger." He yanked my anchor rope.

A flash from the past aimed three guns at me on Zeb Turley's farm. Lucas lunged. All the hot red wrath of that thieving day in East Tennessee stirred itself into the horror of the icy Mississippi waters. Locking reason in my guts, I met Hank Lucas head on. We grappled on the tilting deck as the churning current turned our flatboat halfway around. Chilling water drenched us. I felt Lucas push me toward the edge, his hands grappling to choke me. I jammed my knee into his groin. He screamed in pain. I aimed for his ribs, but the motion of the boat deflected my second blow. He had hold of the rope around my waist, one hand gouging at my eyes. I flung my right arm hard against the side of his skull.

The boat tilted sideways. Thrown against the handle of my broadhorn, he kicked the small of my back. Pain shot through every nerve of my spine. I turned and with all the force I could muster kicked the bastard just as the boat lurched to the other side and sent him reeling across the deck. He smashed into Levi Lee working his sweep. Levi had seen us. Although he could not leave his post to help me, he swung around, smashed the end of his sweep into Lucas's stomach. The scoundrel doubled over in a vomiting heap.

* * *

The flatboat shot out of the whirlpool, twisted through the Devil's Race Ground. The river channel still turned in endless contortions. From a southwest to south course the current changed abruptly to north by west, then south by southeast. A second large bend churned and boiled back to the north, then swirled to south by east, east by north, through the Devil's Elbow, where the river formed a left-hand point. Again our boat jolted and turned, uncontrolled, in a wide circle.

Dead ahead huge chunks of earth tore loose from the banks and tumbled toward the river surface. Mud and rock landed on our deck. Poling hard, we saved the flatboat from being jammed into the bank. Snags and planters clawed at the side of the boat, but the current and the efforts of us militiamen kept it moving. We jabbed our sweeps into a low sandbar, prevented the boat from grounding, then poled quickly to avoid drifting into a mass of floating debris and wood the size of an island.

Hours later, the Mississippi River straightened its twisting course. The channel broadened. We had conquered the Devil's Race Ground and the Devil's Elbow. Exhausted, Levi and I sprawled side by side on the deck. Men on every boat in sight dropped in heaps onto decks.

"Keep an eye on that Lucas. He tried to kill you," Levi warned.

"I know. He almost shoved me overboard."

"What's he got against you?"

I thought first of holding back, but why not tell Levi? "He stole my farm."

"Took your land? The bastard."

"Yes. At gunpoint."

"Briggs and that other fool?"

"Rather not talk about it. They just hate." I expected any minute to be called before an officer because of *my assault* on a white man.

Soaked by the icy river water, splattered by the mud, our hands and wrists scarred, our muscles strained, our bellies skinned and raw from the ropes that had raked us, Levi and I lay spent. We lacked energy to keep our eyes open. My back stung from the Lucas attack.

My life, a calm river flowing onward? No. Like my flatboat in the Devil's Race Ground, my life bashed against the boundaries of hell. Like the old Mississippi River, my life rolls and twists, rages one day, calms the next.

The day sped. The overcast thinned. The late afternoon sun warmed our bruised bodies. Mercifully, no officer belted out *One,*

Two, One, Two. All across the decks of our flatboats, men sprawled, too done in from working the broadhorns to care. I did not know the militia penalty for total inability to respond to an order.

Hours later, I flipped through maps in *The Navigator*, saw where we had been, conjectured where we were going. The next important place seemed to be Council Island. Zadok Cramer wrote that it lay three miles long near the middle of the Mississippi where the river turned suddenly to the left, the right chute choked with dense growth of young green willows, "their leaves dancing with the wind in springtime." Cramer got poetic at times. During years past, on that island with its good beach, numberless councils of Chickasaws, Chocktaws, and other Indian nations had met to settle disputed tribal matters.

From what Cramer had drawn on *The Navigator's* pages, it appeared as if for the next five hundred miles the Mississippi River would flow a straighter course. Fortunately, for none of us wanted another struggle like the one we had through the Devil's Race Ground. And I wanted no more of that confounded Hank Lucas jumping me in the worst stretch. Lucas and Old Turley, Briggs and his farm hand—to make up for every hateful one, it takes a thousand Levi Lees.

* * *

Our flotilla drifted onto a broad beach, for a change more sand than mud. The officers allowed a rest period, although a few captains took advantage of the open ground and put their units through drill. Far into the west stretched a broad prairie, its tall grass green and silver yellow. Against the skeleton of an ancient sycamore splintered by lightning, a wild rose climbed skyward, its branches heavy with dark red hips. I picked a handful of hips, sniffed their pungent spice, chewed the fruit, its cinnamon flavor reminding me of Mahala's jelly making. A warm feeling swept into my soul. For a moment I stood in the Philadephia kitchen of my boyhood, a vase of pink wild roses in the middle of Mahala's table, so real I could almost reach out and touch the soft velvet blossoms and hear her chiding Jonah.

Late that night, my greatcoat pulled close around me, I looked up at the stars, heard the rush of the river. On solid ground, I wanted to sleep as many hours as the officers would permit; but the night filled with the same nightmares that had bedeviled me at Sam's house. Riding again with the spirit, I saw the faces, first of Sally, then of Isaiah. I could not relax. I took my bedroll far from the rest of the men, lay down close to the shattered sycamore with its rosebush.

I let my thoughts slide back to Sam and Sally, heard their rich voices speaking the patois of the slaves. When I first had ridden to their house, I could barely understand their words, even had the foolish idea I ought to teach them some decent "Philadelphia English." But before long, I realized they talked with a language from far back in time, an accent older than any I knew. Intelligent people, Sam and Sally had no schooling. Of course, plantation Brown did not believe in educating his slaves. No doubt he agreed with the white folks of Richmond, Virginia, who a few years past, in 1811, had rid themselves of a man teaching slaves by confining him in the insane asylum.

At first light the next morning, my ear against the ground, I heard rumbles through the earth. I puzzled, Shots? Thunder? No, they were hoofbeats. Listening a few moments, turning toward the direction of the sound, I stood up, caught sight of wild horses racing to drink at the river's edge. Glossy, long-legged, liquid muscled, the creatures seemed fantasies from another world, wild ones beyond human reach. The morning sun swept over them, gilding their backs golden brown, creating a painting no artist's brush could put on canvas. An urge to ride, ride across the prairie into the wilderness swept through me. The power of the horses held me in its grasp, drew my every thought into the joy of racing with them in wide open spaces. I stood breathless, knowing the slightest motion would fracture the moment.

Then shouts, curses, noise from the militia camp ruptured the clean, crisp stillness of morning. Rearing up, heads tossing, nostrils flaring, the magnificent wild creatures turned, galloped westward toward the wilderness, disappeared into freedom.

* * *

"You plan to lash boats together? To drill?" An officer shouted to General Carroll in the lead boat. "You can't be serious. Not unless you think our men can walk on water."

"No problem," William Carroll responded, ignoring the attempt at humor, true to his reputation of being devoid of it, a man whose life focused only on work. "A common practice on the western rivers. Lashing boats." He paused, his feet braced on the deck. "In peacetime, lashed boats provide space for floating trade fairs and dancing. In wartime, we'll use the decks for drilling. So, Gentlemen, time to lash the boats together."

At both ends of each flatboat sturdy wooden pegs had been set into the planking, pegs tapered in the middle to retain the rope when coiled around them. Catching a rope thrown to me by the man from the preceding boat, I and a couple of slaves tugged hard to close the gap between the two boats. We pulled and wrapped the rope tight around the large peg at my end, securing the flatboats to each other. One of the slaves who helped me, Robert Franklin, strong muscled, was as white as most of the white men who rode the river with us.

"Son of his master, Judge Franklin, from up Nashville way," Levi Lee had told me a few days earlier. "His two older brothers had been sold at an auction to pay off the Judge's gambling debts. The Judge always rides with the militia. Outfits his own squad."

From the flash of Robert's angry green eyes, I doubted he would stay slave forever.

Looking across the decks of several boats, I estimated the total length, judged we had a tolerable distance for marching practice. We would feel better moving over more space. But march on tilting, jerking flatboats? Skeptical, I scanned the length again as I took my place with my squad.

Captain Lewis and his orderly appeared before us men of the 5th Tennessee Regiment. "Today, we will drill the companies by marching. You have learned to step in cadence, in place, all of you as one man. You will now march together over equal distances, in equal amounts of time. Is that clear?"

No, it was not clear.

One, Two. One, Two. One, Two. The men stomped feet. *One, Two.* The same old cadence stuff, I thought.

"Short steps. *Forward, March*! Step even. In unison. Snap to." The command, a new one, sounded impossible. I hesitated, looked at the man on my right. Then I stepped forward with the other men. *One, Two. One, March. Two, March.* Short steps. Our column moved forward, stepped onto the next boat. *March, One. March, Two.* Better keep count. I stomped short steps with my column across the deck of the second boat and forward onto the deck of the third one next up front.

I hoped to God the officer remembered the command to turn us around before I had to test my ability to walk on water.

One, Two. One, Two. Halt! About Face! Forward, March! The column stomped across the boat decks back to the point where it had started, then reversed, repeated. Back and forth, the drill repeated on commands: *One, Two. One, March. Two, March. One, Two. One, Two. Halt. About Face.* The drill continued across boat to boat. The men marched, halted, reversed, marched, until I, for one, gave up trying to keep the count, let the officer's *One, Two, One, Two* work on my instinct. A rhythm was beginning to take hold of my body, the counting still necessary to keep the pace, to bring our steps into unison.

March, One. March, Two. One, Two. One, Two. March, March. One, Two. We militiamen stomped back and forth across the flatboat decks, moved together on the repeated commands, our rhythm still ragged. *March, One. March, Two.*

* * *

Following that drill, we listened to more William Duane:

> "The soldier stands firm, his eyes to the front, his left hand down by his side, not constrained, but straight; his right hand fingers in front of the firelock, the butt of which is close to his right foot and dressed with it; the barrel rests against the right shoulder, the thumb of the right hand behind the barrel, the arm bent a little."

"The British will wear red uniforms with white straps crossed on their chests," Captain Lewis lectured more than once. "Aim your musket an inch above where those white straps cross. That is your target. Dead center on a man's chest."

"Simple as a turkey shoot," a man back of me laughed.

My stomach tightened, and I saw Levi flexing the muscles of his jaw, both of us thinking ahead to the British veterans, the fighting, the killing.

Each day our officers intensified the drills. Each day Robert Franklin, Jim Dunbar, and other slaves substituted for their owners in the marching. Each day militiamen forced themselves to match their length of stride with those of the men next to them. Short, quick steps demanded by our limited space. Ahead of me I saw men mince, sway their hips, in their way burlesquing the entire operation as if we were putting on a parlor performance. My squad kept the count, every man taking pride in instant reaction to orders. We marched equal distances in equal time with every other man.

The men from the sunken flatboat had trouble keeping up with our crisp cadence. After the drill, they received new duty assignments. I held the rope for a waiting rowboat, Hank Lucas lowered himself into it. I sneered loud enough for him to hear, "You couldn't keep up with us. You weren't good enough. You stinking bastard."

* * *

One afternoon, an assignment to help with food duty varied my boredom. Butchering had been a familiar task back in Philadelphia, but on the squad's supply flatboat the hot humid air mingled with the odors of the penned-up critters. Cooking fumes and fireplace smoke at one end, half-wet grain and molding hay added to the stench. A huge carcass lay on the boards, and the cutting-up job seemed endless. For a moment the sickness that long ago had plagued me on board Captain Stevenson's sailing ships swept through me. Trying to breathe as little as possible, stooping low to swab up the warm sticky blood and guts, I could not hold my insides from churning. I retched. Slopping a bucket of the animal gore against my leg, I rushed to the edge of the deck, relieved myself into the Mississippi River, a giant privy flushing itself southward to the sea.

* * *

Our river fleet floated past the mouth of the Yazoo River, flowing from the east, marking the north boundary of Mississippi Territory. Then about noon on December 12th, we passed Walnut Hills, a dried grass ascent rising gradually several hundred feet from the river level.

December. Dried cornstalks and withered pumpkins lay strewn on the once lush green fields of summer. The pilots told us to keep well in the middle channel to avoid the large eddy near the left shore. We took a salute from the soldiers at Ft. McHenry cheering us southward.

On the shore of the Mississippi, I saw lines of flatboats and keelboats tied up waiting to move south—loads of timber, farm produce, boats with goods for trading. If the British blockade of New Orleans could not be broken soon, all the farm foodstuffs piled on boats would rot.

Goods for sale: Human beings with spiked collars around their necks and legs, men, women, and children lay chained together in forty-foot coffles bolted to the deck. We passed close. In each person, I saw Isaiah. And as we left the slaver's boats behind, in the distance, I heard echoes of Isaiah's unforgetable rich laugh, now streaked with a haunting but defiant tone.

* * *

Early one morning, a sound I had never before heard spread a strange rhythm across the river, an eerie soughing caused by the wind. Sunlight played through moss hanging like old men's beards from tall deep green cypress trees.

"Spanish Moss," Captain Lewis said, "a certain sign we have floated into the Southlands."

The trailing moss gave off an odor as decadent as the air in a prison. The smell irritated my nose. The mysterious soughing of the moss spooked me, made me uneasy. With my broadhorn, I swept in and grabbed a branch of moss drifting with the current—strange material, springy but cloying to my touch. Some men chewed the moss. I tried but spit it out, the taste bland, the shreds of it clawing at my tongue.

Worthless, the moss appeared to me, but Levi said different, "Pack a mattress with the stuff. Moss makes for softer sleeping than horsehair or corn stalks."

Its blades sharper than most hunting knives, twenty-five feet or more high, the canebrake stretched from the riverbank as far as I could see.

I heard Will Briggs laugh. "Good stuff. It'll cut down any slave running through them."

Not caring to hear his wisdom, I moved to the other side of the boat.

Flocks of geese and bittern and crane, disturbed by the flatboats, flapped wings, rose high from secluded habitats along the marshy banks. Taking imaginary aim, I followed the flights of teal and other ducks, game birds flying from the north to their winter home. On a low neck of sandy land, a large flock of swans held their ground. Men who knew said that swans were numerous along reaches of the lower river. Those were the first swans I had seen. They did not take to flight as did the game birds. Most of the swans stood on the sandy strip, but a few moved across the beach, slowly with grace. Proud birds, they were not intimidated by our parade.

As we floated deep into the Southlands, the Mississippi River turned darker, mysterious. Fog often overhung from bank to bank, shutting out view of land during the day and stars at night. Only the sounds of water rushing against the flatboats or the soughing of moss in cypress trees broke into our thoughts of what lay ahead as the river flowed endlessly southward.

The drills never ceased. *One, Two. One, Forward. Two, Back. One, March. Two, March. One, Two. One, Two. One, Two.*

* * *

Our fleet drifted through the country of vast sugar plantations, a region of white-pillared mansions built by black hands. The dark soil of fields along the riverbanks showed recent plowing and tending. The fertile acres stretched from the river's edge far beyond the range of human eyes, land ready for the spring planting.

Broad acres of the Southlands supported the thieves of human liberty, one of the largest being General Wade Hampton, a Carolinian who owned nearly four hundred people. A crop year could produce him 500 hogsheads of sugar, 1,000 bales of cotton, all worth some $150,000, among Americans a vast fortune. I knew, of course, General Hampton shared none of his profits with the slaves who produced his wealth. I knew he saw the spiked iron collars, leg irons, chains, as a burden on his plantation, an annoying expense caused by the man, woman, or child who ran.

And past the sugar plantations, I rode the flatboat southward with *One, Two . . . One, Two.* I had mustered into the militia to protect the plantation ilk.

But floating toward New Orleans with the Tennessee Militia, I saw admiration and envy for the plantation owners of the Southlands riding with us. Harry Jenkins, a store owner, had moved to East Tennessee from North Carolina where he had feared the Garvin slave insurrection back in 1790. He believed that to keep slaves in their place whites had the right to use any means, inhumane, violent, or otherwise. He admired the bullwhips, the spiked collars and leg irons, the chains. More often than not, Jenkins began his tirades with a dissertation on the care and feeding owners provided the slaves, then turned his talk onto us free men.

"That Tunnell made a big mistake gittn' a free nigger into this here militia," his voice carried back to me as Jenkins, Briggs, and their white friends walked to the side of the boat, our drill for the day ended.

Will Briggs motioned toward slaves in a field. "That clabber belongs out there. Chained and whupped."

Another farmer-slave owner, a backwoodsman originally from western Virginia, boasted, "Yes'n onc't they've seen a dead nigger, too, makes it easier so's n' 'ey don' try nothin' ever."

I looked at them, fought to stay calm. In an even voice, I broke in as casually as I could. "You know, I had a white friend in Philadelphia who wasn't scared of Negroes."

"Scairt? You say I'm scairt? You bein' smart with me," spewed from Jenkins.

I heard the force in the voice but read the insecurity in the eyes.

"Sit down, Clabber!" ordered Will Briggs.

I ignored Briggs, my eyes locked on Jenkins. The insecurity in the man's eyes shifted into a smoldering hate as a twisted grin formed on his mouth.

"Tha's right, sit down there. Now, Boy," rasped a couple of other voices.

"You make George Bush sit down? You have to make me sit down, too," the words shot from schoolteacher Levi Lee. He bit hard on the stem of his corncob pipe.

"Well, you two are in for some trouble, and you better watch your tracks. I saw you attack Lucas, Boy." Will Briggs stance and voice dared me to touch him. Leaning back against the flatboat railing, he sneered, relaxed, no doubt thinking because he had shoved me overboard once he could do it again and get away with it. Levi and I turned away and walked down the deck, our swagger as insulting to them as we could make it.

The next day, a Sergeant whose name I did not know called from his rowboat to Briggs, Jenkins, and their friends, "General Carroll wants to see you-all. Now. At once."

In front of General William Carroll, the men stood at attention. "In battle, you fellows keep your guns pointed only to the enemy or you will be executed," Carroll ordered. "I am in command, and I aim to knock off the British Army. I don't care a whit about your personal dislikes. When the British attack our lines, we must be totally disciplined and focused against them. George Bush is a sharpshooter. I know what happened to him upriver. I am warning you now. You are dead men if he gets a bullet that is not from a British gun. Dismissed."

I knew Andy Jackson would back Carroll. He had ordered six militiamen shot for disobedience in the Creek Indian War.

* * *

"Wednesday the 14th we landed at Natchez," wrote Levi Lee while I cut the thirtieth notch of my plank calendar.

The flatboat fleet bearing our three thousand Tennessee militiamen had floated and rowed to a point six hundred ninety-five miles south of the mouth of the Ohio River, still about three hundred fifty miles north of New Orleans. The flotilla tied up something less than a quarter of a mile north of the wide open city of sin known to every boat pilot as Natchez-under-the-Hill. The port crouched at river level below the civilized Natchez of fine homes on land high above the Mississippi.

"Ya-hoo! Shore leave!" Militiamen shouted at sight of perhaps the most notorious spot along the entire Mississippi. We had men sick with fever to put ashore.

At the landing we saw the keelboat *Pittsburg*, a trader's vessel that had floated downriver alongside us on several different days. From rumors, we figured its cargo included the five thousand stands of arms with flints and thirty thousand musket cartridges ordered by the United States Army for the defense of New Orleans.

With other freight for sale on board and unconcerned about either the war in general or the defense of the Mississippi Valley, the *Pittsburg* skipper made stops as he chose. He ignored the urgent call for supplies, took time to put dollars into his pockets by private trading at settlements and wharves along the rivers . To do so was his privilege, the way he figured.

General Carroll charged that the keelboat captain was failing to carry out his contract with the U. S. government to deliver promptly supplies urgently needed by Andrew Jackson for the defense of New Orleans. In General Carroll's mind, the demands of war were the first duty of every citizen, suppliers no less than us militiamen.

* * *

"Forward to board!" Mist hung along the Natchez waterfront as we stepped from the wharf to the *Pittsburg's* deck. Part of my squad marched to one side of the supply boat ready to work the broadhorn, the rest of us took posts to guard the entries to the lower deck. *One-two, One-two, One-two* pulled us to our duty.

A lone figure climbing out of the hold of the keelboat stopped, jerked erect, when he saw our shadowy forms. "What the hell is going on? You stupid fools, coming on board without warning." The keelboat captain started to lunge at me, pulled up short when he realized that I held aim straight at his chest. "I am in command here. Get off my boat. Every blasted one of you!"

Several militiamen surrounded the angry captain. General Carroll's order barked crisp in the misty night, "We're here to take the guns and ammunition for the United States..."

"The hell you say! Not till I git to New Orleans and git my pay." The *Pittsburgh* captain lunged again, that time toward General Carroll. "I'll put you in chains, Carroll. Boarding without permission."

Levi and Robert Franklin seized the keelboat skipper and pinned his arms behind his back. With several guns pointed at his head, his mouth open, the man could only glare.

"Take the *Pittsburg* alongside our blacksmith boats," General Carroll ordered.

We pushed the heavily laden boat from the wharf and poled upstream to the militia fleet, our poling punctuated, first, by the keelboat captain's obscenities against Carroll's heritage, then, by the slurp of the current against the bow. Gusting cheers poured out of us. We transferred the guns and ammunition to the care of our blacksmiths. The unexpected assurance of guns and shot spread confidence through everyone.

With the U. S. Army's supplies in our possession, we returned the captured boat to its berth at Natchez-under-the-Hill. In high spirits, we withdrew as the skipper's final threat boomed, "Just you wait, damn you, Carroll, till I report you to Andy Jackson. You thieving son-of-a-bitch."

I roared aloud as never before on that river ride, roared with laughter till my sides nearly split. The episode so fired up the entire Tennessee Militia that shouts and guffaws and "Huzzas" thundered in swells across our decks, a mighty tide sweeping away an enemy.

* * *

During the few hours at Natchez, little could be done to give precise medical attention to our sick men.

"The General and the Captains have done what they could. But they have no medicine. No laudanum or blue pills. An awful situation," Levi said, then turned silent as he scribed in his diary with me looking over his shoulder:

> ". . . Fryday 16,th the[y] Buryed 2 men at night and while the[y] was doing of it a nother man died, on the same night we floted till have after one oclock whan was fired of five minute guns, that was the signal when a boat was in distress . . ."

I heard that one of the dead was Hank Lucas. Much as I hated him—devil he was—the man had suffered a dismal end far from wife and son. But, in truth, I could not say I felt sorry Lucas was gone.

Captain Lewis ordered our sergeant to put three men to digging graves.

One man complained, "They's a powerful lot of other people's that can dig. What about that lazy guy from Jackson County? And that East Tennessee darkie? He better git a shovel before you tell me to git off the boat and wade around in that muck. I ain't diggin no graves. Not till he's done it."

The sergeant clenched his teeth, snarled, "I've worked sixteen hours today. I'm not taking any guff from you, you son-of-a-bitch. Besides, them's the Captain's orders. Git at it now."

They dug the graves, dropped in the dead men.

The next morning, reaching for my pack, I found its draw strings neatly cut by a knife.

* * *

While floating south toward New Orleans, Levi told me how he planned to make his lessons back in school more interesting by explaining to his pupils what we learned about the British in U. S. waters. My friend Levi noted in his diary:

"Between Sundown and and darke we Rec,d General orders that Lord hill was seen near the Cat Island And for us to make no delay till we got to orleans And we floted on about 4 hours in the night and a boate run on a sandbar And got in distress and fired of 5 minute guns."

* * *

Beginning about December 15th as our flatboat fleet neared New Orleans, the war began to move into final stages of preparation. An Andrew Jackson scout on land in the vicinity of Cat Island off the Louisiana coast watched British Admiral Cochrane anchor the powerful enemy war fleet. At least fifty British warships bearing one thousand naval guns spread across the open sea. The towering 80-gun *Tonnant*, captured from the French by British Lord Nelson in the Battle of the Nile, led the invading fleet into American waters.

General Jackson's scouts reported that Creek Indians had been seized by enemy scouting parties. Brought on board the British naval vessels, the Creeks handed over American rifles to enemy captains. Those weapons were longer than the British muskets and fired a smaller ball. The foreign soldiers sneered as they inspected the guns. They spoke with mocking words about men who could think of fighting battles using squirrel-hunting rifles.

The British navy anchored off Cat Island might fix on us Americans its contempt and smugness about our weapons. But all the royal trappings failed to ease the penetrating wet cold that wrapped around the invading army as it moved from shipboard at deep sea anchorage onto Pea Island, sixty miles closer to New Orleans. For ten hours, the British foot soldiers sat or lay cramped in open barges during the row across shallow waters. Rain slashed them, rain laced during most of the row with small, stinging ice pellets. Seamen suffered at the oars. Their orders to transfer soldiers allowed little rest between ten-hour stretches of rowing the heavily-laden barges. The new base on Pea Island provided no tents or other shelter. [I read later, Englishman George Robert Gleig wrote that the torrential deluges were "such as an inhabitant of England cannot dream of, and against which no cloak could furnish protection."]

On the flatboats many miles north of New Orleans, we American Tennessee militiamen drew our greatcoats and blankets around ourselves for warmth. We complained to each other about the endless drilling and confinement. Louisiana's raw winter winds and ice storms numbed us.

* * *

We bumped to a stop about four miles above the city of New Orleans at Avart's Plantation, the place designated by General Andrew Jackson as the base for our Tennessee Militia. My calendar plank received its thirty-sixth notch, my final one.

> "... on the 20th of December we landed at New orleans on thursday the 22nd of December we marched out and piched our tents ...," noted Levi Lee.

Weathered and toughened by wind and sun, we squinted through wind-swollen, blood-shot eyes at the few people who watched us land. Huddled in our greatcoats, blankets, whatever clothes we happened to own, the entire Tennessee Militia was a filthy looking bunch. One man looked different from the next one only in the shades of hair and whiskers that waved in the breeze.

Lean and fatigued from the weeks on the rivers and the intensive drilling, I knew I looked as tough as any one of them. My whiskers, matted and long, hid the fatigue lining my face. Hair, tangled by wind and sweat, hung wild around my neck. Knuckles, beaten by the broadhorns, bore nasty scars. Hunting jacket and pantaloons hung torn and dirty. I felt grimy, smelled worse. I wanted only to clean up, crawl off somewhere, sleep for a month. I had lost the clean, washed backwoods look and smell of the East Tennessee farmer.

Strange what had happened to me those last few weeks. That glide the backwoodsman learns slipping through the forest had served me far better than my clipped Philadelphia gait. Even without a grog-blossom, in spite of the "white male citizen" militiamen, I found myself becoming "Tennessean." I thought like one. I walked like one. I talked like one.

We had come to save the people of New Orleans who knew only the Louisiana military men dressed in smart clean uniforms parading with polish and spit. Seeing us Tennessee militiamen, New Orleanians first jeered, then shouted as they dubbed us, "Dirty Shirts."

9

Rain-sluiced wind tore through our militia camp on the stubble fields stretching across Avarts Plantation north of New Orleans. For a day our Tennessee Militia held immobile. My linsey-woolsey hung soaked on me. My blankets smelled musky, and I spread them on sycamore branches. Everything I touched felt damp, moldy. My grits had turned mealy. The smoked pork tasted rancid.

My nightmares returned. The Spanish moss soughing in the night mourned with Isaiah's cries, and I saw again his anguished face the night he was stolen in Philadelphia.

Rumors spun in thick layers as we swore at our generals and officers for rushing us down the Mississippi River, then forcing us to wait and fight our personal war sleeping on soggy ground. I was not alone in misery. We all grumbled, not always under our breath.

General Carroll used every drill in his *Handbook For Infantry* to keep us disciplined, our muscles toned, our senses keen. Drilling us from first light to sundown, the General allowed no quarter for rain-soaked, wind-whipped bodies.

"Aim an inch above the crossed belts," the order dinned at every drill. I began seeing that spot "an inch above" on every tree, every passing boat, every tent. When I began clothing my comrades in red jackets with white crossbelts and spotting "an inch above," I knew action must come soon.

* * *

General Carroll sent a messenger to General Jackson's headquarters at 106 Rue Royale in New Orleans asking for orders of the day.

Old Hickory replied, "Stay at ready."

* * *

After midmorning drill on December 23, Levi and I were the messengers, and I saw for the first time the famed Andrew Jackson. I stood a bare arm's length from him, so near I could smell his sweat-soaked uniform. I heard the gravelly intake of his breath. Lanky, straight and tall, small-boned, steely white hair on the wild side, blue eyes penetrating, Andy Jackson looked to be a copy of Captain Stevenson.

Levi and I held at attention. Shoulders back, arms straight down along the side of my linsey-woolsey, I pressed my hands flat against the rough soaked wool, felt it scratching my legs. I bit the inside of my cheeks so hard I tasted blood. My entire being riveted on the General. It was as if he held my life in his hands, long white hands, so thin the weathered skin seemed grown into his bones. Andrew Jackson, the man whose land speculation ads in the Philadelphia papers had drawn me to Tennessee. Andrew Jackson, the man who promised one hundred and sixty acres if I joined to fight the British.

Levi close beside me, I spiked up my nerve, steeled my mind to speak to Old Hickory.

At that moment, Major Gabriel Villeré and Colonel de La Ronde rushed into the room. Their uniforms were stained with mud, sweat rolled down their faces. Their breath spilled out in short gasps. Gabriel Villeré shouted, "The British have seized my plantation house and grounds! Only eight miles from New Orleans!"

General Jackson reacted at once. "Gentlemen, we must fight them tonight." The orders issued, he directed all of us messengers to alert our officers.

* * *

Back at camp, General William Carroll called us Tennesseans into ranks. "General Andrew Jackson's orders are to proceed at once to Bayou St. John. He believes the British will attack New Orleans from there, using the Chef Menteur Road. Our companies will move into position. *Forward, March.*"

Gusts of wind drove deep into ears and noses, numbed hands, pecked eyes. High in the night sky, the moon spread dim light through puffed cloud layers.

A dull boom sounded, muffled by distance. Another cannon shot rumbled, died away. Then, the booms began sounding, regular, and with a rhythm as if promoted by the devil. The next day and deep into the night of the 24th at top speed, we chopped trees and barricaded Chef Menteur Road.

An order passed through the dark, "Every man ready."

My stomach tightened. Make a clean shot into the chest. An inch above the crossed belts. How can a man see a crossbelt at night?

We waited. Cold chilled. The dark night threatened.

Toward morning, a messenger slipped into our lines. Colonel Booth listened to him, then spoke to us. "The enemy is not coming by Bayou St. John. They have attacked on the Plain of Chalmette below New Orleans. Skirmishes have broken out. General Jackson needs us there. On the double! *March! One, Two. One, Two.*"

Of our forced night march, Levi Lee recorded in his diary:

> ". . . it was after night, and the[y] marched us onto the Battel ground, [But the Battle Commenced about dark and continued Some time] and the[y] marched us right in betwixt the two armyes and we stood under arms all night and in the morning the General with drew his Army two miles and left us standing thare and at sun rise the[y] moved us back and the General formed his brest workes . . ."

* * *

Assembling troops along the Rodriguez Canal, an abandoned millrace a scant five miles below New Orleans, General Andrew Jackson began on December 24th to form "his brest workes." I respected the General for the choice he made. The Rodriguez Canal had natural advantages for a defense line. It cut through open ground called the "Plain of Chalmette" and provided our defense the narrowest line stretching from the bank of the Mississippi River into the thickly wooded cypress swamp to our left.

Jackson's order pulled every available man in New Orleans to the duty of digging and piling mud for a solid defense line along the canal's north side. New Orleans men streamed onto the site to celebrate our pick and shovel Christmas building the Rodriguez Canal rampart. Bartenders and free Negroes. Southland storekeepers, farmers, clerks, laborers. Mud-caked New Orleans dandies. LaFitte and his Barataria pirates. Editors, lawyers, doctors. Even a few bankers dug as if they knew how. Jackson's order set nine hundred slaves to the labor, and through the day I searched every face. No Isaiah.

We dug the shallow canal deeper, piled the mud high, carried more mud from the field, packed it on the wall for a barrier against the British. We tore apart fences on the Macarté plantation grounds and pounded the posts into the Rampart for reinforcment. We framed apertures for cannon, lined them with cotton. Finally, we backed the canal defense with two more lines closer to the city.

Andrew Jackson's Christmas gift to us had been his command to construct the defense line by deepening the Rodriguez Canal and increasing the width and height of the rampart which that morning had reached only waist high.

Our Christmas gift to Old Hickory was doing it. Shovels thudding against frozen mud were the bell chimes I heard on Christmas day 1814.

* * *

By January 1, 1815, we had built our earthen defense wall three to four feet high. The ditch in places eight feet deep and twenty feet wide, the Rodriguez rampart stretched from the Mississippi River nearly eight hundred yards to the impassable swamp.

Lying on logs, we snatched sleep between shifts. Time drifted. Exhaustion blurred men's shouts and the noise of shovels and picks.

Behind the Rodriguez Rampart, at the end nearest New Orleans, sat the Macarté plantation house, commandeered by Jackson for his field headquarters. From its upstairs dormer, the two-story Macarté mansion provided a sweeping view across the Canal to the cane fields and ditches of the Plain of Chalmette. In the distance, I could see the Gabriel Villeré mansion seized by the British.

* * *

We felt confident that we had built a strong rampart for the action. But nothing cheered us Tennessee militiamen as thoroughly from coonskin caps to boot tips as did the news about the errant *Pittsburgh* trader. The day he set foot in New Orleans, he swore to the authorities, "That goddamn Carroll and his ruffians boarded my boat at Natchez. They stole the government arms and ammunition I had the duty of delivering to Andy Jackson. I want them jailed."

Old Hickory promptly ordered the trader jailed.

* * *

Stepping back from the walkway along the barrier, I talked with militiamen lounging on the Macarté plantation field. Many were sitting on logs or standing in small groups, their talk low. Some smoked. Several swilled home brew, their grog-blossoms grown dark red from rum and wind. One Tennessean jigged, and his friends joined him mimicking a dance they had seen on the streets of New Orleans. We all drank the strong coffee trailing its steam into the frosty air.

Facing back, Levi and I stared across the Rodriguez rampart onto the Plain of Chalmette. We saw the British drilling in front of the Villeré mansion, their bayonets glistening in the sunlight. How soon would those white crossbelts become our militia targets?

Levi and I dug a shallow pit and lined it with leaves. We built a fire, burned sticks until they became glowing coals. We fished the river, then wrapped our catch in wet leaves and dropped them onto the coals. In a short time, we had roasted Mississippi catfish, succulent, smoky, fresh.

> "You're now to fight with Yankees,
> I'm sure you'll rue the day
> You roused the sons of liberty
> In North America."

A few of us hurled our song at the British, but not as lustily as we had on the Nashville campground. We knew that in front of the Rodriguez Rampart a battle was closing in on us.

10

Before first light, January 8, 1815, I rolled onto the ground from my blanket. Swinging my arms for warmth, I headed for the Rodriguez Rampart to stand watch duty. Most of our men on the Macartè plantation field had not yet stirred. Dominique You, brother of Jean Lafitte, commanded the pirates on the Canal. Their crew kept pots of coffee boiling at their station near one of the cannon, a twenty-four pounder.

Although not yet three a.m., General Jackson stood close to our mud rampart, his thoughts no doubt drawn as tight as the lines of his face. He looked more gaunt every time I saw him.

"Doesn't the man ever rest?" Levi Lee muttered to me.

Jackson paced the walkway, made a last minute check of Beale's New Orleans Rifles, the unit closest to the Mississippi. Next, the U. S. 7th Infantry. On its left, the Orleans Battalion. The Louisiana Free Men of Color. The Saint Domingue Free Men of Color. The 44th Infantry. A company of the U. S. Marines at the center. The other half of the line, our Tennessee Militia, then the Kentuckians. At the very edge of the cypress swamp, more Tennesseans, General Coffee's men. At the several batteries, the Baratarian pirates. Choctaw Indians at the swing end of our lines.

The General relaxed, talked with Lafitte's men. Only a few steps away, their voices carried, strong and clear on the still air.

"Where do you find coffee that good?" the General asked. "It smells much better than any I've had."

No pirate answered.

General Jackson continued, "Maybe you smuggle it in?"

Dominque You laughed, handed Jackson a mug of steaming liquid, but offered no explanation. He knew how tenuous a position the pirates held with the General.

"Hellish banditti," Andrew Jackson had stormed when he first had learned that pirate Jean Lafitte and his men were volunteering for American service. Our hard-hitting General, who had earned his militia fame by pushing the Creek Indians off their land, harbored a pious streak. He opposed the "immoral" pirates joining his command. But New Orleans civic and government leaders had persuaded him that the pirates were well provisioned, heavily armed, badly needed. And deadly fighters.

* * *

Thicker than I had seen it before, the fog drifted across our lines, hung low over the earthworks. My uneasiness and uncertainty doubled at sight of the white haze masking the enemy.

Back of me voices sounded almost like soughing of the Spanish Moss. Two men stepped into sight, one was Captain Lewis, but I did not know the other man in a Kentucky officer's militia uniform. Studying a map, they pointed across the barrier.

General Carroll stood below the ramparts talking to his captains. General Jackson rode by. Two scouts covered with mud ran to General Carroll, and he at once stopped his discussion to listen to them.

Bits of hurried conversation sifted through the air: ". . . pickets . . . great force . . . British . . ."

". . . columns . . ." One of the scouts pointed across the barrier, then took a step, his hand tracing an arc toward the woods at the edge of the swamp.

"About a half mile in front . . ."

". . . captains on horse . . . thousands of men in columns marching . . ."

". . . muskets . . . bayonets . . ."

General Jackson dismounted and stepped up to the barrier beside his chief engineer, Major Latour, and General Carroll. Old Hickory looked so scrawny, so sick. Reports had it that stomach upsets plagued Jackson, that he existed on only a few spoonsful of rice a day. I wondered about the man's strength. What made him leave his comfortable home, his good land, his Rachel, to stand in the cold? His hatred for the British was legendary. Hatred would not be enough for a rational man to suffer months of bad food and sodden clothes. Need for glory? Perhaps. As Tennessee's favorite, Andrew Jackson had known glory enough for one man. Patriotism? Perhaps. Yes, patriotism must have been it. Old Hickory was a patriot. In the Revolutionary War, his mother and brother had died for America, and his face bore the scars cut by a British officer's saber when he was a fourteen-year-old prisoner of war.

I figured a patriot believes in a cause worth dying for. I looked at that emaciated form, watched his nervous stride. Old Hickory believed in America. Aye, written all over Andrew Jackson was one emotion: patriotism.

"Major Latour, when will this fog lift?" Jackson asked.

"Within an hour. Perhaps, a little less," Latour answered.

Jackson directed, "Awaken the troops. Move them into position. No noise."

In an eerie silence unusual for us militiamen, we carried out the order within minutes. Captain Lewis and our other officers set us Tennesseans into three lines, one behind the other along our sector of the Rampart.

As my squad waited on the walkway, Captain Lewis issued instructions. "You sharpshooters on the first line, fire on command from General Carroll. Step back immediately and reload. The second line step up with guns loaded. Then, the third line, in turn. Keep up the rotation. Each line keep firing in volleys until further orders."

Hearing the words, "Fire on command," my brain stopped working. Hot, dry parch crawled around my mouth, down my throat. Fear passed through me as if lightning had struck. A shiver burned along my spine. I felt ashamed, looked at the man next to me. He looked as scared as I felt. I held myself ready for the order.

How long must we stand waiting? Levi Lee cursed. Squinting into the semidarkness, I squelched the urge to aim and fire without any order.

A strong gust of wind tore strips of fog from the Plain of Chalmette. Directly in front of our Tennessee Militia stretched line after line of veteran British in columned formations across the open field. Easy targets? Men in red uniforms, chests marked by white crossbelts. Close to the riverbank, stretching far back, another column waited in formation. British redcoats by the thousands fronted toward us!

The enemy first line stood about a quarter mile away. The second marched into position close behind it. During the night when our pickets had reported the sound of shovels and muffled noises, the British had pulled up cannon.

A rocket shrieked into the sky toward us from above the British lines near the cypress swamp. Near the river, a second rocket arched upward, belching its flame and whistle at us. The battle on the Plain of Chalmette began before dawn.

"They're coming. The British are coming," the man behind me yelled.

"Roll on Jordan, Roll on." Levi Lee jumped to the top of the Rampart and blasted out the song with full voice. I pulled him back as shells from the British cannon shrieked over the Rodriguez Rampart.

The British lines strode forward. A crimson wave advanced to engulf us. A wave of enemy shells swooshed so close overhead I felt the heat of the blasting. American cannon thundered back. Gunsmoke and burned powder stench swirled into my nose. Cannon blasts became one long endless rolling thunder.

Fire now? I questioned myself as the clean, tall, red columns moved straight toward us. Still no command from General Carroll. "Wait until they move within two hundred yards," he had said. We held position, muskets loaded, ready. The mass of redcoats covered the Plain of Chalmette, spread out in one solid crimson block.

"Look at them come," I rasped, my eye sighting one inch above a crossbelt.

"Oi," croaked a militiaman to my right.

"Our cannon are ripping their lines," I yelled.

"Look at all those men staggering . . ."

". . . falling to the ground."

"But see," another man shouted. "They keep coming!"

"Watch those bright spots, over there." I pointed with my left hand, gripped my Jaeger, loaded and ready, with my right, "Whenever their cannon . . ."

"Yeh, but their cannons do not fire as quick as ours."

"You can't really tell. I . . ." The man's voice drowned in the booming of cannon and the shrieking of shells and rockets.

Dull thuds beat into our ears as cannonballs slashed the mud wall of Rodriguez. Close by, two American cannon fired at the same time, smoke spurting from gun barrels. A shudder rolled through the earthen walkway. It seemed to roll through my feet and up my legs, lodging in the pit of my stomach.

Red-clad figures lunged forward, hung an instant motionless, then keeled over onto the ground. Stomping over fallen comrades, other soldiers pushed closer. Our cannon firing blasted them. Scores of enemy dropped in bloodied heaps.

Some place I had read, "The glory of war. A battlefield is a beautiful place to die." Even though they say they hate it, men have always loved war. I did not want to die. I saw no glory in the scene before me. No beauty. Without the men, the guns, the cannons, the smoke and shattering gunfire, the Plain of Chalmette would be a good place for a summer picnic: the open field, the blue sky overhead, the Mississippi River flowing alongside, the distant cypress swaying in the breeze, the soughing of Spanish Moss.

* * *

Against that sweeping tide of red, a feeling of great compassion reached out for the men who stood beside me, a feeling of love and brotherliness, a oneness extending even to the men whose beliefs I despised and railed against. We had a common cause. Defending America.

The British looked so well armed. Invulnerable.

Not real. But they kept coming!

My stomach cramped. My mouth tasted last night's cornbread and grog. Clamping my teeth to keep from screaming, I stared at the advancing cross-belted red columns. Real, unreal, I could not be sure. *A British shell crashes into me. I seem to hang suspended in space. Where, I cannot say. The British shell has cut me down. A skelton-framed Death claims me. I lie bleeding. My glazed eyes stare at the Rampart. Isaiah stands looking down at me. A few feet away, a Britisher lies bleeding, torn by my Jaeger. Moans drift from sightless heads, heads that spit puddles of blood upon the Plain of Chalmette.*

Death cheated, the unreal passed into the real. An icy cold swept from my feet up through me. Muscles in my face twitched. My shoulder ached. Unknown words spilled through my clenched teeth. My gun primed and ready, I smelled its fresh gunpowder. I gripped my Jaeger so hard the bones of my hand seemed ready to burst through my skin.

The distance to the British front line? Two hundred yards? Probably less. Still, we waited for the order to fire. My head pounded, one thought pushing another aside as images crammed my mind: Philadelphia, East Tennessee, Quaker blab school, Captain Stevenson, Matthew, Sam, Isaiah.

Then General Jackson's voice, clear and forceful, cut through the stark image formed on drifting fog. "They're near enough, Gentlemen."

General Carroll raised his arm. "Ready."

At the officer's command, my month parched dry. "Artificial instinct" erased all thoughts, all doubts. "Artificial instinct" triggered the single purpose of driving my Jaeger's shot into the spot one inch above the white crossbelts on a red uniform.

I braced myself, gun at my shoulder.

"Aim." The trigger—that tiny bit of polished steel—made love to my finger, hot, scorching, tingling.

A redcoat's chest came into my line of sight. I was thrust with the speed of a bullet back to East Tennessee. I seemed to have a lifetime before me. I felt my horse under me as I rode along the quiet stream bordering my pasture.

"Fire!"

My finger stroked the trigger, evoked a moment of love, a movement so slight it raced through me, a desire only.

Explosion.

The red-clad figure in my sight lunged forward, head jerking backward. His arms flailed upward, his body twisted. My mark fell to the earth, a twitching, bloodied heap.

The booming roar of rifle and musket shot deafened me, forced tears down my cheeks. I felt a charge as if I had been hit. Fright. Shame. Terror. Death? Whatever drove through me, I could not wait to aim and fire again. To hit that spot an inch above the crossbelt. *One, Two* . . . *One, Two* . . . Across the Plain of Chalmette, the enemy ranks splintered under the blood-drenching blasts of a thousand Tennessee rifles.

I stepped back from the Rampart. The next line of our militiamen stepped into place.

"Ready. Aim. Fire!" General Carroll's commands called forth the second volley.

The thundering volley of muskets, rifles, and cannon drove more tears down my face, blasted sharp pains through my head. Men shuddered, agonized by the racket. Not one of us could wait to step onto the line again.

Artificial instinct held me in its grasp. I did not exercise a will of my own. A powerful force reloaded my Jaeger, ready to sight an inch above the crossbelt with no sympathy for the falling human being who grasped his chest in death agony. The drumming in my ears, the hot bursts on my skin, the wetness from my eyes draining onto my cheeks, rose from fear slashing at my deep insides, fear I had never before known, fear I had seen in the eyes of a deer fallen in its death moans in the East Tennessee woods. Thoughts for life, for survival, rose above all else. I clung to the idea of simply staying alive. I jettisoned all decent feelings for that other human being striding across the plain toward me, his killing weapon aimed at my head.

* * *

Quick to man the Rampart, the second Tennessee Militia line on the walkway shot its volley, then gave way to the third as Colonel Tunnell triggered the volleys with the order, "Fire!"

Our first line stepped back to the Rampart. The sharp crack of my Jaeger sliced the air, sharp amid the dull beat of musket shots. We militiamen were detached from reality. Origin or rank or color no difference, men out there on the field taking our fire pitched and swayed like the planter trees buffeted in the grasping waters of the Mississippi River.

White crossbelts stained crimson, red-jacketed Britishers lay in rows, in bunches, in front of us, in jumbled, undisciplined, stained heaps across the Plain of Chalmette. Amid the din and smoke, British officers shouted orders. The columns had shrunk to half their number, but the enemy soldiers closed thinning lines, merged ranks. They pushed toward us, bayonets fixed. I saw their mud-covered boots, their grim faces. Scared, ashamed of the massacre, I could not wait for them to drive closer so I could fire an inch above another white crossbelt.

* * *

In the storm of firings that surged from Jackson's defense line, our volleys lost discipline. The crisp timed orders crumpled. Pushing shoulder to shoulder onto the Rodriguez walkway, groups of us

Tennessee sharpshooters began firing at will. I aimed and banged away on my own hook. Joy overrode fright. Joy that we were decimating the crimson tide. Joy at the deafening thunder roaring from our guns. One continuous barrage of killing gunfire poured across the rampart. Smoke choked the Plain of Chalmette. Commands became useless. But we had our orders to keep our firing unbroken. "*One, Two. One, Two. One, Two,*" I shouted in my loudest voice.

Out on the field, red-clad figures turned their backs, ran from our defense line. I was conscious that the roar of our muskets and rifles was lessening. I began to hear shrieks, anguished cries, piercing yells of fallen enemy. Human beings no different than me, men out there lay gutted like animals in a slaughterhouse.

It was hell. Hell was a beautiful killing ground.

"We're driving them back," Levi yelled.

"They're taking to the ditches," I answered.

For those moments, the battle seemed to draw to an end. Militiamen around me were shouting, "Huzza!" Their yells swelled along the Rodriguez Rampart as many joined the outburst.

The band struck up "Hail, Columbia." In response, our militiamen cheered.

But we hailed Columbia too soon.

* * *

"They're coming again!" Men around me shouted.

From my post, I saw the British columns, thinned but regrouped into a solid front, advancing steadily toward me. I aimed and fired, simultaneously with bursts of musket fire crackling to my right and left. The foremost lines of the rigid column staggered, splintered, fell to the ground, their human contents shredded, torn apart, spilled in bloodied heaps.

"Look at those two British officers on horseback, out there, waving swords. They're trying to drive their soldiers this way again," I hollered to Levi.

"That officer. He's gone mad," Levi yelled back at sight of a British officer smashing the flat of his sword across the backs of soldiers stretching themselves in a ditch.

"None of them will make it over the Rodriguez Rampart." Yelling to Levi, I flattened my body against the back side of the mud barrier. "They'll never make it. Gaps in their lines. They keep closing ranks." I wondered, What forces them on? I knew the answer. They have been drilled and drilled by their officers. Artificial instinct took command of those men.

Gunfire belched in constant volleys from our Tennessee guns. Cannon thundered. Heaps, ragged lines, of crimson uniforms lay nearer the Rampart. In those moments, we "Dirty Shirts" knew power. Power of death over life. Power that lifted us above our mean humanity into the stars. Gods of war ordered our lives. We were their servants.

We Tennesseans heard only our own guns. But the constant waves of cannonballs, musket and rifle shot all along the Rampart, stabbed into the torn, irregular British lines, spilling more bloodied bodies onto the ground.

* * *

Through the smoke above Chalmette, I glimpsed an enemy squad carrying facines. Days before, we had seen them tying those bundles of sticks to throw into the Rodriguez ditch to support scaling ladders. Those men intended to storm our barriers. Even if any of the British could have clawed their way to our ditch, put up ladders, it would have been suicide to climb the wall under our fire. But those men, down there, certain targets, must have been beyond brave, must have made their pacts with death. I knew they had crossed the line beyond human reason. Their fears hid behind masks of unreality. Gun fodder, expendables, they drove their suicide missions in the name of the King. They obeyed *artificial instinct*. Insanity reigned across the New Orleans battlefield.

The British lines before us splintered into disordered fragments. Their regiments decimated by our blazing fire, the enemy began to realize they could not repeat at New Orleans the victories they had won on the battlefields of Europe against Napoleon's veteran legions.

Rockets screeched overhead. Hunching my shoulders, jabbing my chin down onto my chest, I stepped off the walkway a moment. Those rockets were doing little damage, but I hated their whistling shriek. None of us could predict where one would end its flight. I looked back to see a shelter on the Macarté field burning from British cannonballs. My Jaeger reloaded, I jumped back onto the walkway, found a target, fired again.

Across Chalmette, a new crimson column angled toward us. I wondered, Is their no end to the number of men the British can waste against us?

We learned later that the 93rd Highlanders had been ordered to support the battered main columns retreating in confusion from our shattering musket and rifle fire. I saw the Highlander commander fall at the front of his men. His first company wiped out within moments, his men carried their fallen chief to the British rear.

A few Highlanders crawled into the Rodriguez canal, huddled below our mud rampart. We poured shot down into them. After the battle, prisoners told us that Colonel Dale had handed his watch and a letter to a surgeon, requesting, "Give these to my wife. I shall die at the head of my Highlanders."

* * *

Hours no longer framed reality. Reloading and firing possessed me. How many times I fired amid the booming and clamor, I do not know. Gripped in the savage power of the *One, Two, One, Two* beat, I loaded, aimed, fired as fast as I could. We Tennesseans at the Rampart, grim-faced sharpshooters, swept our muskets and rifles across the field, guiding our shots like unrelenting sickles mowing rows of grain, each of us squinting to pick out forms through the drifting haze. Militiamen jostled each other, stomped back and forth. Shouts, yells, curses punched the air. A few jokes threaded the clamor.

There seemed no end to the number of Britishers. They kept driving toward our defense barrier. Our fire dumped them in mounds and ragged lines on the Plain of Chalmette. We shredded each new formation but seemed short of power to stop the advance of those thinning crimson ranks.

Much closer to our Rampart, fragments of the British units regrouped. Our muskets and cannon streamed a fearsome killing hail into them. Men twisted and fell, struggling with life's last step to make their way closer to us. The numbers advancing melted away like snow in blazing sun.

In a last desperate effort, a few Britishers charged to our earthworks, dug in their boots, tried to mount the few ladders they managed to bottom in the ditch, only to fall back, shot in the face or chest. We pulled over the top men who raised their arms in surrender. Would-be English conquerors became American prisoners.

* * *

"See that officer on the big horse? Still shouting orders for the column to move forward again," broke out of me as I saw him through the smoke. "Jimmers, he's been hit."

The man stiffened, rose upright in the saddle, tumbled to the ground. Several red-clad figures rushed to the spot, carried the officer to the rear, and eased him down under a large oak tree. British commander-in-chief, Sir Edward Pakenham, fatally wounded in the groin, died within minutes.

A few feet behind our walkway, as he rode by with Andrew Jackson, I heard William Carroll say, "Magnificent, Sir."

"Yes, it is magnificent," General Jackson agreed.

Magnificent. The enemy had come to the Plain of Chalmette, an enemy we had feared was mighty and unbeatable. Our accomplishment?

"Magnificent," the General repeated.

My mouth dry, my body by spells chilling, numbing, then boiling, I could not keep from trembling. My mind played through me disbelief at all that spread before me. Horrible what lay destroyed in the mud and cold, though enemy they be. Horrible to see what we sharpshooters had done from our side of the Rampart. Slaughter. Like shooting down animals. But far worse, the redcoats were human beings.

But we, the victors, remained the living.

Small groups of enemy soldiers scattered, ran to the rear. Many of them fell, hit before they could dash beyond range of our continuing deadly fire. Along the ditches and in the patches of sedge on Chalmette, I saw men lie down, try to hide behind dead comrades, any means to escape our blasts of cannonballs and rifle shots. One group broke toward the cypress swamp, but General Coffee's Tennesseans ripped them into bloodied flesh and bone.

British fire withered to almost nothing. We did not know enemy intentions. They could have been regrouping for another assault. Wary, we kept muskets and rifles loaded. We kept cutting down anything across the Rampart that moved.

* * *

Then we spotted a courier carrying a white flag toward us across the Plain of Chalmette.

"Cease fire!" The order came from General Jackson. His words rolled along the Rodriguez Rampart from the cypress swamp to the Mississippi River.

Our rifles, muskets, and cannon fell silent.

The smoke lingered.

From the courier, we learned the enemy had lost so many of its ranking officers that the message came from General Lambert, a junior officer who, out of necessity, had on the Plain become the British acting commander. He requested a truce in order to care for their wounded and bury their dead.

In the lull, we viewed the extent of the carnage in front of us. Gutted, headless, legless men lay one on top of another in rows and heaps. Movement soon stirred in some of the piles as first one, then another, blood-covered Britisher shook himself free from his dead brothers and staggered to the rear.

An awful silence settled over the scene, broken only by the moaning of the wounded, the last wheezing gasp of the dying.

As I drew back my rifle from aiming over the Rampart, a British soldier raised himself over the mud wall, holding above his head a sword bearing a piece of white cloth.

"Grab him," yelled the militiaman on my right.

Dropping my rifle, I leaped on top of the Rampart and seized the young British officer who sagged exhausted, unable to climb farther. Levi and I carried the wounded Britisher to level ground behind the wall.

"Loosen his coat and belt."

"Here's a canteen of water."

Raising the soldier's head, helping him drink, I eased him back to rest against a pack under his head.

"Sav... My... wife..." He died.

Britishers began surrendering. First, ten in number. Then, eighteen. Twenty-six. Thirty-three. Forty-one. And more.

High-pitched shrieks close by drew me to the top of the Rampart. Below me, red-clad figures lay in the brush and water in the canal. Blood oozed from the neck and mouth of one man as he raised his arm to me. Blood streaked the arms and shoulders of a second man. Blood flowed from the legs of a third. Blood dripped through the stiff cloth of uniforms, from the cuffs, from the sleeves, from the nostrils of dying Scottish Highlanders.

"Here. Get them out of the ditch." I motioned militia comrades to help me, and we pulled the badly wounded Britishers onto the walkway of the Rampart. "Careful, easy now. This one has a bone sticking through his pant leg."

The enemy, a broken man, dug his fingernails into my wrist. "Dear God! Holy Jesus! Help me!" Raising up against the arms of the men carrying him, the wounded enemy gasped, then slumped back, dead.

"God A'mighty," broke from my lips, prayer not oath. Mutterings spread from comrades lifting and carrying enemy wounded. Driven by "artificial instinct," we moved at a subconscious, unaware level of existence. In that zone where time had no reality, lifting and carrying bodies, we no longer knew concern for human endurance.

For the British wounded resting behind American lines, we provided water, loosened clothing, tendered emergency treatment. Back and forth across the Rodriguez barrier, Tennesseans and Kentuckians worked trying not to hear the cries of pain, the screams of terror, the rattling death throes.

Sick at what I had done for "160 Acres of Land," I stared across the Plain of Chalmette, unseeing. My head filled with sounds rising in the far distance, cries not human. My land would be stained crimson with the blood of men I had killed.

Insanity.

In the grim, set faces of my Tennessee comrades before the firing had begun, I read the same insanity. Us grim sharpshooters had answered the British challenge with "artificial instinct." In the grasp of that insanity, we killed—the goal of war. For the soldier in combat, *bravado is the mask; fear is the reality.*

* * *

According to Levi Lee and his diary, we had left Nashville on November 22nd and reached New Orleans on December 20th, a trip that had lasted a month. Decimating the British had taken us less than half a day, not counting the stand-off skirmishes of the weeks before January 8th. We had traveled from our homes in Tennessee swearing, singing, joking, quarreling, drilling, many of us "half seas over," all of us cheering, celebrating the coming glorious event.

More than twenty-six hundred Englishmen lay dead or wounded on the Plain of Chalmette. Our losses counted thirteen Americans killed, thirty-nine wounded. An irreverent thought flashed through my brain: Odds a Tennessee betting man would not find sporting. I shared my thoughts with no one.

The "magnificent event" had come to its end.

The British asked for our help.

We carried their wounded and dead to a line designated on Chalmette as the divider between them and us. We helped bury their comrades in two-foot deep ditches. It could not be the usual six feet because of the high water table near New Orleans. The burial squads did their best, but arms and legs stuck out of the ground, sad reminders of the price of war. Somewhere I had read that Europe's battlefields blood-drenched by centuries of battles grew lush crops. The Plain of Chalmette could expect a high yield of corn.

* * *

After a gruesome set of burials the next morning, the total horror of the battle hit me. I was afraid I would crack, go beserk in front of everyone. I needed to take myself in hand. I asked permission from Clovis, a sergeant from a New Orleans Free Negro battalion who was in charge of my section of digging and burying, to leave the field for awhile. I knew he thought the reason for my request was physical. I let him think so.

I could not shake off the killing. Images of blood draining away a man's life flowed through my mind. I tried for other thoughts, but I kept seeing that spot above the crossbelt on a crimson jacket. On the barrier facing the British, I had not thought as a separate being. I had moved, mindless, in the deadly control of the militia guns. I wondered if I had stood by myself, alone, Could I have fired to kill? With the men standing together, molded into one, I was part of that deadly beast, a huge savage who know only the *artificial instinct—aim, fire.*

Upriver at a quiet spot away from the activity among the boats, I found myself staring deep into the muddy Mississippi. Strange, the grasp that rivers have on me when the ocean had little or no appeal. It must be the ever forward motion, the fact that somewhere at the source the rivers start out small, a trickle, then work their way through the countryside swelled by numberless streams and tributaries.

America is a mixture, rich, muddy, deep . . . deep as the rivers . . . and as turbulent.

* * *

"Sir Edward Pakenham's guts were cut out of him. Buried under those twin oaks yonder." Levi Lee paused as we lowered one of the last litters. "His flagship will carry his body to England for a hero's burial. Sealed in a cask of rum."

"Cask of rum? How do you know, Levi?"

"A junior officer from Pakenham's division told me. I found him lying near the swamp. His leg shot to pieces. He talked a lot. Kind of delirious. Told me Pakenham was their commanding general. The King of England had promised that he would be governor of Louisiana. A reward for capturing New Orleans. The officer I talked to had been promised a big job in the government down here."

"Know the man's name?"

"No. He expected to be a general soon. Said generals get the best treatment. They'll bury Pakenham in an important church in London."

"Some ending, Levi, for the King's plans! Sir Edward's guts dumped under those Chalmette oaks. His body pickled in booze. God, I'd hate to be the thirsty bloke who opens that cask to filch a drink of rum in midAtlantic."

* * *

Days later, on orders issued by General Andrew Jackson, our militia established itself at a new base camp. The orders held all troops on alert. Old Hickory believed the British might stage another attack. We left the Plain of Chalmette behind, not certain of the enemy's intent, and it would be our fate to fertilize another meadow. Our bodies as well as our uniforms stank with mud, sweat, and British blood.

For the first one-quarter mile toward Camp Henderson [a mile or so north of Avart's Plantation where we had landed in December] I marched with an awkward, out-of-kilter gait. I felt as if I were an old man, a man as old as the ancient Spanish moss hanging from the cypress trees. I had trouble responding to the officers at first, felt out of joint, paralyzed. No one caught the count. No one kept it. We stumbled along for miles. Finally, the cadenced rhythm of the officer count took over, and we men responded with a sharp *One, Two, One, Two*, back to our new bivouac.

"Lordy! Lordy! I gotta git that battle out of my head," I overheard a militiaman say as he grabbed the grog bottle after stowing his gear.

"Me, too." His companion swilled down a mugful in one motion. "I wake up nights and see them redcoats in front of me, running and screaming like hell."

I agreed. My mind was full of the battle. I had to quit thinking about the killing, or I would swill the whiskey and sprout a grog-blossom like the puffy rum noses on the veterans who drank too much. Even that engulfing sense of comradeship, of oneness, that had washed over me during the battle had drained away. My old feeling of loneliness, of apartness from the other militiamen, again ruled me.

"Hey, George, you got that *Navigator* handy?" Levi sat on a log, writing notes in his diary. "Would you help me? Some of those places along the Mississippi, I'll forget them if I don't write down the names."

I rummaged in my sack, found *The Navigator* still intact, though a little mildewed from being packed away damp. On the map, we searched out names.

Levi asked, "What's the town with the Spanish name? I wrote down only, Earthquake, 1811."

"Let's see." I found the name on the map, pointed out the location.

"Horrible mess." Levi squeezed the name New Madrid beside 1811.

"Hey, you." One of the men from Levi's outfit joined us. "Hear you lost a bet, Mr. Lee."

"What bet?"

"Word just come. Andy Jackson's horse, Pacolet, beat Doublehead. Beat him good and easy."

His head in his hands, Levi groaned. He had bet against Pacolet that day on the Mississippi when we knew the horses were running in Nashville. I neither won nor lost. I was one up on Levi Lee. I did not bet on General Andrew Jackson's Pacolet.

11

"Let's take leave and go to New Orleans. A lot of the fellows have already headed in to see the city," Levi greeted me a few days later. "Besides, I got bets to settle."

"Yeah! And after you pay up your gambling debts, maybe you'll have money enough left to buy me a drink." I had no bets to pay, but why rub that into Levi?

"Sure. Anyways, I've heard several of the men talking about finding some cockfights. I'd have better luck picking roosters than horses, I'll lay a bet on that."

"No deal, Levi. I wouldn't want to steal your money." I slapped Levi on the shoulder. "You know, Levi, while I'm in town, I'd like to take Sergeant Clovis up on the invitation to his house. Be interesting to see how a Louisiana man lives."

On the Plain of Chalmette, after we had put the British on the run, Clovis made special point of getting acquainted with me.

"He seemed like a decent fellow. I'd like to know him better."

"You should visit him, George. First, let's go to a tavern and have a drink together." Levi's glance told me he had left unsaid, *If we can.*

"Let's get our passes and move out," I agreed, but I knew we both had doubts we could find a place where we could sit across the table.

Above a Bourbon Street shop, a woman waving from a window that opened onto a wrought iron balcony shouted her friendly, "Welcome, Dirty Shirts," and blew us a kiss.

"You've never seen the best of Tennessee till you've met George and me," Levi tossed up to her for both of us. We waved our broad-brimmed beaver hats, swaggered a little that we had won acceptance even at a bloody price.

What an accomplishment, winning over the people of the city, I thought, recalling the jeers branding us "Dirty Shirts" when first we had marched into that port on the Mississippi.

Farther along at St. Philip and Bourbon Streets, two men nodded, smiled at us as they entered a blacksmith shop constructed in the old French mode, brick between posts.

"Something familiar about those two, Levi."

"Should be. They're Lafitte's men. Remember? They manned one of the batteries on Rodriguez."

"Yep, not far from us." I spotted a sign on the corner. "LaFitte's Blacksmith Shop. It's right here."

"Let's hang around," Levi suggested. "Maybe we'll see Jean himself. He probably carries on his less-than-legal deals with the local gentry from this place."

"See Jean LaFitte? Man, I want to talk to him."

"You?" Levi's grin spread over his whole face. "Reckon you'll join his Baratarians?"

"Not me. LaFitte puts in too much time on the high seas." We had joked about what an inept sailor I had been on Captain Stevenson's ships. Besides, the LaFittes were slavers. But I did not want to discuss that curse, so I said, "Remember, Andy Jackson called those fellows 'hellish banditti.'"

"Right. But you know, George, New Orleans loves Jean and Pierre Lafitte and their gang. They smuggle in jewelry, china, gold, fancy clothes from Europe. Wines, laces, perfumes, too. For all those rich folks. So, the New Orleans officials pretend they keep things honest by jailing a pirate now and then."

"Hell, Levi, those jolly rogers supply so many merchants and bluebloods, there's always bail to put them back at work. Like my old Quaker reader said, 'Greed buries the conscience.'"

"You bet it does," Levi laughed. "And just over a year ago, the Governor of Louisiana posted a five hundred dollar reward for the capture of Jean Lafitte."

"Ha! LaFitte tossed back a challenge, branded the Governor cheap. He said he would give a five thousand dollar reward to anyone delivering Governor Claiborne to him at pirate headquarters on Grand Terre."

"The hullabaloo stirred up would fill a book. The District Attorney even resigned over that fracas."

We stood on the street talking, hoping for sight of the notorious Lafitte. No more "Hellish Banditti" came by.

"Let's go. We do enough waiting at camp." I saw no point in lazing on the street just to pass time.

Under my heavy linsey-woolsey shirt, my skin itched from the humid, close day. As friendly as New Orleans had been, I needed more than anything else to move out to Tennessee's fresh mountain air before the sticky Southland climate turned hotter and muggier.

"Jimmers!" I gasped. "What's that stink?"

"Ach. Down there." Levi pointed to the open gutter, clogged with city refuse and sewage.

I stepped to the corner of a building where the breeze relieved part of the stench. "You see, Levi, the mess has no place to go. New Orleans dumps its sewage into the Mississippi like every other town along its banks. Remember on the flatboat? I said then the river is a giant sewer flushing itself to the sea."

"No doubt about it, Friend. And we contributed our part all the way down the Mississippi." Levi thumped me on the shoulder.

* * *

In fine spirits, we strolled along the plank walk beside the ditch, past the clutter of square buildings two and three stories high beautified with filigreed wrought iron gates and railings, most of it created by Negro slaves gifted in ironwork. Back of the fancy, expensive buildings leaned squat, ramshackle slave quarters, plain and unadorned.

"Stop!" I swung my arm straight out, held Levi back. A few feet away an alligator crawled toward us from under a house built on stilts. We jerked back, we "brave" militiamen. Ignoring us, the creature wriggled its way to a warm spot, settled down to snooze in the sun.

"Damn if New Orleans doesn't have everything." Levi's voice quavered a bit.

"We're near enough I'd like to see the Cabildo. That's where the transfer of the Louisiana Purchase from France to the United States took place." I sneaked a look back. The alligator, unimpressed, had not moved an inch.

"You're on." Levi headed for the intricate wrought iron gate into the old building flanking the St. Louis Cathedral. "A first-rate idea. I'll go back to teaching, you know. It would be a great history lesson to tell my students I stood in the same room where the French agents handed the Louisiana Purchase papers to the American ministers. That deal more than doubled the size of the U. S."

"Sure enough. You can tell your pupils many important events besides wars and battles make history." As we climbed the stairs to the second floor of the Cabildo, my mind stirred among long-stored readings in Captain Stevenson's library. "Napoleon needed money bad to fight all over Europe. He sold the whole Louisana Territory to the United States for fifteen million."

"Fifteen million dollars? That's one huge stack of money."

In the Cabildo Council Chamber, a long narrow room that faced St. Peter Street, awe held us silent. We imagined seeing the men who had made history there.

"In this very room, Levi. The agents for each government signed the papers and made the transfer. On December 20, 1803, if I remember rightly."

"Do you suppose they signed on that big old table? Sat in these chairs?" Levi slid onto a high-backed chair with rush seat, braced his elbows on the table's shiny surface. "Maybe some of the importance will rub off on me. Any notion how much land we bought?"

"Let's see. Mmmmm . . ." I thought a spell, pulled from memory what I had read. "Over five hundred seventy million acres, and . . ."

"Gott in Himmel!"

Gott in Himmel. I had always suspected that German blood ran in my friend's veins. We had grown close in the militia, Levi and I. Perhaps under our different skins we did share common ancestry. On the trail long years ago, I had not quipped to the German immigrants about my mixed genes. But I had learned to trust Levi, so I laughed, "Well, here we are, Brother. I am part German, German like you sound."

For a moment, Levi looked at me as his own cheer met mine. "Sure thing, Brother." He clapped his arm on my shoulder, and we went on figuring what we had coming.

"Levi, if five hundred million acres shocks you, listen to this. Assume the government paid our land bonuses—one hundred and sixty acres out of the Louisiana Purchase for our militia service. One-sixty to you. One-sixty to me." My thinking sped on with another calculation. "The U. S. Treasury will be out less than $4.20 for each of us. Think of it. Four dollars twenty cents. The total cost for each one-sixty. And if I figure correctly, that's less than three cents for one whole acre. Not a bad deal for the politicians and generals to pay off us militia veterans, would you say, Teacher?"

"Not bad. Not bad at all. You earn a grade of one hundred percent." Levi stood up, his broad grin showing he had grasped my point right away.

Shouting "Gott in Himmel" together, we bolted down two stairs at a time, then out the door, nearly bumping into a man backing his wagon of firewood into the Place d'Armes. "Look at him. He's fixing to sell his wood here."

* * *

Rubbish, stones, and junk lay scattered about the plaza in front of the Cabildo. The Place d'Armes, a historic spot, deserved better, and its mess insulted my Quaker sense of order. The disarray did not fit with the grand buildings. Worse, it appeared that anyone could hawk his wares there. The proud old St. Louis Cathedral faced the square, flanked on one side by the Cabildo and on the other by its look-alike, the Presbytère parsonage for Cathedral priests, each structure a jealous sentinel disapproving of intrusions into its open line of vision across the parade ground to the Mississippi. Almost on the point of telling the man to take his junk and move on, we decided against it. New Orleans ought to clean up its own mess.

"Levi Lee on the levee." I laughed as we walked onto Levee Street, a low embankment of earth packed solid to keep the Mississippi's high waters from overflowing into the city. "An elegant walk" the local folks had for years spoken of Levee Street while ignoring the dirty, sweaty task of unloading boat cargoes, taking on new ones.

Sailing ships from many parts of the world rode at anchor. Upriver, I could see numbers of flatboats, perhaps some from Tennessee. In a jovial mood, we strode the New Orleans waterfront. The day carefree and happy, I wanted nothing to intrude, but scenes of the Philadelphia waterfront swam in and out of my mind.

We paused several times, amused by the banter of the traders plying their customers. Some merchants and traders sold their goods and wares from piles on the street. In a number of small shacks built to display the clothing and furs, produce and supplies, merchants and buyers dickered to gain an advantage on prices. Listening as Levi bargained with a trader for a couple of items, I picked up a trapper's knife that lay on the counter. Its worn and knicked handle spoke of the many seasons it had served skinning beavers. Hundreds of slaves tramped ship planks, sweating as they bore the heavy boxes and bales onto the levee. Sight of the endless procession of black bodies glistening under the January sun tempered my jovial mood. I searched each line of slaves. Not one bore even close resemblance to Isaiah.

That port, that city. I wondered. We had freed ourselves from the British years before in 1789. If they had won our Second War for Independence and taken over Louisiana, would they have freed the slaves? Did I fight on the wrong side? Or would that Sir

Pakenham as Governor have found some excuse for keeping people in bondage? As England did in Jamaica?

Deliberately, Levi and I had put the battle behind us. Nor did we discuss British schemes. It was as if, for the day, we needed to free ourselves of those particular concerns. We were two militiamen on leave looking for fun, needing to erase the bloody battle from our heads.

* * *

As we crossed a side street toward the city jail, a strange, hollow, misery-laden half cry, half laugh, an almost insane wrenching sound, rose from the building, hung in the air a moment, then silenced. A vibrating note in that cry-laugh jerked me back to Philadelphia and a boy I loved as well as if he had been my blood brother: *Isaiah*. I stopped, stared at the barred window. Every muscle in my body tensed. Shivers stung my spine. I felt that Isaiah stood beside me, that I could reach out and touch him, his presence almost as strong as the reality of Levi.

I started toward the jail door, but Levi grabbed me. "Let's get out of here. That jail spooks me." Levi shook my arm. "Gott in Himmel, George, you look as if you'd seen a ghost. What's the matter?"

Seen a ghost? Heard a ghost? The humid hot air from the New Orleans waterfront stifled me, and I dared not answer Levi.

Forcing myself away from the jail, I walked some distance with Levi. At the intersection of Chartres and St. Peter Streets, across from the Place d'Armes, the Black Code of Louisiana strode between my friend and me. Levi went into the Tavern of the Suckling Calf to celebrate and settle bets. Wrought up as I was from struggling to hide my thinking I had heard Isaiah, Levi saying he would meet me later stuck wrong in my craw.

* * *

As I stood alone on Rampart Street, a cabriole drove around the corner, its horse high-stepping in the mud, its occupant a young woman, her ruby-red cloak glistening in the sunlight. Jimmers! A flash in my mind plants me back on a faraway hilltop. Yesterday becomes today as I envision a Tennessee redhead silhouetted against the blue sky. I see Isabella James riding in the cabriole in a ruby-red cloak. With my Philadelphia money, I could put Ibby in clothes like those the woman in the cabriole is wearing. That is the way Isabella could look. My fantasy turns the woman's black hair to strawberry red as the rig hurried up the street and passed from sight.

Pull yourself together, George Bush, I scolded. Stop hearing ghosts and seeing them. First Isaiah, then Isabella. Careful, Man, the East Tennessee Militia has no place for a lunatic.

* * *

"Yes?" A woman filled the door of Sergeant Clovis's house. Tall as I, long-necked, skin purple black, her nose even with mine, chiseled ebony features failing to conceal a fierce expression, her eyes raked every inch of my six-foot frame.

"Y . . . e . . . s?" she drew out the word, her eyes narrowing. Her disapproval of my backwoods linsey-woolsey, muddy boots, and long hair showed in the curl of her lip.

I stared back.

Instant mutual dislike pecked at each of us.

True, I was ragged and unkempt appearing: at least twenty pounds lighter since leaving Sam's cabin, eyes sunken in, lips parched, hair tangled. But I'll be damned if you can put me down, I thought as I looked her over. A weird figure of a woman in a shapeless dress, around her head she wore a plain cotton kerchief with knots all pointing straight up. The overbearing tone of her voice, her insolent stance, added up instantly to the difference between that Southlands creature and my Philadelphia Mahala.

It took me a moment to respond to her insolent greeting. "I came to see Sergeant Clovis. Is he home?"

"Mister Clovis is home, but you . . ."

Behind her stretched a hall with its shining floor.

Then, Clovis called, "Who is it, Veta?"

"A man." She turned from me, but her voice carried. "I did not ask his name. My land, you should see how bad . . ."

"Well, well, George. George Bush." Sergeant Clovis stepped to the door and greeted me, his hearty welcome a sharp contrast to the woman's scorn. "Come in."

Clovis ignored Veta, but I caught the malice in her scowl.

"I wanted to be sure I could find your house. I'll come back another time." Uneasy, I wondered about the woman's place in the Clovis household.

Clovis grabbed my arm. "Come right in."

I followed him down the hall, my boots tracking Veta's polished floor. The man looked different from the days when he had worn the uniform of the Saint Domingue free blacks carrying litter cases across the Chalmette battlefield. A bit of a potbelly, a little stoop-shouldered, older than I remembered—but with all that, trim in his pin-striped jacket, gray trousers, shiny leather boots. From what I had seen so far, my friend Clovis had to be one successful man.

In the first room off the hall, Clovis turned to me. "I want you to meet my family. George Bush, may I present my wife, Maria."

A gracious lady rose to greet me. She stood a few inches shorter than her husband, her finely woven white cotton gown setting off a sensitive cinnamon face.

"Mr. Clovis has told us about you. We welcome you to our home." His wife held out her hand to me.

"And may I introduce Jeannette Giroux, my stepdaughter?"

Slender, satin amber skin tinged with palest rose, cheekbones tracing an exquisite contour across her face below smoldering amber eyes, hair a high-fashion pile of curls, her dress of the latest French style [a Jean LaFitte import?], she barely reached my shoulder height.

If the Clovis family heard me catch my breath at meeting Jeannette Giroux, no one let me know.

Men at camp bragged about the women they saw in New Orleans. What the devil did they say? "Stylish?" "Beautiful?" "Elegant?" That was it: "Elegant." Seeing Clovis's stepdaughter, I added my own words: Stunning. Exotic. Gorgeous. I had faced the British guns across the Rodriguez Rampart. I had stood firm on the line and fired. Facing Jeannette Giroux, I felt as if I would cut and run.

Politely, the family tried to put me at ease. I was caught, struggled to make conversation, my words jerky and meaningless. One hell of a mess I had gotten myself into. Those people must have thought I had no manners, a "dirty shirt" in their fancy sitting room.

Jimmers! That Jeannette Giroux. George Bush, you should have bought new clothes before coming here, I scolded myself. Finally, I mumbled an excuse about duties at camp when the family asked me to stay for the evening.

Clovis followed me to the porch, ignoring my embarrassment. "Come and spend an evening with us next week."

"Thanks. I would like to, but I doubt I'll have time to find decent clothes. We couldn't bring anything extra from home. I've lived in these linsey-woolseys so long they're pretty rank."

"Clothes? Don't worry, George. Didn't I tell you, tailoring is my business?" He stood back, his professional eye measuring me.

"But I don't . . ."

"New Orleans is yours, young Man. No cost to a Tennessean. You stopped the British. Here, now, let me use my tape. When you come next week, I'll have a jacket and trousers for you."

* * *

The ghostly laugh-cry from the jail had haunted me all afternoon. Before heading from New Orleans for camp, I took a roundabout way past the jail, stopped across from it, waited to hear that mangled sound. But the place lay still. Needing to rush through the gate, push open the door, and inquire after Isaiah, I stood on the boardwalk debating my best approach. If I burst in, asked for him, the jailkeeper would deny Isaiah was there, then run me out. If I stood around too long, no doubt I would be yanked in for vagrancy.

Absorbed in my thoughts, I did not take direct notice of a man angling toward me until he demanded, "You there! Looking for your master, Niggah?"

The young dandy's open coat revealed the butt of a pistol. "I said, 'Looking for your master, Niggah?'" His voice insulting, demeaning, his hand moved to his gun.

Surprise, then anger, tortured my face. Squelching those reactions, relying on the fact that the militia gave me my best protection in New Orelans, I answered as evenly as I could. "I'm heading back to the Tennessee Militia at Camp Henderson. I'm a sharpshooter in General Carroll's command, Sir." The last word came hard, but I forced myself to say it.

"That so. Sharpshooter, huh? You liar. You free?"

"Yes, Sir. I am *free*." I hit the word free.

"Let's see your paper."

By choice I would never let my paper into another man's clutch, but I knew a white had the right, anywhere, to demand proof of my status. Reluctantly, I reached inside my shirt and pulled out the most important document of my life—my freedom paper. Grasping one side, I held it so the seal of the Philadelphia Clerk showed clearly. The stranger read, a sneer working his face. What the devil, is he going to yank my freedom away from me? If the white grabs your evidence, you are finished, George Bush.

Without warning he let go of my paper, lunged toward me, swung his fist. He smelled like a saloon. "Why the Hell you hanging around here? Too many of you black northern bastards running loose in New Orleans to suit me. You ought to be locked up."

Flashing through my mind sped wild thoughts. Swing at the drunken fool. Hit him hard. Slug him good. Smash his face. Get yourself locked up in that jail. Probably in the same cell with

Isaiah—if he is there. We could break out together, me and Isaiah. Head North. Far North.

Oh, Jeez, I needed right then to show the New Orleans dandy how I could shoot out the red center of the bull's-eye. I ducked his blow, stood an instant glaring at him. My own hatred boiled, driving me to the brink of lunging. Then, as if they were real, I felt iron chains. *The chains that bound Isaiah fastened my arms to my side, kept me from slugging the bastard.*

Back on the Mississippi flatboat, I had not been disciplined for the fight with Hank Lucas. Even though General Carroll had not said a word to me about Briggs and his gang, I know he sided with me because he dressed them down. But I was not with the militia on the Mississippi. I was in New Orleans. Little would it take for the Black Code to destroy me.

Hiding the hate that still seethed, unclenching my fists, restraining again my impulse to strike out, I started to walk away. The man blocked my free passage on the boardwalk, and I had to step down into the mud and around him. I expected a shot in my back or one at my heels for the sport of making me jump. Rage rode my shoulder with every stride.

I might walk with the pride of a Tennessee Militia sharpshooter, but I could not carry my gun on the streets of New Orleans or any other city without a certificate. The dandy could have killed me right then. I would have turned up a week later, no questions asked, just another sodden body from the river.

No shot came, but that walk back to camp was the longest one I ever made. No place to run for shelter from the "gentleman" and his gun. No place to hide. I felt exposed, naked. A woodpecker could hide in the forest but for the tap of his beak. I could hide in Louisiana but for the color of my skin.

* * *

As late January settled muggy, sodden days onto February, our militia officers cancelled leaves. Around-the-clock guard duty and swamp fever or whatever, no doctor dared fix on an opinion of the disease, made the camp near to intolerable. The hospitals stuffed with hundreds of wounded British and a smattering of Americans, General Carroll arranged for transfer of our worst medical cases to Natchez. Carrying men on litters to the boats, I was thankful for my robust health, cursed the officers for not getting us out of the fever-infested Southlands. Overlaying everything, my mind pulled me toward Isaiah. After hearing that, haunting cry, I was nearly insane for not taking action.

We Tennesseans had signed into militia service for the emergency created by the British invasion. We had expected the fighting to wind up within a few weeks, and then we would be on our way home. But the calendar was rolling through February, and our stay dragged on. Monotonously, our officers repeated that we would likely not leave for many weeks and kept ordering more drills to fill the endless hours we spent merely hanging onto time.

Though I grouched out loud with the other men about the bad conditions, I was relieved at the delay. I had good reason for staying. That laugh-cry reaching out to me could only have come from Isaiah. It beat its own never-ending wild cadence through my head as I listened to the gripes. In my heart, I recognized that laugh from our Philadelphia days although the cry carried a haunting tone that made me shudder through the drills in the Louisiana cold. I would not leave the Southlands until Isaiah walked free.

"Why can't we close down this mess? Get on home? Hell, we've licked the British." The litany always began and ended with the same gripes.

"Damn if we don't know that. But Andy Jackson won't let up till he has official word from the President that the war is over."

"Men everywhere has got the fevers. Bad, they are. And it's taken all the camps."

"Hundreds down with dysentery. Many will die."

"What do you expect, crawling in this wet, God-forsaken swamp?"

"Yep, I could be the next man down with fever. But I'll turn into an officer-eatin' alligator if they bury my bones in this here bog."

* * *

At the time the British had finally withdrawn on January 18th, the citizens of New Orleans had acclaimed Andrew Jackson their hero. Believing that with the British driven away from their city they were free of martial law, people had jammed the Place d'Armes and the streets. They cheered from balconies and rooftops at the celebration honoring Old Hickory and his troops, Tennesseeans included. Then, those citizens, angry at General Jackson for burdening them with martial law after winning the big battle, breached his honors with a fresh level of irritation. Some even spoke open defiance. Their lack of understanding brought Old Hickory's rage to explosion. He ruled the city on the river with an iron hand.

Rumors of a peace treaty and the city's irritations to the contrary, Old Hickory held New Orleans under his nine-o'clock curfew. His scouts brought word that two veteran British regiments had arrived in American waters to add strength to General Lambert's army. A few days later they brought news of the surrender of U. S. Fort Bowyer to the British forces concentrated on Point Mobile and its occupation by General Lambert. Clearly, Andy Jackson had reason to believe that a continued enemy threat lay offshore.

As much as the next militiaman, I wanted the war finished so that I could get on with my life. But I saw no logic in moving out for Tennessee, then being ordered back to fight again. Until he received official word directly from President James Madison that the peace treaty had been signed, General Jackson dared not relax vigilance or dismiss military units. I figured he had to be right.

Because the martial law and curfew disrupted their business, anger festered in the New Orleanians. They maligned General Jackson. Their friendliness toward us cooled. Their voices curdled again when they called us "Dirty Shirts." I sensed that the greed to carry on trade and put dollars into pockets overrode the strangling fears of those days just past. Then the life of the city had hung in the balance threatened by the massive British military force on our shores.

Into this turbulent setting came Rachel Jackson the middle of February 1815. Bringing two flatboats loaded with food and provisions, she had floated down the Mississippi. The General's wife proved a boon for Andrew Jackson's health and a bridle on his temper.

His delight in her became evident as they danced at the ball honoring Old Hickory. The chatelaine of his Tennessee Hermitage seemed to be accepted by the New Orleans society ladies. But cutting through the polite facade as they followed her plump figure around the floor, some snobs laced their observations with an old French saying, "She shows how far the skin can be stretched. Mon Dieu. Mon Dieu. A trubtail."

* * *

Its nutmeg-red bark luminous, contrasting with the gray-white birches I knew in the north, a tall river birch tree shadowed the bathhouse in the corner of the yard behind the Sergeant Clovis residence. Across the lawn, blossoms of two round-topped magnolias showed creamy white against oval charcoal-green leaves. The Louisiana spring rang with songs of marsh wrens, goldfinches, mockingbirds.

On pegs in the bathhouse hung fawn-colored trousers and a jacket, deep blue with braid on the lapels. Two buttons fastened the belt across the back. Beside them hung a shirt tailored from fabric as fine as any of Captain Stevenson's. On the floor stood shiny leather boots. For a long time, I soaked in the tub of hot water. I wondered if I had really heard Isaiah's cry from the jailhouse that day with Levi. No sound like it met me when I took time to saunter past the city prison again on the way to Clovis's house. Strange. Could I have been so nerved up my first visit that

I imagined hearing my friend's rich, vibrating voice? Swallowing my discomfort, I rubbed myself with the rough washcloth, my bath a lush contrast to the dips in the cold Mississippi water that often left more grime on the body than a man could wash away.

Dressed, I stepped outside. The tight fitting jacket confined me, made me uncomfortable, uneasy about what lay ahead. With exaggerated motions, I tried to get a feel for the clothes, hoped my stretching was not obvious to Clovis then intent on showing a servant how to transplant a small, pink-orange azalea bush. I tried by an awkward maneuver to relieve the itch of my left shoulder blade. Then, two small boys, arms and legs rotating in simulated military style, marched from the kitchen door toward me.

"Did you bring it?" One of them asked as they halted in front of me.

"Bring what?"

"Your gun. Grand-père says it has silver on the stock."

Sergeant Clovis left his servant with the planting. "George, these are my two grandsons, Emilé and Armand. Jeannette's twins. Armand, you know Mr. Bush can't carry his gun through the streets of New Orleans."

Twins? I hid my surprise. Jeannette's twins? No one had mentioned that Jeannette had children.

"We want to see your gun. Bang! Bang! Bang!" The boys aimed imaginary weapons, fired imaginary shots, and took up playing battle again before Clovis could stop them.

The Sergeant laughed. "I laid it on about the fighting, George. How you and I beat the British. The more I explained, the more it sounded like we won the big battle ourselves. Just you and I."

"Bang! Bang! And the redcoats kept a-comin'!" Shouts drowned Clovis's voice.

The twins darted behind trees and shrubs. They looked alike, dressed alike, shouted alike. I could not tell one from the other.

Watching the boys play, I relaxed in my new outfit. I realized that the jacket was not tight. A well-fitted garment, it was a contrast to the loose backwoods clothing I had worn since leaving

Phildelphia. My body would have to adjust to confinement in tailored city clothes.

"The redcoats kept a-comin'! Bang! Bang!"

As I heard their boy-voice commands and watched, their play drew memories through my head. Two Philadelphia lads on the banks of the Delaware River fought the Revolutionary battles, claiming the entire victory for Crispus Attucks.

After thanking Clovis, I asked, "How much do I owe you? As soon as I'm back home, I'll send you the money." Questions about the boys' father kept prodding to be said. For then, I masked my curiosity.

"George, I don't want any pay. I know what this war has cost you. Take the clothes as small thanks from New Orleans and me to George Bush and to Tennessee."

"March along!" The two small, would-be troopers interrupted. They passed between us, pretending to guard their captured prisoners.

Clovis shook his head. "My young marksmen have many questions for you, but they'll have to wait till another time."

His tailor's eye measured me. "You look great. I figured you were one of those men who could wear the new style fawn-colored trousers and blue jacket."

"I'll admit I feel more New Orleans in them than I do Tennessee."

"It appears to me like the trousers need to be tightened a little around the waist. Let's step inside and I'll take a quick tuck for today. Tomorrow, I'll have them recut at the shop."

To the boys, Clovis directed, "Run along. We'll see you later."

With a tailor's needle and linen thread, Clovis stitched a couple of tucks in the waistband. As I slipped into the jacket again, he lifted it by the shoulder seams, adjusted it to hang properly.

I started toward the door, but Clovis stopped me. "One more thing. I don't want to be rude, but let's finish your haircut."

I had shaved off my beard and trimmed my hair at camp. The result had turned out uneven, ragged. I felt the strands scrapping my neck.

"You a barber, too?" I laughed and settled down on the bench.

"Well, in my business you get a lot of experience." Draping a towel around my shoulders to keep clippings off the new jacket, Clovis cut my shaggy mass with his straight-edge. "The French barbers tell me that a man's hair should be shaped to follow the contour of his head. Makes a better looking product than the old round-head style."

My tailor-turned-barber stood back, looked me over, whistled. "My shop doesn't often cut a suit for such a tall lean body. Your wide shoulders and narrow waist were a welcome relief for us. It takes a chunk of our time to design and fit clothes to the paunches and sagging muscles my New Orleans customers pack around." Clovis thumped his own potbelly, chuckled. "My workmen say you have the figure of a country gentleman—long legs, slender body, wide shoulders, and at least six feet tall. Right handsome man, you are, George."

A bell tinkled. Embarrassed by his compliments, I was thankful for the interruption.

"That's Veta." Clovis stepped around to my other side again. "Two or three snips more and I'm done. We don't keep Veta waiting dinner."

* * *

That New Orleans table: damask cloth, wine glasses, silver forks and knives, carved French-style chairs, the bouillabaisse, the shrimp with corn croquettes, and coffee that never had known a campfire pot. It was ". . . a fer piece . . . ," as they said in Tennessee, from our militia camp chow—a chunk of salt pork with hard biscuit and strong coffee often laced with grog—gobbled down while I sat on a damp log by a smoking wood fire. The dishes cleared away, dinner finished I thought, our talk compared Philadelphia and New Orleans.

Then, Veta brought fresh coffee and a platter of square crisp-fried rolls, "beignets" the family called them. Made of heavy, sweet dough the beignets did not have as delicate a flavor as the pralines that Jeannette passed to me next. Our hands touched. Our eyes held a moment. When I raised my glance, Veta's hostile stare renewed the mutual dislike that had risen between us the first time she confronted me at the door.

To her stepfather, Jeannette suggested, "Let's go to Congo Square and watch the dancing. Why waste this beautiful afternoon inside?"

"Good idea," Clovis agreed. To me he added, "I'll wager you never saw slave dancing in Philadelphia."

Slave dancing? Had I heard correctly? These people enjoyed watching slaves dance? But I had other questions, too. Who was Jeannette? Did she have a husband? Where was the father of her children? Why had no one mentioned him? Dared I show an interest in her? Escort her during the afternoon outing? No one volunteered the information. I was not certain why, but I held back my questions.

As we left the house, Clovis explained. "The authorities permit slaves to gather at the public square and dance. They have set the hours on Sunday afternoons."

Jeannette walked beside me. "The dancing gives the slaves free hours away from their work. Once every week. Anyone can come and watch the entertainment."

"'Joyful exercise for them,' folks claim." Maria's voice carried a caustic tone. "But the police are always around the Square with guns. They watch every move, so dancers can never carouse or break away."

Joyful exercise? How could dancing be "joyful" guarded by armed police?

Near the corner of Rampart and Orleans Streets, we worked our way through the large crowd. Congo Square throbbed with moving bodies, the air with sounds I had never before heard. French? New Orleanian? African? Caribbean? I did not know much about music, but the powerful beat saturated the air and wrapped around me. I watched Jeannette, a half-smile on her smooth, amber-colored face, a faraway, dreamy expression in her eyes as she listened to the music, its rhythm offbeat, syncopated, beats half sounded, rhythm with missing beats. No matter to her, it seemed, if I were dressed backwoods or New Orleans or even stood beside her. Evidently, she was thinking of someone else.

"Watch the drummer on the far side of the Square," Clovis broke into my thoughts. "He beats out the rhythm for the dancers."

The drummer half crouched at his drum, a bamboula, made of calfskin stretched over an open barrel and held down with staves. His body undulated up and down, side to side, in time with the slaps of shined-up calf bone drumsticks. Onlookers clapped their hands, their bodies swaying with the rhythm. The drum rolled. The sounds pulsated.

A rasping noise punctuated the rhythm as a younger drummer raked his small turkey bones up and down on the staves of his bamboula, counterpointing the older man's beat. The men in the Square stomped their feet, jumped and kicked their legs, shouted, twisted and rolled their bodies, shook glittering pieces of metal on ribbons tied around ankles to sprinkle the beat with metallic sounds. Women swayed, gyrated their hips, seldom moved from one spot. The dance was sensuous, primal, cadenced by chants not French or English as I first had thought, but a patois of sounds, a language that belonged to Congo Square alone, made up of words that must have come from our common source, Africa.

The dancing fascinated. The pulsating throbs, the chants rising to high pitch, dropping, repeating, spoke to me of many feet marching forward, many voices calling with longing and sorrow for freedom. I could not understand the words, but I did understand their message. *Freedom spans the abyss.*

I tried to make polite conversation as we watched, held back from speaking my mind about the police who milled around the Square. As they paced from one corner to the other through the crowd, each time they passed me, their eyes locked on my face. The police knew I was a stranger.

Joyful time for the slaves? A sham, that pretense of freedom under guard. In St. Louis Cathedral a few hours earlier, many of the white watchers had listened to the priest's words of love, compassion, and justice. At Congo Square they stood in the sunshine entertained by that spectacle of human beings in bondage pretending happiness.

"Lemonade! Ginger Cakes!" Hawkers with large trays mingled among the spectators, their cries promoting a brisk business for them. I, for one, had no desire to eat. I had seen enough of that "joyful dancing." I had enjoyed the Clovis hospitality, but the dancing presented a strange situation. I sensed conflicting forces weaving through the talk and actions of my hosts. And what was Jeannette's situation? Was the twins's father dead? I held my tongue. My Philadelphia manners dictate that a guest does not pry into the lives of those in whose home he visits.

* * *

The tortured laugh-cry ripped the air again, freezing me in place. High-pitched and agonized, vibrating a moment, the cry swelled, beat at me, insane, a familiar powerful note. The lash of a whip curdled the air. The anguished laugh cut short. That haunting plea bore more substance than it had before.

Isaiah. Isaiah, how can I get to you?

* * *

Hurrying around a corner late that afternoon, I came upon Negro convicts from the calaboose. Spiked iron collars circled their necks, chains hobbled their ankles. Whips coiled in the hands of white guards threatened lashings. Driven to clean an overflowing sewer of New Orleans, feet buried in gutter filth, each man looked the same as the other.

I stopped in my tracks. Searched the faces of the chained men. Waited to hear the laugh again.

Isaiah. Isaiah?

A guard's whip whistled short of my ear. "Move along you black fool. Or I'll chain you."

Stiffening, I jerked, stepped back, yelled, "Isaiah?"

"Get the hell out of here if you know what's healthy for you." His pistol buttressed the guard's threat.

"Isaiah? Isaiah!" His name simply exploded from me.

As the click of a pistol hammer backed me away, eyes from the third man in the chain met mine, stared. Lips moved. No words.

I had found Isaiah.

Rush in. Cut his chains. Action that would end both our lives. I did not have to read the Black Code of Louisiana to find a reason why Isaiah, why any of those men held prisoner, cleaned New Orleans's gutters that beautiful Sunday. Whatever crime he had been formally charged with, any whim could have locked Isaiah in those chains.

Free Isaiah? You cannot even see him at the jail. You cannot even speak to him. George Bush, you cannot touch that emaciated, ragged, fear-ridden human being sloshing in gutter filth. The thoughts nearly drove reason from my mind. I fought against running to that third man.

Pretending to heed the guard's threats, my heart pounding, I strode away gulping deep breaths. I stopped as soon as I rounded the next corner, tried to plan a course of action. I had not yet learned how Clovis fit into the Southland city scheme of things, but he was the only New Orleans man I knew. I had found no opening to make acquaintance with other Saint Dominguians much as I had thought about asking their help to find Isaiah when I was still back in Philadelphia and Tennessee. I could not expect to unload that heavy problem on any of them at first meeting. Perhaps, the Sergeant could learn the charges saddled on Isaiah. Perhaps, we could figure means to free him. Trust Clovis, I must.

As I ran back to find Clovis, I remembered men at the Free African Society talking about tragic endings. In the crazymaker that is slavery, kidnapping as well as selling or buying stolen people being regarded even by decent white folks as dirty business, no respectable man could risk getting caught with stolen goods. That day by the sewer, I saw that my friend had been abused almost beyond recognition. I knew slashings of the whip had forced him into submission. I, an outsider, dared not say the careless word, take the hasty misstep, commit the rash act, that would end Isaiah's life.

Knowing that my leave ended with the fall of night, I rushed into the Clovis house, drew the Sergeant outside, unloaded my story on him, demanded his help. He glanced away, mumbled to himself, clearly uncomfortable.

Agitated, a sharpshooter on the edge of hysteria, I yelled, "I have to do something, Clovis. Tonight."

He turned to me, his voice firm. "George, you better go on back to camp. If that is your friend Isaiah, . ."

"I know it's Isaiah. I saw him, I heard his laugh. We knew each other too long in Philadelphia. We grew up together. I couldn't mistake him."

"In your rage, George, you dare not walk the streets yelling about a stolen Negro. You'd be struck down, your freedom papers taken. You'd wind up in chains yourself."

Finding Isaiah. Pure accident. Freeing Isaiah. Impossible? No. It had to be done.

"George, I could go to the jail and ask for Isaiah. Little good it would do. He cannot talk to me. The guards will not know him as 'Isaiah.' New names are always forced onto stolen people. He could be Tim, Reuben, Joe, Clay. Any name. So, we can't start there. More serious, I'm sure you know, if he dares speak out claiming he is a free man, before we could spring him, he would be whipped senseless. He would be carried in chains to a back-country plantation where we would never find him."

The Sergeant's logic buttressed what I already knew. Although his calm manner almost maddened me, I tempered my tongue. No use attacking him and driving his help away.

"I understand what you're telling me. So, before you can help, you'll need to know what Isaiah looks like. Come on, I'll show you."

On the street where my friend slaved, unseen by the guards, we slipped between two houses, waited a moment.

"He's the third man from the far end," I whispered.

"I'll walk by and take a good look at him. Fix his face in my head. You go back to camp, George. Don't hang around here. Give me a few days to figure something out." Clovis, the sergeant again, gave his order.

Wanting to stay, fearing for Isaiah's safety, holding myself in rein, I obeyed.

Without a chance for me to ask more of him, Clovis sauntered easily along the street, pausing and glancing at a nearby house as if he were a prospective buyer.

Lingering a few moments in the shadows, I heard him ask the guards, "You men know who owns this place?"

Endless, it seemed, the time it took the whites to look him over. Then a drawl, "Naw. You better check the parish books to find out, Boy."

Clovis walked into the yard, glanced around, squinted as if the chain gang did not exist. I knew he took in every detail of Isaiah's features. Then he turned away and strolled homeward.

I forced myself away from the slave line and headed toward camp. A rawhide whip snapped on the back of a man, and shouts from the guards pierced the late afternoon quiet. "Git on with it! Move your ass, you black Heathen!" Agony rose and hung on the air from a voice I did not recognize. Isaiah knew I was there on the street for he kept his head down, bent to the work, avoided drawing attention to himself. After all the years of waiting, searching, then seeing him almost close enough to touch but having to force myself to walk away, not to seize him in my arms, was worse than facing the fire of the British cannon. I considered running after Clovis, demanding that we free Isaiah at once. How unrealistic could I be?

Proof of Isaiah's free status could bring him home, justice for him, for the Curry family. But how to get that proof, and bring it to New Orleans in time to save him? As I have often reminded myself, the solution to injustice is justice, but too often the law blocks the solution. Governor Sieur de Bienville and the framers of the Louisiana Black Code back in 1724 wrote the words they knew would keep my people down. And there I was on his namsake street, Bienville. Joy at finding Isaiah. Bitterness that I could not simply head to Philadelphia with him free of chains. Turmoil in my soul. A contradictory day. In the sky bright sun. On the horizon dark clouds.

Walking fast, sometimes running, I was hit by the enormity of what had happened that afternoon. The Quaker bible readings came to mind. I knew exactly how those folks who had lived in bible times felt when Jesus raised their brother Lazarus from the dead. Did I know, oh, did I know! "He lives, he lives," they cried. Isaiah lives! Pounding with my every step, the litany: Isaiah lives. He lives. He lives! What words can describe absolute joy? Absolute jubilation? No word majestic enough came to mind. "Isaiah lives!" Those words sufficed.

"Lordy, I feel good," I laughed to myself. My Clovis clothes fit with the city, but I was glad to be again in my loose-fitting linsey-woolseys. I felt free in them, light of foot, light of heart. Mysterious how the mind weaves in and out of memories, and I recalled the time in Nashville when William Carroll had read Jackson's order describing the uniforms for our militia.

> . . . dark blue, or brown has been prescribed for service, of homespun or not, at the election of the wearer—hunting shirts or coats . . . with pantaloons and dark colored socks . . ."

A loud whoop and holler from all of us had greeted the words. Old Hickory understood the state's poverty and for official militia uniforms had ordered our everyday wear. No man would be left behind for lack of cash to outfit himself.

* * *

Early one morning, Colonel Booth, 5th Regiment, East Tennessee Militia, assembled us to hear a message from General Andrew Jackson read by his adjutant.

> "Citizens and Fellow-Soldiers,
> "The enemy has retreated, and your general has now leisure to proclaim to the world what he has noticed with admiration and pride—your undaunted courage, your patriotism, and patience, under hardships and fatigues. Natives of different states, acting together, for the first time, in this camp; differing in habits and in language, instead of viewing in these circumstances the germ of distrust and division, you have made them the source of an honourable emulation, and from the seed of discord itself have reaped the fruits of an honourable union . . ."

Listening to the words, I wondered if the General would make good on his promise of the hundred and sixty acres.

> "The pride of our arrogant enemy humbled, his forces now broken . . ."

The land? The one-sixty for our services?

> ". . . your country saved from conquest, your property from pillage . . ."

The adjutant's voice rambled on monotonously,

> ". . . the consciousness . . . done . . . duty . . ."

The officer read nothing about the promise. The flowery words matched the debris cluttering the Place d'Armes. Too much had happened during the past several weeks. I would not be turned aside by phrases gilded with praise. Every militiman had earned his piece of land. I sure as hell would hold Andrew Jackson to his one-hundred-sixty-acre promise.

I wanted that land so badly I had blotted out the nagging thought always sitting in the back of my mind that Jackson's promise was not sincere, written particularly to lure the free Louisiana men of color into the fighting. Back at the Knoxville muster, I had taken it as my invitation, too. I needed to talk to someone soon on how to proceed. I figured to see Colonel Tunnell. Through all the weeks of my service he had kept his word. Like he had said to me that day at the militia muster, "Nobody wastes his time as a waiter where we're going. It's sharpshooters we're needing . . . the only reason we enlisted you to go to New Orleans. I give you my word."

Sharpshooter. I had done my part of our bargain.

I followed Jackson's words closely. "Every man will continue to carry out fully his assigned duties until further orders from the Major General. Dismissed." The adjutant finished the message. I had not heard a single hint of the land bonus.

Most of the men broke formation immediately. Some stood in groups talking. For several minutes, I remained bound to the spot, upset over Jackson's failure to mention his land promise.

During the boredom of militia camp the next few days, my head boiled with the question: Would Andrew Jackson's honor drive him to direct the government in Washington, D. C. to grant our land bonus? Old Hickory's sense of honor was renowned. Twice, he had dueled over insults to his wife. One dead man, and his own shattered left shoulder, grimly reminded that Andrew Jackson would duel for honor. And that same sense of honor had led him through the Battle of New Orleans.

Surely, that honor would compel him to perform his pledge to the "black sons" he had called to the flag. Surely, that honor would demand that the nation come through on his pledge of one hundred and sixty acres for each militiaman. Back in Tennessee, I had acted on the General's promise. At the Rodriquez Rampart, I and hundreds of other Africans had done our part. Each of us had offered our blood for that bit of freedom.

Of course, Jackson and I had never shaken hands. But we two had a deal. I had performed my obligation.

* * *

What of Clovis? Waiting with lessening patience, I wondered if my obvious disgust over the slave dancing had cancelled me out with the family. Perhaps the sergeant considered the task of freeing Isaiah a risk he would not take. Through the days with no word, my spirits sometimes soared with certainty that he would help. But as often they lay dashed in the mud with my fears that Clovis would wash his hands of us. I argued with myself the wisdom of taking leave in order to act on my own to free Isaiah.

Then, a message arrived for me: "Sergeant Clovis is at the company clerk's tent. He needs to see you."

We walked beyond hearing distance of the men. Without wasting time on small talk, Clovis said, "I have learned very little that will help you. I have spoken with Gregory Hamilton. He is a trader from Illinois who headquarters in New Orleans a good part of the year. I know he deals in several lines of merchandise, but I'm not sure about all of his activities. He does have a clean, straight out reputation. Never goes back on his word."

"What can he do for Isaiah?" I knew my voice sounded impatient.

"I'm not certain. It will take . . ."

"We can't wait. You have to . . ."

"George, slow down. You need to talk with Hamilton. He can do more than a dozen others here in the city. Speak to him. Judge the man yourself. Decide if you want to plan a course of action with him."

He left me with the invitation, "Come for dinner Sunday. We want you to join us. If you can, stay overnight. I'll get hold of Hamilton and arrange for him to meet you."

Not wanting to berate Clovis for so much time lost and then coming to camp with no more than talk of meeting some stranger, I said, "What the devil, Friend. Isaiah's in that jail. I don't know how long I can hold myself back."

Again the Sergeant's disciplined voice tried to calm me, "George, take care. You're on the thin edge. You're an outsider here in New Orleans. Don't explode and ruin the chance to free Isaiah."

12

"Tonight we will take you to the voodoo ceremony. Sanité Dédé leads quite a show," Clovis said.

"Please, Sir, who are you talking about?" I asked as we finished the meal with steaming hot coffee served in fine porcelain cups.

"Sanité Dédé. The voodoo queen," Marie answered.

"I'd like to have you come." Jeannette smiled across the table at me.

No mention had been made of either Isaiah or Hamilton. Uneasy, I wanted desperately to press Clovis into action. But I obeyed an undefined sense of restraint, chafing that I must bide my time.

What was with the Clovis family? They had stood and watched the slave dancing in Congo Square, seeming without a touch of feeling, entertained like the rest of the crowd by the slaves under police guard. What about the sergeant himself? On the Plain of Chalmette, he had shown the same shock as I had over the British soldiers' agony. Did he not have any concern for the slaves' agony? For a kidnapped free man suffering slavery?

For a block or two, deep in thought, planning how to see Clovis alone, I walked behind the family. Ahead of me, Jeannette and Maria talked about voodoo, the Queen's powers, and words drifted back about her ceremonies as a time for our people to relax with each other.

"This belief in voodoo power is in your mind. You want something to happen to you or to someone else. You make yourself think it happens. Then it works." His hand flat and extended, Clovis curled his fingers upward as if he held a ball. "Take apart a gris-gris—that's their special charm bag. You will find no magic potions, only small pieces of torn cotton, powdered ochre, cayenne pepper, maybe bits of snakeskin. Or, in another one, nail pairings, scales from an alligator hide, dung from a dog or cat, and gunpowder. Let's just say the voodoo will give us an evening of fun." Clovis looked back at me, a smile on his face. "Come on, George."

"You mean if I pay Dédé to leave a gris-gris by your door in the dark of the moon, you won't be so scared you'll drop dead?" Jeannette faced Clovis, poked him playfully.

"Not me," Clovis chuckled. "But it happens to people. Mighty strange things do take place."

Although Clovis's words might seem to scoff, I sensed that he half believed the talk of spells, charms, love potions and amulets that could be purchased from voodoo sorcerers. Did he think voodoo would free Isaiah?

Voices of people unseen on the path ahead drifted back to us. In the distance, a dog howled. Occasionally, a frog croaked. Jeannette stepped back to my side, the soft scent of her hair purling around me. Marie walked ahead with Clovis. His lantern lighted a twisting path through the tall grass and weeds of an abandoned brickyard off Dumaine Street. Above us, the branches of ancient magnolias blocked out the stars, the early blossoms scenting the spring air. The night of crisp beauty held excitement for the Clovis family, but I lost its magic although Jeannette walked close. The revulsion of Congo Square still nagged. I hoped this performance would not repeat the one that other Sunday with slave dancing under the threat of guns in white hands, the same threat that ruled Isaiah's hell-hole.

Even though I was a guest, I finally spoke out. "Clovis, I have to know. Will this be more slave dancing?" I did not care that my voice sounded curt. I intended to be blunt.

"No, George. We are not going to an exhibition." The lantern light ghosted Clovis's face. "You will see rituals. Most of them coming from Saint Domingue. Different ones from Jamaica. From other islands in the Caribbean. They're all performed by free people, island refugees, and a few Louisiana slaves. When refugees come to a new land, they bring along their customs and beliefs. Voodoo has come here from Saint Domingue."

"George, the rites trace back to the dim beginnings of us all. Our African religion." Maria's voice trembled. "I object to the slave dancing as much as you do. But remember that our heritage from Africa is freedom. Listen to the chants. Pay attention to the words. You will hear voices crying out for freedom."

"Whites do not know what the rituals mean. They think it is just heathen mumbo-jumbo. So the authorities overlook it as long as the rituals do not directly disturb the city. Or no one files a complaint." Jeannette slipped her hand into mine. "Listen to the bamboula."

I became conscious of drumbeats, low, measured, calling through the shadows from a building dimly outlined under the starlit sky. Then, another sound, rattling, insistent, reinforced the lone drum. The tempo quickened.

Clovis motioned us inside.

Flickering light, cast by flares high on the sides of the room and by fires blazing on a brick dais at each end, wove shadow patterns across the walls. The potent odor of burning cypress bark and herbs almost suffocated me. Staring at the human-sized figure hanging close to the wall across the room, I crushed Jeannette's hand in mine. It took every ounce of discipline to keep from screaming at the sight of the woman hung from the rafters. Human sacrifice? Did these people carry on forbidden rites?

Appalled, my body rigid, I shuddered, my eyes fixing on the figure. Around its neck hung two chains. One, the dressed skin of a snake, flashed scales in the torchlight, yellow, then black, now blue-green, then pure green. The other, a larger chain, glistened with polished white teeth torn from a dead wildcat. I stared awhile, then felt foolish when I realized that before us hung only a human-sized, black doll clothed in a golden-green fabric on which were embroidered huge occult symbols. If the voodoo required that the doll set the stage for terror, it had succeeded. Jimmers, I hoped the Clovis family had not seen its first effect on me.

"Hideous," I whispered.

"Hideous?" Jeannette drew back. "George, remember the crucifix in the St. Louis Cathedral? The little statue, a doll really, of a man nailed to two crossed boards? And what father in the Old Testament burned his son as sacrifice to God?"

"But those were religious . . ."

"Don't you understand, George? That's what I'm saying. This ritual is religious. Older than Christianity. Watch and listen."

Below the doll, a voodoo attendant poured corn flour on the red brick floor. Then, on hands and knees, he drew the intricate symbols, called vévé, tracing them through the flour to expose the dark red color. As he completed each pattern, an elderly woman placed a piece of dried maze or fruit on that section. Another woman dedicated the offering with a sprinkle of rum and the shake of a calabash. Creation of the vévé took quite some time. Completed, the designs portrayed tracings of hearts, flowers, sabers, dishes, figures of twin children for good luck, a boat, a servant, blending symbols from the folklore of ancient Africa with those of the Caribbean. Works of art, the vévé patterns reminded me of the wrought iron scrolls adorning the galleries and fences of New Orleans.

In the center of the room, two men in loinclothes drained blood from the slit throat of a slain goat into a ceremonial bowl on the floor. The drummers, joined by two banjo players, quickened their tempo.

"George, I've been talking to you, but you are not listening." Jeannette tugged at my sleeve. "Watch Queen Sanité Dédé. And Nepo, the man on that huge drum."

From a seat raised so that everyone in the room could see her, the Queen of Voodoo signaled with a majestic wave of her hand. The two men dragged the lifeless goat from the room. As another man moved to the drum, Nepo stepped away, swept up the bowl of blood, circled three times around the six initiates standing before Sanité Dédé.

Jeannette prodded me. "Think, George, about the priest's incantations for the 'blood of the lamb' in the Christian church. Is this any different?"

"The goat will be roasted and eaten toward morning during the feast." Clovis drew us back to reality. "They waste nothing."

"Shush." Maria silenced him.

We watched as Nepo drew a cross in blood on the forehead and on the high point of the breastbone of each initiate. He scattered the remaining blood into the altar fire, and it threw off a luminous purple glow. Alongside the vévé in front of the doll, Nepo flattened himself, head touching the floor. For a moment or two he remained prostrate. Then, in continuous motion rising to his knees, he stretched his hands upward and outward, chanting, "Doujou, Santou! Doujou, Santou!"

Sanité Dédé answered. "Doujou, Santou!" Then she signaled the assembly to take up the incantation.

"Doujou, Santou! Doujou, Santou!" Voices responded from all parts of the room. "Doujou, Santou! Doujou, Santou! Doujou, Santou!"

With a shriek louder than the chanting, Nepo rose to full height, seized a snake from a cage in back of the doll. Holding the serpent high over his head in both hands, he whirled before the Queen. The drums rolled, sharply staccato, then cut off. Silence bound everyone in the room.

Jeannette whispered in my ear, her eyes glittering in the flickering light of the flares. "Watch Sanité Dédé closely. She will get the power."

Nepo began a hypnotic, monotonous chant as he stared into the snake's hooded eyes. For a few moments the head rested on the coils of its body, then slowly the neck lifted, stiffened, poised rigidly almost a foot above Nepo's hand. The man moved with deliberate steps toward Sanité Dédé motionless on her seat, eyes fixed on the doll. At the moment Nepo touched the snake to the forehead of the Queen, the scaly reptile opened its mouth, the tongue darted out. With the serpent's kiss, an intense tremor struck Sanité

Dédé's head, surged through her body, arms, legs, until her whole being pulsated into a shaking mass.

My imagination? Was I seeing the impossible? The doll gyrated with the same rhythmic motions.

"Doujou, Santou! Doujou, Santou!" Distinctive, patterned phrases repeated themselves, many voices interweaving the chants.

"Now Dédé has the power." Jeannette's voice strained against the incantations.

Her voice and mine blended with the others, chanting mysterious sounds and phrases of the voodoo. I sensed each sound meant more than just old tribal jargon.

I looked around the crowd. The spirit of the voodoo had drawn me into it. Its rhythm pulsed through my heartbeats. I felt it in my temples, my breathing. No longer hideous, it had become filled with mysterious sounds and rhythms. The powerful sounds and rhythms reaching out spoke to me. Maria's "Listen, . . . pay attention to the words" stayed with me. I began to recognize meaning in the voices and the happenings as the ceremony unfolded. To the chanting I added my own, "Free Isaiah. Free Isaiah. Free Isaiah."

Folks responded to the ceremony in different ways. Some struck with religious fervor called out to a diety. Others shouted, twisted, laughed, enjoying a social outlet. A few seemed to draw strength from the rituals, embraced each other, clasped hands as if mending old insults and wounds. As Maria had said, "You will hear voices crying out for freedom." Her words were true. In the chants, I could identify masked cries of freedom for our enslaved people.

"Free Isaiah. Free Isaiah. Free Isaiah." My own litany kept blending with the cries.

I respected the performers' courage, for I was certain they risked the presence of an informant. In fact, all of us, assembled together, were committing acts the law branded illegal, but acts authorities condoned as long as everyone obeyed the rules, "kept their place," and hid the true meaning of the rituals in theatrics.

Sanité Dédé raised both arms upward and outward. The crowd stilled. The scent of burning herbs and bark saturated the air. I wondered what the quiet portended.

"Watch how she passes the power to her initiates." Jeannette turned to me as I slipped my arm around her waist, drew her close.

All eyes centered on the Queen holding a majestic scepter with ornate wrought iron lacework at the top. Dressed in a loose-fitting robe, poor like the people over whom she reigned, the voodoo Queen wore as her crown a kerchief with seven intricate knots pointing toward heaven. I had seen the same on Veta's head on my first call at the Clovis house.

Rising, signaling the initiates to kneel before her, Sanité Dédé rubbed two fingers of her left hand on the spot touched by the serpent's tongue. Then, with a sweep of her arm, she reached out, stroked with the same fingers the blood mark on the forehead of each initiate. When the last girl had "received the power," the drums, the chants, burst into the deafening, throbbing beat that drove every thought from my mind and held me in its hypnotic spell. In rhythm with those about me, I chanted, twisted my body.

I stole a look at Clovis. His face drawn into a closed expression, he tried to scorn the sight before us. Maria swayed with the beat.

Jeannette moved with my every motion, her body against mine, seeming part of me.

Nepo zigzagged around the initiates, his steps matching the tempo of staccato notes the drummers struck with buzzard bones on small calfskin drums. Then, with giant leaps Nepo whirled the length of the room, the serpent held high overhead.

Another gyrating, twisting figure danced into the other end of the room.

"It's Veta. Jeannette, it's Veta!" I blurted out.

"She always dances with Nepo. Just keep your eye on her, George."

Her six-foot figure swathed in green fabric, Veta whirled in concert with Nepo as she transformed before my eyes into a glittering, writhing human serpent. For several minutes the pair performed their synchronized dance, fast, exotic, flashing in the light of the flares.

The room throbbed with drumbeats, movement, chanting—a cacophony of sounds against which I struggled to retain my hold on time and place. A vision of Isaiah in chains, gyrating, writhing, flashed before me. The cry of the people became his cry.

At the instant Nepo flung the snake into the open-pit fire, Veta sank to the ground at the feet of the doll, her head touching the outer tip of the vévé. For a moment the fire darkened, then I heard a crackling and smelled the burning sacrifice. I tasted the strong fragrance of burning incense that drifted around me. The music and chanting ceased.

Jeannette pressed closer to me. I would have been content to stay forever as we were.

Then, the Queen's voice commanded attention. Holding high her scepter, Sanité Dédé rose to her feet. She instructed the initiates in the precepts of the voodoo ritual. Many words, phrases, sometimes whole sentences spilled out in languages I did not understand. I could not sort out the Spanish from the Saint Dominguen and the French. The mixture added up to the patois I had heard on the Mississippi waterfront.

As the Queen pointed the scepter at the doll, I caught words that described the figure as the symbol of immortality, of a people's soul temporarily bound by chains that we must break to achieve freedom. Her voice lowered. She pointed to the vévé on the floor. She praised spirits that had gone before us, the spirits that send us their strength and love. The serpent symbolized the evil that encircled and enslaved our people. The kiss? Her eyes swept across the silent crowd. Then, she threw back her head, held out her hands, her voice defiant and vibrant, no longer couched in veiled language.

"By that kiss I take the power from the serpent, add it to our own inner strength and power. I create greater strength for each of us. Not for us to endure suffering for all time but to overcome the evil that binds us. I have passed the power to you initiates. I charge each of you: Use your power. Break the chains encircling our enslaved people." The Queen paused, resumed her seat. "Now, my Children, let us commune and refresh our strength."

Voodoo attendants brought flasks of the sugar rum called "taffia." They served the Queen and the initiates, then, Nepo and Veta, who disappeared outside into the night; and finally, the worshippers and us onlookers.

When handed the small flask, I hesitated, then found the heavy, sweet drink palatable, tasting of molasses. Above the babble of voices sounded the twang of banjos and the rattle of pebbles in gourds.

During Sanité Dédé's interpretations and instructions to her initiates, I had observed that Clovis became increasingly uncomfortable. He did not join the conversation. On cue, the attendants gathered the empty flasks. The beating drums and the incantations again throbbed and reverberated as men and women swirled across the floor following Veta and Nepo.

Clovis edged toward the door, calling back, "It's time we go."

Jeannette clung to my arm as we strolled back along the path. Her body close to mine, the scent of her perfume drove my mind into an imagination that we were gyrating, twisting in a voodoo dance all our own.

* * *

Long after the family had retired, I stood by the window unable to sleep. Tortured by images of Isaiah chained to the floor of the jail, fretful at Clovis's seeming indifference to Isaiah's plight, voodoo scenes played through my mind. My reactions puzzled me. First, I had held back, skeptical about going to a voodoo performance. Then, I looked on the affair as entertainment, ready, like Clovis, to scoff. But the chants, the symbols, the voices reached back, far back beyond my cautious Quaker, white-man upbringing and touched my deepest African instincts. Streaming through the voodoo ritual, I heard powerful cries for freedom, cries masked in language no white man could understand. In them, the haunting scream of Isaiah rose above his clanking chains. The ceremony stood as proof that the soul of my people, rooted in its ancient African religion, had survival power.

Thoughts shifted to Jeannette. Who was that woman? Her two boys? What man had fathered them? Who provided their support? Clovis had a good business, but that household displayed more wealth than I figured he made.

The fragile lines of Jeannette's body, the scent of early magnolia blossoms from the tree outside my window, the same musky sweetness she . . .

The door opened.

"Jeannette!"

"I couldn't sleep, George." She hesitated. "You can send me away, if you want."

Questions about her present, her past, dissolved. In my arms, her body pressed against mine, our lips met, our embrace tightened. My mind tore loose from its Quaker moorings.

We lay together, breathless at first, fingers tracing endless véve patterns on our bodies, hands guiding us to the source of our own intimate voodoo magic. Our whisperings fed the need to release passion long confined, a taste of passion we had restrained until those moments. An interweaving surged through us, rising from the fires of our depths, pulsed and surged and pulsed again, rose and fell as emotions drained us, repeating into the early morning hours, merging the desire of weeks into a misty soft and fragrant forgetfulness.

*   *   *

The next morning, my head was torn between wanting to spend the hours with Jeannette and planning action to free Isaiah. I figured to see Clovis first thing, but he had gone to his shop early. He had left a request that I meet him at the Café des Exiles, a place hospitable to free Negroes, he had told me. As I folded the note, I wondered how much he knew about Jeanette and me. I wondered, too, why he had not said for us to meet at the Café des Emigrés. Many refugees from Saint Domingue frequented that drinking spot. Perhaps Clovis had chosen an eatery where customers or others would less likely recognize him or stop for a few words.

In the Café at the corner of Royal and St. Ann Streets, a one-story restaurant covered with a Spanish tile roof, the waiter seated me and showed me the menu board.

"Just coffee for now. I'm waiting for a friend."

Thankful for a few minutes alone before Clovis arrived, my mind and senses full of Jeannette, I had to admit that I did not really know her. Whenever I had been with her, my questions, my doubts, had been pushed far aside. The past night had convinced me she belonged in my bed the rest of my life. Why not take her to Tennessee with me? Wouldn't we . . . ?

Clovis strode into the Café. "Sorry I'm late, George. We are shorthanded at the shop with some of my men still out on Jackson's guard duty. One customer was particularly fussy. I had to help my assistant with the man's measurements. God, I wish the General would turn lose the militia. I need all my men back in the shop."

"I haven't been here long." It would have suited me to talk about Isaiah or Jeannette right away. Clovis being my host, I felt uncomfortable jumping ahead.

Our orders for beignets, gumbo, and coffee given the waiter, Clovis lighted his cigar. We ranged over several topics: the war, the climate, the voodoo, the Black Code of Louisiana, the success of free Negroes in New Orleans despite the Code, the need for people of our race "to keep our place." Everything but Jeanette and Isaiah.

"I have a good business, but at my age I can't afford trouble, suspicion. None at all." Clovis suggested we keep our conversation low, warned that we did not want anyone to hear us talking about our rights and the laws. "George, I must keep my place at all times. That's what I do. Like it or not."

"The same for me. Back in Tennessee, I had my own adjustments to make. One of the most frustrating, the registration paper I have to carry just to cross the line from one county to the next. I feel damnable. But as you say, 'Like it or not,' that's what I do."

"My family has never had any trouble with the authorities. The middle 1700s, before the big revolt in Saint Domingue, they saw the smolderings that preceded the bloody outbreaks and fled to Louisiana. We lived here as free people. Helped build this city. We've enjoyed freedom for decades."

"My father got his freedom under Pennsylvania law. And Captain Stevenson himself cleared the way for us. His will provided freedom forever for our Bush family."

"I think a lot about my family's place in Louisiana, what's likely to happen to our people. I don't ever want to give up being a free man. Most of us believe we are free. But, George, I know we are just 'free Negroes.' Totally different from being 'free people' and citizens. We don't have citizen rights," Clovis continued, his voice firm but low. "I know you think I'm slow acting, but this is what I live with." Then the Sergeant quoted from memory the Louisiana law: "'Free people of colour ought never to insult or strike white people, nor presume to conceive themselves equal to the white. On the contrary, they ought to yield to them in every occasion, and never speak or answer to them but with respect, under the penalty of imprisonment, according to the nature of the offence.'

"That's the mandate for me to keep my place, always. Regardless of causes or circumstances, George. So, I cannot walk into that jail demanding to free Isaiah. I would be giving insult to the white man who claims to own him. A clear offense by me. And it would not help Isaiah."

I had no words to counter the criminal purpose that had written those lines into the Black Code of Louisiana in 1806.

So we rambled on, coming to no solution for Isaiah's problem.

Then, Clovis shifted our conversation. "Jeannette and her boys, they are part of our family. Mine and Maria's. Women like Jeannette have a very difficult position in life, George." He watched my face intently. "I . . . I don't know how to begin."

"If you don't want to discuss her, . ."

"You should know what we are like." Clovis drew on his cigar. "Take Jeannette. A beautiful quadroon woman. I hate to put it this way to you, but she was raised for one purpose only. To become the mistress of a wealthy young white man."

My breath came in short, sharp gasps. I had not suspected such a blunt statement.

Clovis did not look at me. "All of her growing up years. Like most quadroon women. Her training. Dress. Table manners. Talk. Bedroom graces. All French. I guess you'd say she was groomed for display at the Quadroon Balls."

"Quadroon Balls?"

"Yes. Special dances where trained girls of mixed blood are shown off before young whites who choose them for paramours. They dance, talk. The men eye the girls, then make a choice of one to live with."

Was I hearing Clovis straight? An apologetic tone in his voice? I would be blunt, too. "Sounds like a fancy cattle auction."

"You hit it right. A fancy auction. We mask reality. Everyone in the city takes pride that only men from wealthy and respected families are invited. The balls are elegant, they dominate the social scene."

What the hell had I gotten myself into? Jeannette, one of the women the men at camp made the butt of obscene jokes? I did not want to believe she was one of the light-skinned mistresses of white men with fine family names.

Hide your confusion, George. Careful with your tongue. "What of such liasons? Do they last?"

"Yes. Some continue many years. The man sets his woman up in a house in the Rampart district of the city. You know, like the one we live in. Most of those trim white homes hide quadroon mistresses."

"The way you explain it, Sergeant, New Orleans condones mixing of the races more than Philadelphia does. That surprises me. Doesn't the Black Code here prohibit such relationships?" I spoke quickly, thinking of my own Philadelphia heritage. My black father and my white mother had carried on a backstairs pleasure that produced me. In New Orleans, Clovis faced me explaining, "The elegant, polite society promotes these liaisons for the gratification of their men."

Either situation bred the same result, children of mixed blood who must live forever in that undefinable zone between races. No race to claim our own. The past had created us. The future would create many more, so many that the race of the future might well be the race of mixed blood. As General Andrew Jackson said, "White, black, or tea."

"Let's say the practice does not square with our laws but has become a well established custom. One you can be sure the white men will never change. They take it for the custom of convenience it is." Clovis's voice shook. Perspiration covered his face, and he could not hide his agitation. "Of course, the white wives pretend the mistresses do not exist."

"What about Jeannette?"

"At her Quadroon Ball, Jean Devereaux chose my stepdaughter. He comes from a wealthy, respected old New Orleans French family. Jean had money to build a house and furnish it with the best, in order that he and Jeannette could live together in the style of his family. At his convenience, he came and went as the master. Jeannette devoted her life to him. Loved him. Saw no one else." Clovis hesitated. "Maria had lived the same kind of life but with a man of less wealth. After Maria's white man broke off their relations, I married her. When Jean Devereaux left, Jeannette needed her mother. We moved into Jeannette's house to help raise her sons."

"What do you mean, Devereaux left?"

"As I said, for several years, she enjoyed Jean's whole attention. His protection. The twins were born, and for a time Jean saw only Jeannette. We thought he loved her. Hoped he might make the home with her permanent. Some men do. Then, suddenly, or so it seemed to us, he entered into a marriage arranged by his family with the daughter of another prominent Creole family. A good connection for him. As custom demanded, he made a financial settlement with

Jeannette. That included the house and its furnishings. Jean and his wife sailed to France to attend to family matters on the Continent. His abrupt marriage and leaving nearly killed Jeannette."

"My God!" I struggled to keep my composure. Instead of the shock of Clovis's words turning me away, desire to be with Jeannette surged again. I did not see her as a one-night woman. I wanted her for life.

Deep in thought, Clovis spoke slowly. "For weeks, we feared she would do something drastic to herself. Finally, we succeeded in helping her take an interest in her twins. Now, she seems to enjoy life again."

"What will happen to the boys?"

"As part of the settlement, their father agreed that he would find a school suitable for their education. In Europe, perhaps in Switzerland."

"Well, one good thing ought to come out of all this. The boys will be ready to make a decent living when they come back."

"George, Emilé and Armand will never come back to Louisiana." He stared at me, his face looking as bleak as his words sounded.

"What do you mean?"

"When the boys finish their education, they will take their place in Europe as gentlemen. Gentlemen of means. Of culture. In a foreign country. Maybe France. Maybe Switzerland. Rich, well educated, as light-skinned as the boys are, they will pass into the white world. Women like Jeannette have that goal, that their children pass as white."

"I have heard of that kind of thing happening. But . . . Kings? Emperors? More liberal than our Presidents? Europe more accepting than America?"

Clovis motioned for silence. "You see it for what it is, George. Here in Louisiana, once her lover leaves, the mother has only one choice. She must get her children out of the city so they will not cast shadows on the white families they came from. They are bastards their white fathers will never recognize publicly. Or she will be forced to send her children to a back-country plantation. Brutal. But the reality of life down here offers no other way out. So, better a mother like Jeannette let the father send them to Europe. There, as educated young men, Jeannette's sons will have the freedom you and I can only talk about."

The impact of Clovis's words sickened me. He made the tragedy so impersonal. I had difficulty accepting what he had been saying, so I repeated, "How can a mother bring herself to send her boys to another country? Never see them again?"

"Like I explained, George, a woman in Jeannette's situation will do anything, agree to anything. She does it so her children are not forced to bury themselves in the backcountry. Mothers like Jeannette want their sons and daughters to pass into the white world," he repeated. "Sending them to Europe provides the way. It's been done for so long that it's accepted as part of what goes on down here in the Southlands. I used to wonder myself. But, now, I realize on the Continent they can have a future. Their prospects here are nothing."

The implications were deadly. "A woman will not likely get over the hurt for years, if ever. I do not see anything reasonable about it. Isn't there any other choice?"

"Impossible. She can think and hope for another way out. But in the end she forces herself to accept the inevitable, a last gasp in a mother's desperation. Jeannette has become one of the many victims of the brutal system. It permits New Orleans gentlemen to satisfy their egos and their sex. I have seen it happen over and over again. And we will not see the end of it in our lifetimes."

Our coffee chilled. Our gumbo glazed with a fatty covering. I was about to bring up freeing Isaiah when Clovis picked up the talk again.

"I have more to say about the family, and we have so little time. I know you have Isaiah on your mind. I see it in your eyes. I have arranged for you to meet Gregory Hamilton. When we leave, I will take you to his office." Again, he changed the subject, "I know the militia will be heading home soon. But do you have to go back to Tennessee?"

His question surprised me. "What do you mean? Not go back?"

"George, stay in New Orleans. The city has shortcomings. But in spite of them, free men of color are getting ahead faster here than any other place in the country." He eyed me intently. "I know you are interested in Jeannette, and it appears mutual. She is a fine person. The two of you can forget the past. Maria and I did. We have talked about you staying in New Orleans. Being part of our family."

What had been Clovis's purpose? To pressure me? Certainly not merely to explain his family. He "invited" me to be part of it. One thing I knew clearly, I would not spend my life in New Orleans. I could never fit into that slave city, the constant demand "to keep your place." If Jeannette would go back to East Tennessee with me, we could overlook her past, build a life together. No, I would not get trapped into a hasty commitment here. No marriage for me until I had a few matters figured out. Besides, I had to clear up another question.

"Clovis, what about the people who work for you?" I asked even though I had surmised for some time they lived in bondage in that house. I almost blurted out "Slaves?" but I wanted to hear how Clovis explained them.

He did not respond at once, looked away, his face drawn, then said quietly, "Veta. Doby. The rest. Our slaves."

Hearing from his mouth that my friends had bought and enslaved people, our people, shocked me. More devastating to me than Jeannette's story. I could work out the past with her, but I could never accept slavery. I had been wrong to pass his people off as servants. Wrong not to face from my first visit that they were slaves. Deep in my heart, I had known better. But I did not want to believe that a Negro family held in bondage Negro men and women. My people enslaving my people?

Reading the disgust on my face, the Sergeant's voice strained. "Many of us free Negroes buy slaves. It is our way of helping them. We protect them. They become part of our family. We provide them a more decent life than they could have with white masters. We train them."

I ought to have stayed and reasoned with Clovis. My leave time was passing, and to meet the mysterious Gregory Hamilton took over as my most urgent need. Somehow, before I received orders for the militia to move out to Tennessee, I would make time to see Clovis again, alone. Persuade him he must free his slaves. And like Captain Stevenson, give them a generous share of his means to make their own lives decent.

As we rose to go, through all the thoughts and confusion about Isaiah and Jeanette tumbling in my head, Veta's angry face glared at me. I blurted out, "Why does Veta hate me? What's her problem about me?"

"You have noticed?" Clovis appeared relieved that I did not press him further about his enslaving people or seeing Hamilton.

"I can't ignore her."

Outside, on the corner, Clovis responded. "I'll be brief. Veta's family has been slaves to the Devereaux people for generations. Veta's loyalty belongs to Jean because she is still his slave. When he loaned her to Jeannette, he promised Veta freedom if she would keep all other men away from Jeannette. She has jealously carried out her duty. Now, she sees you as a threat for Jean's return to Jeanette's life. A threat to her own hope for freedom." We started down the street. With a half-smile he continued, "As you saw last night, Veta practices voodoo. How deeply she involves herself, I'm not certain."

Veta did hate me! And through his slave, the will of Jean Devereaux reached into that home. That explained Veta! I could understand Clovis's reaction to the voodoo chants of freedom. He held slaves, and the people knew he did. No wonder he acted so uncomfortable at the ceremonies off Dumaine Street.

"Enough of our problems, George. Forgive me for taking so much time to explain my family. I felt we owed you that much. Now, Gregory Hamilton is waiting for us at his office."

* * *

Past barrels of merchandise, rolls of cloth, crates of hides and leather goods, following a dim passage between stacks of sacks and boxes, up a broad, worn warehouse stairway, Clovis led me to a small office crowded with more boxes and sacks and left me alone with a man seated behind a paper-strewn desk. On the side wall hung several theater masks, a number English, a couple French, faces laughing, crying. Tragedy? Comedy?

Gregory Hamilton, the man I had waited impatiently to see: Thick hair, husky build, a bland face that would likely never be remembered on the street. A few white hairs streaked his dark bushy eyebrows. His jacket hung on a peg. His India cloth shirt sleeves were rolled elbow high. He certainly was not a dandy.

Hamilton's "Here, sit down" sounded friendly enough as he opened what must be one of the strangest, and what I thought at the time, the most pointless conversations in history.

We skirted around every facet of Philadelphia, its streets, its businesses, my history, my family, my childhood, my experiences in Tennessee, my fighting the British. We talked on every topic but the one I had come for, to plan how to free Isaiah.

He rambled on with considerable involvement about himself. He was born in Boston, had lived in New York, had built a passable business in New Orleans in trading goods and materials to merchants, had a brother in Kaskaskia, Illinois, who was a trader-blacksmith. He disliked the British, hated slavery, cared little for money. An illogical man? I was not certain. An unlikely white man hiding behind a mask? So he seemed that first meeting. Slightly on the daft side, I thought.

Then it dawned on me. All the while he had been speaking, his eyes were riveted on my face. He had neither missed a word I had said nor lost a nuance of my expressions. I felt as if the stranger had checked me out thoroughly, knew everything about me. I was puzzling how to accept him. At that point, believing he was simply being polite because of my Clovis connection, figuring he had no plan, I stood up, ready to excuse myself and leave.

A direct question brought me up short. "And how do you mean to free your friend?"

"I . . . I don't know. I'd like to bust him out. But I need your help. Clovis said you . . ."

"Yes, I can imagine what Clovis said."

Still seeing no help from that unlikely man, I started for the door.

"Stay. Sit down." The rambling, inquiring talk had ended. His voice shot out the words, "How do you know he is a free man?"

"His father and mother are free people in Philadelphia. Everyone there knows Isaiah is free. Even white folks. They can prove it. His whole family has freedom papers."

"What happened to him?"

I dredged around in the horror of the night Isaiah was stolen and gave Gregory Hamilton the succinct facts.

He sat quietly, again studying my face as if reading me to find out if I spoke truth. "It is not an unusual story. Too many kidnapped. Sold into slavery. God, how I hate the system."

Even with his words speaking what I believed, countless doubts and questions crowded in. Who was Gregory Hamilton? What if he bought Isaiah, then failed to honor his word and kept him slave? What if he spirited Isaiah away for his own use on some faraway plantation? How could I know if he was mixed up with slave traders? Would he sell Isaiah to make a profit? Was I myself opening the way for another chain to bind my friend? What purpose did Gregory Hamilton have in helping us Negroes?

Trust. Trust a white man? Who else? I had no one except Levi. But the problem of freeing Isaiah was far too risky and too complicated to open to Levi. And Clovis had made it clear that he dared take no hand in the matter.

Skepticism must have been etched on my face, for Hamilton said, "You don't really know who I am, George. For now, I will simply say my business down here runs to more than selling merchandise. The plan you will hear may seem overly simple. But my brother Ira up in Kaskaskia, Illinois, and I have helped free men and runaways often enough to know the dangers and make the right moves at the right times. The fewer details you know, the better for everyone involved."

Hamilton had put in considerable effort checking on Isaiah, had learned that a man named Marvin Pryor, the master of a huge Red River plantation, claimed to "own" Isaiah. He had saddled his new slave with the name "Jess." Hamilton learned also that Isaiah had run three times and been recaptured. Angered at Isaiah's fourth escape, Pryor turned "Jess" over to the Sheriff to work the chain gangs as punishment.

Because plantation owners mistrusted runaways, more particularly those who were repeats, it was Gregory Hamilton's thinking that Isaiah was less valuable to Pryor and could be bought. Sam's chopped off foot flashed. Isaiah's feet had been so deep in the gutter filth I could not see if one had been butchered.

Someone "owned" Isaiah. Isaiah could be "bought." Dreadful the logic, but there it was. To have worried all those years about his being in bondage had been one thing. It was a crazymaker blow to face the reality of the words: "Owned." "Bought."

We talked far past curfew. Our plan to buy Isaiah seemed practical, because to wait while someone brought his freedom papers from Philadelphia would take far too long. I warned Gregory what could happen. I called his attention to the case of Elijah Morris, sold in Nashville and shipped south before a friend could bring his freedom papers. I did not want to chance Isaiah being spirited further into the backcountry before we could provide proof of his free status.

When I told Gregory Hamilton that the Free African Society had a paper authorizing it to draw from my Philadelphia bank funds to help free Isaiah Curry, he stood a long time again reading my face. Shaking his head, he said, "It will likely take quite a sum to buy your friend. If you are willing to put up all that money, I believe you have told me the truth." Apparently, he had harbored some doubts about my sincerity.

We talked details of working out the plan. It was then I realized the deep commitment he had against kidnappings of free people. He told me that he and others, including his brother Ira, "in the work" kept funds from which he could draw to buy stolen people and help runaways. It was important to the cause that the funds be paid back for future help. He made it clear that he would do the necessary without fee to himself. In return, I wrote a note to Reverend Allen explaining about Gregory Hamilton and me working together to free Isaiah and Hamilton's willingness to advance the cash necessary and receive reimbursement from the Society.

When we had finished talking, Gregory headed with me back to camp for I could not be caught alone at night on the streets of New Orleans without a white protector. We passed the streets lighted with huge lamps swinging from crossbars nailed to posts, smoke of their burning oil strong on the air. Beyond the city, darkness covered us. As Gregory Hamilton and I neared camp and our talk drew to a close, my first inkling of trust for him that sprouted at the warehouse had grown to a more solid feeling. I prayed his actions to free Isaiah would never diminish my trust.

I had convinced myself. Our plan was simple and certain. Gregory would buy Isaiah, then free him. I would have a place for him in East Tennessee.

I put my trust in Gregory Hamilton. We shook hands on our understanding.

13

Like shards of broken procelain suspended in the night sky, fragments of clouds revealed, then concealed, the half-filled moon. Soughing of Spanish moss in the cypress trees along the Mississippi breathed mournful, eerie sounds as I stood guard duty at Camp Henderson.

Much had happened those last few days. Isaiah. Slave dancing. Voodoo. Devereaux. Knowing Clovis enslaved people. Hamilton. My powerful attraction to Jeannette. Love? Not yet. I was certain in time it could be. For Isabella James, call it what you will, love had hit me at first sight. So! I admitted it. Yet Ibby was a Tennessee wild flower. Her words to me, "Shoot him?" She was white, she was forbidden. Jeannette was a New Orleans hothouse flower, her life complicated and involved. She was quadroon, she was available.

Through the soughing of the moss in the cypress, I seemed to hear the voices of Emilé and Armand. I remembered my visit early in March. As I had turned the corner to Clovis's house, I heard "One, two! One, two!" The twins had marched along using the plank walk for a flatboat deck, the muddy Rampart Street for the Mississippi River.

They had run toward me. "We've been drilling like you did on the flatboats."

"Did you bring it with you this time?" One boy had asked, which one I could not be certain. They still looked alike to me.

I had hesitated. Before I could answer the brother had retorted, "You know he can't carry his gun through the city. Grandpère has told you not to ask."

"But he says you have a fancy gun." The twin nearest me had taken my hand.

"Yes. Like your grandfather has probably told you, my gun has silver inlay. I call it a Jaeger."

"What a funny name. Where'd you get that?"

"My kind of gun got its name from soldiers who were sharpshooters, the best shots. The men were called Jaegers. They were German soldiers, and they fought in the wars in Europe. Some of them came to the United States and fought with the British against us in the American Revolution. After that war, many deserted and stayed in Pennyslvania. They began making more of their guns and called them Pennsylvania rifles. I had one made for me. I call mine a Jaeger."

The other twin had edged around, taken my free hand. "Grand-père says it shoots better than the guns the British had."

"That's right. The gunsmith back in Pennsylvania bored the barrels with spiral grooves so the shot would spin out faster and faster. Older guns, muskets they are called, are smooth on the inside of the barrel. They don't put any twist on the shot." I had stopped. I remember thinking, Foolish of me. Small boys cannot absorb a lecture on weapon design. I must learn how to talk to them with words they can understand.

They had made it easy for me, they changed the subject. "Did you see any pirates on the river?"

"Not on the Mississippi. But I know way back on the Ohio River bad pirates have a hideaway at Cave-in-the-Rock. They sneak out and rob people headed down to New Orleans."

Four shining eyes had held mine. "Can we go with you and catch them?"

A lump in my throat, I had put my arms around their shoulders.

The feel of their taffy-colored curls, their eager questions about life in the woods of East Tennessee tapped at me. How did I answer them? I could not promise them anything. Rays of moonlight flashed on my Jaeger that night when I stood watch at Camp

Henderson. The cold and deadly barrel chilled my hand. The cold and deadly system that would banish Emilé and Armand to Europe chilled my heart.

"Rumors of the past several weeks have become fact. President James Madison has sent official word from Washington City. England and the United States have signed the peace treaty," Colonel Edwin E. Booth addressed our 5th Regiment. "Major General Andrew Jackson has ordered all units to assemble for review tomorrow on the parade ground at New Orleans. We will leave Camp Henderson at twelve noon. Dismissed!"

* * *

Holding his horse with taut reins, the Commanding General of America's Southland armed forces angled across the parade ground to a point directly at the front and center of the men assembled before him on March 14, 1815. Old Hickory saluted his field officers, then drew a document from his inside jacket pocket. His voice at times breaking with emotion, Andrew Jackson read the commendation he had written for us. "The major general is at length enabled to perform the pleasing task of restoring to Tennessee, Kentucky, Louisiana, and the territory of Mississippi, the brave troops who have acted such a distinguished part, in the war which has just terminated . . ."

To the right, my eyes checked down the long line standing erect. Gun butts rested on the ground in ramrod rows, our militiamen as straight as the lines of the regular army. I was intent on Andy Jackson's message, anticipated that at last we would have word about the hundred and sixty acres earned by our service. If Jeannette went to Tennessee with me, I would need that land more than ever.

The General concluded his speech, saluted his field officers. Men around me shouted, cheered. Someone pounded me on the back. But I had heard nothing about my land. Why did Jackson continue to ignore his promise? Would I have to fight another battle to get my land? Our officers silenced the militiamen temporarily and ordered us into ranks for the return to camp. Songs, jokes, shouts, "Huzza! Huzza!" broke the formality.

Fog crept over us as we marched across the cane stubble fields. Undecided where to look for a new location for my farm, I was unsure about my future. One thing I did know, complicated as her life had been, I would overlook the past, marry Jeannette, blot Jean Devereaux out of our lives, bring her and the boys north as soon as they could come. With her away from New Orleans, we could make a home without all those side influences.

My thoughts abruptly fractured. Tennessee, too, had its complications. The faces of Zeb Turley and Hank Lucas appeared and disappeared, weaving in and out with those of my tormentors on the flatboat, mocking me as I stared into the dusk. And Sam had sweated forty years under the whip to buy freedom.

Before I could take leave and ask Jeannette to go north, a message came from Gregory Hamilton: Please come to my office. No explanation, no indication of the subject.

* * *

As I hurried up the warehouse stairs, my hopes for Isaiah climbed with me. I thought, Jimmers, could he be here? Waiting for me? Already free?

Inside his office, Gregory stood facing the window. Alone.

"George, sit down," he said, turning toward me. "I've heard about Jackson's orders. I know you will be leaving for Tennessee very soon. I wanted to talk with you before you left."

Sunlight through the window played shadows across the masks on the wall, the images coming alive for me. As my eyes fixed on the mask of the laughing face, Isaiah's features seemed to spread over it, fade a bit, then sharpen. As from a great distance I heard his rich, vibrating voice.

"Where is he, Gregory?" I needed to know right away.

"I've seen him. He's still in the jail. I've made my first offer for him, but there's been no answer from Pryor." A frown swept over his face. "I have concern how soon we'll get Isaiah."

"What do they say at the jail?"

"The guards can't tell me a thing. They don't know a man named Isaiah. But the word is that Jess, you and I know him as Isaiah, has been a repeat runaway from the plantation. The fourth time now. Bringing him back has cost Pryor a lot of money."

"Didn't we sort of agree that should make Pryor more willing to sell him?"

Hamilton's concern showed on his face. "Yes, we did. But it depends on the kind of slaveholder Pryor is. Some masters would use Isaiah as an example to his slaves. Take him back to the plantation, order the slaves together to watch the overseer..."

"No. No. No."

As the words wrung from me, the implications of what Gregory was saying about the cruelty of Pryor and his overseer too awful for me to accept, the mask of the crying face stared down, tragedy reaching out for me. I denied it, pushed it back.

* * *

The stillness in the office pressed in. As I had pondered many times at camp, I questioned again, Why don't I stay here and free Isaiah myself? Leave the militia right now? Don't depend on Hamilton or anyone else to do what you ought to do yourself, George Bush. Go get him. Buy him. Steal him. Head north.

Even as I sat in the crowded office, I knew where I stood with the militia. I had tried a number of times to obtain my discharge in the Southlands so I could work personally with Hamilton in freeing Isaiah. The answer always being "no," I had contemplated simply walking away from the militia. That would not solve the Isaiah problem for I would be judged a deserter. Most of us volunteers knew that Andy Jackson, in January just past, had ordered six militiamen executed for desertion. Jackson had ignored their need to leave their units and return home, needs legitimate concerning families, crops, creditors, landlords. Even more disturbing to me was the case of seventeen-year old militiaman John Woods, a boy newly replacing his older drafted brother. Unfortunately, his squad was known for disorderly conduct during the Creek War. John had threatened his officer with a gun and been found guilty of mutiny. Harsh it was, but General Jackson approved the death sentence decreed by the military court.

For me, a free black wanting to rescue a slave claiming freedom would carry little if any sympathy. I could dredge up no reason the officers would grant leniency to me if I walked away. George Bush dead would certainly slam shut the main door to Isaiah's freedom.

Gregory Hamilton and I talked for a couple of hours or more, explored every means we could think of to pull Isaiah out of his hell-hole if our plan to buy him failed. My wild thoughts of stealing him just that, wild thoughts. Through our talk, no preaching, no moralizing, no bragging. Plain straight-out words proved to me again Gregory's unusual commitment to saving a free black man.

His last words deepened my trust in him. "Any news I have, I'll send to my brother Ira in Illinois. We have developed a roundabout way of writing so the wrong people will not understand what we mean." His faced tightened, and for a few moments Gregory seemed to look beyond me. "When Isaiah is free, I will send him north to Ira."

We said good-bye. Despite my wrenching anguish that Isaiah was not free, I left Hamilton's office still believing our plan to buy Isaiah was stronger than any other means.

* * *

"George, the days, the weeks, drag terribly when I don't see you." Jeannette snuggled against me as we walked into the parlor of her house on Rampart Street. "I knew you would come today."

"I couldn't stay away. But I'm afraid I have to count my days in New Orleans. The militia has been ordered home."

My frustration must have been common to soldiers of all ages, everywhere. A man needs time to plan, but duty and orders squeeze in. We force decisions in a few hours, make commitments for life. Then, we rush away, driven by the whip of the winds.

"No one gets leave now without good reason. So, I told the sergeant I had urgent business to finish in town."

"He accepted that?" Jeannette laughed, but her voice sounded worry.

"Seemed reason enough to him. I didn't tell him my urgent business concerns you. Jeannette, I want you to come to Tennessee. Live with me on my farm."

She pulled away, searched my face, dropped her eyes. "We've had our very special times together, George. But aren't you taking a lot for granted? Just asking me to come with you . . . without . . ." Her voice trailed off.

I puzzled. It took me a moment to realize my goof. "I failed to stop and think . . . It did not . . . Jeannette, I want you to be my wife."

"George . . ." Her accent softened the hard phonetics of my name. She buried her head against my shoulder, drew me close, her warmth and scent enveloping me. Never had I savored a moment as deeply fulfilling as that brief pause in my life when Jeannette whispered, "Yes." I was aware of nothing else in the world. That instant fixed itself in time as nature treasures the perfect raindrop shimmering on an early spring leaf.

For an hour, two hours, we planned. After returning to Tennessee with my militia outfit and finding a new location, a matter perhaps taking three or four months, I would rejoin Jeannette and marry her. She and her mother could arrange the details.

"Buy furniture. Anything you think we need. I'll send the money. Chairs. Tables. Kettles. Dishes. Silver. Whatever you want." It all sounded so good, I grew expansive toward Jeannette. "I'll hire a flatboat to get us back to Tennessee."

She listened, then questioned. "Why buy new things, George? Don't I have enough? I like my furniture, and nothing has begun to wear out."

"No, Jeannette. For our home, I will buy what we need. Don't you see? Another man bought what you have."

Jeannette paused, ran her hand along my arm, smoothed the collar of my shirt. "If I have to, I can leave my furniture with Mother. At least for now." Then, in a voice so quiet, I could scarcely hear her words, "I'll just take John and Doby and two of the women."

On my feet instantly, I braced my hands on the back of the sofa where she sat, my face close to hers. "Jeannette, I have told you before, 'No slaves.' One thing for certain, no slaves will come north with us."

"But, George, why do you force me to give up everything? My furniture? My silver? My people?"

Time drifted. We struggled with words, patched conversation together. Wanting Jeannette, trying to avoid appearing heavy handed, I made a decision. "Bring your furniture. I realize you will feel more at home."

"That's sweet of you." She kissed me, played her hand through my hair.

I drew back. "Those are things. Bring *anything* that will make you happy."

"Everything, George?"

"I said *anything*, Jeannette. But not *anybody*."

"I did not know you could be so stubborn." She slid from under my arms, stood facing me. "Old Doby and John, the women, belong to me. They have no one else. No place to go. They depend on me. You can't expect me to turn them out."

"That's not true, Jeannette. You must leave them here. Free them. Give them money to start a life for themselves."

"I can't. They won't know how to live, being free."

"Teach them. While I am away."

"I can't."

* * *

Our voices must have carried down the hall because Mrs. Clovis suddenly appeared through the door, closed it behind her.

Without giving me a chance to explain the plans, she waded into the argument. "George Bush! You speak lightly of our relation to the slaves. You have never lived in Louisiana. You know nothing about our life." Irritation crackled in Maria's words. "White men hold total control. Families like us, we came here generations ago. We learned to survive. To fit in. Keep our place. Negro folks here face constant danger. Those of us who have the means provide the only protection our poor people can depend on. That's why we buy them."

Our eyes locked. We stared at each other.

"You're not free, George. You're a Negro."

"I know my freedom is not perfect. But I am a free man, and I will not tolerate slavery. I do not believe there is such a thing as one human being owning another. Even if you say you bought people legally, how can someone own another human being? No. Impossible. Free your slaves. That's the only way you can be free."

Maria screamed, tears running down her face. "You do not understand, George. Slavers drag our people in here chained. Whipped. Afraid. We take them in and . . ."

"But you 'buy' the men and women. You make them your slaves." Her implication that they took in our people out of kindness insulted me.

"We protect them," Jeannette joined her mother.

"You do not understand, do you? As long as anyone buys slaves, one human being claiming to own another, no difference whether the masters are white or black or green, none of us in this country can honestly believe we have freedom."

"But, George, great people, important people, have slaves and treat them more kindly . . ."

"You are both blind. George Washington. Thomas Jefferson. James Madison. Presidents of the United States, but slaveholders every one of them. How can any of us change the system when it is embedded at the top? The whole matter hinges on color: white on the top, with all shades in between, down to black on the bottom."

Side by side, they poured out the time-frayed excuses of slaveholders everywhere.

"They need us."
"We feed them."
"We clothe them."
"We provide homes for them."
"They depend on us."
"We nurse them."
"They have been with us a long time."
"Freedom is dangerous for them."
"Cruel to turn them out."
"We are responsible."
"Clovis trains them."
"We love them."
"They love us."

The same line of false mouthings white men spouted to bless evil with virtue. Defensive nonsense. Blindness. Denial of simple justice. Always a tearing apart, never a mending.

They love us.

Sam had told me how folks looked on their "masters," on those who enslaved them. "They be only degrees of dispisement."

I broke into their litany of defense. "Mrs. Clovis, at the voodoo ceremony, you said, 'Listen, . . . you will hear voices crying out for freedom.' You were one of those voices. Didn't you believe what you said? Freedom."

"You dare question my sincerity? Of course, in that hidden building we could sing and chant of freedom. Dream of everyone being free. Share our hopes for a few hours, together. But the reality we face every day of our lives forces us to care for our people. We save them. We buy them so the white man can't."

Amazing, the capacity of human beings to rationalize evil into virtue. None of us touched Veta's tea. We groped for understanding but failed. In an effort to break the impasse, to bridge the gap between Jeannette and myself, I decided a compromise might possibly resolve our difficulty. "Jeannette, we must be reasonable. We want to make a home together. I'll agree to take the slaves north with us. Then, in Tennessee, you and I can free them. I'll provide the money for them to live. If necessary, I can send them to Philadelphia for schooling and work. That way..."

"No, George! No!" Her eyes smouldered amber-yellow with anger and hurt.

A sense of defeat, frustration, despair seized me. I feared that I had lost Jeannette and the boys. Ironic. Walking into town, I had imagined rescuing the twins from the forces condemning them to Europe, imagined them in buckskin and linsey-woolsey riding through the Tennessee woods with me. In the Clovis house, I realized the bitter fact that the mere mention of their going north would create more hard feelings. I saw no way to bridge the gap between us.

As quickly as the fresh spring raindrop slides from the leaf and shatters, my instant of elation fragmented. I realized I could not change Jeannette. Her words beat into my head, "I can't. I can't." Of course, Jeannette could not free her slaves. She was not free herself. Only free in name, bound to Jean, chained to her slaves, she could not teach anyone else how to live free.

One hope remained. If I reasoned with Clovis, perhaps together we could find the means to mend the tearings that threatened to separate us.

* * *

In front of a building on a street a few blocks from Clovis's tailor shop, well-dressed men crowded in front of a newly constructed platform. Others dallied in carriages or lounged on horseback smoking fancy cigars. Sprinkled among them, a few women twirled lacy parasols. Laughter, loud voices, the stamp of hoofs overlay low moans. To one side a huge poster nailed to a tree advertised: "A fine cargo of Negro males and females. All young and strong." I knew, cargo from Jean Lafitte's slave ship.

A slave auction. Behind their masters stood barefooted men, dressed in dingy, gray-colored plantation gear. Slaves broken to field service, they carried chains to bind any new properties their masters might buy. Police armed with guns and lashes patrolled the block. The "young and strong" merchandise would be permitted no break for freedom.

At the auctioneer's invitation, "Step up and inspect the goods," a number of buyers strode to the platform. Intent on improving their stables of Negro slaves, as if looking over a bull or other animal for the plantation breeding stalls, they jerked open mouths of the captives, pulled at teeth, pried legs apart, prodded genitals, fingered and squeezed breasts. Nameless cargo and no more, dumped on the docks of New Orleans, the men and women captives shrank back, tried to draw themselves out of sight. Shackled, they could not run. Weakened by months of imprisonment in the outlaw slaver's ship crossing the Atlantic from Africa, suffering in excrement and vomit, naked except for torn fragments of clothing, they had no choice but to bear the abuse. Fear, loss of hope, total despair oozed from every pore of their bodies.

Turmoil churned within me. My fists clenched. I restrained myself from screaming out, held back from rushing to their cages to free them. I had no gun. And I would have been dangerous right then carrying my Jaeger. For a moment, my mind blotted out reality. I hunched with the prisoners, felt myself strain against the bonds grinding into my heart, tearing through me. I was one with them as we broke out and fled together. Had I reached the point of honor when a man gives his life for what he believes?

But, no, I felt myself a lesser man rooted to that spot, a spineless nonentity. I stood stiff and sweating, offering no helping hand. Those caged men and women would be sold into slavery anyway, and me, a blob in that insane humanity would be dragged from the street, lifeless and discarded. How long must I put up with my rational mind warning me against rash sacrifice?

In the New Orleans sunshine, framing the chatter and laughter of white voices, the moans of the chained people sounded an anguished dirge. Then, the words of the auctioneer rent the air, "WhatamIbid? WhatamIbid? WhatamIbid?"

Head down, unable to watch, I started away. I thought my face had turned to stone, but the rage within me must have flowed across my features. As at the slave dancing, a policeman eyed me, his right hand stroking his whip.

"WhatamIbid? WhatamIbid? WhatamIbid?"

Crisp, resonant words answered the booming chant. "Five hundred dollars."

My head snapped up. I knew the voice. It could not be. Pray God it could not be. But there stood Clovis in the line of men closest to the platform. I did not want to believe what I was hearing. "Five hundred dollars."

"FivehundredFivehundredhere. Gimmesix Gimmesixhundred Six Six. Gimmesix."

"Six hundred." A cigar-smoking horseman streamed smoke from his nose, and in a lazy drawl raised the bid.

"SixhundredSixhundred. I'mbidSixhundred. NowSevenSev..."

"Seven hundred," Clovis called out.

Maria's and Jeannette's arguments hammered in my skull. "They need us... They love us... We love them." Then, the Sergeant's words at the Café des Exilés, "I teach them a trade. They know nothing when I get them. They learn from me. I teach them everything they know."

For what, Clovis? My mind repeated the question: For what, Clovis? For what? To be your slaves? Who profits off them? You take everything, Clovis. You slaveholder. Your brand of concern will sure as hell sink us all.

Shocked that my friend bid for another slave for his shop or household, hurt that my dream of a home with Jeannette had been destroyed when I had reached the point of thinking that the two of us could unite our lives, but most of all anguished by the turmoil seething through me that I stood mute at the auction and did nothing, I tramped the streets of New Orleans. I headed in a direction opposite the house on Rampart Street. The bitter knowledge slashed. My friend Clovis, slaveholder. No wonder he shunted aside the burden of freeing Isaiah.

Take hold of yourself, George Bush. You best face the facts. People in New Orleans pleasure in the way they live, the ease of having slaves do their work. None of them will change. You cannot persuade those you have drawn close to here in this city on America's great river to mend their ways. The bustle of buying and selling goods along the waterfront failed to draw my attention. Quite another style of business a few blocks away dominated my thoughts. The bidding for slaves.

Duty to report back to camp pushing at me, I needed to get my linsey-woolseys from the bathhouse. I needed to face Jeannette, tell her the end had come for us. I would not leave without making my position clear one final time. I turned back to the Clovis house.

* * *

The New Orleans trousers and jacket that Clovis tailored had turned me into a dandy, a man I was not. Made me pretend I was something I could not be. Like Clovis said, "A gentleman." If being a gentleman meant enslaving other people, to hell with it.

What kind of a two-faced bastard had I been in New Orleans visiting the Clovis house the past weeks? Talking about freedom for everyone. Never using people for slaves. Letting Jeanette's sweet bed blind me to what went on in her household every day. New clothes. Warm water in the bathhouse. Delicious food. Freshly washed sheets. Every bit of it the work of slaves. I had avoided facing the facts. Dishonest with myself. With the slaves. In my enjoyment, I had dumped the problem in the corner of my mind. My Quaker moorings tightening around me, I charged myself: George Bush, don't you ever again stumble along being a hypocrite.

* * *

The fine town clothes shucked and hung again on their pegs, my worn boots and honest linsey-woolsies turned me back to the man I had been. The door of the Clovis house stood partly open. Restored to my rightful person, I walked in and up the stairs resolved to pull aside the blinders cutting off Jeannette's vision, to draw her away from her narrow New Orleans trail.

Jeannette turned from the window, tried to smile, her face drawn and tear streaked. I resisted the urge to grasp her, swallowed the longing to feel her warm, soft body against mine.

"Our militia will leave for the north directly. Jeannette, I have to be straight out with you. Unless you free your people, we have nothing left."

"No, George, no!"

"You won't do right by yourself, your boys, shipping them off to Europe."

"Don't talk to me that way." She steadied herself at the side of the dressing table. "I had hoped we would . . ." Her voice faded to a whisper.

We stared at each other.

"You're a slave yourself. Enslaving human beings."

"No, George, no!" She screamed.

Another argument! I had figured to be diplomatic, but her defiant words heated my anger to boiling. Abruptly, I turned from the room. My last glance took in her dusky, amber face framed against the dark green magnolia leaves shading the windows.

Along Bourbon Street, my hand brushed against a lump in my pocket. Strange! Nothing in there that morning. Whew! The odor of garlic, gunpowder, sundry other stuffings reeked from the voodoo ball Jeannette's slave must have hidden in my clothes. I flung the gris-gris against the side of a tavern. It burst. Its contents scattered at my feet. I kicked them into the gutter.

14

In the spring of 1815, my Tennessee Militia slogged homeward on the Natchez Trace through its steaming swamps and river crossings, over rock outcroppings, up ridges and rough hill country. The "Notchey Road," as local folks spoke of the Trace, linked old buffalo and Indian paths stamped out in ancient times by herds of bison following instincts between watering holes and feeding ranges. The trail wove through forests of chestnut, persimmon, and blackwillow. Vines entangled those aged trees towering over our struggle, mocked our plodding pace as we followed stretches twisting across the land. We stumbled along sections of the Trace tramped deeper below ground level than the height of two men. Only a spectral glow guided us through tunnelled recesses as nature's tangles screened out the sun's brightness.

Tough canebrake halted our steps. Slimy swamp mud clung to us. Insects stung our exposed flesh. Five months ago we had lived and slept on flatboats. But on the Trace, thinking of the monotony we had griped about on the Mississippi River flatboats, our minds booted those river days to the level of luxury. Our exhaustion from dawn-to-dusk marching over the hostile terrain scourged us with drudgery that matched the vigor of our hatred for it. The physical demands dropped us each night with numbed feet, aching backs, burning muscles. If we militiamen had held any doubts why General Carroll chose the Mississippi flatboats in November, I understood fully, there on the Natchez Trace, why he had ignored orders "to march with all speed to New Orleans."

* * *

Why didn't General Carroll send us home on boats headed up the rivers? Perhaps lack of funds. I never heard the reason. He did board the militia on schooners to cross Lake Ponchartrain, damn well saved our feet miles and miles of slogging through the canebrake and swamps of the Southlands when we first lit out of New Orleans. Even so, we had a bad trip. On the Lake, severe winds and lashing waves turned the greater part of our militia ill. I had to hold my guts down part of the time myself but got across still standing up.

I shudder to remember again how fever had spread through Camp Henderson beside the Mississippi above New Orleans those last days waiting for Jackson's order dismissing us. The nameless graves held three or four hundred of our men dead from the fever. They added up to fifteen to twenty times our battle losses, figuring we had eight killed and only fourteen wounded. That same swamp fever had dogged us northward. From across the Lake, we marched several days along the Tchefuncte River to its confluence with the Bogue Falaya. There, at the town of Wharton we established another hospital. What the devil, I had wondered, How many will die in these insect-infested tents without enough laudanum to ease their pains and delirium?

On the Tchefuncte riverbank, several of us put in our free time fishing, hooked bass and rockfish. We built a fire, and for that one meal ignored our oversalted pork. The look of utter disbelief on the face of the hospital cook when we handed him a large mess of cleaned fish for the sick men provided the only happy memory I have of that dismal delay.

During nearly every stop Levi wrote in his diary, shared his notes with me. Watching my friend scribe his words, I tried not to laugh aloud over his creative spelling.

> ". . . we went on borde of a scooner and we roed down to the Lake Cast anker till morning on the 19th of March we

set sail for the muth of Chefunkey on the other side of the lake ponchertrain which is 27 miles we was driven to the levee 15 miles, on the 20th, at night we landed at Chefunkey, Then we marched 4 miles and Crost Chefunkey, we marched 2 miles and in Camped then we left The Sick at Horton town, then we marched on two days and left 50 Sick men, Then on Satterday the 28th we arived at By shears and left more of the sick."

* * *

March 28, 1815.

Colonel Edwin Booth rode up, anger in his voice as he addressed General Carroll. "What in hell happened to our supplies? Jackson ordered deliveries here. But there aren't any. You know the men have eaten all the stuff we took on at New Orleans."

My belly growled its hunger and displeasure. I knew firsthand that our slim rations were failing to cover the energy spent tramping the Trace.

"War Department suppliers are contemptible, as always. Putting profits ahead of men's lives. They ought to be shot." General Carroll raged. His voice rang across the campground at Turner Brashear's way station on the Natchez Trace, some two weeks out of New Orleans.

"Yeh. We have a couple thousand hungry men to feed. But count on those bastards to make money first. Like that devil trading from the *Pittsburg* at Natchez." Colonel Tunnell's rage matched Carroll's. "Holding government supplies while he bargained for dollars. Damn his hide, we had to use force to take our own guns, shot, and powder, war matériel Jackson needed. Hope that fraud never gets out from behind bars."

"They're the problem. Those suppliers. More greedy than loyal. We'll have to buy what we can from the Choctaws and sign for the government. Tell the men to forage the rest." General Carroll's worry sounded through his rage. "Issue the orders."

Even though hundreds of men had dropped from our ranks, we still numbered over two thousand, each one a hungry, growling belly. No doubt about it, our militia needed food. No way could we cover the Trace that stretched four or five hundred miles from Natchez to Nashville without mammoth stocks.

* * *

After involved bargaining with the Choctaw people for supplies, charging them to the United States government, we took up the homeward march again, tramping the Trace from Brashear's Station northeasterly toward Grinder's Stand. Our wagons and horses packed with supplies, foraging as we moved north, we gained confidence we would make it back to Tennessee. The officers rationed the food by strict measures to assure we would have enough to match the days ahead.

Yep, we had supplies. And when we rested, Levi noted:

> "... and that night we drew one pound of Beef and one gill of meal to a man. Then we marched on till the next night and drew one half of a pound of Beef and no meat nor salt Then we marched on to By Shears on the Natchey Rode which is 200 miles from Camp Henderson and drew a quarter of Beef to the Company, and about a gill of Chopt Corn to a man, .."

Levi's hesitation as he wrote, glancing at me a few times, suggested that he was thinking of taking me on as his assistant during his next teaching term. Of that move, neither of us could ask the other.

> "... Then we drew 4 days rations of Beef and no salt, on Satterday the lst of Aprile we drew one pint of flower and then we Started on our way that night and drew 3 pints of flower, on Sundy night we drew one pint and half of flower and a half of a pound of pork on tusday night we drew 2

pints of flower, and about 6 pound of pork to the Company on wednesday the 12th we arived at tennessee river which is 223 miles up from the Chocktaw agents . . ."

Although the spirits of most of the men had revived, I did worry about Levi. His long black hair matted against a face that became more peaked every day. He complained of a head cold and an aching back but insisted that he would walk home on his own two feet. Surprisingly enough, despite his coughing spells, every day he matched steps with his squad.

Few human beings met us on the Trace. Some days a couple of men, then five or six, rode by on horseback. Another day, a wagon or two of settlers filled with family and belongings, cows tied behind, passed greetings. Sometimes, a mounted Indian pulled into cover at our approach. Never once did the thieves saddling the Trace with a bad name attempt pillage against us. Our numbers must have kept them lurking in the dimness beyond the trail.

For the Tennessee River crossing on the ferry owned by Chickasaw Chief George Colbert, our officers charged the expense to the military accounts of General Jackson. They complained loudly that Colbert exacted an enormous sum for our passage.

* * *

Near Grinder's Station, General Carroll ordered the militia to attention at the lonely grave of Captain Meriwether Lewis. In silence we stood bareheaded, patches of fluffy clouds casting shadows across the burial spot. We honored the leader who had shared with William Clark command of the expedition that had braved the unknown regions of the Louisiana Purchase and beyond. Ascending the Missouri

River, wintering among western Indian nations, Lewis and Clark had followed the Columbia River to the Pacific Ocean. They had mapped rivers and mountain ranges, collected botanical and mineral specimens, assembled Indian artifacts before returning to

Washington City in 1806 with detailed data and reports for President Thomas Jefferson. The expedition made Meriwether Lewis a national hero.

Later that day, finishing our salty pork and corn pone, we speculated on the fate of that Captain Lewis. Some said he had killed himself, despondent over vicious, unfounded charges that he mismanaged the territorial governor's office at St. Louis. Others branded it outright murder, asserting that ambitious men had lied to open the way for them to take over Lewis's post. Circumstances and fact mixed, clouding definite conclusions. Tragic, the insult to his integrity. Meriwether Lewis, the national hero, lay alongside the Natchez Trace in a nearly forgotten wilderness grave.

"He tried to run an honest office," I drove home the point.

"I agree. Too many out there lining their pockets with government money. Just like our war department suppliers." A sergeant threw his frying stick into the fire.

"Sure thing." The man next to me spouted tobacco juice into the flame. "That Meriwether Lewis made it tough for those bastards to carry on their crooked deals."

I swallowed the last bite of the hardest pone I had ever rammed down my throat. "And he was on the way to Washington City to report how much the crooks at his headquarters were stealing."

An old veteran across the campfire blasted, "Captain Lewis had been Jefferson's aide for years. Lived neighbors to the President. Jefferson knew he was honest and had wilderness experience. So, he chose him to lead the exploring out west. Made him the captain. But the President of the U. S. could not save Lewis from those crooks in St. Louis. Don't make no sense."

"Will any one ever know if his death was suicide or murder?" Colonel Booth voiced the question all of us had.

Revolting. Men's fortunes change overnight: A hero one day, villified the next, destroyed the third. For what purpose? How can greedy, dishonest men so quickly bring down a man as honorable as Captain Meriwether Lewis?

Human beings have a sinister talent. Almost at will, without risk of just punishment to themselves, the schemers, the crooks, can drown any decent man in the muck they create. I felt the old urge to pontificate but held back further words.

* * *

I had my own problems, so I stayed on "alert." I could not forget that Will Briggs and his ilk tramped the Trace with me. After the "execution" threat by General Carroll on the Mississippi flatboat, Briggs had ignored me. We had fought together in defense of our country, but I was certain the "our" ended the minute we had stepped off the Rodriguez Rampart. Carroll's threat must have deterred them for they kept their "place," and I kept mine.

As I walked the ancient Natchez Trace, moving farther away from New Orleans and Gregory Hamilton, doubts kept rising about Isaiah's fate. Every step of the way home was plagued by the misery of my thinking I should have freed him myself.

Nightmares struck during my sleep. One night, I jumped to my feet, grabbed my gun. *The redcoats sneak past our sentinels! They are charging us! I can't see the spot an inch above the white crossbelts! But they keep rushing the mud rampart! I hear the gunshots, the curses of Lucas and Briggs, the screams of the wounded and dying. The sobs of two taffy-haired boys alone on a ship, storm-tossed on the ocean, mix in the screams. I hear the auctioneer's, "Whatamibid! Whatamibid! Whatamibid!" Clovis's crisp, "Seven hundred dollars." The slave he bids for is Isaiah. And through it all Jeannette screams, "No, George! No!" Then disappearing into the background, the skeleton on a big horse drags Isaiah away in chains.*

Breaking out of my sleep, I dropped my Jaeger to the ground. My heart pounded. Sweat ran down my skin, chilled me. One hell of a nightmare—it took several moments to come out of my fright. All around me blanketed men on the ground tossed, turned. Some muttered, others cried out in their own tortured dreams. Far across the camp, I saw that a few men were walking the night away. Nightmares stalk the dreams of men who survive combat.

The tragedy of Captain Meriwether Lewis had been boiling in my mind when I fell asleep, stirring the pains of the past weeks, sharpening the images of people who would live with me in my memories forever. To settle myself, I paced a few yards down the Trace. A night breeze rustled the leaves overhead. In the distance a mockingbird sang. An engulfing sense of loss swept through me. The thought haunted me that if our lives had come together at different angles, Jeannette and the boys and I could have been a family in Tennessee.

Beside the campfire a lone figure paced, a moving shadow silhouetted by the flickering light. Hearing my boots crunch on the vines and twigs on the path, he turned. "Who's there?"

"Private Bush."

I sensed a momentary hesitation by Colonel William Tunnell.

"George Bush." He poked at the fire. "I couldn't sleep, either. Returning to Tennessee and so many of our men left behind. It plagues me."

Difficult, the duty the Colonel faced to inform folks their son, their husband, their brother was not coming home. Glad I do not have to carry those messages, one good thing about being a private, I thought.

"What will you do after you muster out?" Tunnell shifted the subject, passed his mind off the pain ahead for him.

I hesitated, then answered. "Find my one-sixty acres and start up my cattle trading again, Sir."

"You have some enemies in this outfit, George. But other men tell me you handle your deals square with everyone."

"I aim to keep it that way." Speaking slowly, giving myself time to think how to avoid talk about my plans but anxious to bring up the land issue, I said, "I need to find out about the one hundred sixty acres General Jackson promised in his proclamation."

"Each militiaman has earned that bonus. Make your application."

"How can I do that, Sir?"

"A formal claim, signed by each man, has to be filed. I don't know the exact procedure. We'll have to wait for Congress to act."

"That could take months." My voice sounded sharp, as I intended.

"Yes. I think we'll have to persist for some time." The Colonel stared into the flames. "I've wondered myself how long it will take. A lot of us could make use of the land."

"I'll likely need your help to file my claim, Colonel."

"Get in touch with me. I will be in East Tennessee. I'll do what I can for you." Tunnell's voice lightened. "George, I want to tell you that you are one of our best militiamen. I'm proud to have you in this command."

Nice to hear his words. I had not anticipated commendation.

Then he chuckled before he said, "I have never forgotten that day at the Knoxville muster signing you in. Your upset."

Aye, Colonel, you may chuckle over "waiter."

Men began to stir. A couple of grog mugs banged together.

"I've orders to make out for the day," the Colonel closed our conversation.

So, my Colonel William Tunnell connection came to an end. I did consider him an honorable man. His words had matched my trust. He never gave a hint on the entire mission of my doing "waiter" service.

General Andrew Jackson's honor remained to be tested.

* * *

The next morning, crossing the border into Tennessee, we shouted hellos and huzzas. Spontaneous singing broke out. As they had done on the Rodriguez Rampart, some men jigged. Forgotten were our hungry bellies and the last miles when shoes wore out and bleeding feet stained the trail. Even men sapped by fever joined in the milling, boisterous corps. All of us acted like schoolboys, free for the summer.

I was eager to muster out. I needed to grasp Sam's hand, swing Sally around to celebrate with them my survival through the terrible January 8th battle. I imagined her face shining as she lighted the porcelain lamp from New Orleans I was carrying for her in my pack.

Along the route, our officers released men from the militia at the farms and villages they had left to fight the war against the British. I wanted to believe Levi Lee and I might keep in touch. But we both knew too well that the restrictions on me, the dangers of kidnapping if I rode across county lines into strange territory, would hold us apart. The mail service was erratic. I used that as an excuse to cover the real reasons.

"The best to you, George," Levi shouted, waved as he headed toward Nashville. Still coughing, illness preying on him, he needed a companion to walk home with him. He could use my help, I knew, but a feeling buried so deep inside that it hurt to recognize held me back. So, I watched my friend until he turned a bend in the trail and disappeared.

* * *

My company mustered out May 18, 1815, at Knoxville. The Company Pay Roll carried me as "Waiter, Captain Lewis' Company, Col. Edwin E. Booth's Regiment, East Tennessee Militia (War of 1812.) for Nov 13—1814 to June 5, 1815. Commencement of service, Nov 13, 1814. Expiration of service, May 18, 1815. Term of service charged, 6 months, 5 days. Pay per month, 8 dollars,. . . . cents. Amount of pay, 67 dollars, 95 cents. Remarks: Added $18.62 for clothing. S/s Crosby, Copyist."

My pay sure as hell would not buy much. Sixty-seven dollars and ninety-five cents for all those months, plus eighteen sixty-two for clothes I had provided for my own use? Getting myself shot at twenty-four hours a day! Devilishly small amount. I stuffed the money and discharge papers into my saddlebag and headed for Sam's. I chided, "George Bush, you did not enlist in the East Tennessee Militia to get rich. And you still got a hundred sixty acres coming."

* * *

As the trail led eastward, I dreamed of my one-sixty. The sounds and smells and sights of Tennessee spread around me. Robins sang from meadows along the way. Bluejays screamed their mating calls. Even the rat-a-ta-tat of woodpeckers on tree trunks told me I had come back to familiar country. Wild crab apple blossoms. Honeysuckles. Bushes with flowers I did not remember. Trees in bloom. The fresh open smell of spring, scented by all the blossoms. No blood and guts. No fever-ridden swamp odors. No sweat and stench from that New Orleans jail. Even the spring grass seemed to welcome me. Many a time I threw myself down to rest, smothering my face in its green, soft tenderness.

Tennessee in springtime. Home.

15

Sam's house looked neglected, deserted, Sally and Sam nowhere in sight. Nothing appeared changed, but the rooms were empty. Sally's spinning wheel stood in the same spot it had in November, the thread hanging loose. No log burned in the fireplace. Cold gray ashes that lay heaped under the swinging crane, the rusted insides of the iron skillet and kettle that hung on it, showed they had not been used for weeks. Dusting off the small table, I set out the porcelain oil lamp from New Orleans, poured in some oil, pulled up the wick. It looked at home, ready for Sally to light.

The chill of the room disturbed me.

Outside, hollow sounding echoes answered my, "Hello, Sam. Hello. Sally?"

Under the old hickory tree, some distance from the cabin, a figure huddled over fresh lilac blossoms lying on a small mound. Sam looked up at me, tears streaking his haggard face. As he tried to stand, he staggered. I reached out, held him close, heard his mumbled words, "Da lung fevah. In March."

Sam's skinny frame had shrunk to nothing. Weeks of grief had all but consumed my friend. How much longer did he have? Unprepared, shocked though I was at Sally's passing, my first duty commanded that Sam be brought back to health. He would never recover from the loss of Sally. His listless, not caring, almost starved, condition troubled me. The woodenware Sally used for food storage stood empty except for a few of last summer's beans. The butter tub and churn had dried out, crusted on the seams. The wooden mixing spoons hung on their pegs, clean but unused.

"Someones done stole dose hams and bacon from de spring house—all dat food," Sam explained the emptiness. "Chris'mas time, it wus, an' we gone to da church meeting. Den dey came here, stealin'. Made my Sal so sick, dat stealin'. 'Why dey steal?' She cried an' cried, 'I jes' giv dem food iff'n dey be hungry.' An' fer us, all dis wintah we be dead hungry."

Long forgotten adages flitted through my mind—"Man's inhumanity... ," Job's burdens... , the ancient who spent his life trying to push the huge stone uphill. Proverbs and legends might describe my old friend's agony, but they gave little comfort. Early the first day home, I greased the buggy wheels, hitched up, and drove to the store on the outskirts of Knoxville to buy a load of food and supplies.

"Whad yo' up to, George?" Sam revived a little after a dish of warm grits and crisp bacon.

"I plain don't know. Won't until I get my one hundred and sixty acres. The land Jackson promised. Do you remember the proclamation?"

"Yep. I does. Feels guilty. I pusht yo' to inlistin'."

"No, Sam. I wanted to go."

"I done think it ovah. Don' believe de guv'anment evah gives us free mens enny land. Main reason, Jackson, him done got no right makin' dat promise." He paused a moment, coughed before he could finish. "Dat be a trick."

As always, Sam's insight hit right at the core of the issue.

"I hate to admit you damn well could be right." We sat a moment, quiet, seething deep inside. "But I have to believe General Jackson meant what he said. He's big on honor, you know. I also believe Congress has to back him up. So, I'll keep at it till I get that land."

His face inscrutable in the flickering light, Sam stared at the lamp, did not suggest lighting it. He knew I had brought it for Sally. Difficult for Sam, those moments when he slid back into memories. But within several days of my return, he pulled himself out of his worst grief. "Tended bettah, dis place'ud make a real good fahm."

"Reckon Brown would sell?"

"I donno. But we sho' as hell kin try." Sam's shoulders sagged. "You kno' I gots no money."

"No need for you to worry. I can handle the deal."

He stared past me, his eyes fixed on a point beyond my shoulder. I was certain he wanted to ask how we could buy the place, but he took me at my word even though he knew nothing about my money banked in Philadelphia. We talked late, planned our offer to Brown.

The next morning the old fellow hurried the chores, spoke about changes he would make when we owned the place. I hated to slow him down but could not let him overbuild his hopes. "Sam, we have a lot of work around here. Each of us must have a good horse. Too bad the pack horse is gone, but he was old when I bought him. Now, if I can borrow yours today, I'll ride in to town and fit myself out."

"Son. De one in da pasture. He's still good, and he's your'n."

"Not now. Remember? When I joined the militia, I gave the horse to you."

His wan face tried to form a smile. "To keeps till you com'd back. Like da cows. We keeps dem till you com'd back. An' now you done . . ."

"No. Sam. If we work up any kind of a cattle business, each of us will need a horse."

* * *

In Knoxville, I made the rounds of the stock pens and stables looking for a strong-muscled, high-spirited riding animal. Each horse trader tried to impress me that he owned the best in the country. I did not have to look hard to realize that their sales spiel hid the facts, some obvious, others less open. No use wasting time on neglected, untrained, or spavin-jointed stock.

About ready to head home, I stopped at a place across town. To my surprise, a well-proportioned young horse, head high, circled the pen, anxious to get out and run free. I checked teeth, knee joints and feet, prodded his back. Riding him long enough to learn how he would handle, I decided he had good blood and plenty of spirit.

"You know how to pick 'em. That's for sure." The owner stepped closer. "Who you buyin' him for, Boy?"

Boy. For a long moment, I was tempted to say Old Man Brown. To mask my resentment at being called "boy," I dragged out the inspection. The bastard assumed I was just some white man's lackey or slave. Forcing my voice, I controlled each word. "I'm buying this horse for myself."

"That so? You lookin' at an expensive animal." His eyes narrowed. "You got the cash on you?"

We dickered. I talked slowly, held back, guarded against the chance the man would pull a trick to get his hands on my money before we came to terms. My pride insisted that I leave; but needing the horse, I stayed and bargained. It took a couple of hours before we settled on the price, a strong effort on my part to work him down from what I knew was an overpriced deal. Grudgingly, the horse trader conceded a saddle.

From my pack I counted out the right sum, waited to hand it over. "I'll want a bill of sale."

"What'll you do with a piece of paper like that? Just give me the money, and you take the horse. Nuthin' more necessary."

Most honest men offered a handshake to bind the deal. That horse trader failed to suggest even such minimum formality. With doubts rolling to full tide, again I controlled my disgust at his effort to take advantage. "You may think that's enough. But you know I need proof this animal belongs to me."

"Don't trust me, do you? Listen, Niggah, I been dealin' around Knoxville going nigh onto ten years." From deep in his eyes the hard core of the man bored into me. "I'm a reliable business man. Got to be in these times."

Our eyes locked. Through my mind flashed the faces of Lucas, his wife, his son. I heard again the shots fired close overhead. I sensed that the man wished he had not made an issue over the bill of sale, that he would back down to get my cash. He talked about his breeding stock a few moments, finally broke the impasse. "Guess there ain't no real harm fixin' out the paper."

The man obviously had nothing to write on, if he could write. Taking paper from my pack, I scribbled a few words, read them slowly to him. He persisted in having me read them again. Neither of us trusted the other. Over the space where I had printed his name, he marked his "X" with a flourish as if to tell me I was buying from an important person. Then, he reached for the money. I held on to the writing that proved my deal and slipped it into my saddlebag.

The ride home seemed an ideal time for a quick workout. Tying Sam's horse to a tree, adjusting the saddle girth on my new mount, I tested his responses, reined him in. I turned him left, then right. I galloped him back and forth along the trail. The horse showed class. Spirit. I had not seen an animal as choice since leaving Philadelphia. Once in a while, life can be wildly exciting. In the sheer pleasure of racing, I set to rest my latest insult, exuberant that I had taken topside in the deal for the horse. The wind whipped across my face as I let him go full speed.

"Ha! Pennsylvania!" I shouted in my best Philadelphia Quaker accent. "I christen thee Penn!"

He pricked up his ears, pawed the earth, then tossed his head as if to say, "Penn. That's fine by me."

In the yard, Sam walked around both horses as I dismounted, then stood back, eyes on my purchase.

"You done git yo'sef a mighty fine an'mal."

"Took longer than I planned. Didn't see all that much good stock." As I talked, Sam's horse nuzzled him. "You see? Your horse is a smart beast. He knows where he belongs."

"Mebbe so. An' I fix't him wid a name you'd nevah guess." By his deep chuckle I knew Sam had something special to tell me. Across the rump between us, his worn face smiled. "Give'd him da bigges' name a hoss kin carry. Bigger'n your'ns gits."

"I wouldn't lay a bet on that. Not with you," I laughed back at him, warmed to see my friend enjoy a shot of pleasure.

"Old Sam heah tuk a while figurin' out how to ride. Nevah done rode a hoss. Not in me whole life." Swinging into the saddle, he continued. "Tuk a real long time. But he larnt me good, yo' hoss did. Sally watch't us. Kept askin' why I had sich a battle wid 'im." He caught a few breaths. "I com'd off so stiff some nights I cain't sleep. Guess da problem jist me. Mebbe at me age a man don't larn easy like yo' does."

"You must have had a battle, the way you tell it."

"Yeh. But one day I stay on. An' Sally sez to me, 'Sam, you done gone trou' da bigges' battle of yo' life. An' I gots dat hoss a name.' I asks her what. An' she tells me real serious, 'Armageddon.'

"Done stump me for a spell. Den I see da reason. Big battle I done had, fittin' me to dis yere hoss. So, he git 'Armageddon' fer his name. Big battle, 'twas."

"Armageddon. Some name. Good for me, Friend, that I didn't lay a bet with you."

* * *

Before daylight a few mornings later, Sam prodded me, "Let's try Brown fo' da lan' today."

He had the horses saddled before I was out of the cabin. We rode into the plantation as the first slaves headed to the fields.

"I'll see." Brown glared at his former slave, eyed me with suspicion, perhaps affronted by our temerity in asking to buy his land. He brushed us aside. "Maybe later."

Sam had told me Brown was one East Tennessean who figured to make his land into a rich plantation. From what I could see he had "a fer piece" to go.

Fall passed into winter. The landlord accepted my presence on Sam's place. But every time we offered to buy, Brown refused to discuss the sale, would not even name a price. Perhaps he did not believe I had the cash. I felt that Sam's deal with Brown smelled Turley-like, but Sam did not seem to have the same concern. So, we kept working on the place.

Although I tried to spare Sam the hardest labor, he put in long hours, some days outdid me. Our cattle thrived. We bought scrawny ones. They fattened and sold for a good profit. Together, the two of us planned more purchases. I did the buying. Underneath a loose stone at the corner of the fireplace, Sam hid our money. His pride in the growing herd of cattle seemed surpassed by his delight over our increasing hoard of cash. Sam had never held money in his hands. Every few nights, as he counted the silver, his easy words of satisfaction informed me more than anything else that healing was building deep inside him. He was beginning to mend.

Just as I thought he had no problems, late one evening, Sam appeared troubled, finally turned to me. "George, I gots to talk wid yo'."

I wondered what was bothering him.

"Yo' 'members, dat day way back, Sally an' me an' yo'," he coughed, "we talks 'bout our famblies. N' Sally sez her niece still slaves ovah on da plantation?"

"Sure do. Sally took it real hard when Brown's overseer refused to let her visit her niece. I remember he threatened to use the whip. He refused Sally being a freed slave and coming back."

"Well, I gots a few personals Sally wan' he' niece to hab. Tied 'em up in he' bandanna." Sam wiped his hand across his eyes. "Not now, but some time, mebbe you kin tek da passel to her."

"Whatever you want, Sam, will be done."

He did not add, "Befo' I dies." The message it implied focused clearly in my mind.

Another time, Sam turned our talk to the niece. "Some times, me and me Sally said you mebbe ought to fix on marryin' wid Li'l Sal. She mos' pretty." Sam bringing up Sally's wishes showed me he had her on his mind, always. Me free marry a slave? In my own thoughts, Isaiah constantly haunted me. Some nights I saw him safe in the Curry kitchen. The New Orleans anguish lacing his voice seemed in the past. I wanted to believe that a good omen for I did not yet know what had happened to him.

In my memory, too, lay the loss of Jeannette, a loss less poignant for me back in East Tennessee than months ago when I had camped only a few miles from her, a loss less grievous than Sam's but one that I might never have the discipline to bury completely. Images of Emilé and Armand kept surfacing. In my nightmares, I heard their sobs as they sailed from New Orleans for Europe alone. Again, I heard Sally crying at night for her children sold down the river, a grief that had seared every day of her life. Ah, Jeannette, what of your grief in the years ahead?

During the days, Sam spent most of the time outdoors with me. The hard labor consumed his energy, and he slept through the nights. Occasionally, we leaned on the pasture fence, admired our herd, talked of plans. No one challenged our rights to land or cattle. Old Brown stayed away. But deep in my thoughts wariness nagged that some day, when we had the place in good shape, Brown would pull a Zeb Turley and sell it out from under us.

Neither of us mentioned again my marrying Lil Sal.

* * *

In a Knoxville tavern I met the Hawkins brothers. Farmers had told me the men had two-year olds for sale. Sam cautioned that if a man kept his wits he could buy average critters from the brothers. "Dem two be a couple of dirt farmers always lookin' for cash. You gots to be real kerful cause they'll beat you out of anyting de kin."

At the Hawkins place, Amos greeted me first, then Zacharias.

"We've got real fine animals." Amos chewed a straw, squirted juice between his teeth, giggled. "Damn good stock like those in the pen by the barn."

The brothers climbed the rail fence with me, and we inspected several lean, young animals.

"How many you be wantin', George?"

"Only three this time."

"Let you have all seven. At a damn good price." Amos pushed the deal for the brothers. "Our boy Noah's herdin' the rest over yonder behind that thicket."

We dickered about numbers and prices. They both pressed me to take the lot, but I had already set my mind that for the first time around with the brothers I would buy only three from them. They finally agreed.

"You got to put money down to hold them critters. Three or four dollars a piece'll fix the bargain between us."

Aye, the deal had to be clean. But the sickening, calculating looks that passed between them drew my wariness to the surface. I knew they were scheming a way to best me. But more than that, just seeing the way they sat together on the fence made my skin crawl.

I despised the thought of doing business with their ilk, but I needed the critters. Besides, I would never show money to the Hawkinses without a witness. "I'll bring Sam with me Monday to help get 'em home. We'll settle up then."

"That ain't no way to do business, Boy." Amos turned nasty, reached for a couple of muskets leaning against the fence, tossed one to his brother.

"You got to put money down to make the deal. Right now," Zacharias sneered, a slimy laugh spilling out as he eyed my saddle pouch and squirted a thick stream of tobacco juice toward me.

"So, why you here wastin' our time, if you can't pay like we want today?"

"I said I'll come back..."

"The hell you say. You ain't got no money. Too many of you free niggahs running' loose with your schemin' ways." Amos moved to cover me from his side.

"Git out now. Else we'll put the sheriff on you fer trespassin', you Clabber Bastard." Zacharias fingered the barrel of his musket, an ancient left-over from the Revolutionary War days.

As I rode away, the Hank Lucas-Zeb Turley deal spilled around me. But at least by the time the Hawkins brothers crossed my trail I had wised up, was smart enough not to hand them any money. Down the draw, I glimpsed a slave herding cattle. Must have been the one they called "Noah." I did not linger to get a better look at him.

A sleazy pair. I had seen the traits in my first talk with them in the Knoxville tavern. For weeks, the Hawkinses branding me a clabber bastard trespasser rankled. It raked open old scars. What am I? Black? White?' In my head, their jeers echoed, pounding me no less sharply as the days passed, beating a clop, clop, clop over the lesions in my mind.

The incident surfaced all of Sam's old griefs: Losing Sally... Brown's refusal to sell the small corner of ground... Lil' Sal being held in slavery. And as he lived the Hawkins insults with me, Sam seemed to slip back into the depths that had nearly smothered him by the time I had ridden in from New Orleans. I tried to ease his burdens, regretted that I had told him anything about the insults I took from the brothers.

Nothing had changed while I had been in the Southlands. The new put-down mixed with my old defeat. I felt again the confusion, the hatred, of the day Hank Lucas stole my land. Back then riding to Sam's cabin, my mind in turmoil, my free status a sham, I had doubted that my life had direction or purpose. Sally had shaken me out of my self-pity with her challenge, "What's the matter, City Boy, you got both yo' feets chop't off?" That second time, no Sally challenged me.

Spells of frustration, rage, helplessness plagued me. I threw the pitchfork at my tormentors whenever I imagined their faces leered at me from the corner of the barn or the gate into the pasture. I blasted away a few precious ounces of gunpowder target practicing deep in the woods. Looking for land? More cattle buying? What good? For Old Brown to seize at his convenience? Me, a free man? Free for what?

* * *

Despondent by spells, avoiding people, Sam and I stuck to the place. Since my return from the Southlands, the old fellow had begun reviving. A bad event, the Hawkins insult took the last of his heart, and he began losing interest in our work. Never before conceding his need for the "Beulah Land," he longed only to join Sally, slept or dozed most of the time, ate little. His thoughts turned confused, his words became ramblings.

One day, as if making a last request, Sam charged me to deliver the bandanna parcel to Li'l Sal, seemed fearful I might throw it away. Violent coughing spells again erupted from him, but he brushed aside help. My efforts to talk about our cattle, to count the money with him, meant nothing. I knew he was very ill. Hope had deserted him.

Sam failed to rise one morning. I buried him beside Sally under the hickory tree. A few days later, I carved a small wooden cross for the two who had become my family and burned into it: "Sally and Sam Bush. Peace." I gave them my name "Bush," because I knew those two were destined for Heaven. I feared that Saint Peter would choke on the name Brown.

Frequently, I stood bareheaded by their graves, drawn there at dusk some evenings, aware of an inner spirit between us that had spoken no words. Two intelligent people capable of contribution to this world but hobbled a lifetime by bondage. Sally—compassionate, sensitive, direct. Sam—courageous, perservering, insightful. The wooden cross would not survive many years. I would carry with me forever the memory of their friendship, their trust, their home in a remote corner of the East Tennessee hill country.

* * *

As yet, I had formed no plans to move. Attempts to buy the farm for myself failed. Grudgingly, Brown did agree to a year's lease.

My request to write it out drew another insult. "Boy," he sneered, "you don't need any paper. We made a deal. You can trust me."

A couple of weeks later, losing sleep over his refusal to give me any writing, I rode back to the plantation. The discussion again gained me nothing, and ended with Brown's, "Now, listen once more. Careful as you can, Niggah. I have given you my word. You have the place for one year. If you don't want it on my terms, say so now and move your stuff off my land tomorrow."

Trust you, Mister Brown? Like trusting Old Turley? The Hawkins brothers? You, a slaveholder who kept Sam in bondage forty years before you let him "buy" his freedom?

I cannot trust you. But this time I will use you. While I wait for Gregory to free Isaiah, your land will feed me and my cattle. I need this time to go after the acres that Andrew Jackson promised when he wrote "To every noble generous brave freeman of colour volunteering to serve . . . one hundred sixty acres in Land . . ." Without so much as a nod, I reined Penn around, my face, my muscles, hardening as inside me bridled rage seethed every foot of the path across Brown's plantation.

* * *

Trips to the courthouse about my one-sixty acres produced no results. The clerks had no claim forms to fill out. Perhaps they withheld documents from me, I don't know. Their vague responses buried my inquiries, our talks fell apart, and each time I walked away angry. My dander up, I wrote Andrew Jackson at home in Nashville knowing he was immersed in accolades for winning the battles. Public sentiment had spread his hero image far beyond Tennessee. Many men said he should run for President of the United States. Neither my letters to Jackson nor to Washington City brought answers.

For the sake of knowing that Old Hickory's promise did in fact exist on paper, some nights I pulled out the Proclamation. Reading aloud to hear his words ". . . one hundred sixty acres . . ."

seemed to reassure me that my imagination had not created a false promise for land where none actually existed. As always, my every thought lay with the idea that landowning was the key to freedom, independence, happiness.

* * *

For Sally and Sam one duty remained, delivery of the packet to their niece. What few times they had mentioned her, they called her "Li'l Sal." I had formed a mental picture of a miniature Sally, an urchin, no bigger than a six- or seven-year old, with Sally's sparkling black eyes.

On Brown's plantation, the slave who stood beside my horse asking questions about her aunt and uncle did not at all match my image of a child. Grown up since her two relatives had left Brown's plantation, as Sam had said, she looked exactly like a young Sally. The same pert nose and soft features. The same musical tone to her voice. The same eyes, but without sparkle, searching mine. Her up-turned, haunted face could not force a smile. Sensitive like Sally, hurt lay on her in deep layers, unheeled and seeping.

Watching her, thoughts ranged through my head. Grab the girl, ride away with her. Let whites worry about free blacks stealing their slaves. That's just what I'm thinking of doing. But the old caution, the lifelong wariness, took over. The wrong move, and she would die. For her sake and mine, I had to free her legal. To protect her, I would send her north. She would be safe with Mahala and Jonah. Marry her, like Sam suggested? No. That would not work. I could not marry her in spite of Sam's wishing it. Not yet, anyhow. Marrying should be for love. I did not love her. I did not even know her.

Another barrier to marrying Li'l Sal, even if I were so inclined. The law did permit a free person to marry a slave if the slaveholder agreed, but I knew Brown would never consent. In spite of it all, I would never abandon Li'l Sal. In the name of Sam and Sally, in the name of my own father, in the name of my Curry family, I knew I must free her. Buy her, send her home to Mahala. Provide for her schooling with the Quakers.

Standing close to Penn, hiding Sam's bandanna parcel in the folds of her skirt, she talked easily to me. Through her words, I heard the music of Sally's voice. Then, abruptly, she drew away, fear in her eyes, as Percy "Pork" Herrod, Brown's overseer, rode toward us swinging his bullwhip.

"Sal, git yourself back to the kitchen. You got no business lollygaggin' here." Herrod reined his horse around to face me. "Git off this plantation, Boy. We don't allow no free niggahs. You jist cause trouble." One hand snapped his whip as the other slid down to the butt of his pistol. "Don't ever let me ketch you on our land again or messin' with any of Brown's slaves."

A special purpose had brought me here, but telling him everything would not be wise. "The girl's aunt and uncle are dead. She needed to know."

"Don't give me no lip. Damned if I wouldn't put you northern niggahs in jail. We got things hard enough, herdin' a passel of slaves, without you bastards agitatin' among our hands."

If Pork Herrod intended to pull a Hank Lucas on me, he would have to try another day. I turned Penn away. "I'll ride to the house and see Brown himself." Before he could object, I kicked my mount in the flanks as I caught sight of Li'l Sal running across the yard to the slave kitchen.

* * *

Riding Penn toward the big house, I addressed the dichotomy of East Tennessee. A region of small landowners, most of the people did not have the means or the will to own slaves. But here was Brown, one man determined to build a plantation worked by many slaves under the whip of the overseer.

"We can still do business, you and me, George. But you got to understand one thing. I know you're a free northern niggah. Somehow you got hold of money. All the storekeepers in Knoxville say so. The farmers tell me you deal fair with them. But that don't give you no license to mess around my slaves. All my men have orders to shoot on sight any free niggahs hangin' around the slave quarters. No questions asked. No other way I want it."

Brown fingered his cigar, flicked off the ashes as he laid out the rules of his plantation, his jacket flap not quite concealing the butt of his pistol. "I might as well be blunt with you. Don't go wenchin' with my property." His voice thickened. "Don't spout free talk around them. Just stay away from my niggahs. Especially young Sal."

A plan for Li'l Sal had been forming in my mind. I had intended to take my time, work into it gradually. With Brown's threat, I acted on the spur of the moment, blurted out an offer to buy Sally's niece.

His refusal relayed a final, brutal message. "Sal is a breeder. Out of my best stock. I've got the biggest black buck in the state of Tennessee to work on her. He's done her real good. Should be some mighty fine slaves drop from her." Brown sneered, puffed his cigar. "Nope. I'll never sell her. Nohow."

Blurting out my offer to Brown, not waiting to think through my plan, plagued me. I did not make a practice of pushing ahead recklessly. Festering for days over Brown's abuse of Li'l Sal, prodding myself with memory of Sally and Sam, I stored deep in my mind the threats to me at the plantation. How much Brown had heard about me, I did not know. No doubt he figured me for a man panting over a woman, for he could know nothing of my bigger purpose of freeing Li'l Sal and sending her north. I read Brown as a brutal, arrogant hardnose who would always talk down to me. I made up my mind that the next time he would find me tougher. Enough cash should persuade him.

Over Sally's grave, I promised myself to keep after Brown till he sold Li'l Sal to me. My plans had to be well set before another attempt. I knew her abuse went on every day, but I figured my only course lay in letting Brown cool down before I tried again.

* * *

Efforts at planning ways to get my land bonus often overshadowed the proddings to do what I must for Li'l Sal, for Isaiah. Work consumed long hours, but an occasional free evening provided time to write and rewrite letters to Colonel Tunnell, Captain Booth, General Jackson, and the War Department in Washington City.

To Gregory Hamilton in New Orleans, I tailored inquiries with care in the cautious manner Hamilton said he wrote. And I spent days writing a long letter to the Currys telling them to hang onto hope, for I would return to Philadelphia with Isaiah.

Levi Lee? I wondered whether he was any closer to his piece of land than I was. I missed him those first months back in East Tennessee. As near as for any white man, I had felt kinship with Levi. Maybe his being a schoolteacher, seeming to have an open mind, he could understand my people's feelings. We had shared the fighting and some of the good times in New Orleans. More than that he had proved a true friend when trouble came my way on the Mississippi. The letter I knew I should write Levi, I put off to another time.

Weeks, months, passed. All my inquiries about Andrew Jackson's promise of the "... one hundred sixty ..." went unanswered, except for a few lines from Colonel Tunnell saying that, so far as he knew, the government had not established a procedure for filing the land claims. His answer carried well wishes but offered no encouragement.

* * *

Sally and Sam, and especially Li'l Sal, intruded constantly into my thoughts. If the plantation kept Li'l Sal until she had the child, she would be stuck there the rest of her life birthing one slave after another. Brown had refused me. At the next rent payment, I decided to tackle him again.

"Damn your hide, Boy, I told you I'd never sell you any of my property. You've got to understand that simple point. Listen to what I say. The wench ain't for sale."

The smoldering anger that spread across the slaveholder's face sharpened my senses. Watch it, George Bush, I told myself. A mistake now could bring you to a brutal end.

"You don't heed warnin's. None of you arrogant northern niggahs do," Brown snarled. "Take one step toward my slave quarters, and I'll put you in chains. Have Sheriff Dunbar jail you. You cause trouble, agitatin' my slaves. You got no business in Tennessee. None at all."

I held my ground. "I have the cash to buy Li'l Sal right now. You won't . . ."

"The Devil take you! I've told you she's my best breeder. I aim to keep her producin'. Now, git your stinkin' ass off my land, Boy!"

Snapping his riding whip, the tip barely missing my face but chipping skin on my left hand, Brown galloped up the curving drive to the mansion sunning itself in style on a knoll surrounded by aged hickory trees. The only way out for Li'l Sal rested on what could be done to help her escape. A matter of stealing? In the eyes of society, Brown's right to "own" her came from the law itself that classed her "property." I hung onto my temper. Best that I put stealing out of my mind. Keep to legal means first. If buying Sally's niece failed, I would figure the other way. I saw it clearly.

* * *

Any man who talks about injustice, and does nothing, shackles his allegiance to that injustice. Aye, provisions in the law books protect the slaveholder, make defiance of the law illegal. My rights as a free Negro were limited. But in spite of the risk to my freedom, recognizing that America had realigned the paths to justice, I knew I would disobey unjust laws to free the Sam's and Sally's of my country.

Never would I concede Isaiah "slave."

Injustice came through to me as arrogance in the law. The registry law one of the most insulting, the most arrogant. I simply did not list my name in the county registry when I returned to Tennessee. I refused to carry letters of identity and commendation from white men as protection in case whites might stop me and demand proof that I was honest, upright, and free. I considered it demeaning, humiliating, insulting. More than ever because of that registry law, I knew I must always hang onto my freedom paper.

Trying to be independent, having learned bitter lessons from the Turley-Hawkins ilk, I kept myself to a straight line, wary, cautious, vowing never to owe another man money, not for one day. I dealt in cash, figured that would keep my deals too clean for a single complaint. Never would I permit the flimsy whim of a white man to conjure up cause for jailing me.

16

One day I read and carefully reread a poster for a farm auction. Everything not loaded onto wagons would be sold as the family aimed to head west and settle in the Missouri Territory. The sale included cattle but no slaves. I planned to attend.

Bidding developed into the sharpest competition I had faced in months. At one side a lanky young man kept an eye on me. He vaguely reminded me of someone, but I forgot him in the heat of the bidding for two-year olds. I lost every bid. A disappointing sale for me.

As I tightened Penn's saddle girth for the ride home, the young fellow approached. "We got a few head to sell on our farm. Can you look at them?"

The faint recollection stirred in me again. "Do you have any yearlings?"

"Mostly. And a couple of two-year olds."

"I'll ride over some time next week." I looked at him. "Tell me where you live."

"You came twice before." He grinned, saw my uncertainty. "I'm Ben James."

Then, I remembered. On the hill farm before I had enlisted in the Tennessee Militia. "Did I buy two cows from your Ma?"

"You sure did."

"You must be one of the kids who drove them from the pasture. Jimmers, how you've grown."

His red hair and blue eyes rekindled memories perhaps not buried as deeply as I had thought. An illusion flashed before me of a redhead on a hill, the reason I had avoided the James farm even though hearing from time to time of animals for sale by Mrs.

Preacher James. No cause to hang back from buying cattle because of errant feelings about Isabella. They had been put to rest, I was certain, by time and distance and Jeannette.

* * *

The Tennessee hills blossomed with spring flowers, everywhere dots and clusters of color, yellow, red, orange. Some day I would take time to learn all their names, but I did recognize the Dogwood, perfect, pristine, wild, that dotted the hillsides. The stream along the trail sparkled with water from melted snow. The James farm showed little improvement, although spring freshness cloaked the place with a happier appearance than I remembered from times past.

Ben and I rode through the pasture, cut out a couple of animals that suited me. Then, all hell broke loose. A barnyard fracas. Perhaps the younger boy, David, had left the pigpen gate open, I do not remember. The yard filled with squealing, running pigs, David and Ben chasing them. The big boar charged between the boys, changed course, veered for the house with me in pursuit. We raced across the garden patch, trampled the new turnips and mustard greens. I could not head him. Straight to the cabin. Through the door. A shriek. I burst in after him. Heard a girl's high scream as the boar crashed into a butter churn, turning it over. Cream spilled out, greasing the floor. My feet slid out from under me. I took the most undignified fall of my life at Ibby James's feet. My head smashed into the stone fireplace, and I snapped into darkness.

Tresses of red hair hung over my face. A voice close to me asked, "Are you dead?" Her hand touched my forehead. I kept my eyes closed, wondering how in tarnation I could extricate myself from that ignoble position stretched out on her floor, half-churned cream soaking my pants.

I had fantasized Isabella, never expected to see her again. But to knock myself out? Lie at her feet? Put me back on that flatboat down the Mississippi. Even on the pitching deck of one of Captain Stevenson's sailing ships. Anywhere but here.

Drifting in and out of consciousness, fuzzy one moment, sliding out the next, I heard a sharp demand, "What's going on?" Mrs. Preacher James yanked Isabella to her feet. "Ibby! My stars! What do you think you are doing with him?"

Nothing I could say would make sense. I had to get out of there. Dizzy, my head pounding, I struggled upright. Mumbling my apology, I backed through the door, scraping cream off my linsey-woolsey. Halfway from the cabin to Penn, I stumbled, caught myself.

"Wait!" Ibby called. "Your hat. I brushed it for you."

"Sorry for the commotion. I tried to head the pig back to the pen. He got around me." Taking my old beaver hat from her, I fiddled with Penn's reins.

"Your head must hurt. You took an awful crack on the fireplace."

"Feels like I have a lump big enough to last quite some time." I managed a shaky laugh, felt myself sway, grabbed the saddlehorn.

Mrs. James had been watching. "Hey, there," she hollered from the cabin door. "Don't leave if you're hurt bad."

Through the fog I heard her, thought to myself, She does have a good bone in that crusty old body.

"David, git him some cold water," she ordered. "Now, you sit and rest a spell."

Ben loaned me a pair of his patched old trousers, a couple of inches too short for me. When my head cleared enough to walk without feeling dizzy, I rinsed my pants in the stream and draped them over a stump to dry.

Mrs. James invited me to stay for a meal, grits, black-eyed peas, and fatback. As she began cooking, Mrs. James told David, "Go down to the spring house. Bring some milk and butter. And some cheese. Our company looks as if he could use a decent meal."

Lucky, I thought, they had some spare butter. I had ruined the day's churning. We sat on the stoop. A strange family: mother smoking her corncob pipe, daughter wearing a shapeless cotton dress, two boys with arms sticking way beyond sleeve lengths, a still absent father. Isolated, in the Tennessee back hill country. "Poor, but proud," as the saying goes, they extended an unforgettable kindness. Time had brought great change for me since the day Ibby had taunted me with the words, "Shoot him?"

David and Ben fired endless questions about the battle at New Orleans, the way armies fought each other, General Jackson and the militia. Plainly, the Tennessee Militia would have two more recruits at its next call. I sensed they had difficulty forming a mental picture of the Mississippi River, its great length, its whirlpools, the tremendous power of its current, the flatboat trip. At first, Ibby and Mrs. James listened, sitting quietly back of us. Warming to our talk, they began asking about New Orleans and Philadelphia, the people, skeptical how so many thousands could live crowded together in a city. In their excitement, the boys kept questions flowing until their mother reminded them they had chores early the next morning.

Darkness settled over the hilltops and into the clearing. As time passed, the stars glowed brightly, seemed to draw some nearer. In the cabin, Isabella set out a grease lamp, its tiny beam spreading friendship in the dark room. At Mrs. James's suggestion, with relief because my body felt sore and stiff and my head still ached with a dull throbbing, I unrolled my pack on a pile of hay and slept in the corner of the barn.

* * *

From the James place to my cabin, the trail wound for many miles over hills and along small streams, through hardwood forests and across patches of wild grassland. My new cattle, skittish, often balky, strained on their lead ropes.

The trip extended into the morning of the third day. By noon, if all went well, we should make it home, my purchases turned loose in the pasture, Penn fed an extra ration as reward for his patience. I missed Sam. He and Armageddon could sure help. My pants and the sleeve of my shirt smelled a sickly sour from cream particles lodged deep in the material. I must have cracked my skull a dinger on the James fireplace, for at times a pain, sharper than I had ever known, struck through my head.

* * *

A sound wavered on the still air. I drew rein quickly. The cattle plodded into the rear of my horse. A guttural moan, a cough, a catch, a choking. A strangled intake of air, drawn out, rose, then cut off. Must be human. I had heard that kind of moan on the Plain of Chalmette—the anguished distress of a man, wounded, not fully conscious, choking, gurgling his death agony.

Tying Penn to the tallest sapling in a grove, I parted the branches. Edging forward, I avoided making any noise likely to attract attention. Deep in the grove, ropes twined around a tree, two hands dangled, one on each side of the trunk. A young black lashed to the tree moaned again. And for a moment, I panicked. Isaiah? Cannot be. He is far away in the Southlands.

I turned away, sickened by the bloody mass of the boy's head hanging down against his chest. An ear had been cut off. Flies buzzed around the wounds that slowly oozed bloody pus through the crusted surface. Should he be taken down? Might make it worse moving him. He appeared too far gone for help, but I could not leave him there to die. My stomach twisted, my throat tensed. Fear rooted me to the spot, fear for him, for me, in case his attackers watched from behind bushes waiting to shoot or grab us both. Moaning seeped out again, dull, plaintive, the call of the unconscious for help, then stopped as if somewhere inside him human sensibility knew that help had come.

Listening for a spell, satisfying myself that the calls and songs of birds bore no cautionary notes and that we were alone, I moved fast. The tough hemp ropes hindered me, but I finally hacked through them, braced the wounded boy's body against mine, slowly eased him to the ground. The movement forced fresh blood from the side of his head. His back dripped bright red, raw and torn, a network of many lashes laid one over another. Placing the body face down, I gently turned his head so that the ragged remains of his ear gaped upward.

On my hands and knees, I listened for the sound of breath or moan. He seemed more dead than alive. The bleeding had to be stopped or he would not have a chance. Ripping off my shirt and tearing strips from it, I folded them into thick padding, covered the wound and bound it securely, tied cloth over other cuts. The body shuddered. A movement. Shallow breathing.

He was alive.

I relaxed a few moments, my back against a log. Through my mind pounded the words the clerk at the courthouse had read from the Tennessee law book, punishment prescribed for runaway slaves: ". . . ordered by the court to have one ear nailed to the pillory . . . and the ear cut off . . . and the other ear cut off at the expiration of one other hour; and . . . thirty-nine lashes well laid on, on his or her bare back, at the common whipping post." Whatever had happened, the boy's mutilation looked far from official to me. I believed some scoundrels, out for backwoods revenge or willful mayhem, had laid the misjustice on him.

"Better not delay getting away from here. Those devils could still be on the prowl in these woods," I muttered to him. Of course, he could not hear. Then, I said under my breath, "They might sneak back to cut his head off and spike it on a fence as a brag or a warning to us blacks to keep our place." I unpacked my Jaeger, loaded it, wary for what might strike from the thickets.

Stories flooded my mind, tales whispered among my people, circulated by word of mouth, most often by slaves who had escaped or been freed. I remembered tales of grandmothers wise in the art of mending the human body. They knew how to bind flesh cut open by the tips of leather whips, to heal knife slashes on slaves who had displeased their masters. Always, they cautioned, "Cover a wound with a poultice of sycamore leaves." I could fix a poultice from leaves of the large tree near my cabin.

I should have listened more carefully back in Pennsylvania to learn what the grandmothers had done for a body torn as badly as this one. Or to Sally who knew so much about herbs. The ginseng roots—what did she use them for? My mind, trying to picture the events that had brought the young man to his tragic condition, slowly recovered from its shock. I concentrated on the task of moving him. His life depended on immediate care.

*   *   *

Suddenly, I heard boots crunching through the underbrush. Concealed behind a clump of bushes, hand on my knife, I grasped my gun as two men poked their way through a grove a short distance from us. I entertained, but quickly rejected, the urge to capture them, slash off their ears. Showing my face would mark me. Two of them could run me down like an outlaw. I had survived my own crises, still had too much to do, to end my life by reckless action.

When the men reached the edge of the clearing, I decided. "Stop! Or we'll shoot!" My voice boomed in the best of my acquired Tennessee accent. "Drop your guns!"

Startled, they stared, raised their muskets. But I was hidden and they could not see me.

"You heard the captain. Drop your guns!" I shouted, cloaking my words with the much different accent of Philadelphia boyhood, so the marauders would believe they faced more than one gun.

"Ready. Aim. Fire!" Presumably the captain's order, and I put a shot in their direction, high and wide.

For the first time they reacted, one, then the other, letting their muskets slide to the ground as they backed away. Jimmers, one was Amos Hawkins! My mind flashed to that day he had spattered shots at me. The other one hidden in the brush looked like Will Briggs from the flatboat, I could not be sure.

Moving quietly several feet, keeping myself hidden by the bushes, adding a gruff, throaty tone to my voice to imply that still another man stalked them, I yelled, "Listen to me. We have a good look at your faces. Get out or we'll move in on you. We'll shoot on sight if we ever see you hereabouts again."

Both men turned, took a few steps, crashed through the woods. Picking up their muskets, I followed, screening myself from them. After several minutes they stopped at the bottom of a hill, their eyes scanning the slope toward me. Making my voice forceful, but raising its pitch in order that they would assume yet another man pursued them, I shouted, "Keep moving," and fired one of their guns into a tree and close above them. Both men fell over a tangle of bushes. Straightening, they took off as fast as they could run. I got a full face look at the second man.

Will Briggs. Aye. Brave mutilator of a boy. I would not be any man's cold-blooded murderer, but I sure could put spurs to his soul. Faster than I had fired my Jaeger for the bull's-eye test at the militia muster, I reloaded, fired. Grabbing Briggs's musket, I fired a shot at the heel of his boot, a second one just past his left ear. He jumped sideways six feet, it seemed. Watch the white man dance. Once in a man's lifetime, fate hands him the chance to tread the winepress and drink its sweetest wine. Huzza! Huzza!

Trailing Briggs and Hawkins a considerable distance to make certain they had been scared away, I sized up the situation. They must have horses tied within walking distance. What if they rode back with more men and guns?

Most urgent remained the task of mounting up, carrying the maimed boy home. From past experience, I knew the Hawkins ilk ran loose, ruffians as tough as our worst Mississippi flatboat pilots. Best keep your guard up from here on, I warned myself. Let them surprise you, and the boy and you could end up a double murder.

On the way back to the clearing, a troublesome concern nagged. Anyone could take me for an armed bandit, stalking the trail with a knife, my Jaeger, and their two muskets. Me carrying an arsenal of weapons? A clear violation of law. No explaining that to the authorities.

I adjusted my pack, shuddered at contact with the torn body. He hung limp, a dead weight, difficult to handle. The hideous injuries still horrified me as much as had the first sight of them. With him finally secured across the saddle by loops of the hemp rope, I took to the trail, an eye out for signs of pursuers. If anyone jumped us, tried to take the boy again, I would kill him, that I knew.

Of my limp bundle, except for strangled moans, the question kept repeating, How will you survive, cut up the way you are? Anywhere, any place, you will be a marked man. If life hangs on appearances, the best of luck will not pull you through.

A stench clung to him. Flies buzzed around us, settled on his blood. We stopped many times. The jostling on horseback loosened the crude bandages, blood-soaked and difficult to retie, while my hand swept away for brief moments the gnats and flies that hovered over us. Each resettling of the body over the horse took extra effort. My patient needed water but did not realize that someone raised his head and tried to help him drink. No other walk in my entire life had been as exhausting. My new critters tied to ropes pestered all the way, tried to break away to freedom.

* * *

Late that night, the unkown boy resisted being lowered onto Sam's old bed. If only Sally and Sam could help me. Who else could be trusted? None of my people lived close by. Brown? Hell, no. Mrs. James? She would be against such violence, but I could not load that burden onto her, not with her struggle to survive. No choice but to tough it out myself. If anyone learned of my helping a runaway, my life would come to a bloody end. The Hawkins and Briggs muskets offered damning evidence.

Figuring how to ease the boy's pain, I remembered Sally saying, "Da ginseng. Dat's good medicine fo' what ails yo'." I had watched her clean the ginseng roots the day the young Alabama freedman stopped for a spell, listened closely to her. "Ginseng do much curin'. Makes fo' sleep. Settles da head when yo' gots big worries. Heps da stomach upset. If'n yo' hab a bad pain inside, it cuts da pain. I keeps it in da house all da times. Mix wid hot watta, drinkin' it jes makes yo' feel bettah."

Poking around in her baskets, I found a cloth sack with crushed and powdered bits of the root. Sally had brewed ginseng tea for Sam whenever he lacked the zest she thought he ought to have. "Drink dis to fix youse'f up."

I brewed a pot, but the young man refused when I held him up and tried to pour some of the healing liquid into his mouth. He dropped back, listless and unseeing. So, I drank the brew myself. I needed fixing up, too.

Thoughts of an attack, of the need to keep the extra weapons, prompted me to conceal the two muskets. I hollowed out space from the top of Sam's grave, wrapped the guns in old cowhide water-proofed with tallow, put boards under and over them. A place no one would think of searching. Smoothing out the grave and tossing dried leaves onto the ground, I clearly heard Sam's wry chuckle for my choice of hiding place.

* * *

Uneasy through the night, dozing by spells, alarmed when the young man cried out in the stillness, I eased him back down when he attempted to stand. Perhaps realizing that he had found help, someone who would not hack off his other ear, he finally sagged on the cot, a limp heap the rest of the night.

After tending my stock in the gray hours before sunrise, with pails of water fresh from the creek and rags torn from the rest of my shirt, I washed off the caked blood, applied packs of sycamore leaves to the wounds. The boy tossed in restless, fevered sleep, still could not take a drink. At times his eyes opened wide, stared wild and unseeing around the room, my words not understood.

His ravings told me very little: "My papers . . . my papers . . ." Or "Noah. Gotta catch Noah."

"Who's Noah?" My question, asked between his ravings, brought no answer. That name? Where? Jimmers! The Hawkins brothers! Noah was their slave! I had seen him in the draw the day the bastards shot me off their land.

"Noah. Gotta catch Noah." He tried to raise himself, fell back.

A pause, more fevered ravings, "The papers. They're mine. Gimme my freedom papers, Noah."

Overlaying the face of the unknown on the cot, Li'l Sal's image faded in and out. I feared I had let too much time slip by before confronting Brown again. Then, Isaiah's face flashed before me. I could not stand the thought of Isaiah being mutilated like that young man. Had Gregory Hamilton waited too long? My patient held me in the cabin, but I had to get Li'l Sal away from the plantation stud even if my plan fixed on stealing her. I wanted to lunge out, then checked myself. Rage could force me into a careless move. Stealing Sally's niece required planning, caution. I would be Brown's first suspect.

Rags soaked in cool water soothed the oozing wounds, painful and itching. Plans formed in my mind of what to say, how to handle myself, if anyone set foot on my place. Each plan seemed less than satisfactory for avoiding trouble, but I kept trying. One thing for sure: White men would never take us alive and cut me up the way they had done him. In the event of an attack, shoot to kill. *Artificial instinct?*

"Come back, Noah. Gimme my papers . . ." More often than not, the scarred young man's words, agonized and incoherent, smothered in moans. At times he screamed in terror, struggled in semisleep, shook as if fighting the men who had slashed his body.

The stench of decaying blood and flesh, the odor of a dying boy, hung in my cabin. A few times he roused, cried out, "I'm free! I'm free!" Between ravings, he would lapse into deep senselessness. Too weak even to crawl from the bed, he could not defend himself against an intruder. The door had to be tightly secured during my absences for chores and hunting.

From the torn boy's few words, I pieced together his story. Freedom must be new and precious to him, he raved so often, "I'm free." He never once said his name, but clearly Noah had to be the Hawkins slave. The brothers had said that day that "Noah" was herding their cattle. Noah must have run, met the young man in the woods. Then, while his new friend slept, Noah stole his freedom papers and lit out, leaving this unknown one to be caught, beaten, and mutilated as a runaway slave.

* * *

Nights haunted me more than days. Did that different sound in the darkness signal the approach of Amos and Zacharias? Will Briggs? Did the distant baying of hounds mean they had picked up our scent? Recollections disturbed me. Slaves tortured into unconsciousness, backs slashed, fingers cut off, testicles crushed, rapes, faces knife-marked. Sam's foot half chopped off. No wonder Noah ran. No wonder African men and women risked their lives as runaways. No wonder freedmen hereabouts seldom made contact with each other, just kept their place.

Jimmers, I had thought this is a great country for raising Jeannette's boys?

As infection spread through the young man's body, death picked at him, sapped his strength. The ravings became less frequent, weakened, finally ceased. Obsessed with the name "Noah," he seemed to have no need to speak his own. Unnamed and unknown, he died in my cabin. Whatever presumed healing power the sycamore leaves might have, they proved inadequate to repair his injuries. Under the sycamore tree, the earth tapped flat, leaves and chips from my woodpile scattered and kicked over it, the unnamed lies in a grave nobody can find.

* * *

"You may think you're one smart cattle trader. But we'll larn you to keep your place." Pork Herrod leaned forward in the saddle, rasping a whip against his saddle flap. "Brown and me, we've both told you enough times to stay away. But you keep turnin' up here. A true-to-hell devilish nuisance. Mebbe I'll tie you up and take that other horse you got in tow."

Cursing, Herrod reined toward Armageddon tied behind Penn for Li'l Sal to ride if I could buy her. He started to speak, but the sound of hoofbeats interrupted. "What you got, Herrod? I told you before, I don't want no trouble around here." Brown called out, pulled his mount to a stop.

"We got a simpleton on our hands. Best we tie him up in the barn and git the sheriff first thing in the morning."

"What you want here this time, Boy?" Brown sneered at me, flicked his whip.

"Sir," my voice choked on the word, but I had made up my mind to be polite, humble, ingratiate my way into Brown's agreeing to sell Li'l Sal. "Sam said you were always kind to . . ."

"If you're leadin' up to buyin' my slave wench, hear me again. The answer is NO. Same as always, NO." His voice burned like the hot branding iron searing flesh. "She's prime breedin' stock. A mistake ever lettin' my old Sally go. Never again." Brown's eyes bored into me. "I aim to make this place a first—rate plantation. I need every hand and every acre I can get."

Before my few words about buying Li'l Sal could be spoken, they had cut me off. I tried again. "Sir, any man has a price for a piece of property. You must have a price for her. Just name it. You'll be paid. Right now."

"Even if you got the cash," Brown tilted his head, "I would never sell a slave to a northern free niggah. Not under no conditions. Sure not when I got a purpose to keep her." Brown turned to Pork. "Report him to the sheriff tomorrow, Herrod. And if the blockhead ever sets foot on my land again, shoot him on first sight."

They rode away together, leaving me with no doubt of Brown's intention for me. A sense of failure spread through me, a recognition of loss akin to my defeat in failing to persuade Jeannette that she must free her slaves.

* * *

At the edge of the barn, a man hammering hot metal on an anvil straightened, eyed me a moment, his expression and a bare shrug of his shoulder conveying the message that he had heard us. As I kicked Penn's flank and headed away, I recognized him. Jim who had pulled me out of the Mississippi River the day Briggs and his cohorts had attacked me. Jim who had ridden the flatboat to New Orleans and served as another stand-in-place on the Rodriguez rampart. I had seen him blacksmithing at several farms where I bought cattle. Sheriff Dunbar earned cash for himself by hiring Jim out by the day horseshoeing for other farmers. Not likely Dunbar would ever permit Jim to buy himself. Without a word, he turned back to his work, and I rode on. We both knew the law barred me, a free man, from speaking to a slave.

* * *

The months linked one onto another, months with a fresh round of my letters about the one hundred and sixty acres unanswered. Aye, I did receive a single reply from Captain Lewis. Like Colonel Tunnell, he offered nothing definite, only suggested, ". . . keep writing the military department in Washington City."

A sense of defeat preyed on me. Chagrin fevered me for being played a sucker. I had bit on the promise of one hundred sixty acres. I had performed the required militia service. Sweat broke over me every time I thought again that no one intended to hand over land, not to a black man. I wanted only to pioneer in the East Tennessee wilderness. Plow land. Plant crops. Raise cattle. I cursed in my barn, cursed at my cattle. I kicked the milk bucket, stabbed the pitchfork into bundles of hay.

"Damn the law. Damn Andrew Jackson. What a fool I am."

Penn shied away from my outbursts. I nearly missed the saddle a half dozen times.

Everywhere, whether in town stores or in remote cabins, people talked of Andrew Jackson, how he had won the Second War for Independence against the British at New Orleans. Men promoted Old Hickory for the office of President of the United States:

"Andy will get rid of the crooks in Washington City."

"He's one of our greatest leaders."

"Andrew Jackson will fix the nation's problems."

"A man what beat the British can lead the nation."

"Old Hickory represents all the people."

With the many national issues pulling at him, what would Andrew Jackson do for us Negro militiamen? His regard for the men of his corps had always been high. That day at the Cabildo, in the midst of the grand Southland celebration, he gave thanks to God but praised his troops for the victory. Then he ignored us. He forced us into a corner to be forgotten, the same as he had forced the Creek Indians to live in a corner far from ancient tribal lands. His indifference to the suffering of the Creeks turned them into a people neglected and forgotten. In his treaty terms with them, he seized twenty-three million acres for the United States.

We war veterans needed land. Praise is good, but you cannot plow it.

My mind harbored an awful nagging that had begun back on the Knoxville muster ground, a rising doubt that the passage of time was beginning to settle into certainty. There would never be a land bonus for me. My apprehension rose into certainty that a clash with Brown would end my tenuous hold on his piece of ground. I saw no ready solution to either concern. Anger rode me as my cattle business took me across the countryside, sometimes to the Preacher James farm.

* * *

We accepted each other easily, the James family and I. We laughed together over my feet-first, butt-skidding entry into their cabin. An easy companionship grew among us, similar to mine with Levi Lee. Friendly as our times together were, they never became as open or as direct and family-like as with Sam and Sally or the Currys. Ben and David shared their favorite fishing holes. We stalked game in the breaks along the river. In the evenings around a warming fire, they questioned me about the world beyond Tennessee. We talked again of New Orleans, Philadelphia, the sights that only a city offers. Experiences around the country, commonplace to me, transformed into tales of adventure for the boys. Then, the sight of wild horses on the western slopes up from the Mississippi River flashed across my memory. Laughing over my story of their graceful speed and wild neighing, we three agreed we ought to shuck our chores and ride west to chase the wild beauties.

Some trips I brought a load of provisions. Although she had so little to do with, the first time I brought gifts, Mrs. James had said, "No. You don't have to git anything for us."

"Sharing comes from both sides," I had countered. "You have shared your home with me. Let me share these with you."

Ben had overheard the conversation, walked to his mother's side. "You do enough, George. Always working around here."

We turned as David, pulling at my pack, whooped, "Hey. These pants look like mine. I'll take 'em."

From then on no one questioned my sharing with a household bare by all standards. To avoid undue show of interest in Isabella, whenever my pack contained something special for her, it also held an item for every other member of the family. Tools for the boys. A shovel for the barn. A copper kettle for cooking wild apple butter. A can of pepper, unheard of in the James kitchen. A new tin pail. Oilcloth to cover the bare table. Pewter dishes for the house to replace the handmade clay mugs and plates. A family-sized, heavy Dutch oven for Mrs. James. The day I had given it to her I saw a tear or two on her cheek and heard her say under her breath, "Oh, Lawd, to own one of these." In it she later baked a sea-pie, a feast of ham, bacon, small bits of jerked beef, fresh squirrel, dusted with sage and pepper, encased in a thick crust of butter, lard, and cornmeal.

The gift I felt Isabella treasured the most was a mountain dulcimer, its tone sweet and pure. I had it carved from an ancient chestnut by a Tennessee musician.

As I rode toward the James cabin one afternoon, Isabella sat on a stump, her hands behind her back. Mrs. James stood at the side of the door, smoke curling from her pipe. David and Ben leaned against the fence. Evidently, the family had been waiting for me.

"Here. Ma and I made this for you." Ibby's eyes glowed. She laughed as she handed me a new coonskin cap, a splendid tail hanging from its back. "Ben shot the coon some weeks ago."

"Jimmers! You've read my mind. I been figuring how to make one. But I'm not the best hand at working fur." Swiping off my old beaver felt, I settled the coonskin on my head as the boys ran whooping toward me.

"Now you look like you belong in Tennessee." Isabella had been holding her dulcimer. As she picked the notes, the family sang folk songs I had never before heard, tunes familiar to the Tennessee hill country people.

Then Isabella tossed her red hair to one side, faced me, "What is your favorite, George?"

Together, we sang the oldest of songs:

> "Greensleeves was all my joy,
> Greensleeves was my delight.
> Greensleeves was my heart of gold,
> And who but my lady Greensleeves."

* * *

Work around the place never quite ceased, but the boys and I slipped in fishing and swimming in the river, mostly on weekends. With my help they repaired fences, dug a pit in which to bury slaughtered animal parts, cut a shorter trail to the river. Mrs. James's friendliness matched that of her sons.

At times, Isabella joined us. On sunny days the two of us hoed in the garden, carried water from the creek. Once in awhile our hands touched. My eyes met hers. In their sky-blue depths, I read a hunger equal to my own, my feeling for her no longer fantasy but a reality that I had bridled to keep from action I knew Mrs. Preacher James would never condone, a reality unmentioned between Isabella and me.

Sometimes, the redhead dared me to a race. We would speed down one slope, up another, running far from the cabin and into the hills, racing free, the wind brushing our faces. Late on an afternoon I still remember, our race across the pasture took us over the rail fence. She tripped, fell to the ground. Quickly, naturally, I lifted her up. Easy it would have been for my black and white halves together to rest her against my chest, to keep the redhead in my arms. I wanted to! Oh, did I want to!

* * *

A Sunday morning.

Mrs. James met me in the yard. Red-eyed, brushing tears from her cheeks, she choked, "Ibby. She's gone."

"Isabella gone?"

"Pa and me, we sent her with Pa's brother Robert. To work for his family."

"Where?"

"Don't know where they'll stop. Just headed west a fer piece. Lookin' for a new start. Mebbe out west in a place called Missouri. Lots of Tennessee folks goin' there."

"You and the boys will sure miss her." My attempt to cover shock and dismay sounded flat. So much more I needed to say.

"I know." She hesitated. "But I'll be straight out with you, George. Last time when Pa came home, he complained he didn't like you bein' here so much. Said it meant trouble for Ibby. For all of us." Looking away, she continued, "I seen how it was for you two. Had to stop it before things went too far. Best for both of you."

The air of friendliness had chilled. My young fishing partners, usually the first to greet me, put in no appearance. Further talk, argument, would change nothing. Mrs. James and Pa had made the decision for Ibby. For me, too. Without another word, Mrs. James turned her back on me. At the door to her kitchen, she paused, half-turned as if to say something, tears on her cheek. But she stepped inside, and the door closed on unvoiced dreams of Isabella and me.

* * *

Red sunset splashed against a cloud-dusted blue sky. Red hair blowing free in the wind, blue eyes, a white homespun dress fanned against tiny breasts of a long-limbed girl standing high on a Tennessee hillside.

A dream? A vision? Mind wanderings?

No.

I first saw her that morning long ago, heard her never-forgotten words, "Shoot him, Ma?"

Never again would Isabella James race me over the Tennessee hilltops, our hands brushing against each other, her strawberry red hair streaming as the wind whipped our faces.

No letter came from Gregory Hamilton.

A hawk swooped down, seized a rabbit in its talons. My eyes followed the predator's flight up and over my pasture, his gray earth tones blending him against the hillside. He swept high above, carrying his helpless victim. The figures outlined sharply against the depth of cloudless sky as they hung seemingly motionless an instant before the predator turned back in his flight. The bird a speck in the distance, my thoughts fixed more on Isabella James than on my work. A sense of loss, sadness, defeat walked with me every day since her parents tore her from my life.

17

In the distance, where the trail rose over the far ridge, a man rode toward me, his horse at a lope. I reached for my Jaeger, eased my grasp when I heard Jim's call, "Bush? George Bush?"

Why had he come? Always, we could only silently recognize each other at Brown's plantation or at the farms where I had seen him at his blacksmithing. Few words had passed between us during the river descent to the Southlands. Never could we make contact in New Orleans in spite of the fact he had saved my life that day on the Ohio.

"Don't worry none, George," Jim extended his hand. "I need to talk to you. Can we git inside somewhere?"

Inviting a slave into my home, I, a free man, broke the law.

"Sure. Let's sit in the cabin."

"I can't take much time." He closed the door, lowered his voice. "Risky, me coming here. Terrible risky. But I has to warn you about the . . ."

"What do you mean, warn me?" Surprised at his bluntness, I could not hold back my question.

"George, don't go back to Brown's plantation. Never again. Not for no reason." He searched my eyes. "Day before yesterday, Brown, he come to the jail. Sheriff Dunbar and him, they be plannin' to trap you. They say next time you come demandin' to buy Li'l Sal, they'll fix you. They'll get you. For trespassin'. For agitatin' around Brown's slaves. Brown, he's real mad. He say he'll git up a patrol with Will Briggs and other men. He said you're one northerner what won't keep his place. They joked. They goin' to treat you special for wenchin'. The way . . ."

"But, Jim, I have never . . ."

"Jes' lemme finish. Won't make no difference what you say. You know that. Go there agin, and they'll set you up for a 'fair trial' one day. String you up the next, or put you in prison thirty years. 'Pears to me they aim to put you out of the way real soon."

We sipped mugs of steaming hickory coffee, sat in silence several moments. He chewed a slice of my tough bread. His words boomed in my head. The dead Hank Lucas's musket pointed straight at my chest. Hawkins's shots sounded in my ears. Will Briggs snarls threatened.

Jim had saved my life on the flatboat trip. In my cabin, he was risking his life to warn me. Why? Erect at the table, thin and angular, the play of light at times bringing out features like Sam's bony cheeks, he appeared unpretentious. His eyes penetrated, expressed emotion his face masked. His hands ran along the edge of Sally's table, and his gaze lingered on the pile of her patchwork quilts, not touched since her death.

"George, I knew Sam and Sally many years. But since the day they been freed, we couldn't visit none. You know how it is. Freed folks and us slaves, we is in danger if we visit."

"Would you like to see their graves?"

We stood beside the marker. Slowly, he sounded out the words, "Sally and Sam Bush. Peace."

Jim laid his arm across my shoulder. "You got to be all right, George Bush. They loved you like you be their son. Good you gave them your name."

Tears in his eyes?

"Sam worked all them years buying their freedom. He got me thinkin'," Jim continued. "I been savin' money the Sheriff holds back for me. From the jobs him hires me out to. In a few more years, I be ownin' myself, less'n he welches."

"Sally told me about Sam's struggle to keep working. Working so he could buy the two of them."

"George, Sally feared maybe they'd die or something happen before they were freed."

"Sam knew they could not trust Old Man Brown."

"Fearing he'd never let them go free. He kept them slavin' so long."

"Jim, I know a little of what you're going through now."

"Some days my life seems useless. Don't know if I can keep on. There ain't no choice but to buy myself. Can't risk runnin' and gittin' caught." Jim's voice hardened. "I guess you know, every time the Sheriff hires me out, he writes me a pass. Jes' like the law says to do. Today, my pass says for me to go horseshoein' over yonder a piece." Our eyes met, held. "I got to be mighty extra careful. Else, I'll be a slave the rest of my life."

When a few steps from his horse, Jim turned, grasped my arm. "George, people comes to crossroads in their lives. I been there many times. Mostly, a man has to decide by hisself the road he takes. Ain't many what can hep you. Few you can trust." He took a deep breath, his concentration so intense a man could feel it. "Me and you, we can trust each other. I know Li'l Sal was a big worry to Sam and Sally. And now, she worries you."

Jim stopped. His eyes narrowed in momentary scrutiny as if looking inside my soul, searching the core of my being. "I need more time for talkin'. But we don't have it today. I must git on to my work." Then, in a low voice, "You needs to know there's a few of us what keep helping slaves run north to freedom. Li'l Sal done gwine to run next. Her and that big man she loves."

A cold shiver trickled down my spine. For once words would not come. Seldom had a man so quickly earned my respect. Brave, I knew. He had rescued me from the icy Mississippi. Appearing plain, uncomplicated, a slave himself, now he was risking his life to help runaways? Awesome.

"We have plans for Li'l Sal to run north, like I said. She's got to get away. That's why I has to make sure you never go back to Brown's. And I needn't have to say you must keep everything I've said to yourself. Lives depend on it."

"How can you get her away?"

"Best not talk now."

"Can't I help Li'l Sal? I've got money that . . ."

"Jes' you stay away from Brown's plantation. Don't make trouble for her. You face too much danger youse'f. George, I must say agin, Brown means to put you away. Real soon. He may leave you alone a while yet. But he figures you'll keep comin' back for Li'l Sal. That's part of his trap."

"I hate to give up, but I understand what you're saying. If my going there makes trouble for Li'l Sal, I'll stay away. But, Jim, for God's sake, let me help."

I dashed to the cabin, brought him cash from our store of cattle money. Sam would have approved. And I told Jim to send Li'l Sal to the Free African Society and Mahala.

"I'll see to it that Sally's niece gets your money when she runs. It will sure help her when she gets north. Good for her to know she has a place to rest. And I thanks you for her."

Jim tucked my money into his sack, and as he swung onto his horse he emphasized his warning. "I'm not one to tell another man what to do. But I feels real strong friendship for you. George, I know you stand at the main crossroad of your life right now." Jim's eyes searched mine again. "You ain't got no choice but to head out to another part of the country. Fast."

As my friend's figure dimmed with distance, my mind beat with the warning. It drove from one corner of my head to the other as I hustled about my chores. Another day that I wondered about hell. Is hell divided? One part a white hell? One part a black hell? One devil white, one devil black?

18

The night before Scamp had followed Turner to his death, I heard footsteps outside, muffled voices, horses in the distance. Scamp lay dead the next morning at the corner of my barn.

A few nights later, strange hooves beat again, midnight riders. Staring out into the moonlight, I saw shadowy figures slipping along the trail beside the river bordering my pasture. Another late hour, hearing the baying of hounds, I barred the door, made certain no embers glowed in the fireplace, waited. A burning sweat festered on my skin.

Then came the time, riding home from Knoxville, when I had been stopped on the trail, challenged by a slick looking pair on exceptionally fine horseflesh for that part of the country. They had questioned me the better part of an hour before I managed to persuade them of my free state. It had been difficult to keep cool while I hung onto my paper as they read. On the dash home, I pushed Penn into galloping near his limit.

Each jab bred uneasy late hours. Nightmares wrestled me, turned my sleep fitful. I tossed, sweated, sometimes came half awake, bolted upright whenever the cloven hoofs of hell clattered through my dream tortures.

The direct threats to my existence dumped me into a state of numbness. Rage often kept me awake, and I worried about the fate of Li'l Sal. My loss of Isabella cut a deep wound even though I had seen no road we could walk together. I turned inward. Always at the surface, Jim's warning beat at me, plagued every thought of what I wanted to do.

In my worst moments, I doubted my safety. Would I be forced to walk the path Isaiah had walked? Did my kidnapping lie ahead?

My work slowed. I avoided people, quit buying cattle, sold off all but a few skinny ones. The days began weaving a pattern of aimless wandering along the river, across the hillsides, until the sight of pasture land and fields I would never own, a cabin that would never be home, turned life into the worthless puff Clovis had made of Veta's gris-gris balls.

During my absence one day to buy supplies, an intruder nailed a blood-encrusted, dried black ear onto my cabin door. Horror stricken, I headed with Penn to the pasture, but he reared back, whinnied, refused to go. Then I saw the dead cow propped up with poles at the gate. Jim had said my time on the Brown land would be short. The ear nailed onto my door and the dead animal underscored his warning.

Survival could depend on packing up and riding away in a matter of hours. Where to? What state?

* * *

My belongings, supplies, other possessions lay in piles on the floor between the fireplace and the door. Clothes, dried grain, chunks of smoked pork, blankets and my rug, utensils, books, a paper where I had written down Sam's remedies for sick cattle, and a few personal items filled the bags Armageddon and Prince, my new packhorse, would carry. My freedom paper and money I stowed inside my shirt. The remainder of my household goods I flung onto glowing coals. They smoldered, then burst into flames. The muskets buried with Sam? Better not leave them to be discovered. Dismantled, out of sight in the bottom of my large pack with my Jaeger, somewhere across the country they would trade for a fair amount of supplies.

Armageddon and Prince loaded, a single barnyard chore remained. Open the pasture gate. Chase the last skinny cattle into the woods. Let them run wild. Let the critters, at least, have freedom.

One last look inside the cabin. Sally's lamp reflected the light of the dying fire. I flung it against the stone slab in front of the fireplace. Never would its wick shed a glow in that room. The shards scattered across the floor. From the shining pieces, faces stared at me, faces of my people, broken, scattered in fragments across the land. One shard larger than the others caught my eye. Held in my hand, its reflected rays played in and out the faces of Sally and Sam. In memory of the man and woman denied inalienable rights, I slipped the shard into my pocket.

My copy of the proclamation issued by General Jackson in 1814 lay on a bench near the table, a paper wrinkled, spotted, much used for all the readings of past years. My eyes raced over the words, long a part of my memory, my hopes.

> "To the free coloured . . . Your country, . . . does not wish you to engage in her cause, without amply remunerating you for the services rendered. Your intelligent minds are not to be led away by false representations . . . In the sincerity of a soldier, and the language of truth I address you.

> "To every noble-hearted, generous freeman of colour, volunteering to serve during the present contest with Great Britian, and no longer, there will be paid the same bounty in money and lands, now received by the white soldiers of the United States, viz. one hundred and twenty-four dollars in money, and one hundred and sixty acres of Land.

> "Due regard will be paid the feelings of freemen and soldiers. You will not, by being associated with white men in the same corps. be exposed to improper comparisons or unjust sarcasm . . ."

Disgusted and bitter at Andrew Jackson's neglect that had grown into insult, the promise of land bonus for militia service a mockery, I knew then I would never find my one-sixty in Tennessee. For me, Jackson's honor lay smeared under a heavy coat of tarnish. I resisted the urge to burn the paper to ashes, then grind the ashes under my boot heel. Grim-faced, I glared at the words "Due regard will be paid to the feelings of freemen." Slowly, I folded Jackson's promise and stuffed it deep into my pack.

Isabella's coonskin cap on my head, without a backward glance, I headed west into the wilderness.

19

Lacking a definite plan, uncertain about my future, I spent weeks in the saddle, camped in uncounted places at the edge of nameless groves and streams. My destination: unknown, a piece north, mostly west. On sleepless nights, my mind wrestled more than ever with the truth, the facts, of my status in every county and state where I had lived or walked or hoped for freedom. I forced myself to come to grips with the fact that chains bound me to a rootless existence. Me, George Bush, had I become a shadow haunting the countryside? A solitary wanderer without home or country? That ghost on a skeleton horse?

Far from familiar places, I wandered in the wilderness that stretched mile after endless mile in all directions from Tennessee. Wide open country with land waiting to be taken, perhaps I could find freedom in a world away from the settled areas. To keep my sanity, I forced myself to think I could find a world not so sharply white at the top, black at the bottom.

As I headed north, I remembered that Kentucky was a slave state. Hanging in my mind were the slave poster and the auction that had badgered me during my long ago journey from Pennsylvania toward East Tennessee. I set caution on the saddle beside me. I avoided settlements and people, kindled few fires, burned my leavings, beat the ashes into the soil. I rode toward the Ohio River following trails marked only by animal feet.

Keelboats along the Ohio had space for the occasional man and his horses wanting passage. I held wary, for I knew many river men harbored no compunction against slipping a black body to a slaver in return for dollars in their pockets. One or two captains slyly urged me to take a job with them, but I knew from their shifty ways that it was the opening of the trap. I eased away from five or six men, aggressive and ready to make a dollar any way they could, men in whose eyes burned their underlying objection to me. In one captain's eyes, I read hatred that could burn me. I had seen the same look in the eyes of Isaiah's kidnappers in Philadelphia.

It took time. But heeding my wariness, comfortable finally with a captain who talked open and straight out with me, his eyes steady, I boarded. I cared little to what river landings the boat might travel.

* * *

The further west I moved, the more Philadelphia, that place of my origins, kept nagging me. Before I could consider whether to head east, I had to find Gregory Hamilton's brother in Kaskaskia, Illinois, to learn if Isaiah had been freed. Logically, my native city should have been my destination. My roots lay there. Aye, but it was the site of my family's bondage, of Isaiah's theft. To bury that past, I had broken completely from Philadelphia. As I thought of the Quaker school, the Stevenson library, Mahala and Jonah, I found a longing deep inside me to return east, a longing that prodded me time and again. But an old newspaper article proved to me I could not go back. An 1813 bill in the Pennsylvania legislature had aimed to prohibit us free people from coming into the state and to require registration papers. The bill had not become law, but the thinking behind it showed what people had on their minds. A web of attitudes and practices strangled America, a craziness that entangled Pennsylvania as tightly as any other state.

Riding the trails, waking at night, I often caught myself mumbling out loud words from the Pennsylvania Constitution: "All men are born free and independent, and have certain inherent and indefeasible rights . . . enjoying and defending life and liberty . . ."

Did that Constitution, by the trick of assuming that none of my people are "men," cut off rights the white men enjoyed from birth? Like them, we were born with America. We helped build her cities, brick by brick, stone by stone. We black men, free and slave, fought her battles on the Plain of Chalmette.

Crispus Attucks, the hero of Isaiah's and my young lives, a runaway slave turned sailor, died on Boston Commons in 1770, the first American killed by the British in the Revolutionary War. Did he bleed any less red than his white comrades?

Benjamin Banneker, a respected inventor, astronomer, and scientist, served by appointment of the President of the United States on the Commission that laid out the boundaries and streets of Washington City. Were his achievements in science any less significant than those of Benjamin Franklin?

Jean Baptiste De Sable, a fur trader and businessman, built in 1772 on the shore of Lake Michigan the first trading post at Eschikagou, later called Chicago. Was his effort any less courageous than that of the French nobleman Sieur de Bienville in founding New Orleans?

I grieved for my country and for my people.

At an occasional river landing, a fur trapper or two took passage on my keelboat down the Ohio for the Missouri, others headed for the Mississippi and New Orleans. From talk with those trappers, I glimpsed a life more independent than mine had ever been. To hear them tell how they roamed the far west mountains at will searching streams and lakes for glossy beaver pelts, they sounded as if they had a freedom to the point almost of abandonment. Those long past days watching the pirogues from my militia flatboat, I had imagined joining that carefree life. The voyageurs bragged of fortunes reaped from the western furs by the traders Manuel Lisa, a family of brothers named Robidoux, others. Shipments for the eastern markets, the pelts loaded onto barges backed their stories with proof. I could almost feel myself on a mountain stream in the wilderness when I sang with them.

> "Who is it cries in the dawn,
> Cries when the stars go down?
> Who is it that comes through the mist,

The mist where the rivers run?

> "Who is it
> in the dawn
> and the mist?"

* * *

After several weeks drifting the Ohio, I left the flatboat on the north shore past Cave-in-Rock. Not wanting to tangle with the legendary band of outlaws who made that place their headquarters while they preyed on river traffic, I lit out at once on an animal trail leading northwest. And the thoughts closest to the surface in my mind about Isaiah and Gregory Hamilton led me toward Kaskaskia and his brother Ira's smithy.

The prairies of southern Illinois tempted me, but my hopes to own land in America had stretched thin. Illinois, a free state, had its special message for Negroes. I figured to slip through the state unseen and unknown, turn my journey onto a trail into the far west.

Perhaps I could claim a piece of land for Isaiah and me in the unexplored wilderness beyond the Mississippi River. The further from Tennessee my travels took me, the more talk I heard of vast western regions across the Mississippi, beyond the United States. The west offered a land where a man could do as he pleased. He could put down roots, if he should decide to shift into a settled life, without fear of an intruder booting him off. He could own boundless reaches over valleys and mountains and plains where the air must certainly be purer.

My dreams drew me across the great river toward that west and into the high peaks of Northern Mexico country. In my fantasies, I climbed Blanca Peak in the romantic sounding Sangre de Cristo Mountains and fished the cold mountain streams with my boyhood friend.

* * *

As dusk settled one evening, the routine of making camp out of the way, my packs tied to tree limbs higher than bears could reach, a rustling sound in the bushes, the snap of a twig, alerted me as I returned from a small stream with water in my cook pot. Slowly, a head, then shoulders silhouetted against the dull glow of my campfire. A stranger sneaked from the trees bordering camp, reached for one of the packs. At the moment he raised his hand to cut the rope, I yelled, "Drop your knife!"

Startled, he swung around, crouched ready to spring, slashed his knife through the air. A skinny boy's scared eyes glittered at me, his clothes in rags, his hair matted and dirty. A runaway? The thin, drawn face told me he had not fed well for a long while.

I stepped toward him, my gun pointed at his chest. "Drop your knife."

His body quivered, his voice squeaked, "Don't shoot." The knife slipped from his hand. "Food, Mista. I needs food."

"You a runaway?"

"Me? No runaway. Me free."

"Show me your papers."

The boy avoided my eyes, looked to the ground.

"I said, Show me your papers."

"Los'. Los'." His voice a whisper, he turned his back to me.

I found it uncomfortable challenging another human being about freedom papers. Countless times I had suffered the same insult. Demeaning, that question asked by Turley's clerk, the sheriff, cattle traders, the New Orleans dandy.

I dropped the question, asked, "What's your name?"

He hesitated, screwed his chin back and forth. "Noah."

My grip tightened. "You said, 'Noah'?"

The name brought back vivid images of the young man in my cabin, ears slashed off, life seeping out of his lacerated back. I heard his cries "Give me my freedom papers, Noah."

"You're lying to me. I know you got freedom papers. You stole them."

He dashed toward the trees at the edge of the clearing. My rage boiling, I rushed after him. He stumbled, I grabbed his legs. Dragging him to the campfire, I set him upright, held him by the shoulders, forced him to look me in the eye.

"Tell me whose freedom papers you stole." No more hesitation to ask about them.

No response.

"I ought to throw you into the fire. Let you burn."

Shaking, Noah burst into moans, sobbed, mumbled words, incoherent and unintelligble.

Unable to control my wrath fired to scorching flame by memory of the mutilated boy who had died in my cabin, I slapped the intruder. I knocked him down, picked him up. My fists hammered his body. He dropped to the ground before I realized how hard I was pummeling him. I eased up but tied his feet so he could not run away. Eying me with hatred, fear, suspicion, he gulped down chunks of bread and salty fatback.

Refusing to answer my questions, he pleaded through sobs, "Jes' lemme go, Mista. I won' bother yo' no mo'. Lemme go."

"You'll stay here till you tell me whose freedom papers you stole."

I was certain the pitiable creature had caused the death of the unknown boy in East Tennessee. The wretch could name the unmarked grave under the sycamore.

Calmed by the food dulling his hunger, the tenseness in his face eased. I glared at him while he glowered at me like a cornered rat.

"Did Amos and Zacharias Hawkins own you?"

No answer.

"You were on the Hawkins farm. I heard them call you when I tried to buy some cattle. I saw you in the draw when I rode away."

Still no answer.

"Noah, because of you, Amos Hawkins and Will Briggs caught that other boy. Cut off his ear. Slashed his back with whips. I found him tied to a tree. He had nearly bled to death. Finally, I got him home. Couldn't save him. He was out of his mind. Kept moaning, 'Noah, Noah, give me back my freedom papers.' Now, blast your hide, Noah, what did you do with his papers?"

Screwing his face tighter, looking more than ever like a starved, cornered rat, the boy stared at me for a long time, his eyes tiny pinpoints. As I glared at him, his tough boy defiance began crumbling. All pretense gone, he rolled over, his sobs wrenching. My anger burned hot as I watched him across the fire, anger fueled by the certainty that he was the Noah who had stolen freedom papers from the boy who had died in my cabin.

What should I do with him? Turn him in to the sheriff as the law required? Of course not. Helping a runaway meant breaking the law, but the whole rotten system had to be broken before change would come. If he were the slave Noah from the Hawkins place, as I suspected, I would never send him back to the brothers, nor would I have any part in the law forcing him back.

The rope around his legs cut loose, wrapped in one of my blankets, he passed into a deep sleep. I thought he would run during the night. But when I rolled out, he had a good fire blazing, sat on a log waiting.

"Noah, we got talking to do."

"Yessuh."

"If that young man were alive, I'd take you by the scruff of your neck, and we'd go find him. Give him back his paper. But he's dead. You helped him get killed. You stole his only chance to live." My wrath boiled again. With effort, I held it in.

"I'se sorry. Cain't hep now."

His response, "I'se sorry. Cain't hep now," slashed me the wrong way with its no caring attitude. I knew the Noahs of this world live in slimy gutters, victims so caked with abuse no compassion reaches them. Still, even in the depths of the most despairing human should live a shred of compassion for another suffering person. As beat down as that boy appeared to be, How could I reach him?

"He's dead. No help in being sorry. It's too late. But I warn you. Never again steal a man's freedom papers. They're his life." I pulled carefully from the seething in my heart, knew I must stay calm to reach him. I had to lead him to understand the gravity of his theft.

Without a word, he reached into his dirty bundle, handed me a crumpled paper. "No kin read."

Across the page in scrawling letters stretched the name "Aron Davis." At last, the unknown boy who slept under my sycamore tree bore a name.

Perched in space I fixed among Prince's packs, Noah rode with me the next several days. At night, he stuck close to camp, fearful of my turning him over to a sheriff. Usually, we covered the miles on the trail in silence. Even around campfires, talk did not come easily.

* * *

Time dragged on, the progress slow as I forced Noah to talk to me. Usually he sat, eyes half closed, watching, never offering a word about his parents. Obviously, he must have been a leftover from some auction, his family separated, each bought by a different slaveholder. Whenever I walked near him, he shrank away. He withdrew more than my pounding seemed to warrant and kept evading my questions by speaking in a low voice and not answering directly.

"The Hawkins brothers. Did they beat you, Noah?" My question caught him off guard.

"Yessuh."

"Don't 'suh' me any more. I'm not your master. I'm trying to help you. Call me 'George.' I told you that before."

His lips formed the word "George," but he did not speak it aloud.

"So they whipped you. Why?"

"Dey . . . Dey . . ." He looked down, would not meet my eyes.

"Why?"

"Dey tie me on da bed. Whip me an' play with me . . . Down here."

My turn to feel sick. "Go on. What else?"

"So, they lie on bed. Togethah. Make me whip 'em. Not too hard. An' dey play wid each other, awright. Same as dey done me. Make me stan' an' watch." His words came slowly, forced. "If hot day, I gots to fan 'em."

I hated to press him further, but I had to ask, "Will Briggs, was he a friend of Hawkins?"

"Yes. Him come dere. But me nevah fanned him."

So much for Briggs.

More questions were unnecessary. Impossible. For a long time, saying nothing, we sat across the campfire from each other as I struggled for the right words.

In Tennessee, Louisiana, everywhere, sickening rumors circulated the countryside of the evils perpetrated upon slave children. Here on the trail, I was hearing of the abuse straight from the lips of one of them. It was tough learning its reality that way from a young boy. Victims dared not talk. Li'l Sal and Noah were only two of the many, unnamed and forgotten. The bastards who abused them sure as hell would never disclose their slimy crimes.

Noah ran away. Like Sam had said, the slaves who would not tolerate the abuses ran.

One morning, Noah asked, "You dat big free man what lives wit Sam?"

"Yes . . ."

"I gots to tell yo'. Las wintah, the Hawkins, dey stole all Sam's food. Said dey meant to starve him and Sally out. Said dey din't want no freed slaves in de country. Let dem starve, dey said. Dey made me go wid dem, whupped me when I said, 'No.'"

The lonely house on Sam's acres. The empty woodenware. The cold fireplace. "Starve them out," the Hawkins brothers had bragged. And Sally's spinning wheel, thread hanging down, flashed through my mind, the first thing I had seen when I returned from the fighting at New Orleans.

* * *

Faced with necessity of dealing with a young man damaged by years of abuse to mind as well as to body, theorizing about equal rights, simple justice, seemed without purpose.

Finally, I plunged ahead, a plan coming together for handling the boy myself, outside the law. "Noah, bad as you've had it, make yourself forget. You must think only of how you are going to live free. To begin with, right away, you must do two things. First, your name. You've got Aron's freedom paper, and . . ."

"Don' take da papah . . ."

"I won't take it. Aron is dead. Buried back in East Tennessee. His papers can't help him now. You're here. Alive. But you are a runaway."

The old fear flashed in his eyes.

I lowered my voice, made it as stern as I could, poked my finger into his chest. "From now on you must be 'Aron Davis' every minute of your life. Never Noah again."

"Me Noah." He puzzled. "Me nevah Aron."

"I know you are Noah. Not Aron. But you stole Aron's freedom paper. Now, you better use it. If you don't, you'll get yourself jailed."

"No!" His voice, thin, high-pitched, screeched, "Don' let 'em take me."

"Then, listen. Think what I'm telling you. If you want to stay alive, if you want to be free, you can never show Aron's paper and tell anyone your name is Noah. Never. Never. Never." I paused. The boy clearly had grasped nothing of the mortal wound he had inflicted on Noah. He had no understanding that he must become the person named on the paper. "Anyone will know you stole the papers. Figure you for a liar. The sheriff will put you in chains and drag you back to the Hawkins for sure."

God, if I had been a Baptist preacher, right then I would have dunked the boy in the river as "Noah." Baptized him as "Aron." Washed away evil memories that would terrify him the rest of his life. The thought hit me, Give the idea a try. Something dramatic might help Noah make the change.

"Here. You can have this shirt and pants. And these boots. Throw away your old clothes. Jump into the creek. Scrub yourself hard. Get off all that old stink." I plunged on. "Wash away 'Noah.' Come out 'Aron.'"

Some of my talk must finally have sunk into him. He shucked his ragged garb, splashed into the stream. I made him rub the dirt off his skin, then grabbed him, one hand steadying his back. We stared at each other, his eyes filled with fear, their questions and his stiff body telling me he had not yet come to the point of trusting me. But he did not pull back.

"We'll wash Noah away forever." I dunked him into the water, lifted him up. Dunked him again. "I name you 'Aron Davis.'"

As smoothly done as a preacher baptism.

Over the next days, we practiced his new name, repetition after repetition, my same questions seeking the same answers. ["One, two . . . One, two." Memories of the flatboat drills down the Mississippi.]

"What's your last name?"

"Me Davis."

"Now your first name. What's your first name?"

"Me Aron."

We drilled, drilled, drilled, drilled.

With my finger, each evening, I traced the words on the freedom paper, slowly sounded out every letter of every word, had him hold the document and repeat several times, "Aron Davis." At first, his slowness discouraged me, but by the middle of the second week he seemed to have made the transition, was beginning to understand that his survival depended on keeping the name he spoke consistent with the name on the paper.

"Me Aron Davis." Promptly, he answered my question. His voice sounded the first trace of the pride that I had hoped he might attain. Even more encouraging for his safety was the chance that he would fit in somewhere. A strength long buried within and unknown to him began to surface. Having established a safe identity, he pulled himself free of a few vines of the fear entangling him.

I believed Aaron Davis would find meaning in hearing about Isaiah. In simple words I explained slowly, paused for questions, finished with adding that I had handled him like I did because of Isaiah. To my surprise, he seemed to understand. Perhaps his slave experiences had given him a deeper insight than I thought he had.

Several days later, my mind setting squarely on the western country, I told the young man our trails would soon part. "I'll not be staying in Kaskaskia. It's time for me to head on west, Aron. The second thing you must . . ."

"I won't stay heah. Me ride with you. I gots no friends but you, George." The boy's tone of voice bore his old fears.

"No, Aron. Listen to me. Remember, way back, I told you the first thing was to get your name fixed in your head. Now, the second thing important for you, we have to find a place where you can live free. And you must work to provide what you need.

"We are in Illinois, a free state. No slaves allowed. No Hawkins can touch you here. I'll help you find a friend and work. In the town ahead, it's called Kaskaskia, I know of a man." I passed over saying the Hawkinses could not likely take him legally from Illinois, but I knew the country harbored kidnappers and patrollers. I had to find Aron a safe place.

"Not here. Me ride with you."

"Aron, where I'm going will not be safe. You have to stay here. I will help you set down in Illinois."

* * *

At Kaskaskia, the blacksmith brother of Gregory Hamilton welcomed us. While the smithy reshod my horses, we talked. The man I faced held a slight height advantage over Gregory. He packed quite a few less pounds. His pants and jacket even more frontier than mine, Ira was "a fer piece" from the city-cut clothes of his brother. His heavy eyebrows were identical to ones I had seen before—dark and bushy with a few white hairs. If I been looking at that one feature alone, I could not have told Gregory and Ira apart. Heavy eyebrows appeared to be the special mark of the Hamilton clan. His hands firm and sure with hammer and hot iron, his voice determined, Ira Hamilton appeared to me a man forged to more decisive ways than Gregory.

Evidently he had heard from his brother in New Orleans for Ira knew a few things about me. In those first hours with him, I confirmed that he like his brother had no use for slavery, that he despised the system and the men who practiced it. For hours after Aron had fallen asleep in the hay loft, I trailed Ira through details of the young man's tragic life, the abuse inflicted on him by the Hawkins brothers. After hearing Aron's full story, asking the boy a few questions and receiving straight answers, Ira said he accepted the freedom paper as satisfactory identity. Ira understood that it would take considerable time to build trust between them and to create confidence in Aron where none existed. He needed a hand and was willing to train Aron. I felt no doubt that Gregory Hamilton's brother would protect the young man still seeking his path to sanity.

A third horse would have been excess baggage for me at that juncture. Aron accepted Prince with a handshake and his biggest smile yet, thanked me for my few dollars given to cover his needs until the job began to pay. I felt it prudent to warn the young man again always to hold onto his freedom paper, to fight if necessary to keep it.

"Losing that paper can mean you'll get killed. I warn you to guard yourself day and night against kidnappers. Men like the ones who stole Isaiah. Never let go of your freedom paper." As I talked that night, I believe Aron finally understood the reason for the pummeling I had given him.

Before our conversation ended, Aron surprised me. Without urging, he volunteered, "Aron promise. Nevah again I steal a man's free papah." He looked squarely at me. I saw in his eyes the beginning of change. His childhood had been erased once the Hawkins brothers began using him as slave. Here in the free state of Illinois, he looked forward to a job with Ira. I had created hope where hope had lain dead.

* * *

Stretching, moving one candle to an old table, Ira drew from the drawer a sheet of paper and handed it to me without a word. Leaning toward the other candle, I read, my heart skipping beats when I saw the handwriting. The letter from Gregory was brief:

> "Dear Bro. Ira,
> "I re'vd your shipment of blankets and cloth for the shops. Came through a little late, but in good condition. The young man from Philadelphia I wrote about before will not be going home. He no longer works his job here in New Orleans. There's much call for food and grain. Send all you can get your hands on. I've a market for every pound. I have no knowledge of the present whereabouts, so that fellow must be back up river on his old job at his old place. I tried, but I could not help him. It's sure a relief for trade and for our business to have the war ended. The river boats can come right in and unload with no delay like the damn British caused. You may have a caller. A young man you can trust. Originally from Philadelphia. Tell him his friend is still in Louisiana. And you can say whatever's on your mind to him. Hope things in Illinois go well. Business looks good here for a long while ahead. I may plan to come north sometime soon and take a large pack of goods up with me.
> "Your Bro.
> "Gregory Hamilton"

The lines held me, and I read them again and again. Despite my wavering the past several months between convincing myself that

Isaiah was already free and questioning whether anyone could ever break him out of Southland bondage, the letter hit me like a hail shower bending the traveler by its icy pellets. The truth exploded in my mind. Isaiah was not free.

By Ira holding his silence while I read the letter, I knew he understood my shock.

As he pulled a packet from the drawer, Ira said, "Gregory wrote a letter to the Free African Society in Philadelphia and sent it with yours. Sometime back, I received these with a message to hold them until I heard from you."

Hesitating, fearing what I would find, slowly I slid out the papers. A letter from Reverend Allen expressed the hope of those in my home city who had been trying to will Isaiah's freedom. A shorter note from Mr. Curry accompanied a copy of his freedom paper and Isaiah's freedom paper. Several testimonials from important white people as well as from men of the Society certified Isaiah's good character and free status.

"I think, George, you are faced with one choice. A lot of time has passed. You must return to New Orleans. Buying Isaiah failed. You and Gregory have to work through the law to win Isaiah's freedom. These papers should be sufficient evidence for the court." Ira's thoughts seemed to leap far away, perhaps to his brother's warehouse.

We sat facing each other, silent for several moments. "Stash your things and leave your pack horse with me. They'll be safe here. I would go with you, but I don't know influential men there. Gregory knows people in New Orleans. Helping slaves run north takes time and people a man can trust. There are many risks. George, trust my brother Gregory. He doesn't talk much about what he does, but trust him. He's a quiet hero."

20

On my second float down the Mississippi, the early morning sun blazed crimson across the eastern sky above the Missouri prairies. As our flatboat drifted southward, through the crimson robe I saw an image of Isabella James. In the silence of the dawn, her voice drifted with the notes of her chestnut dulcimer, "Greensleeves was all my joy, Greensleeves was my delight . . ." For an instant, her hair glowed wild strawberry red. Then, the glow faded as had our joy for the moments we had raced hand in hand across the East Tennessee hillside. I wondered, Where on those endless Missouri prairies are you, Isabella? Forbidden to me, yes. But no one can forbid your returning time on time to my memory.

The flatboat bearing me to New Orleans suffered damage from batterings among sawyers in more than one congested schute. I chafed over the extra days it lay over for repairs at Natchez-under-the-Hill. I chafed knowing Isaiah waited.

That trip no wild horses drank at river's edge, then raced westward, manes flying. Again the song of the voyageurs kept calling me long after an occasional pirogue bearing those mountain men had disappeared in the haze far upstream. The melody stirred anew the spirit of the western wilderness where men roamed as they willed.

Far down the great river, the soughing of the Spanish Moss draped an eerie feeling around me. We glided past Avart's plantation. The Mississippi teemed with greater activity than during militia days—numerous flatboats, people bargaining wares and sundry goods, huge quantities of boxes and stacks of goods on the banks. A new feature of travel south, their stacks emitting smoke, a couple of steamboats presented a strange sight amid the flatboats. New Orleans had become the thriving gateway of interior America to the world's markets. It appeared that other traders besides the Lafitte brothers offered slaves to plantation owners, whether done legally or illegally.

* * *

I hurried from the waterfront to Gregory Hamilton's warehouse office with my two small packs, the one with the Curry papers grasped in my right hand and held close under my arm. My concerns mounted, cut across the sharp edge of an excitement, an anticipation, I had not before experienced.

Gregory welcomed me, and I sensed that he felt relieved I had come. In the span of time since my last visit there, the man appeared not to have aged, his bushy, dark, a mite curly eyebrows seeming that day to shadow a tense face.

As before, his words lay on the air with a calm, matter-of-fact clip. "I'm sorry. I have little to go on, George. The very day Isaiah's sentence on the chain gang ended, Henry Pryor carried him with three or four new purchases to his Red River plantation." Gregory pursed his lips, stroked his hand several times through thick hair. "Pryor has made no response to my offers to buy Isaiah."

Silence sat with us in that room the next several moments. I noticed the old masks were gone from the wall, and I wondered why but did not ask. At the window, Gregory looked down over the busy street where men hurried into favorite taverns to drink and celebrate finishing a deal, unaware of the crisis entangling us two upstairs.

"Gregory, I brought evidence that should win Isaiah's freedom."

He wheeled around, "How? What?"

"Your letter to the Free African Society in Philadelphia, along with mine, stirred people to action. When I got to Ira's, he had a packet with a copy of the Curry's freedom papers, several testimonials, and Isaiah's paper. Papers that witnessed freedom for the family beginning at least as far back as their fathers and mothers."

Silence again took up residence in the crowded office while Gregory studied the papers.

With a heavy sigh, he said, "Just might do it, George. Just might. But a man of Pryor's mentality will never concede a single point without a battle. Plantation owners are all tough, their property their first concern, I've learned. You never know for certain the key to besting them. It's time now we hired a lawyer who knows the game. One we can depend on to file the proper papers and battle in court. I know from experience we can trust Mortimer Tompkins."

The old word "trust." Mortimer Tompkins? Mortimer had never stood by me in a tough spot. *Trust?*

21

Judge Pierre Fauré leaned forward on his desk in the New Orleans courtroom. He had discussed several points with our lawyer and the state's counsel during the *habeas corpus* hearing to gain Isaiah's freedom. After listening to the personal testimony of plantation owner Henry Pryor on his purchase of the slave Jess, he called Gregory Hamilton to the witness chair. Staring straight at Gregory, the Judge asked, "Mr. Hamilton, do you personally know this individual you claim to be Isaiah Curry? Have you ever seen him?"

"Your Honor, I have personally seen this man Isaiah Curry. I would never forget him."

"Where?"

A slight pause gripped Gregory before he seemed able to answer. My hands tightened on the edge of the bench where I sat at the back of the courtroom.

"I saw him when he was working on the chain gang here in New Orleans. I also talked to him face to face in the city jail."

"Mr. Hamilton, on what basis do you claim that the nigra you saw was in fact Isaiah Curry, when the jail has no record of him?"

"I am satisfied the man called Jess is Isaiah Curry."

"Satisfaction is a most nebulous experience, greatly varying in individuals, as you well know, Mr. Hamilton. Did you yourself ever see this slave Jess as the so-called Isaiah, a free man?"

Gregory's eyes fastened on my face. In those eyes I saw misery.

"Mr. Hamilton, the Court instructs you to answer the question."

"Your Honor, no. But in Philadelphia, he is known to be a free man."

"Objection, Your Honor. That is unresponsive to the Court's question. And it is hearsay." The state's counsel leaped to his feet as he spoke.

"Objection sustained. The Court asks you again, Mr. Hamilton. Did you ever see the so-called Isaiah Curry as a free man? Did you ever know him personally prior to seeing the slave Jess in jail? Yes or no."

"No, Your Honor."

"Then, can you personally establish identity between your so-called Isaiah Curry and the slave Jess?"

Hamilton paused, dejected, then in a scarcely audible voice said, "No."

"If you have nothing further, you may step down, Mr. Hamilton," the Court directed.

Mr. Tompkins motioned me forward while passing me a warning glance. Turning back to the Judge, he requested, "May it please this Honorable Court, we do have a witness who can establish the link of identity the Court believes missing. He will swear from personal knowledge that the slave called Jess is in fact the free man Isaiah Curry."

As I moved toward the front of the courtroom, Tompkins continued, "This witness grew up as the boyhood friend of Isaiah Curry. They were constant playmates in the city of Philadelphia in the free state of Pennsylvania. In fact, the witness I wish to indulge this Honorable Court's discretion in hearing was with Isaiah Curry the night the kidnappers seized him. This man can tell you details that only an eyewitness would know. He clearly identified Isaiah here in New Orleans as the slave Jess on the chain gang.

"Unusual though it may be, I most respectfully beg permission of this Honorable Court to call the witness George Bush. He was born free in Philadelphia and carries with him his certificate of free status. He fought as a sharpshooter in the great Battle of New Orleans as a member of the Tennessee Militia. George Bush risked his life to help save our historic city from the British invaders. And I most respectfully . . ."

"The Court understands your concern, Mr. Tompkins, but the Court cannot accept as admissable evidence that which by statute is barred and therefore inadmissable. This witness is a nigra. He cannot testify against a white man in the courts of Louisiana. It is clear, then, that we cannot permit the nigra to testify against Henry Pryor, a white plantation owner."

I stopped. I looked into Judge Fauré's eyes. The Judge was killing Isaiah. I barely heard Mortimer Tompkins's voice fighting back at the Judge. I stood there ready to go forward if Mortimer Tompkins won his objections. Was my lawyer's tirade only a rehearsed act? A prologue to defeat? As I waited Mortimer Tompkins strode to the bar in front of the Judge.

"Now, Mr. Tompkins, is there or is there not any other evidence you wish to present?" The Judge's words rang sharply against my ear.

"May it please this Honorable Court, the equitable power you can exercise in your discretion . . ." Lawyer Tompkin's voiced carried respect as he fought for my testimony to be heard.

"The Court has ruled the testimony of George Bush, nigra, inadmissible. I will not allow him to testify in my Court. I order him to his seat in the back of the courtroom." As the Judge ruled, he pointed his finger at me and glared, motioning me to the rear.

"I strongly object to the Court's . . ."

"Overruled. Do you have further evidence? Or do you rest?"

Striding to the clerk's desk, Tompkins picked up a handful of papers. "Your Honor, these documents you have read are certificates proving Isaiah Curry's free status, his family's free status," he said in a tone diplomatic, reassuring, while I sat on my bench with my heart in my boots. "Genuine documents, Your Honor, for they bear the seal of the county clerk in Philadelphia. Documents in due and proper legal form. As I have already explained to the Court, these documents are testimonials from whites and Negroes of Philadelphia who know of their own personal knowledge the fact of Isaiah Curry's free status. Each of these statements is witnessed by two white citizens of the state of Pennsylvania. I request their admission into evidence."

"Objection!" rang sharp and stern from the state's counsel. "We do not know if these documents are authentic. Papers can be forged and fabricated. And these here papers totally fail to establish any link between Jess and Isaiah. With or without them, Jess and Isaiah are still two different individuals. The documents and the petition are nothing more than an attempt to create a specious, self-serving claim. A claim that will rob a legitimate owner of his property. Property he acquired by due and legal process."

"The Court has studied the papers submitted. They bear the seal of the Pennsylvania court. Therefore, I accept them as authentic. But on the issue of the link of identity, as the state's counsel quite correctly points out, they do not and cannot establish that the slave Jess is the so-called free man Isaiah Curry."

"Do you have anything further, Mr. Tompkins?"

"Your Honor, I enter strong objections to the Court's line of reasoning. Some of these documents are by white men. All of them are witnessed by white men. They do prove who Isaiah Curry is. The eyewitness, George Bush, supports these white men's papers and can prove the link of identity. As I have told the Court, George Bush personally knows Isaiah as well as if they were brothers."

"Objections overruled . . ."

"But Your Honor, I must object again. The Court does not . . ."

"Overruled, Mr. Tompkins. I have ruled. Any further waste of the Court's time, and I will find you in contempt."

Lawyer Tompkins looked at me a moment, a deep frown lingering briefly on his face, then disappearing. I sensed that a crust of frustration enveloped him. Gregory sat with his head in his hands. An errant gust of wind stirred the papers on the clerk's table, papers now useless.

In the silence, I could hear the flies buzzing on the ceiling. In that Louisiana Court of Justice, I stood chained within the boundaries of hell.

* * *

"There being no further evidence, the Court rules as follows. Under Louisiana law the presumption that a nigra is a slave is given great weight. The only evidence the Court has admitted supports that presumption. This evidence comes from the sworn testimony of Henry Pryor, a respected white citizen of Louisiana, a man whose credibility before this Court is without question. Mr. Pryor has presented uncontroverted evidence of his legal purchase of the slave Jess by a judicial sale of a court of this state, a purchase he personally attended to in every detail.

"Under the basic principles of law in Louisiana, the slave Jess is an object of property, a thing. Mr. Pryor's testimony conclusively establishes that he bought this piece of property called Jess. There has been no evidence accepted by this Court that contradicts his testimony. And such a sale by judicial decree is final and binding upon all persons.

"Moreover, no evidence establishes that the two names, Jess and Isaiah, identify the same individual. Your witness Gregory Hamilton failed to establish that link of identity.

"It is clear to the Court that the slave Jess is nothing more or nothing less than the property of Mr. Pryor. The Court so rules.

"On such a state of the record, owners ought not be subjected to having their titles to property questioned by nigras, most particularly by their own slaves.

"In this case the only question was *liber vel nonò*, free or not. The question *liber vel nonò* is clearly found in the owner's favor. This Court must and will give judgment for Mr. Pryor without further inquiry as to source of title.

"Petition for writ of *habeas corpus* to release the slave Jess is hereby denied. This Court's decree is here and now entered accordingly."

The Judge crashed his gavel on the desk. With it crashed my hope of justice for Isaiah.

* * *

Blustering, swearing about the decision in the privacy of his office, Mortimer Tompkins declared that he would take Isaiah's case to a higher court, believing he had grounds for reversal of the decision and the granting of a new trial.

The shock of Louisiana Judge Pierre Fauré's decision burned in me while I strove to think rationally and to begin planning my next move. That judge denied our writ of *habeas corpus* on the ground that we had not established a link of identity between Isaiah and Jess. Humiliating for us, he had branded our evidence untrustworthy and immaterial. Yet, I knew the papers contained the truth about Isaiah Curry.

The law's presumptions had weighed too heavily in favor of slavery. Gregory and I had little to say to each other. We knew that Judge Pierre Fauré held the belief that a Negro was presumed to be slave, so the black person always had the burden to prove otherwise.

Failure of identity, fatal flaw in our proof, bound our hopes as bondage bound Isaiah. Irony snapped at me, for I could supply that identity.

* * *

Back in Gregory Hamilton's office, he and I assessed our legal options, the claimed gap in my friend's identity bludgeoning our thoughts. Seeing ourselves jammed into a corner, turning to me, Gregory broke from deep in thought. "A court appeal will likely be lost. Take far too much time." Then sharply, he asked, "Are you prepared for the risks of stealing Isaiah?"

"Gregory, we will not be stealing. We will be freeing Isaiah Curry."

Gregory studied my face as he had when we first met and made our plans. I knew he agreed with me. He had already acted to free other slaves.

Both Gregory and I knew the underlying premise for holding people in slavery is wrong, dead wrong. We did not recognize anyone's right to buy and sell human beings.

"Isn't it ironic that Isaiah himself was stolen and we have to steal him back?" I could not stop, for pouring through me flowed my Philadelphia law readings and discussions with Captain Stevenson. "It's a crime to steal property. A boat. A cow. A horse. A roll of cloth. No one can pass legal title to stolen goods. So, if they claim Isaiah property, no man can sell him and give a good title. Isaiah being stolen, if we take him back, we are only doing what is right. Making him free will . . ."

"I'm with you, but tell that to the Louisiana sheriff hereabouts." Gregory held up his hand to stop my rambling. "I believe every word you say, George, though I must caution both of us again. Under the law here in Louisiana, slaves are property. So, we would be taking another man's property. Just remember, Judge Fauré ruled that Pryor owns Jess by a judicial determination that binds everyone. But stealing is the only way . . ."

Without hesitation, I cut in, "We'll do it even if we risk the wrath of a dozen angry slaveholders. Gregory, I will not head out of Louisiana again before freeing Isaiah. I have promised the Currys I would return with Isaiah." On myself, I placed blame, George Bush, you should have taken Isaiah home long ago.

"All right, George. I suggest waiting until the dark phase of the moon. Just a few days. Then, we can move under cover of night. I will take with us a couple of men who know Pryor's plantation area in detail. They are free brick masons who through the years have done work on his buildings and finally quit, sick of his cruelty to slaves." Turning from the window, Gregory continued, "I will see one of them in the morning and arrange for their help."

22

Late one afternoon the fourth week of my stay in New Orleans, Gregory was pacing among the packs of goods stacked on the floor below his office, waiting for me.

"Pryor may have reached the point of selling the slave he calls Jess. He sent a message that he would see me at his house. I plan to ride up river tomorrow. I'm not certain how he will take to another man coming with me, but I want you there, George."

"I'm ready now. I couldn't stay here."

We rode for hours along the trail bordering the Red River. In fields stretching to far horizons, my people, men and women, yes, even children, bent to hoeing and weeding cotton. The midday sun, the humidity, the flies wore on Gregory and me although we two had free movement. A mild breeze brushed our faces.

At the gate to a sweeping semicircular carriage drive, two black men in livery attended to letting us enter. By their demeanor, their eyes questioning my presence, I knew they wondered why I rode open and free with Gregory Hamilton, obviously neither servant nor slave.

Majestically gracing a knoll bordered with magnolia, willow, and beech trees, a pillared mansion faced the Red River. A pool mirrored one wing in clear water, its fountain in the center spouting cool spray high into the humid air.

At the massive carved door, Henry Pryor's house slave greeted us. His words formal, they hung stiff on the air as he tried to frame them with a friendly tone. His eyes clung to me a few moments. I read fear in them as we walked to the arched entry of the high-ceiling great room.

Henry Pryor, a man definitely of Spanish origins in spite of his English name, imposing in his finely tailored suit, an arrogant mannered "Southern gentleman," grasped Gregory's hand. He looked straight through me without seeing me. "My pleasure to have you visit *Le Grand Domaine*, Mr. Hamilton. A pleasant day, isn't it, now that the heat is not as oppressive as it has been the past week. May I offer you a cool drink?"

"Yes, it has been a hard ride." Gregory's voice carried no warmth. I knew he despised such an obvious attempt to press the meeting into the frame of a host and social guest rather than that of two men meeting to discuss a serious business proposition.

From where I had been left standing just short of entry into the great room, I scanned its rich decor. The furniture, finely carved and covered with satin, had been imported from Europe. Damask draped windows, the curtains drawn back, looked out to a green pasture with blooded horses being groomed by slaves. I wondered if I would soon see Isaiah's ebony face. Beyond lay the Red River winding its way through the wealth of *Le Grand Domaine*. I gritted my teeth over the pretension I felt that name implied.

For over an hour, Henry Pryor plied Gregory with small talk. No doubt he questioned my presence but raised no issue with his guest. The master of *Le Grand Domaine* made it clear that he was ignoring me. I was invisible to him. Rambling at great length about his plantation, an ancient land grant from the French monarchy passing to him through his mother's family, he strode out the entrance. Without letup, he bragged of his fields, the rich soil of the Red River valley, his riding stable and horses.

From the corner of the white-pillared veranda, I listened.

"Mr. Hamilton, you made me an offer some time ago for my slave Jess. He's strong stock. Does his work. But he's of a mind to run. And my overseer, Jake Bunyon, figured if Jess ran once more, we'd stretch him and break him for good. Now, the niggah fool has run to the canebrake again. In fact, he's run since I sent you my note.

"I had decided as I said in my message that I would sell Jess. Not for what you offered. But you can take him for ten thousand dollars when we catch him." Pryor sipped his cool drink, and for the first time looked at me.

Gregory stared into the distance, and I saw the muscles of his face tighten. "I'm prepared to buy Jess. But not at that price. No slave in the entire Southlands could command a sum anywhere near that amount."

Robbery, I knew. But Pryor actually saying he would sell, I had to pick up the offer, so I burst out, "We will pay . . ."

Pryor brushed me aside as if I did not exist. "You are the one, Mr. Hamilton, who made an offer in the first place. You insisted on buying him. I heard about you poking around at the jail. I ignored that. But when you filed the *habeas corpus*, I knew you aimed to seize my slave without paying for him. A great expense you have put me to. And, I must say, an insult to me and to *Le Grand Domaine*. Harrasssment that I do not intend to let pass without fair and just compensation."

"Mr. Pryor, your claim is baseless. We know this slave is in fact a free man. I would never . . ."

"You have your choice, Mr. Hamilton. You practiced a fraud on me claiming that Jess is someone else. I do not take lightly to . . ."

Hoofbeats pounded the gravel of the circular drive. Dust devils rose from the hoofs. A horseman leaped from his mount. He threw the reins around the hitching post, a carved statue of a smiling young black boy in red and gold livery.

"I have to talk to you, Mr. Pryor."

"You will excuse me, Mr. Hamilton." Pryor sneered at Gregory. "I must speak with my overseer."

Henry Pryor's fine leather boots, polished to mirror brightness, shone as he passed me without a glance. For several moments, the two men of *Le Grande Domaine* stood in the shade of an old weeping willow. Striding back to the veranda, Pryor snapped his riding whip toward me. An arrogant tilt to his head, he barked at Gregory, "We've caught Jake. My dogs flushed the niggah out of the canebrake, and he's not leaving the plantation again. We have nothing to discuss, Mr. Hamilton. You may as well ride out now."

Pryor's haughty dismissal of Gregory Hamilton drew a sharp response. The men parted without a handshake. In silence, Gregory and I mounted our horses delivered to us at the edge of the carriage drive. Our eyes met, faces tense. We knew our next step would be stealing Isaiah.

* * *

A couple of miles from the mansion, the moans of men and women began streaking the late afternoon stillness.

Whips cracked.

Dogs barked.

The sight brought us to an abrupt halt as field slaves met us along the road, heads down, arms hanging limp. Guards prodded them with clubs and whips.

Impaled on a pole close beside the dusty road, only a few paces from the beautiful Red River, an ebony head stared from a single eye, the other gouged out. Blood dripped down the pole from the neck. The face clawed and bruised almost beyond recognition, the lips twisted with words that would never be spoken.

Isaiah.

23

Penn's whinny raged like a mighty wind. He reared, pawed the air with his front hooves. In a complete circle, he shied to the left away from Isaiah's head and the smell of blood.

I clung to the saddle, my body horizontal to his back as a frenzied Penn bolted down the road from the Pryor plantation. There was no slowing him. Gregory raced close behind at the same breakneck speed. Hoofbeats pounded. Anguish rode us like that mighty wind, shattering the forest, tearing off boughs.

Dust clouds rose, choked my horse and me.

A bitter sickness numbed my brain, filled my soul.

Miles away from the Southland plantation, Penn slowed beside the river. Too deep for wading, thirty yards or so across, the river proved no deterrent. My horse, then Gregory's, plunged in and began swimming. Blood surged in my forehead. I squinted up the river while through my brain rang the words, "This river stained by the blood . . . this land soaked . . ." The current swept against me. Isaiah's happy Philadelphia face laughed at me, then disappeared in the undertow. I heard again Mother Curry's cry for her lost son. Crazymakers stalk the land.

* * *

As our horses climbed dripping wet out of the river, the bitterness rose to delirium. I sweltered as with jungle fever, lost in another world. Gregory feared my reason had flown, for my ravings bore no rational thought or word. He watched me closely during the next several weeks, fearing for my sanity.

* * *

Long ago, Sally had said, "Dey's mendin' in a poultice of sycamore leaves." Somehow, I wrapped Isaiah's memory in a sycamore leaf and enshrined it deep within my heart. But in that poultice festered the knowledge that I had not acted soon enough. I had not acted with courage. I had failed Isaiah.

Intruding without warning into my days, Guilt clamored for redemption. In my nightmares, *Guilt circles through my mind. Guilt turns me into a skeleton striking its spurs into a white horse. I reach into the shadows drifting around me but feel nothing. The lightning of a Southland thunderstorm burns my eyes. A stench dumps an acrid biting into my mouth. I face a nameless masked judge. His gavel striking the desk hard batters my ears. His flint-stern tone fractures my urge to speak out. "I pronounce sentence upon you, George Bush. Guilty. Guilty of the murder of Isaiah Curry."*

* * *

A voyageur rows his pirogue in circles on the river that runs in my mind. "Who is it cries in the dawn, cries when the stars go down? Who is it in the dawn and the mist?" Those haunting songs of the fur trappers beckon, draw me toward escape into a far wilderness.

"I have made my decision, Gregory. I mean to escape into another country. Escape to fur trapping in the mountains of Mexico." In his warehouse office, I sat across the desk from my Southland friend.

I saw the pain of failure sketched across his face. But I knew from past action that he had the strength required to meet the risks his action incurred. I believe I drew on that quiet strength for I said to myself, He will go on helping other men and women to freedom. Not a man shouting his success, he never stormed long over his failures. I see Gregory Hamilton for what his brother said, a quiet hero.

"Gregory, before I ride the trail west, I have an obligation to see the Curry family. I have to make a journey to Philadelphia."

How can I tell the father and mother about the beheading of their son?

24

During my last week in New Orleans, Gregory completed arrangements giving me passage on a steamship bound for Philadelphia. It carried a load of furs, svelte and rich and soft, that Gregory had sold for his business customers, the Robidoux Brothers of St. Louis, Missouri. My stay in Philadelphia would be short for I had passage on the steamship's return trip. I had heard of the agitation against free blacks. I knew Philadelphia was no longer my home. On my return to New Orleans, I intended to find out more about the far west and the source of those furs.

The closer the day came for my journey to the Currys, the more I dreaded seeing the family I loved. I searched for the right words to tell them about Isaiah. I could find none. All I could think about were those last minutes on that plantation.

A phantom sailing ship plows the whitecaps alongside the steamship bearing me north to Philadelphia. Its great sails glow with a beauty and nobility unknown for any land-based transport. In the moonlight, I see the tall thin form of my father, his white hair and beard streaming in the wind.

The days at sea dragged. We passed the tip of Florida, the port of Savannah, and made calls at other trading stations. The calm I had begun to feel my first days on board the steamship eased little of my torment over Isaiah. I tried, but I could never hear Father's words from the phantom sailing ship that appeared at random in the moonlight.

At a number of ports, I considered leaving the ship while men were unloading cargo for merchants along America's eastern seaboard. Isaiah's face haunting me, the laugh-cry from the New Orleans jail belted me. Always, I drew back from the urge to disappear on a wharf, and continued my journey toward Pennsylvania to face the Currys.

Many evenings, I retreated early below deck to my bunk. My hands played over the blanket, its texture as rough as the blanket I had slept under at Avart's plantation. Headaches born of guilt battered me during daytime hours, raising the sickness deep inside me. Never before had I known any benefit from headaches; but as I settled down for sleep, I could feel my headache easing the nausea that pestered my insides.

No moon shimmered my last night on board. No phantom sailing ship rode the waves beside us. Then, on the night wind streamed the words, *Swim through the whitecaps, George.*

* * *

As the ship turned up the Delaware River toward the waterfront I had known so well, I forced myself to realize that I had only a few hours before I must face the Curry family. I eased my way along Front Street. Sailors speaking strange languages stood on the docks below their ships. Of the foreign flags, I recognized only those of England and France and Spain. I pushed aside the idea of asking for passage with one of the ships. I had to move along. I had come to Philadelphia with an obligation to meet. In only two weeks I must board the steamship for return to New Orleans.

I walked the streets Isaiah and I had roamed. Since leaving Philadelphia, I have traveled a long journey. Seeking a place to put down roots? A tract of land I can take for mine? Always traveling. Walking. Sailing. Flatboat. Steamship. Horseback. An American odyssey, my life.

At the corner of the block where the Currys lived, I paused, set my bag on a large stone at the side of the street. Rubbing my left hand to ease the cramping of muscles, I glanced along Water Street. I still tried to shape a way I could speak to the Currys about Isaiah.

The red frame house paint had faded, but little else appeared changed. The Curry home drew me along the street, and its door opened to my knock.

Mother Curry's taut, worn face peered up to me. Staring past me, she seemed to lean forward. "George, where is . . . ?" Her voice weak, a flood of tears drowned her words. Father Curry pulled her to him as he whispered, "You alone?" His eyes flinched as if he had seen a ghost.

I failed of any words to console the family. The Curry children had been at the table, but they scattered to the back room and out of sight.

Through most of the night, talk came slow and subdued. Thoughts and memories hard to express, they tangled in knots like a rope that twists and snarls when a man most needs to use it. Mother Curry spoke little, then fell silent. I gave details of Gregory Hamilton's efforts to free Isaiah. Father Curry asked questions about the trial in Judge Pierre Fauré's court. He struggled with trying to absorb my words describing the mind that had rejected justice in the Louisiana courtroom. I could feel that cold tremors sluiced along Father Curry's spine for the same kind of tremors iced me. "Friends, I was present all through the trial. I remember what Judge Pierre Fauré said. I read him for a mind calloused, indifferent, prejudiced. Justice is hard to come by in the Southlands."

* * *

After settling details for my accounts on deposit in the Philadelphia bank, I headed to the old Stevenson red brick house I had once called home.

"Land a livin', it's you!" Mahala grabbed me, clasped me to her. "Jonah, come here. George is back."

We three talked most of the night. Laughs. Tears. Memories. Toward morning, Mahala said, "George, will you approve asking the Curry family to come and live with us?"

Jonah echoed her wish, "It is a big house for jist us two."

"Please, George, you tell the Currys." And the gracious Mahala smile I knew and loved filled my heart.

* * *

When I had "taught" the Curry children in Captain Stevenson's library, Isaiah often asked me to read his favorite story of the man of ancient times trying to push the rock up the hill. Isaiah roared his wonderful rich laugh at the rock always rolling down. He pantomined the man trying to push it back up. The day I told the Currys our plan for them to live with Mahala and Jonah it was as if Sisyphus had pushed the rock closer to the top. I felt a great burden lifting.

ABOUT THE AUTHORS

E. P. Roesch is the writing name of Ethel and Paul Roesch. Their work focuses on the collisions of cultures. Authors of the best-selling novel *Ashana*, they are completing a trilogy centering on three families of Việt Nam.

They live in Washington State and travel widely in doing their research. Their commitment to human rights has marked their separate careers—hers as a teacher and a YWCA director, his as a lawyer. They have published articles, short stories, and poems.

They present Book One of *American Odyssey* at this time. Book Two will follow shortly.

More Praise for E. P. Roesch's Ashana

Ashana bypasses the guts-and-glory version of New World conquests for a portrait of the misery and melancholy suffered by the people who became the prisoners of the new settlers. With its grand scope, it should find an appreciative audience in the public library."

Booklist

"A formidable task of viewing North America's settlement through the eyes of the vanquished rather than the victor is vividly achieved in ASHANA . . . Spellbinding . . . inspiring . . . engrossing because it is based on truth."

Seattle Post-Intelligencer

"This splndidly written novel is set in the Alaska of the 1790s, . . . Many of the passages have a lyrical quality . . ."

Newark Star-Ledger

"A little known era of history unfolds in this detailed saga. . . . Vivid details of the land and folklore blend smoothly with lively dialogue."

Rocky Mountain News

Ashana has ". . . scenes of sorrow and shocking violence mixed with bravery endurance and loyalty, a glowing light piercing the darkness of prejudice. I doubt that any American can read this book without increasing appreciation for Athabascan culture and a reluctant rememberance of the mistreatment of Native Americans and slaves from Africa that occurred in the lower 48 states."

Grand Forks Herald

"Notable/Notorious Women in Historical Fiction," by St. Charles Public Library, St. Charles, Illinois, includes the author's bestselling novel *Ashana* in the library's listing of twenty-six women worthy of special literary notice.

BOOK ONE

It is the early 1800s, and George Bush, a true to life free black Philadephian, confronts the collision of cultures that thrives in young America. Rage batters him that his best friend, also free, is kidnapped and sold into Louisiana plantation slavery. Sustained by strength inherited from his father, supported by the Free African Society, George Bush commits his life to finding and bringing home his stolen friend. Heir to a sea captain's fortune, young Bush has the means to make his search, but anti-free black laws force him to take a circuitous albeit adventurous route.

Believing the wilderness best suits his needs, George settles in East Tennessee. A sharpshooter, he musters into the militia "of the white male citizen," fights in the Battle of New Orleans. Handsome, virile, he is enticed by an exotic beauty of Rampart Street and loses himself for a time in passion. Dubious maneuvers and a devastating court trial to save his stolen friend inflame his unremitting rage.

American Odyssey, Book Two, soon to be released, continues the journey of George Bush. He escapes for a time into the fur country wilderness of Northern Mexico. There, George Bush hones his strength and wisdom to challenge the horrors inflicted by anti-black codes as his odyssey takes him across America to the Pacific.